Desert Desperate

By Dana Mentink

Copyright © 2014 by Dana Mentink
Forget-Me-Not Romances

Discover more romance novels at ForgetMeNotRomances.com. A division of Winged Publications.

This book is a work of fiction. The names, characters, places, and incidents are products of the writer's imagination or have been used fictitiously and are not to be construed as real. Any resemblance to persons, living or dead, actual events, locales or organizations is entirely coincidental.

All rights reserved. No part of this book may be reproduced, scanned, or distributed in any manner whatsoever without written permission from the author except in the case of brief quotation embodied in critical articles and reviews.

This ebook is licensed for your personal enjoyment only. This ebook may not be re-sold or given away to other people. If you would like to share this book with another person, please purchase an additional copy for each recipient. If you're reading this book and did not purchase it, or it was not purchased for your use only, then please return to and purchase your own copy. Thank you for respecting the hard work of this author.

All rights reserved.

ISBN-13: 979-8-3485-4345-7

Chapter One

The Arizona desert is lovely in August.

If you're a cactus.

If you're not green and prickly it's like standing in the bottom of a volcano hoping your SPF 15 will do the trick. You can run, you can hide, but there's no escape from the vast, unforgiving sandbox. As I hung up the phone with my Aunt Stella, I wondered again what would possess her to settle in such an inhospitable location. Probably the same thought process that prompted her to call me every year on precisely the same date, August nineteenth -- National Potato Day. I didn't even know spuds had their own holiday, but it seemed to impress my aunt. Every nineteenth day of August she and my uncle had a baked potato feast and called me to fill me in on the action. She's an odd sort of spud, Aunt Stella, but I love her anyway. Sometimes I'd call her up and we'd pray together, even if it wasn't a vegetable holiday.

It was hard to wrap my mind around my aunt's potato details as I clicked off the cell phone. My thoughts were steeped in a much cooler climate; the foggy world of San Francisco. I was planning a wedding: my wedding. Well not just mine, it included my soul mate Doug too, of course.

It was going to be a lovely outdoor affair at a winery in the Napa Valley. The flowers: white roses and lily of the valley. The music: a tasteful combination of harp and string quartet. The food: smoked salmon pate and lobster in puff pastry among other items. And those little square sandwich thingies. What are they called? Canapes, with brie and basil. The dress: a Vera Wang; fitted bodice inset with pearls and a flared shantung silk skirt that was a perfect compliment to my olive skin and black hair.

I could practically feel the soft swish of the fabric around my body as I twirled gracefully. The buzz of an office phone cut through my reverie. I pulled my mind away from these glorious details to focus on the matter at hand.

I was ushered into a tidy office and the editor of Rock Your World read from my resume. She clasped my hand in a bone crushing grip. "Well Miss Greevey, I'm glad to meet you."

"Please call me Simone."

She regarded me over the rims of her electric blue reading glasses. "Simone then. You're coming in on the ground floor of something special. We are an E-zine unlike any other, the first in the San Francisco area. Real cutting edge stuff. We've got readers as far away as New York and Montreal." Audrey wrenched the cap off her sparkling water. "Where did you get that bag?"

The conversational segue nearly gave me whiplash. "My bag? Nordstrom's Sigrid Olsen."

"Cute, it goes well with the shoes. Anyway, we're a Christian medium, but we want to appeal to twenty somethings, not the white haired old ladies who still wear hats and gloves to church."

Audrey, I surmised, hovered somewhere in the middle part of her fifties but old didn't seem to be part of her personal mental picture. She was whip thin, with a helmet of close cut black hair. I bet she ate vegetable protein patties and wheatgrass for breakfast. She looked fit enough to snap me like a toothpick.

"Do you have a boyfriend?" she said.

"What? Uh, yes, a fiancé actually."

"What's he like?"

"He's great. He's a chiropractor."

"Too bad."

"I beg your pardon?"

"My nephew is looking for a girl, but he's a shoe salesman. No contest for a chiropractor." She gulped some water.

"Ah."

"I introduced him to Donna but she's already got a structural engineer."

I wasn't sure whether to offer condolences or the number of a dating service.

Audrey scribbled a note on a steno pad, crossing the t's with vigor. "Like I was saying, the market is ready to recognize that Christian people can be hip too. The younger generation is not the placid, hymn singing fogies their parents were. They wear thong underwear and listen to rock music, just like their non-Christian counterparts."

I tried to picture Audrey in a thong. It caused distress to my synapses so I let it drop. "What exactly will I be responsible for?"

She flipped her bob of hair and slammed back the remainder of the water. "That's it, a to-the- point gal. That's what we need. A young person who isn't afraid to ask questions. You'll start as copy editor in the Leisure Life section. There's some blogging involved too. Alfie runs the department now but he's retiring. Prostate trouble."

"Oh, how sad."

"By the end of summer I want you on board and running things in that section. What do you think? Can you handle it?"

I tried not to leap out of the chair and do a happy dance. Six years of college and two degrees later and I was finally going to be an editor. I took a cleansing breath. Be professional, Simone. Professional. "Definitely."

"Excellent."

She whisked me down the hall to show me my office.

Okay, the gloomy space did look an awful lot like a room used for hanging meat or developing film, but it was mine. I felt around for a chair and put down my bag. "Thank you, Ms. Stanner. I really appreciate this opportunity."

Audrey was speaking into a cell phone. "Yes, I want to arrange a mud bath. Is that mud filtered everyday?" She covered the mouthpiece. "I'll send Donna in to get you started." Before she cleared the threshold she called to me. "By the way, you are a Christian, aren't you?"

***

Donna was also a twenty something with good skin. She had hair the color of apricots and all the subtlety of a buzz saw. I liked her immediately.

"Hey there. I'm Donna. Praise God we've got you on board. I'm developing a squint from doing all this extra work. Men think I'm winking at them." She flopped down on top of my purse, then extracted the flattened bag. "Oops, sorry about that. Hope I didn't squish anything."

I didn't mention my new pair of sunglasses which had probably been reduced to a fetching set of monocles. "I'm Simone, good to meet you. I heard Alfie is having health problems. Have you been helping him out?"

"Helping Alfie?" She snorted. "Alfie phones in from the golf course once in a while with directions. Other than that, I am Alfie."

"I thought he had a prostate problem."

Donna laughed, setting her freckles dancing. "He doesn't seem to think it's as much a problem as his doctors do. It gets him out of the weekly staff meetings though. I'm so glad to have another gal my age around here. Finally someone to hang out with. Do you like the theater? I've got an extra ticket to see My Fair Lady next week."

"That sounds perfect. Count me in."

"Good." She looked at my left hand. "Are you married?"

"Engaged. His name is Doug."

She grinned. "That's great. I'm still just cruising the singles scene but my boyfriend is really tops. Maybe we can double date or something. What does your fiancé do?"

"He's a chiropractor."

"Oh man. I could use a good back cracker after scrunching over the computer all day. I look like Quasimodo by quitting time. Does Doug like the Forty Niners?"

"With a passion."

"Excellent. Our men will get along famously."

A tiny beep sounded on Donna's watch. "Is it eleven-thirty already? I've got to go. We can chat some more this afternoon. Anyway, here's a computer you can use for the Bloggin' With Brandi deal. We've got a laptop around here somewhere for you to use."

"Who is Brandi?"

She blinked at me. "Didn't Audrey tell you? You are."

"I am?"

"Well, I have been for the past six months but I'm passing the keyboard to you. Congratulations. I never really got into the whole dual identity thing. I keep signing the thing Donna instead of Brandi. Anyway, just update the blog weekly, you can introduce a new topic then if you want. Have you blogged before?"

"Sure, but just with friends." The phrase sounded ridiculous once it passed my lips.

Donna smiled. "Then you're well qualified to do this. Basically, you're just an ear to listen and a spiritual guide when necessary. It's not usually anything too taxing. We average about two hundred hits a week but we're hoping to increase those numbers. Ask me or Audrey if you get anything you can't handle."

I wondered if I was qualified for the spiritual guide part. Fashion tips yes, counseling, not so much. I'd have to call up Aunt Stella if I ran into anything too sticky. She always seemed to have the right soul soothing verse right at her finger tips. Donna's last sentence sunk in. "Did you say Audrey gives people advice?"

"Actually, she's only chimed in once. She told someone to put on their big girl pants and deal with it. Come to think of it, maybe just ask me if you need help." She consulted her watch again. "I gotta go. I have a lunch date with a friend. Do you want to come? There's a place down the street with unbelievable falafels. I'll buy."

I looked around at the small space, cluttered with files and papers. Even in the gloom it was hard to miss the overflowing trashcan and the spilled container of paperclips on the desk. "No thanks. I really should get settled in here."

I was Simone Greevey, professional editor type person and soon to be chiropractor's wife.

It was time to get cracking.

***

Three months and six days later, my life was turned upside-down in Sunday school. Isn't that just the way things go? Who would think you could experience catastrophe in a church room filled with miniature chairs and dozens of safety scissors?

That particular Sunday I was in good spirits in spite of my teaching assignment. I'm not in tune with the natural vibrations of children, so I avoided Sunday school duty like people skirt mysterious fluids on a bathroom floor. But desperation is apparently visited on the clergy as well as civilian people and the pastor's wife pleaded with me until I agreed to one day of service in the preschool room.

She beamed at me, tucking a flyaway strand of hair back into her braid. "Don't worry about a thing. All you have to do is sing a song, read a story and serve snack. It will be an hour, tops. If worse comes to worse, get out the Play-doh. The kids are dolls; you'll love them to pieces."

Having seen some of the little darlings running around the church sanctuary, I was not confident in this assessment, but I figured they couldn't get too crazy in the space of sixty minutes. All I had to do was watch them play and try to slip in a little Biblical gem in between snack and story. No problem.

When the fateful day arrived, I showed up full of God's grace and a bucket of Play-doh under each arm. All seven children filed in and sat in a circle on the carpet. I had to admit, they did exude certain cuteness, especially the girl with the pink pinafore and the fancy hair dealie bobbers. My confidence swelled. Simone Greevey, preschool teacher extraordinaire.

"Hello boys and girls." I consulted my notes. "Today we are going to talk about David and Goliath. Does anyone know that story?"

Ralph Sarnecky, the boy with plump cheeks and a missing front tooth spoke up. "Oh yeah. Everyone knows that story. We heard it a zillion times. It's the one about David, this wimpy kid who kills this big ugly giant with a rock." He pantomimed smashing a skull with his fist.

"Yes, that's right." I read the script from my booklet. "David was a young boy who was called by God to do great things."

Jon Jon shouted, "Yeah, yeah. But what if he didn't use a rock? What if he used a light saber?" He leaped to his feet, wielding an imaginary weapon around the circle.

Two boys and a girl jumped up to join him. "Cool!" a curly haired kid shrieked. "I want a Lifesaver too."

"Not Lifesaver, light saber, dummy," Jon Jon said.

"Hold on there kids," I began. I was pretty sure the people in charge wouldn't condone the use of light sabers in church. My eyes landed on a helpful poster on the wall. "We should use our inside voices and gentle hands."

A tiny blonde girl stuck three fingers in her mouth and began to cry. I gave her a pat on the head. "It's okay. Don't cry, honey."

"I want my Mommy," she wailed in a range that made the windows vibrate.

Jon Jon whirled to slay another hapless classmate. One of his elbows caught me in the ribs. "Jon Jon, that's enough. Everyone sit on the carpet." I might as well have had a cone of silence on my head for all the good it did me. The class was attempting mutiny. If I didn't act quickly, I'd be tied up and forced to walk the plank.

"How about a song?" I scrabbled through the annals of my mind to come up with some sort of happy tune. Mac the Knife? No. The one about the ants and the rubber tree plant? I couldn't remember the words. Ah ha. Brainstorm.

"Just sit right back and you'll hear a tale, a tale of a fateful trip."

Their little mouths fell open.

"That started from this tropic port, aboard this tiny ship."

"I never heard that one before," Ralph said.

"I have," said pinafore girl. "It's about a shipwreck."

"Cool! A shipwreck!" Jon Jon shouted. He began to make loud storm noises and careen his ship from side to side.

"The mate was a mighty sailing man, the skipper brave and sure," I hollered.

Ralph jumped up and down. "I love ships. I'll be the pirate. Look out. I'm going to chop you with my sword."

I stopped singing. "Hold on. There were no pirates on Gilligan's island."

"What did they have there?" a chubby girl asked.

"Uh, well, coconuts, little grass huts and the odd visitor."

Jon Jon crashed his vessel into my chair. "Well if they had visitors, how come no one rescued 'em?"

"I, uh, I don't know."

They resumed their mayhem.

Kids crawled under the tables, seeking cover from Ralph's cannon fire. One kicked over a tower of blocks sending them flying. A bunch of girls began to tickle each other until there was a pile of giggling small people in front of my feet. Even pink pinafore girl joined in the brouhaha. She didn't look so angelic when she put her classmate in a headlock, yelling "arrggghh!" all the while.

"Boys and girls, let's sit on our bottoms and listen to the story. Look at this great picture of David." I thrust the book out for them to see.

They were under whelmed.

"I've got a wedgie," Jon Jon said, pulling at the seat of his pants.

"We'll you're going to have to take care of that yourself," I told him firmly.

The chaos continued.

After several useless verbal corrections I gave up. I announced in as loud a shout as I could manage, "Snack time!"

As if by magic, the children lay down their invisible weaponry and put away their tickly fingers. The pile of children untangled itself and stood up. Then the pirates materialized at the snack table and folded their hands. It was nothing short of a miracle.

"Heavenly Father..." I began until I noticed Jon Jon kick Eddie under the table. "Thanks for the snack, Amen."

"That was short." Eddie rubbed his shin.

"God appreciates brevity." I handed out the napkins.

"What's for snack?"

I held up the bag of fishy crackers.

"Goldfish again?" Ralph wrinkled his nose. "I'm sick of goldfish."

"Me too," Sarah, the sniffly girl, said. "They taste yucky. I want something else."

The scent of rebellion swirled in the air and made my stomach muscles tighten. I could see the plans forming for another pirate sortie. "What do you like for snack?"

There was a moment of silence while they considered the question. I eyeballed the cubbies in search of better grub.

Jon Jon screwed up his face in thought. "Twinkies and ice cream. And Skittles. That would be good."

There was a loud chorus of agreement.

The thought of these children hopped up on Skittles sent a shiver down my spine. "Goldfish crackers are the only thing I can find."

Seven pairs of eyes looked mournfully up at me from their tiny chairs. In desperation, I rummaged through my purse. The search yielded just enough to satisfy my charges. When they were all settled in with a handful of goldfish, one cherry Lifesaver and a minty breath strip apiece, I looked up to find Doug in the doorway.

"Doug." I hugged him like a dieting woman holds onto her last chocolate bar. "Thank goodness you're here. They're almost done with the Lifesavers. Do you know any good preschool songs? What about that one with the ant and the plant?" Doug used to play cello in his college days so I was hopeful he could come up with something. He was a sporadic church goer and definitely not a frequent visitor to the early service but I was too frazzled to wonder why he was there.

"Hey, Sisi." He ran a hand through his sandy hair and surveyed the munching children. "I never pictured you teaching Sunday school."

"Me neither." I consulted the wall clock. "But I've only got thirty minutes to go. So far there hasn't been any bloodshed so I'm doing great."

"I can see that." He took a deep breath. "Uh, Sisi...I wanted to come by and talk to you. I thought I'd catch you after the service."

"We're going to see each other this afternoon, remember?"

"I really can't make that appointment." He smiled, but there was a hint of hesitation on his thin face.

"I'm out of juice." Ralph waved his cup in the air. "Hello? Can I get a refill here?"

I poured him another Dixie cup full. "Doug," I said, handing my fiancé a bag of goldfish to distribute, "the wedding is in two months. We have to choose a disk jockey now or it will be too late. You don't want to wind up with your uncle's banjo band, do you? It was enough listening to them at your last family reunion." Doug had a tendency to try to wiggle out of wedding planning. I had to bribe him with Giants tickets to get him to commit to Raspberry Swirl for a wedding cake flavor.

"Yeah, I know. That's sort of what I need to talk to you about."

I practiced some relaxation breathing. "Can we talk about this after Sunday school is over?"

He poured more goldfish into Sarah's open palm. "I think I'd better tell you while I have the nerve. The problem is, I actually have this other thing going on."

I tried to smother my irritation. "Come on Doug. What other thing? What other thing is more important than our wedding?"

"Before I tell you, I just want to say I'll always love you, Simone."

I experienced a momentary flutter of concern. "What is it? Are you sick? Did you get bad news from the doctor or something?"

He paused for a long moment, twiddled with his glasses and

scratched his eyebrow. "No, nothing like that. It's sort of ...another girl."

The room fell silent. Even the chewing stopped.

I felt my eyes grow to ping pong ball size. "What? What did you just say?"

Doug didn't answer. His mouth opened and closed but nothing came out. He crinkled the goldfish bag between his fingers.

Blood stampeded through my temples. I was sure I hadn't heard him properly. "For a minute there I thought you said something about another girl."

Jon Jon nodded soberly. "That's what he said all right."

"Here kids." My voice hissed out between clenched jaws. "Play with the Play-doh." I dumped the bucket and accompanying accoutrement on the table. Goldfish scattered everywhere. The kids made no move to touch the colorful clay.

"May I see you over here, Doug?" I grabbed his sleeve and pulled him to the farthest corner which was a mere three feet away. "This isn't a great time to joke around. Especially not in front of a bunch of kids. It's not funny."

"Sisi, I'm not joking." His eyes gleamed with moisture. "I don't want to hurt you, really I don't. I will always love and respect you, but I can't marry you. Not anymore. I'm doing us both a favor."

I waited for the part when he would make sense of his crazy utterance. No doubt he had just been to the dentist and his system was still offline due to the effects of Novocain. Or he had eaten too many doughnuts and the carbs had pickled his brain. "What do you mean you can't marry me?"

He spoke to his shoes. "I sort of met someone. She came to my office for an adjustment. She's a teacher for the hearing impaired and she loves backpacking, too." He looked up. "Isn't that great?"

Great was not the adjective I would have applied to the situation. Disbelief clouded my mind. The scene was right out of a bad movie. Doug had met someone else? That was just not possible. We were supposed to be choosing wedding music. "You met someone?" I echoed.

He smiled wistfully, blue eyes sparkling. "I tried to ignore the feelings for a long time, Sisi, I really did. I kept it strictly professional, but then I happened to notice on her chart it was her birthday so I took her out for lunch. Just a friendly lunch, but one thing kind of led to the next and now we're a couple. She's a lot like you Simone: funny, intelligent, good looking."

Lunch? Backpacking? Couple? All I needed was a pinch to snap out of this nightmare. With extreme effort, I kept my Sunday school smile plastered over my gritted teeth. "We have been busy planning a wedding, Doug. You know, matrimony? 'Til death do us part? Cake and presents? Does any of this ring a bell with you?"

"No, *you've* been busy planning a wedding. I hardly had anything to do with it. I should have said something earlier, but you were so into the whole thing, I didn't think you'd even hear me."

I felt as though he'd slapped me. "You sure as shootin' didn't pipe up with this information earlier. You could have mentioned another girl say, before we chose the cake or the lobster in puff pastry. I'm pretty sure I would have heard you then." My whisper edged closer to a bellow.

He looked at the floor again. "You're right. I meant to, Sisi, but I didn't want to hurt you. Rachel insisted that I tell you before we hired a disk jockey."

Rachel, huh? Well wasn't she a thoughtful little maid?

"Thank you for being so considerate of my feelings, and don't call me Sisi anymore." I tried to reduce my volume a few octaves. It was pointless as the whole group of children hung on our every word. To my dismay, my voice faltered. "I thought we were soul mates. I was ready to share my life with you. I thought ...I thought God brought us together."

His mouth opened and then closed. "I don't know what to say except I'm really sorry."

The sight of his puppy dog expression made me furious. "How could you be such an..." I eyed my rapt pupils, "a-s-s..." I spelled.

"I know what that says!" Jon Jon shrieked with glee.

"A-s-s-t-e-r-o-i-d," I finished in a rush.

Jon Jon chewed a goldfish thoughtfully. "Why did you call him an asteroid, Miss Greevey? That only has one "s" anyway," he added, helpfully.

Just my luck to have a child prodigy in class. I clasped my hands together so tightly my nails dug into the palms.

Doug gave me a worried look. "What are you doing?"

I fixed venomous eyes on him. "I am praying that I don't kill you in front of these children." The words came out loud enough to be heard down the hall. I considered grabbing the Play-doh cutter and gutting him like a fish. It might take a while, but it would be satisfying.

"Are you gonna kill him?" Ralph squealed. "Cool! Just like David did to Goliath. Maybe we can find a rock." He began to search under the tables.

"Look, Sisi, I know that right now you think I'm a..." Doug looked furtively at the little snackers, "b-a-s..."

Jon Jon's eyes rolled upwards as he sounded out the letters. I pointed savagely at the boy.

"k-e-t-b-a-l-l," he covered, " but I think that ultimately this is the best thing for both of us."

"What did he spell?" Sarah whispered to Jon Jon.

"Basketball."

"Why does she think he's a basketball?" Sarah asked.

"Doug," I said, sweet as Splenda, "I think you're right. This has got to be the best thing that has happened to me because I have been saved from marrying the biggest asteroid I have ever met. I don't want to lay eyes on you, hear your name, see your car, run across your phone number or even smell that wretched excuse for cologne you wear ever again."

"Hey now." Doug frowned. "What's wrong with my cologne? Rachel says it's earthy."

"It smells like Pine Sol," I hissed.

I don't remember exactly how the Play-doh got into my hand, but the parents arrived to find their children sitting open-mouthed, watching the Sunday school teacher pelt her ex fiancé with purple clay. I believe I was shouting at the time, words which should probably not be uttered in a Sunday school classroom.

I do recall the phrase, "You are a first class basketball!" leaving my lips at a totally inappropriate volume.

Seven sets of parents hurriedly ushered their tots out the door. The pastor suggested that there was an opening in the coffee and doughnut ministry.

As Jon Jon passed by, he stopped. "Are you going to teach next week? That was the best time I ever had in Sunday school."

I gave him the last Lifesaver and walked out of the church.

Chapter Two

Decisions, decisions. Go to grad school on other coast or stay close to home and boyfriend? I love my honey, but can I pass up the chance of a lifetime? I'm torn. I know lots of girls who would love to snap up my hottie as soon as I leave town. Any advice from Rock Your World or anyone else? -- Sister Sue

You'll be cool either way, Sister Sue. But if God has given you a chance to see the world, I say go for it. Boyfriend will hang around if he's worth his salt. We have the internet now plus cell phones. He can always hop a plane once in a while and so can you. Three words honey, frequent flyer miles. Don't you agree, Brandi? -- Cherry B.

Sister Sue, I agree with Cherry B. Take the opportunity God is offering you. If it's not the right door, he'll close it and open another. -- Brandi

I refrained from mentioning that the door might just slam her right in the face. My Dougie door did that. Hey, that was funny. A Dougie door. The laughter welled up in my chest at the same time as a wave of tears. Now was not the time for another bout of hysteria. I gave myself a mental slap and perused the rest of the Monday blog.

Hola, Brandi. How do you know when a guy is for real? I mean, my new honey is adorable, intelligent and a Christian to boot. He drives a gorgeous Mercedes and has a beach house. Is he too good to be true? -- Galpal Glenda

The question seemed to leap off the page to ridicule me. The feelings that swelled in my heart were far from inspirational. I wanted nothing more than to mash the laptop closed and jump up and down on it. Instead I took an enormous slurp of my non fat double mocha latte and slapped out a comment.

Galpal, let me tell you what I know. Guys, Christian or not, are basically bags of pus. Oh sure, they can look good on the outside, and they can sound good, so good that you share your innermost thoughts and feelings with them, but inside, they're nothing but infectious ooze. Don't let the fancy car and the beach house fool you. Atila the Hun probably had a great ride too. So run Glenda, don't walk. Run fast and run far. -- Brandi

My angry finger hovered over the send button.

Donna gazed over my shoulder. "Uh, Simone? That seems a little...harsh. I think maybe you're not striking the right tone here."

I sighed and hit the delete button instead. "I know. Last night I ate two pints of Mississippi Mud ice cream in between prayers and I don't feel any different except I have indigestion along with the overwhelming urge to smash Doug like a bug. Giving the lovelorn the benefit of my experience is tricky right now."

"Been there, done that. It does get better over time. That's about the only wisdom I can share on the subject. Have you told anybody yet?"

"No. I've picked up the phone about a million times, but I just can't do it. It's so humiliating. I guess when people see Doug and Rachel hanging on each other they'll figure it out." I swallowed the bowling ball that suddenly materialized in my throat.

Donna patted my shoulder. Then she fiddled with the pencils on my desk. Then she straightened my pile of papers before stacking the C.D's into a wobbly tower on her way to reposition the pens in the cup on my desk.

Donna is not a fiddler by nature so I looked closer. There were bags under her eyes and a crease between her coppery brows. "What's wrong? Are you okay?"

"Oh, I'm okay, Simone, but you're not." She crossed the room to twiddle with the blinds.

"You can't blame me for being a little nutzo after what happened. How many people do you know who get jilted in preschool? It's just beyond words."

She turned to face me. "It's not that. There's something else you have to know. I can't believe everything is such a mess. I never saw this coming. I need to talk to you about..."

Audrey poked her head into the office. "Ah, good. You're both here. Let's get it done then." She sat on top of my desk, narrowly avoiding my nonfat latte. "I'm sure Donna has filled you in. You have to know there is nothing personal in the decision, merely a business choice. Dollars and cents, that's all. We all think you're great, really great so don't get all worked up about it."

Donna shot me a desperate look. "I didn't get a chance to tell her yet."

A tickle of panic started in my lower spine. "Tell me what?"

Audrey looked from her to me. "Oh. Well then I'll recap. We've decided to promote Donna to the editor's job. She is already making more money than you so we can promote her without any additional cost. You, we would have to offer a raise. So that's it, basically. The Bloggin' With Brandi thing is working out great, so we'd like for you to continue that. Offer up a new subject each week, just to keep things fresh. Work from home if you want." She glanced at the clock. "I'm late for a meeting. Thanks for the good work ladies."

And then she was gone.

I returned Donna's horrified stare.

She crimped her lips together like she was afraid her teeth would jump out of her mouth.

There was an unending silence. I wanted to scream at her, pull the barrettes out of her red hair and stick them up her nose. The old voice box eventually opened up again. "Audrey is giving *you* the editor's job? My job?"

She nodded miserably. "I never expected it. I thought I was being groomed for the technical director's job. I was just filling in until you came on board."

My head whirled like a pinwheel. "How long have you known?"

"I didn't know until this morning. I never really believed Alfie would resign anyway, but he did. Audrey left a message at my home last night asking for a meeting. I had no idea they were going to promote me. I figured they were going to talk about salaries or something. Believe me, Simone. I never would have kept something like this from you. I had no idea they were going to offer me the editor's job. You've got to believe that. We're friends. I'd never do that to you."

"But that job was promised to me, Donna. Did it occur to you to turn them down?" To think I'd been sweating away, putting in extra hours every day in preparation for my big chance. What a joke.

She closed her eyes for a moment. "I'm sorry. I asked them about the change, but I didn't turn them down. Would you, if the shoe was on the other foot?"

I looked into the face of my friend whom I desperately wanted to hate. "No," I said, "I wouldn't."

Tears gathered in my eyes. First Doug, now this. In the space of a few measly weeks I'd been demoted to woman scorned and reject blog queen. Heck, I didn't even need to show up to work anymore. My role as lowly blogger could be done without the need for an office, dark as it was. I could probably work out of a truck in a deserted alley somewhere.

Tears filled Donna's eyes. She clasped my hands in hers. "Simone, what can I do? I feel so awful."

"I'm not feeling so hot either."

"Believe me, I didn't want this to happen. Do you want me to pray with you?"

I removed my hands as gently as I could. "No, thank you. I think I need some vacation time. I'll just take my laptop and work from home for a while." I gathered up my cute purse and cold latte.

"Please don't leave like this. I just can't tell you how sorry I am. I feel like a complete criminal. Let's go someplace and talk. Come on, I'll buy you a falafel."

I shook my head. "No falafels. Take care, Donna. I know you'll be a wonderful editor. Rock Your World is lucky to have you."

She leaped from her chair. "I'm really sorry. You would have been a fantastic editor, better than me."

"Yes, I would have." I slammed the door behind me.

***

What does a college educated, self-reliant woman do when a door is slammed in her face? She picks herself up and grabs hold of life again. She washes her hands of the vile unworthy man who has wronged her, and marches boldly into the future, secure that no matter what sorrows come her way, she will face them with grace and dignity, a shining example to woman everywhere.

What did I do?

I went home to my mother.

Risky move, considering our relationship, but it was the only thing I could think of to get away from the pathetic mess of my life.

It was a two hour drive from San Francisco to Pacific Grove. When I finally eased my Mustang up the smooth circular driveway in front of Mom's pristine colonial I had totally secured all my emotional wreckage. There was not even a tremor in my voice when I greeted Sandy, Mom's long time cook at the door. I gave her a hug and meandered out to the back patio.

My mother was resplendent as usual; the color of her skirt and blouse harmonized nicely with the blue surface of the pool. She looked up from her PDA in surprise. "Simone, honey?" She flowed out of the chaise lounge. "What a surprise. I didn't know you were going to come down. You should have phoned ahead. Don't you have to work on Mondays?"

"Hi, Mom," I said in a thoroughly calm voice. "I just thought I'd pop over for a visit."

She raised an eyebrow but didn't speak.

At that moment my baggage busted wide open. Salty drops began to sproing from my tear ducts. "He dumped me, right in front of the preschoolers. And I'm not going to be an editor. And I've been barred from teaching Sunday school."

My nose emptied itself onto my upper lip. Through the torrent of tears, I saw my mother's face crease into confusion. She took me by the arm and guided me inside. Somehow I was deposited into a chair in the sunroom with a glass of iced tea on the table in front of me. Mother waited, patiently handing me Kleenex until the river ran dry.

"Now what is this about Doug dumping you? Did you say something about preschoolers?"

"He doesn't want to marry me anymore. He told me at Sunday school."

Mother ignored the second comment. "He said he doesn't want to marry you? With the wedding just weeks away? Has he lost his mind?"

"No, he's found Rachel."

"Rachel?"

"Rachel. She teaches the deaf. Isn't that nice? She's kind and understanding and she has a good sense of humor. I believe she's even a backpacker."

Mother took a hefty swig from her iced tea. She had not touched anything stronger than Lipton's for fifteen years. "Simone, are you telling me that Doug met another woman? Is that what you're saying?"

"That's exactly what I'm saying."

"Two months before your wedding?"

I blew my nose into the soggy tissue. "Two months and three days."

Her blue eyes danced little circles to match her mental contortions. "All right. I didn't see that coming, I must admit. I thought he was a fine man. Imagine, such behavior from a chiropractor. I never really did think of him as a real doctor anyway." She shook her head and put down the tea. "Well, it isn't a total catastrophe."

I gaped at her. "How is this not a total catastrophe? Doug dumped me for a girl who thinks his cologne is earthy."

"I just meant that we haven't mailed out the invitations yet. We won't have to face that humiliation. If anyone asks, we'll say he has a disease or something."

"He doesn't have a disease, Mother."

"All kinds of things could be percolating in his body even as we speak. Who knows what he could contract in the near future? The important thing is you don't have to retract invitations and make it fodder for public consumption. I'd say it was a narrow escape."

My mother has always been the beacon of propriety, only deviating from that role when she succumbed to alcoholism after my father died. I remembered exactly one day when she was not firmly in control of her public persona. On that day she broke every piece of china in the house and smashed the tea kettle through the kitchen window, narrowly avoiding the mailman. It was not the destruction particularly that scared me that day, but the fact that Mother wore no lipstick. I had never seen her without lipstick before then and I never have since.

Aunt Stella arrived later that day to stay with me for what would be close to a four month visit. "Your mama needs to go to the hospital for a while."

"Why?" I asked with typical twelve year old bluntness.

"She's got to stop drinking." It had never occurred to Stella to lie about anything. "They can help her do that in the hospital."

"Why can't she stop drinking at home?"

Aunt Stella thought about that one, pulling her long blond hair into a ponytail as she pondered. "I don't know," she said finally. "Can't be helped, Sisi. Now where is the brown sugar? I want to make cookies."

My mother's lipstick was firmly in place as she wrestled with the problem at hand. "Let's see. We've only put a deposit on the reception hall which they get to keep, I believe. You can still cancel the photographer without penalty and the florist hasn't ordered the flowers this far ahead. That leaves only the food deposit and the cake. We can chalk that up to experience." She sat back in her chair, seemingly satisfied to have put the universe back in order.

"But mother," I bleated, "I've been dumped like contaminated rubber gloves. Like a used up tube of toothpaste." I struggled to find another fitting simile. "Like that plastic wrapper on the non fat cheese slices. People will see me as the cheese wrapper girl. And you'll be the mother of the cheese wrapper girl."

"Good grief, honey. That's a little overly dramatic. It's a shock, I know, but it will pass. Don't think of it as getting dumped. Think of it as being spared."

"But...but...I love him" The tears started all over again.

"Do you love him? Still?"

"I think so. Well, I mean I sort of despise him at the moment, but there's an undercurrent of love there. You don't just stop loving someone all of a sudden, do you?"

"I'm not sure, but I would think the humiliation factor would take the edge off your love."

"But we were supposed to be together forever."

She patted my hand. "Honey, nothing is forever. You're young.

You'll find someone else to love."

"You didn't." The words flew out before I had a chance to stop them. I clapped a hand over my mouth. "I'm sorry, Mother," I mumbled.

Her chic layers of hair ruffled a bit in the breeze from the open window. "I never found someone else to love because I didn't want to. Once was enough for me." The soft emotion communicated in that sentence floored us both for a moment. Mother picked at a spot of lint on her immaculate skirt. I guzzled iced tea as if it were the elixir of life. In the distance the waves slopped against the shore.

Sandy spoke from the doorway. "Mrs. Greevey, would you like me to hold dinner for a while?"

"No need Sandy, we're finished here."

***

Over lemon chicken breasts and spinach salad, Mother recalled the last part of my hysterical rant. "Did you say something about your editor's job? How is that going?"

I looked at her unruffled brow. She sliced her chicken into small pieces with the precision of a plastic surgeon. She was the picture of the accomplished woman. For some reason which I cannot fully comprehend, I answered, "The job is going great, Mom. I'm learning so much."

"Excellent. That's how to get into a business, Simone. Work hard and prove yourself. Of course I never understood your yen for writing, but if you can make a career of it I think that's wonderful. A friend of mine just started up a marketing company and she's doing splendidly."

Mother chatted about her ongoing efforts as chief fundraiser for the Cleft Palate Society. She was in the process of arranging a dinner cruise to benefit the fall campaign. I listened, nodding in between bites.

There wasn't much further conversation until she finished her dinner and crossed the knife and fork atop the plate. "It's a pity I didn't know you were coming. I've got to fly to Houston tomorrow. We're consulting on a civic center project."

Mother is an architect in between charity events. She owns her own firm. I've often thought her buildings are a lot like she is: sharp, impressive, beautiful. It was a mistake to think she could be the soft shoulder for me to cry on. I knew better. "Don't worry about it, Mother. I'm actually on my way out of town. I'll just stay here tonight if that's okay and leave in the morning."

"That would be just fine. I'll have the guest room made up. Where are you headed?"

The fictional trip materialized in my mind just in time to stagger out of my lips. "I'm on vacation for a while so I thought I'd head to Arizona. I'm going to see Aunt Stella."

Mother's curled lip spoke volumes.

She and Stella were as alike as bologna and bouillabaisse.

"In Seepwillow? I can't imagine what you'll find to do in that hole in the wall town. It's in the absolute boondocks."

"It is pretty remote, all right." I wanted my mother to ask me to stay, to take care of me, baby me. The silence lengthened. "I guess I'll find something to do there. Aunt Stella is always asking me to come and visit."

"She'll be happy to see you. Please tell her hello for me."

I swallowed an unexpected thickness in my throat. "I will."

"Goodnight, Simone."

"Goodnight," I said to her back.

***

I lay awake, listening to the chime of the grandfather clock in the foyer. When it bonged the three a.m. hour, I got out of bed and wandered down the stairs. As I descended the oak staircase I noticed the view hadn't changed since my childhood days. Mother's taste in fine things was second to none. Lamps accentuated gorgeous oil paintings and the Oriental rugs picked up the subtle color of the sofa and settee. The hardwood floor was cool under my feet.

I ventured outside. The porch looked eerie in the moonlight, all silver shadows and glimmering pearl. A slap of cold fog made me hug my robe tighter. In the distance, heavy banks of gray hovered over the rolling ocean. I wandered up to the elegant gazebo, perched on the top of a slope. My breath caught to see that the chair was still there; the old teak rocker that was my father's favorite. And there, under the concealing canopy of a weeping cherry, was my hiding spot. He used to sit and read the paper. I would snuggle in the leafy cubby and try to read him.

He never knew I was there. At least, I didn't think he did.

I pretended to read my own version of the paper, filled with articles about animals and the newest movies. He perused his own from cover to cover, drinking from his sturdy earthenware mug. I wondered what mysteries that paper contained that would hold his interest until the last drop of coffee was gone.

Some ridiculous instinct made me look around for Oscar. He was a cat, encouraged by me, harangued by mother and ignored by father. I fed him tuna out of my sandwiches. He brought me a rat once as a present. I admired the way he could move so silently, to glide in and out of our lives like a shadow. Oscar was long gone now, except in my mind.

The weather intruded on my memory trip as the cold seeped under my robe. I headed back to the house.

I tucked myself into the guestroom among the down covers and puffy pillows. A photograph on the bedside table caught my attention. My own face stared back at me from my father's. His black hair, his green eyes, the dimple on one side of his smile. He looked as though he was trying to remember something.

Bruce Greevey was precise about everything, right down to the creases on his uniform pants. The last day of his life he kissed my mother and gave her a jaunty salute. "Good-bye, First Mate."

She smiled as she always did and repeated her part in the ritual. "See you soon, Commander."

That day Dad walked to the door and stopped, turning around with uncharacteristic hesitation. He watched me pack up my algebra homework. "Math homework done, Simone?"

"Yes, Dad."

He took a step closer and fingered the edge of my binder. Then he gave me an awkward pat on the back. "Good girl. That hard work will pay off. See you when I get back." His gaze lingered on my face for a moment and then he left.

Yes, Dad.

I thought about those last words. What if I had said, 'Can I borrow five bucks? Or 'you're a jerk to go off to sea and leave us alone again?' You never know which words will be the last ones, that's what made them so powerful. Maybe God has them written down in a book somewhere called The Last Word.

If I had known, I would have said so much more.

If my dad had known, what would he have said?

I turned his picture face down on the table and snapped off the light.

As I drifted off to sleep, I wondered why I had never cried for him.

Chapter Three

There are two kinds of deserts. The first is only marginally hostile, a beast with a tendency towards ferocity were it not for the advent of air conditioning and irrigation. People flock to these forms of desert in the winter, tucking themselves away in spacious ranch style homes with sprinklered lawns and swimming pools. It's the fashionable place to escape from nasty snow covered places. I approve of this.

Then there is the other kind of desert. The kind that brings to mind horror movies of people being picked to death by vultures when they run out of gas amid the sand dunes. The kind where the temperature reaches triple digits and the green of a saguaro cactus is blinding amidst the bleached landscape. The type of desolate spot where only a lunatic would hunker down to watch the sane folks drive through as quickly as humanly possible.

Aunt Stella? She fell into the lunatic category. The name of the town in which she ran a trailer park is Seepwillow. Though willows made me think of lovely shady bowers and grassy knolls, Seepwillow had neither. To further strengthen my aunt's lunatic image, she christened her park, *The Ruddy Duck*. The name sounded more like a yacht or a gentlemen's smoking club, but Aunt Stella swore it came from an actual bird. You guessed it, common name, Ruddy Duck. They aren't very common in Arizona, as far as I can tell, not to this scalded portion of the state anyway. Even ducks have better sense than to hang out there.

I had always known that Aunt Stella was different. I was made aware of this the first time I saw her running barefoot through the Pick N Pack parking lot trying to catch an injured jackrabbit. Uncle Bud picked up her shoes and shouted encouragement until she finally gave up the chase. Though she has nutty tendencies, she is also the one set of arms I can run to and find solace. So when the plan formed in my mind to visit her, I wasted no time in renting a car (there was no way I would drive my Mustang into the belly of Hell), packing my cosmetic bag with extra moisturizer, and tossing in two cases of Avian water. After all, if I could be Bambi the Blogger anywhere, it might as well be in Seepwillow, Arizona.

It seemed like a good idea at the time.

There was no point in phoning ahead to let Aunt Stella know I was coming. She only has two ancient rotary phones in the trailer park and she's rarely there to catch either one ringing. I gave her a cell phone one Christmas and it never made it out of the plastic container. My mother despaired long ago of ever dragging her sister into the current century.

"You can't make a Model T into a Corvette, Diane," I recalled my father saying to my mother as I eavesdropped through the door. "Stella is what she is. Let Simone go spend the summer with her. It will be a great experience."

"Bruce, you know my sister will fill her head with all that religious crap," my mother snapped. "What if she turns her into some sort of zealot?"

"Honey, in this life God is the only sure thing. Let Simone go see her aunt."

Ironic that it was my father, a man I hardly knew, that brought me to Stella and my faith. Strange. I'd never really thought about it before.

The rented Nissan edged dangerously into the overheated range as I zoomed towards Seepwillow. A prickle edged down my leg toward the gas pedal. I fought the ever present desire to floor it, to go as fast as the engine would allow. That was the one thing my father and I shared. The sound of the motor was our common language and our biggest secret. Even Mother didn't know what we did on our occasional road trips.

The gauge continued to creep higher. With a sigh, I eased up on the gas, turned off the air conditioning and rolled down the windows. Instantly, I was sopped with perspiration. My Oakley sunglasses slipped down my nose. The heat hit my face like a stinging slap.

The landscape stretched out in endless blankets of wasteland, dotted here and there with scrubby bushes. In the distance, cliffs cut upward against the brilliant blue sky. I watched an enormous black bird spiral overhead. He floated in endless circles without so much as a twitch of his wings. Probably a vulture waiting for the Nissan to break down, I figured.

I was rethinking the whole idea of visiting my aunt with every passing mile. The skin behind my knees was stuck to the seat. A puddle of sweat formed between my breasts and trickled down to the waistband of my denim skirt. "What would possess someone to live here?" I asked myself for the umpteenth time. Then again, what possessed me to come and visit? Sure I had a few amazing childhood memories connected with this place, but nostalgia will only get you so far. I was a big girl now, with a chic apartment and a two latte a day habit.

Deep down I knew what it was; a childish need for comfort, for reassurance that I was still lovable. Mother loved me in her own way, but it was not the way I needed right now, not in the face of Doug's betrayal and my work disappointment. I needed a strong dose of my zany, unconventional aunt.

A bug splatted on the windshield. It was a good metaphor for my current situation: squished and flattened. Through the yellow smear beneath the wipers, I turned in the town of Seepwillow, population 112. Perhaps the term town was a bit optimistic. Seepwillow covered maybe five square miles. The main attraction was the watering hole, appropriately named The Watering Hole. You probably couldn't get a Cosmopolitan there but I remembered that the soda was nice and cold if the electricity was working.

There was a gas station, a diner, a post office and even a Pick N Pack grocery story. The social gathering place for those who were not in need of alcohol was Katy's Corner. There you could find doughnuts, cookies, soda and cups of coffee. I had consumed many a chocolate doughnut with rainbow sprinkles on those cracked naugahyde seats. Today the Tuesday special boasted a Cup of Joe and a chocolate éclair for a buck.

I passed a few shops that were new to me. A woman's consignment store offered a green sundress in the window and just down the block another wondrous sight; Nicely Icely Ice Cream Parlor. Okay, so the parlor only had a few tables inside but the sign said ten flavors to choose from. Not Baskin Robbins, I'll grant you, but in the desert you take what you can get.

When I stopped at a red light, a chubby woman emerged from the coffee shop carrying a bag. Her gaze was immediately riveted to my car. She bent over to peer into the side window, as if I was a strange exotic animal on display at the zoo. Her face was brown and wide. She called into the open window. "Hello, hon. You look familiar. She placed a meaty arm on the window. "Give me a minute. Wait, I've got it!" she shouted before I opened my mouth. "You're Stella Bernard's little girl aren't you?"

I laughed. It had been a dog's age since anyone mistook me for Stella's daughter. "Actually, I'm her niece. You're Katy Nunez if I recall correctly."

The woman cracked a smile that revealed a missing front tooth. "The same. I haven't seen you since you were a kid. I remember when you were just a little thing with big teeth and braids tearing around on that motorbike. You were the fastest thing on two wheels."

Great. The wizened woman remembered my pre-orthodontic condition and my crazy former hobby. It's a good thing I didn't go to school in Seepwillow or she might recall my brief participation in a frog dissection protest. "I'm on my way to visit Aunt Stella."

She nodded. The heat shimmered on the ground around her. "Good girl. It seems like nowadays the youngsters don't have no time for their kin. You come in for some coffee and a doughnut tomorrow. You could use a little padding on those bones." She patted the car door and shuffled away.

My Nissan wheezed along through six more miles of nothing until we arrived at the Ruddy Duck trailer park. Aunt Stella had been hard at work since my last visit. The split rail fence around the property was painted white and little patches of sickly grass sprouted in front of each ancient trailer. I counted eleven trailers, including the one that served as the office. On the roof of this unit rested a colossal plastic duck. He wasn't new. He wasn't even middle aged. That duck had been up there since the dawn of time. He had so many coats of peeling paint on his body that it looked like he was molting.

A tall woman with long hair twisted atop her head came into view. She carried a paper grocery bag under one arm and a pile of sheets in the other. When she heard my car come to a stop she squinted over at me. A smile more dazzling than the sun bleached sand split her face.

"Simone?" She trotted over to me. "I can't believe it. Simone? Is that you? Honey!" She tried to fold me into a hug along with the sheets and paper bag. "I had a dream last night that you were here. This is just the most amazing surprise."

I took the bag from her hand and melted into her strong arms. "Hi, Aunt Stella. I'm so glad to see you."

She pushed me away a pace. "You look wonderful. So slim and dewy."

"That's sweat, not dew."

"Looks like dew to me, pumpkin. Come into my trailer before you melt away."

I did not need a second invitation to follow. The sun was beating the Macarena on my skull. After two steps I froze, my heart in my throat. "Aunt Stella," I stage whispered. "I think something just growled."

I held the bag at arms length as though it contained grade A plutonium.

"Oh brother," Stella said, retrieving the bag from me. "I forgot about him." She set the sack down on its side next to the shade of the trailer. A hissing, leathery monster about the size of a football marched out. The turtle glared at us with beady eyes before it burrowed under the front step.

"What is that thing?"

"A Sonoran Desert Tortoise. His name is LeRoy and he is the worst fighter on the planet. This is the second time this month I've found him on his back, roasting in the sun. I'm sure he's just the laughing stock of all his compatriots. I'm probably not doing a favor to his species by saving him on a regular basis. He's definitely from the shallower end of the gene pool."

Another gurgling hiss issued from under the porch, followed by some hollow thuds.

"Does he need a drink of water or something?"

"No, no. They can go for a year without so much as a sip, but LeRoy is spoiled. He eats our grass here and has more moisture than any desert tortoise has a right to. Quiet down, LeRoy." The door of the trailer screeched as she opened it. "Come in. Tell me all about everything."

The trailer was not cold, but compared to the triple digit temperature outside it was bliss. My aunt poured me a glass of weak lemonade and we sank down at the battered round table. The place was tiny, worn and neat. On one end was the master bedroom and bath and on the other a cramped kitchen with just enough room for a tiny table and chairs.

In the center of the table was the same squat piece of Indian pottery decorated with flying birds around the rim that had been there for two decades. Over the years I found the vessel to be a constant source of treasures: shiny stones, loose change, the odd bit of candy, and once a barbecued chicken leg that my aunt absent mindedly placed there. I snuck a peek: a few coins, a fat red crayon and a small rubber frog. I felt more at home than I did in my San Francisco apartment.

"Aunt Stella, you look fit as a distance runner." Her arms were tanned and muscular, her face browned to a darker shade than her hair.

"Oh, you. I get along. So tell me why you decided to drop in. Did you take a vacation from the e-zine? How is that going?"

Thanks to the wonders of the postal service, my aunt knew more about my life than my mother. If I could just get her to use e-mail, I wouldn't have permanent writer's cramp. "I didn't get the editor's job."

"Really? I can't imagine why not. Well I know you must be very disappointed, but there's got to be another path for you."

I nodded. "Maybe. I'm just Brandi the Blogger at the moment."

"Sounds like some sort of serial murderer or something, like Jack the Ripper. What exactly is a blogger?"

I tried to explain the dynamics of an online chat group. My aunt smiled with encouragement though I knew she didn't have the foggiest notion what I was talking about. She still wrote all her letters in cursive and to my knowledge had never used an ATM machine. If there's a picture in the dictionary under 'antiquated' it's got to be hers. "Blogging pays the bills and I can take my laptop anywhere I go, even to Seepwillow, Arizona."

"Well there you go." Aunt Stella's eyes were wide with excitement.

"I know you love to travel so now there's nothing to tie you down, except your fiancé, of course. That wedding is right around the corner, isn't it? Uncle Bud and I have to make our hotel reservations pretty soon. How long has it been since we visited you two in San Francisco? Two years maybe? I still can't get the picture of all those hills out of my mind."

I swallowed hard but she didn't seem to notice.

"We wanted to get you both a really special wedding gift. Would you and Doug like matching fishing poles? I thought it would be a great idea but Uncle Bud wasn't so sure. Does Doug like to fish? Well even if he doesn't it might be fun for him to learn. That would give you both a chance to get out of the city once in a while. So how would we get the poles there? We could bring them on the wedding day and leave them at Diane's house. How would that be?"

I couldn't answer.

"No? Oh well don't worry about it honey. We can mail them or maybe you and Doug could come for a visit. Do you think he'd like the desert?"

My eyes filled with tears. As much as I fought against it, my innards began to liquefy until I was a big blubbery mess. "Doug dumped me for another woman," I wailed. "He's gone. I'm not getting married. There isn't going to be any wedding. No Raspberry Swirl cake, no bouquet, nothing."

The rumble of the air conditioner was the only sound for a moment.

"Oh no. Goodness. Well that is sad news. And here I've been going on and on about your wedding. I'm so sorry." Her calloused hand closed over mine. "My poor Simone. How awful for you."

I opened my mouth but no words would come.

Aunt Stella's bushy eyebrows knitted together. Then she said the words I had driven through Hell to hear.

"He will always regret giving you up."

Through a torrent of tears I hugged her.

***

A full box of Kleenex later and I was drained. I paced the perimeter of the tiny trailer, pausing to gaze out the window. The sun was low in the horizon, painting the landscape in brushstrokes of rose and umber.

Stella opened a new box of tissue. "Don't you worry about a thing. You are welcome to stay here as long as you feel like. I'll have Chaz make sure the air in trailer four is working. You can stay there. It's got a new refrigerator and the shower is pretty good if you turn the water up all the way."

"Who's Chaz?"

"He's a nice man who lives here in exchange for handyman services."

I raised an eyebrow at my tender hearted aunt. "He doesn't pay rent?"

"No, but he does plenty around here to earn his keep. You'll like him, I'm sure." She gave me a squeeze on the shoulder and headed to the kitchenette. "You know Simone, I didn't do any shopping this week because I've been cleaning the empty units for the summer campaign."

"What's the summer campaign?"

Her words were muffled as she banged around in the cupboards. "It's a celebration to appreciate the current tenants and to encourage new clientele. It's part of my business plan. Phase one starts this weekend as a matter of fact."

These words did not sound natural coming out of my aunt's mouth, sort of like the Pope giving makeup tips or something. "Have you been reading a book?"

She hurried to the shelf and extracted a battered volume. "As a matter of fact, I have. Your mother gave it to me for Christmas five years ago and I just got around to reading it. Take a look."

"Really?" I was surprised on a number of levels. I never pictured my aunt reading anything having to do with business and I didn't know my mother exchanged gifts with her sister. Imagine. That probably explained the string of dried chillies that had been hanging in the garage for years. I never could picture my mother buying desiccated produce. The book was entitled *One Hundred Ways to Jump Start Your Business*.

Stella handed me a square of paper towel dotted with ink stains. "Here it is, all in black and white. Or maybe blue."

Leave it to my aunt to write her business plan on a paper towel. I struggled to read the inky scrawls. "So you're going to...rent out the three empty units, beef up advertising for the trailer park, increase sales of your prickly pear jam and buy Alpo?"

"Alpo?" Stella peered over my shoulder. "Oh that was part of my shopping list last year. We had a stray beagle living here then. He found a family and moved to Tennessee. He never did eat that Alpo. I had to give him scrambled eggs and hamburger, the stinker."

"This is a pretty ambitious plan. What brought this on?"

She tapped a spoon on the counter. "Nothing. You know your mother has been telling me for years I need to think about the future. She's got such a head for business."

"And?"

Stella is incapable of lying. When she tries, she begins to sputter like a boiling tea kettle. "Well... ah, you know..." Eventually her kettle ran dry. "We have a balloon payment due on this place."

"For how much?"

"Fifty-three-thousand dollars and ninety-eight cents."

My eyes widened to Frisbee circumference. "Wow. That's a hefty payment." I could see why she wanted to put her plan into action but I wasn't sure about her ability to succeed as a business woman. Astute folks with heads for finance didn't let people live rent free on their property. I made a mental note to have a word with this Chaz person. "What does Uncle Bud think?"

Bud was my rotund, jovial, totally scatterbrained uncle currently serving on a mission trip somewhere. He was a good six inches shorter than his wife. As a child I was completely mesmerized by his head which is bald and shiny as a skinned onion. He would eat absolutely anything from head cheese to fried crickets. The only food I had ever seen him refuse was canned peas.

"He thinks the plan is good. God helps those who help themselves is his motto. He is an optimist as you know." She continued to clang around in the kitchen. "How do you feel about Twirly Roni?"

"What's Twirly Roni?"

She moved a pace and I beheld a dizzying array of cans in the cupboard over her shoulder. "There was a sale. And they fit in the cupboard."

"Twirly Roni it is," I said.

We dined on the curly stuff and dill pickles with cans of diet soda to wash it down. As we slurped I looked out the window and saw a older man with skin the color of café au lait and black eyes. His hair was a startling white that seemed to levitate above the browner shades of his face. He scuffled to the door of trailer number six without lifting his eyes from the ground. "Who is that?"

Her eyes followed mine. "That's Mr. Singh."

"He doesn't look happy."

"He isn't. He moved here from India to start a dental practice. Right after they arrived his wife and daughter were killed by a drunk driver."

I watched the man in horror. "That is awful. The poor man."

"Yes." She nodded. "I've tried to get him to come to Bible study on Wednesdays but he's not open to the idea. He's still grieving, I'm sure. Even Bud can't coax a smile out of him."

"How long has he lived here?"

"Almost three years now. He pays his rent on time and works on the grass and shrubs outside his trailer. I just wish we could help ease his pain a little." She pushed her plate away. "Simone, I am so glad you're here. It's just a gift from God."

My cockles were thoroughly warmed. "I really think He brought me here Aunt Stella. I feel as if He led me to Seepwillow."

"Of course He did."

"Mother said to say hello."

"That's so nice. I must write her a letter. I've been so busy but that's no excuse." She continued to chatter.

As I sat in a post carbohydrate slump, my eyelids grew heavy. I tried to stifle a yawn.

"What am I doing blabbering away? You must be just dead tired." She threw our paper plates into the trash. "Let me take you to your trailer. Wait until Uncle Bud hears about your visit."

"Thanks, Aunt Stella. I can't wait to see Uncle Bud. I'll be happy to help in whatever way I can while I'm here. Maybe I can help with the summer campaign."

Her blue eyes sparkled with moisture. "I am delighted to hear that Simone, because I have a big favor to ask you."

"Sure, anything." How bad could it be to do a favor for ones aunt? I knew she would never ask anything that would push me out of my comfort zone.

I didn't have time to regret that thought properly at the time. I was too caught up in the memory that drew me to the window. The sunlight outlined everything in tight shadow. It took me back to a long ago day when I was a child.

When it was me and Dad and speed.

When things were easy.

When I was unafraid.

I felt her hand on my shoulder, bringing me back to the present.

"It's in the shed, honey. Whenever you want it."

"Thanks." I could feel my jaw tighten. "I won't."

She opened her mouth to say something when her words were lost in a horrendous crash. We both dashed into the molten courtyard.

A set of legs dangled from underneath the plastic duck that hovered above the office trailer. On the ground lay the ladder and next to that stood a young child with her middle three fingers stuffed between her lips. As we stood with our mouths open, the child's lips began to quiver.

"Are you okay Jojo?" Aunt Stella asked as I righted the ladder for the hanging legs.

The girl nodded, still sucking the fingers. "I wanted to climb the ladder. It fell down." Tears trickled down her face onto the worn tee shirt. The lashes on her enormous brown eyes collected moisture in a sparkly fringe.

Aunt Stella checked her all over for bumps or contusions. Finding none, she enveloped the girl in a tight hug. When the sobs subsided, Stella looked upward. "Chaz? Are you up there?"

"Uh huh," said a deep voice from beneath the giant plastic fowl. "Everyone okay down there?"

"Yes, Chaz, we're all fine," she said.

So this was Chaz the Moocher.

The legs scrambled for purchase on the aluminum ladder I had propped against the trailer wall. One grubby shoe slipped on the top rung, sending the legs once again scrabbling in mid-air. A shower of loose coins rained out of his pockets followed by a small rectangle that bashed me above the eyebrows.

"Owwww," I said, clapping a hand to my forehead.

A set of black eyes appeared over the trailer roof. "Sorry about that. Are you hurt?"

I grumbled an answer and picked up the tiny book. It was a miniature Bible, water stained and worn. Inside the pages were marked by a rainbow of different inks. Some pages had tiny doodles drawn in the margins. Others were folded at the corners.

"Ewww," I muttered to myself, the book suspended in my fingertips. What kind of person graffitied a Bible? The same kind that wrangled free rent off a softie like Stella. Wasn't Bible doodling along the lines of dragging a flag through the mud? I'd never so much as smudged a page in the Good Book.

Jojo squealed with glee as she darted around retrieving the scattered coins. In the distance I could see a woman trotting towards us as fast as her pregnant belly would allow. She had one hand clasped to her abdomen and the other to her lower back.

Stella steadied the ladder as Chaz climbed to the ground.

The man was roughly the dimensions of an oil tanker. He was a few inches taller than my aunt but broad shouldered and rectangular throughout. His bicep muscles bulged to fill the sleeves of his tee shirt. Two braids of black hair hung out the bottom of a bandana that molded to the top of his head. He smiled and his tanned cheeks dimpled.

My eyes were riveted, first on the big man, and then on the wonder that stood between him and the trailer.

He extended a calloused hand. "I'm Chaz." His eyes followed mine. "You like bikes?"

"Simone." I tore my eyeballs away and took the besmirched hand.

"Are you into dirt bikes?" he repeated, his voice a low baritone.

"Me? Not really." I cleared my throat. "How are the duck repairs coming along?"

He rubbed a finger along his wide nose. "The old bird has seen better days. I think I got the light working under her chin, but that's about it."

Jojo trotted over and grabbed Chaz around the knees. "I'm sorry the ladder felled."

"I am so sorry, Mr. Tagliola," the pregnant woman said, her words colored by a Spanish accent. She panted, looking from him to Jojo. "Are you hurt?"

"No, no problem. I'm fine. Jo's fine too." He patted the child on the head. "I'm just glad she didn't clobber herself with the ladder.

"Anna, this is my niece Simone." Stella pointed in my direction.

Anna turned her attention to me. Through the exasperation painted on her face, her eyes were warm, hair piled up in a curly brown puff on her head. "So nice to meet you. I am sorry Jojo caused a fuss. I thought she was out looking for the turtle."

Jojo nodded. "I didn't find him. He's hiding. Look what I got." She showed her mother the handful of coins.

Anna's face clouded. She grabbed the child's wrist. "Where did you get this? Did you take this Josephina?"

The girl's lower lip began to quiver again.

Chaz smiled at the girl. "It was nothing like that, Mrs. Escobar. Jojo didn't do anything wrong. She picked it up for me. She can keep it."

I huffed silently. Sure the guy had plenty of pocket change; he didn't pay a nickel in rent.

Anna straightened. "No. It doesn't belong to her. Give it back to Mr. Tagiola, Jo."

Jojo handed the coins into Chaz' enormous palm.

"These two are for you." He slid a few quarters into her dirty fingers until he saw the frown that darkened Anna's face. "Jo helped me carry my tools. That's good for fifty cents at least."

Anna prompted her daughter. "Say thank you."

"Thank you." Jojo's mother pulled her back in the direction of their trailer.

"Hey Jojo, I'll tell you when I'm going to work on the sprinklers. Okay?" Chaz called.

The child nodded, and shot him a smile.

"Are you sure you're all right, Chaz?" Aunt Stella said.

"You bet." He flexed his muscled shoulders. "I think I'm in better shape than the duck. At least my feet aren't about to fall off." His black eyes fixed on my face. "I'm real pleased to meet you, Simone. Stella talks about you all the time. She said you used to come to Seepwillow every summer when you were a kid."

I mumbled something noncommittal. His boyish smile made me want to flash one of my own but there was no way he was going to charm me the way he had my kin. Remember all those months of unpaid rent, I reminded myself. Ignore those sultry black eyes. He was a squatter.

"So what brings you to the desert?"

"Do I need a reason?"

"No, uh, I just thought, well, you don't look as though you..."

I wasn't about to let this guy off the hook. "As though I what?"

"As though you're not quite, er, acclimated to the climate yet."

Acclimated? Who could be acclimated to this place? I had to admit though, Chaz looked supremely well acclimated. I couldn't see a single bead of sweat rolling off his wide brow. I noticed that his skin was the exact color of a tan M&M, before that color was kicked out in favor of the flashier blue model. A sudden urge to savor those chocolatey gems overwhelmed me. The heat was getting to me.

"I'm acclimating fine, thank you," I sniffed. "I'm here to visit my Aunt for a few days."

Chaz stared for another moment, shifting from one foot to the other. He slid a wrench into the back pocket of his jeans. "Sure, well, I guess I'll be seeing you around. Let me know if there's anything that needs fixing on your trailer. If it's not poultry, I might be able to do it."

I smothered a smile, ignoring how well his muscular legs looked in those jeans. Repeat the mantra, Simone. Chaz was a moocher. Chaz was a smoocher. Moocher! I meant moocher.

"I've gotta get going." He cast a thoughtful look in my direction. "You should go inside."

The sweat rolled down my face which was probably blotchy from the heat. There was no question that I looked like the skin on a tapioca pudding but I was still more of a gem than this man who used his rugged good looks and boy next door charm to bilk my aunt. He was a louse and arrogant to boot. "I'm fine. The heat doesn't bother me in the least."

He gave me a strange look. "Okay, but you better go inside anyway."

"And why is that, Mr. Tagliola?" I demanded.

"The rain."

I looked up and around. The horizon shimmered gold against the intense blue of the sky. No black clouds. No rumble of thunder. And the temperature was still three degrees past lava. "Really? It's going to rain?" I didn't bother to hide the sarcasm in my words. "Did you get some weather insight while you were up there with the duck?"

His gaze hovered for a moment on my face until it dropped to my Linea Paolo sandals. "I wasn't being smart. I...your clothes are nice and I'd hate to see you ruin those shoes." He picked up a bag of tools with one hand and hoisted the ladder with the other. "I'll just put these back before I take off. Bye, Stella." He gave me a hesitant smile. "Nice to meet you Miss Simone. I hope I'll see you again soon."

"Good-bye, Chaz." Stella waved a hand. "Thanks for tinkering with the duck."

We left him to his clean up.

"You know having him cough up some rent money would help with your expenses. You can't pay off your loan letting people live here for free."

"He does so many things for me. Did you see the fence and the lawns? That's all his doing and I didn't even ask him. I consider it a blessing that he's here." She began to walk towards the office trailer. A sudden breeze picked up her gauzy dress and whirled it around her legs.

My sweet aunt would consider it a blessing if Charles Manson showed up. She would put him to work trimming shrubs and feed him piles of Twirly Roni. "What exactly are his ongoing duties?"

"Oh a little of this and that." She stopped to pluck a scraggly stem of grass. "Lately he's been fixing all the sprinkler heads."

I surveyed the sickly lawns that languished in front of each trailer. "What else?"

"He stayed up all night feeding a baby jackrabbit. That's got to be good for at least a months rent. And there are lots of other things too, that I can't remember at the moment." Her forehead creased in thought.

A strange smell distracted me from my interrogation. I inhaled a whiff of faraway verdure, as out of place as a snowflake on the moon. Stella noticed it too. We stopped in our haphazard march to the office and looked up at the sound of a motorcycle kicking to life. Chaz's muscled arms looked like they were sculpted from glossy brown stone as he maneuvered the handlebars. I forced myself to close my mouth at the luscious sight of a lovely male on top of lovelier bike.

I watched him race away on that sweet, blood red Elsinore.

Just as the rain began to fall.

***

I waited out the storm in the office trailer. Aunt Stella slogged away in search of a bucket to catch the drips in the chapel trailer. The rain slammed so hard onto the office roof it sounded like artillery fire. This place was insane. Molten to muddy in minutes. I watched from the tiny window as water puddled for a few seconds on the ground before it was sucked into the starved earth.

Chaz Tagliola was probably feeling very smug at the moment. My sandals were either ruined or at the very least they would never look quite the same again. How in the name of cheese did he know it was going to rain? Was he some sort of weather savant?

"Okay, so the guy knows the weather," I grumbled to a scrawny spider plant. "He didn't have to be so condescending about it." He knew how to handle a dirt bike too, I thought with a jealous pang. The long ago thrill of reckless speed came back to me so vividly I could taste it. "Get over it, Simone. Ancient history. You're not a biker chick. Put yourself to good use and see what you can do to help Stella."

The nice thing about talking to yourself is there's no one around to argue with you. I made my way over to the messy corner under a hanging lamp. Piles of papers covered the top of a metal desk. Underneath the desk was a box labeled "fuzzy." I didn't even want to know what that was so I went back to the papers on the desktop. I sorted them into two stacks, one for expenses and one for income. The bill pile was frighteningly high but at least the desk looked more organized when I was done. I moved on to the file cabinet.

The top drawer opened after a gigantic yank which cost me a fingernail. The effort yielded three manila files and a can of frank and beans. I put the can on the counter for safekeeping. It might be a welcome change from Twirly Roni. In multicolored folders was the tenant information. As much as I longed to peek in the yellow Chaz Tagliola file, I knew that was private information. Besides, someone might come in and find me snooping. I slid the drawer closed.

The trailer was dingy and faded. It matched my mood. What was I doing in this awful desert again? Oh yes, I reminded myself, recovering from being dumped by the man I loved. Discarded like used dental floss. Passed over like a withered apple in the produce bin. Stomped like...

I was distracted from my list of similes by a tap on the trailer door. It was Jojo Escobar clutching a red and white striped umbrella.

She squelched into the room. "Hi."

"Hi, Jojo. What are you doing out here in the rain?"

"I like rain. Mama said to bring you this." She extracted another umbrella from under her slicker.

"Well thank you. Your mother is so thoughtful."

The girl did not reply. She came into the trailer and stood there, rivulets of water puddling under her. Her big brown eyes fixed on me.

After several seconds of this silent scrutiny I began to fidget. "So, how are you doing?"

"Okay." Her visual interrogation didn't falter for a moment.

I wracked my brain. What sort of topics did little people talk about? "Are you having a good day?"

She rubbed her jelly bean nose. "Uh huh."

"Do you think it will stop raining soon?"

"Uh huh."

"Do you go to school?"

"Uh uh."

"Had any good facials lately?"

The girl blinked and resumed her stare.

"Uh, let's see if we can find something to eat." Sunday school taught me one thing; children and food go together like pedicures and new sandals. Pillaging the desk drawers under the ancient cash register produced a half roll of Lifesavers and a package of beef jerky. I looked around for a clean spot on the floor to sit but the linoleum was pretty much covered with boxes, puddles or muddy footprints. There was one carpeted corner with a stack of folding chairs that served as a microchapel. I hoisted Jojo to a narrow counter under the window and we ate candy and jerky. At least we were getting some protein with all the preservatives.

"Do you like living in the desert?"

She nodded, the snacks seemed to have loosed her tongue. "Uh huh, but not Mommy."

"Why not?"

"She wants a yard for her garden. Mostly she wants a bathtub."

"I see. Are you going to move to a house someday?"

"Daddy says no because he's got too many moths to feed."

I hid a smile. "I think he means mouths."

"Oh." She examined the toe that poked through a hole in her sneaker. "I like it here. Miss Stella gives me candy. Mr. Chaz helps me with numbers."

The thought of the muscled free loader caused my lip to curl.

"Do you like Mr. Chaz, Jojo?"

"Uh huh. He gives me gum and lets me help when he fixes the

sprinklers. He never yells at me."

"Hmmm. What about the other people who live here? Are they nice too?"

"Yes. Only Mr. Singh is scary cuz of the bodies."

I coughed on a mouthful of jerky. "What?"

"I hear Mommy." Jojo hopped down from the counter.

"Jojo," I called to her as she left, "what did you say about Mr. Singh?"

"He puts bodies in his trash bags." She unfurled her umbrella. "Bye Miss Simone."

Then she was gone.

Chapter Four

Brandi girl, I know what Heaven on earth means. I have had the perfect morning. First, shopping in the city for the most amazing pair of Manolo pumps. Then breakfast with Ryan at Tsar Nicoulai. Scrambled eggs with truffle oil and caviar. Ryan said the only thing more delicious than the food was me. Can you believe it? I thank God for him every moment. How did I get so lucky in love? -- Galpal Glenda

I tried not to let the bile swallow me up. The Wednesday morning sunlight danced through the blinds but it did nothing to lighten my mood. A terrible jealous rage swirled inside my head and pounded on my temples, demanding to be released. Lucky in love. Ha. Why should Glenda have perfect Scrambled Egg Man? What did she have that I didn't?

She worked as a dental technician for goodness sake. She spent the day with people's spit on her fingers. To be fair, the woman did seem to have fine taste in clothes, but so did I. My fingernails were always manicured and I was close to being an editor. I had a wonderful sense of humor and good skin, for crying out loud.

My man wasn't perfect. He wasn't even okay. He was evil incarnate. A chiropractor with the heart of a demon. I couldn't recall a single reason why I had fallen for the guy. "Doug," I hissed to my computer screen, "you are a nasty toad and I hope Rachel stomps on your heart like home plate." If there was a shred of justice in the world he would experience what it was like to be publicly humiliated. Maybe she would break up with him via the public address system at the supermarket. It would be justice served.

I grabbed the nearest item and threw it across the room. The empty soda can crashed into the refrigerator with a clatter.

I sighed. The awful part, the really hideous part, was deep down I didn't believe my nasty sentiments. Doug was my best friend and I loved him. I shared everything with him. For some reason which I did not comprehend, he stopped loving me. Or worse, he never really loved me at all.

Ouch.

Hot tears welled up inside my lids.

Doug loved another girl instead of me.

A tiny voice whispered in my brain. "Rachel is lovable. Why aren't you?" I had heard that voice before. Even as a preteen I noticed the whisper of those feelings in my head. The worn packet of letters was out of my suitcase and in my hand before I even realized it. The crisp paper unfolded like a flower.

Dear Simone,

What a lovely lady you are turning out to be. Do you remember when we went to the beach for your birthday? I watched you dance on the waves like a spray of foam. Your hair whirled around you until you fell into the water with a splash. The cold didn't discourage you at all and we made castles and sang in the waves until the sunset. I saw many children playing in the sand but none of them hold a candle to you. I am so blessed to have such a marvelous daughter. I love you, my sweet Simone.

-- Daddy

I knew every curve of the script, every word by heart.

I knew, because I had written all the letters myself.

They were the crystallization of what I knew a father daughter connection should be. Those words held wishes that burned down deep. I wanted to hear them from Dad's lips but I never did. And then he was gone.

A familiar ache rose under my breast bone. Since Doug and I had become engaged, the ache had subsided, buried under a sea of other feelings, I supposed. Now it prickled my insides as strong as ever. I refolded the letters for the millionth time, wishing I could throw them away. Instead, I buried them in the bottom of my suitcase and slammed down the lid.

I leaped out of my narrow bench seat at the rickety table so abruptly I banged my head on the cabinet. An angry march to the buzzing refrigerator yielded nothing for breakfast but a box of baking soda.

Scrambled Egg Man shared caviar with Galpal Glenda and I sat in a decrepit trailer in the desert with nothing in my stomach but a stray Twirly Roni. Doug was probably out backpacking on some breathtaking mountain trail with Rachel, eating gourmet muffins and drinking French roast coffee. Where was the justice in that? I threw myself on the full sized mattress that seemed to be sliding starboard and pressed my hands together.

"God, I am sorry for being petty. I am sorry for all of the countless ways I want to hurt Doug. Please help me to be a loving, gracious person. I need help because I don't know how to forgive him. Really I just feel like smashing him flat. Amen."

I felt not one iota better. I closed my eyes, drained. A fly bobbed and banged into the ceiling above my head. I knew I should respond to Glenda's entry on the blog, but I just didn't have it in me at the moment. My stomach gurgled, reminding me it had nothing in it at the moment either. After a deep cleansing breath I shoved my self pity back into the dark place where it lurked and refocused my thoughts. Someone important said that the best thing to do when life steamrolls you is to help others. "Okay, Simone. Let's just test out that little theory."

Last night Aunt Stella had asked me to help with, what did she call it? Phase one of her business plan set to kick off on Saturday. Secretly I was flattered. I did have a mind for business and it would be a piece of cake to help drag her into the computer age, provided she could be convinced to use the laptop rather than paper towels to formulate her growth plan. I picked up a few tidbits about marketing from Rock Your World that I could put to good use.

Things would be okay. I had been given a mission, a rope to pull myself out of ever deepening self pity.

I returned to the table, tapped open a new Word file and began to jot some notes. Eleven trailers. One functioned as an office/chapel, one for Aunt Stella and Uncle Bud, that left nine to rent. I looked out the dusty window into the sunlight that already blazed at eight fifteen a.m. Time to find out the pertinent business details from Aunt Stella: operating expenses, the cost of insurance and the like.

A gleam of white caught my eye. Mr. Singh shuffled to his trailer, eyes glued to his feet. The shock of white hair hung down into his face. Slung over his shoulder was a bulging plastic bag. With a furtive look around the area, he unlocked the door and darted inside. A strange feeling of unease tickled my backbone. What had Jojo said about bodies in trash bags? Ridiculous, just childish fancy. I pushed away the preposterous thought, turned off my laptop and headed out the door.

Aunt Stella stood along the split rail fence that separated the trailer park from the scrubby wasteland beyond. She stood next to a painfully skinny man who towered over her by a head and a half. He was dusky and dark, with a sweat stained tee shirt tucked into jeans, secured with a thick leather belt. At the sound of my footsteps he whirled around, brown eyes wide with surprise.

"Simone," Stella said, "This is Jaime Escobar. He lives here with his family."

The man nodded, giving me a slight smile that showed chipped front tooth. "Pleased to know you." His voice was heavy with accent. The hand he offered was hardened and dry.

"Jaime's wife Anna is expecting any time now. You met her yesterday." Stella went on. "The kids are so excited to have a new little sister or brother, aren't they?"

Jaime nodded, scuffing one boot into the dry ground. "They hope for a girl, to make things more even."

"How many children do you have?" I asked.

"This one will be six. Four boys and a girl so far. My wife tells me you helped Jojo after some trouble with a ladder. Thank you."

A bead of sweat rolled down my neck. "I didn't do much."

He squinted at his watch. "I need to get to work. Pleased to know you." He marched back to his trailer.

The air was dead still. There was no trace left of the moisture dumped in yesterday's storm. Perspiration collected on my forehead and back. "So the Escobar's are in trailer number...?"

"Three. Next to Mr. Singh."

"About Mr. Singh. What does he carry around in those trash bags?"

She frowned. "Trash, I guess. I never really asked him. Why?" Stella took my arm and we walked back to the office trailer.

"Oh, no reason. I just wondered. So Mr. Singh and the Escobars are long term tenants I take it."

She nodded.

"Are any of the other trailers rented out?"

"Two of them are reserved for the last two weeks of October. That's a nice time to come to the desert." She gazed at the brilliant blue sky.

I remained unconvinced that there actually was a nice time to come to the desert but I refrained from saying so. "Excluding the office trailer and the one you and Uncle Bud call home and the two for Singh and Escobar, that leaves seven trailers available to rent after the October people are gone."

"Six. Chaz is in trailer two."

Ah yes. Chaz and his rent free accommodations. I was about to press her further about him when my foot scraped against something. I looked down and shrieked. I gasped. "Is that...?"

Stella grabbed my hands in alarm. "What? What is it?"

I stabbed a finger downward.

She knelt to the hot earth and gingerly retrieved the half-buried figure. It was a baby doll with empty staring sockets where the eyes should have been. The hands were missing too, leaving sharp plastic stumps. "How grotesque," Stella whispered. "Who would do that to a child's doll?"

"Maybe it belongs to one of Jaime Escobar's children?"

She shook her head. "I don't think so. The older boys are gone most of the time, working with their dad. Anna keeps a close eye on the younger ones. They're good little people. They would never ruin a doll. Goodness knows they have few enough toys to begin with."

I wondered how it was possible to keep your eye on that many children at once. It would be a hefty child to eyeball ratio.

"Must have been dumped by someone, hopefully on their way out of town." I fanned air in the vee neck of my Tommy H. tee shirt. "I need to talk to you about what kind of computer work you are envisioning."

She looked puzzled. "Computer work?"

"Sure. You said you wanted me to help with your business plan. I've never designed a website before, but I know people who can help. The on-line advertising will be a cinch. We can post some photographs and maybe have a contest to give away a free week's stay. There are all kinds of camping groups and we could buy some ads on their sites." I continued to ramble on until I noticed the look on my aunt's face.

"Oh dear. Those thoughts are great, Simone, really. I think we should try all of them, but I was thinking of something a little more low tech, too."

We continued on our way to her trailer. "What sort of low tech?" I said as we piled in.

"Saturday is our kickoff campaign, you see. I mentioned that yesterday. There will be games for the kids, a barbecue, and a prickly pear jam booth. We've already posted fliers everywhere. Folks seem really excited about it. There aren't too many get togethers in the summer time after the July 4th picnic." She went to the closet and extracted a white bundle.

One of my eyebrows prickled in alarm and rose almost to my hairline. "Aunt Stella, just what did you want me to do?"

She twisted the plastic between her hands. "Well there will be lots of children, I hope, and we're keeping with the Ruddy Duck theme you see. We're going to have Pin the Beak on the Duck, Duck Duck Goose and Blind Man's Duck."

A thread of unease rumbled along my spine. "Aunt Stella?"

"So you see, honey, it's just great that you volunteered to help." With a flourish she decloaked the mysterious white bundle. "I was hoping you could be the duck."

The gears in my brain began to grind together. The duck? My eyeballs rolled around in their sockets before my lips could form any syllables. "That looks like a chicken costume," the lips finally managed.

She laughed. "I know. They didn't have any duck costumes, so the chicken was the closest. Just look here. It's got a feather cap and shiny yellow stockings to go with it. I am so happy you're small enough to wear it. And what wonderful timing you coming into town just now." Aunt Stella's smile beamed brighter than a solar flare. "You'll be the cutest thing with a beak."

Cute with a beak?

Perhaps the Twirly Roni had formed some sort of carbohydrate clot in my thinking glands. I looked down at my French manicured nails and tailored shorts. Yep, it was still my body. No one had transported me to some other dimension where duck costumes are the norm. I was definitely awake so it couldn't be some wacky dream sequence.

Dress like a duck?

I wore Manolo shoes and Jones New York jackets. My purses were cute, for heaven's sake, ask anyone. In addition, it was my general policy to avoid any situation that might result in my looking like a complete idiot. "Aunt Stella, I am just not the costume wearing type. Especially not the poultry costume wearing type."

Her beam continued, undiminished. "I just knew God would send someone. I am way too tall and Chaz is too big. Of course Anna is pregnant and frankly, I think she's a smidge too curvy even if she wasn't."

I opened my mouth but my feeble muttering did nothing to stem my aunt's enthusiasm. She had always been relentlessly stubborn in a horrible nice way. Sort of like a big sugary glacier that plows along, leaving a sweet trail of devastation in its wake. Sure, you've been flattened but for some reason you feel as though you should thank her for squishing you.

"Aunt Stella," I began again, determined to derail this glacier.

"You're going to be a superb chicken, honey."

Or maybe a dead duck.

Chapter Five

D-day.

I asked not for whom the duck quacked, because I knew it quacked for me. Five days after my dramatic arrival, the Ruddy Duck kick-off had arrived.

Saturday morning dawned hotter than a habenero pepper. Even the floor was warm where my feet made contact as I rolled out of bed. Aunt Stella fixed me scrambled eggs and toast with prickly pear jam, perhaps trying to sweeten me up for my date with humiliation. Her face was wreathed in smiles as she bustled about moving jam jars, adding stickers to the kids' tables and cleaning the empty trailers until they shone.

I had my doubts about the size of the expected crowd. My internet ads and the new website had only gone into effect a few days ago. How many people would travel to Seepwillow, Arizona to eat jam and make friends with a disgruntled fowl? Then again, many of my San Francisco friends might do it just to get the laugh of a lifetime. The only good thing about it was no one would recognize me in the awful getup.

My mind traveled back to the morning's blog when I tried to deal gracefully with Glenda and her scrambled egg guy.

Dear Galpal Glenda,

*We all celebrate in your happiness. (*God did not strike me dead here so I took that as a good sign and kept writing.) *It sounds like you have found a soulmate* (gulp, sniff) *to walk beside you with your faces turned to Heaven. You go girl. -- Brandi*

I realized when I hit the send button that I was in a Job-ish kind of mental state. The "why me?" zone. Of course, Job had it a lot worse than just being rejected and landing in a chicken suit in the desert. He lost all his children, everything he owned, developed a terrible skin condition and had to deal with excruciatingly pompous friends who told him he was being justly punished. Through it all, he never denounced God.

Go Job.

Job and I were simpatico. I didn't think God had abandoned me either, but I sure wondered why He let my life fall apart. And the chicken costume. Why the chicken costume, Lord? Hadn't I experienced enough character building for one lifetime?

I could feel for poor Job when he asked, "What have I done to deserve this?"

I didn't feel too ashamed about my "why me?" attitude. That was understandable after being dumped in public. And losing a job. And landing in the bottom of a fiery pit. And dressing up like Daffy. It was the other feeling that caused me grief when I considered Galpal and her perfect man. The nasty green "why *her*?" that circled in my gut. Now that was a shameful thing indeed. Catty, petty, envious. None of those descriptors were things I aspired to be.

The ugly truth was I was just plain jealous.

I was jealous of Glenda's perfect guy, envious that Rachel was more a match for my fiancé than I was and positively green that Donna got my job. Frankly, anyone who didn't get roped into wearing a poultry suit was the object of my envy as well.

One of the few positive things about wearing a chicken suit in the desert in August is that there is no room for self reflection. There was hardly room for my nicely toned behind. The polyester fluff encased me like a Polish sausage skin. At nine o'clock in the morning, I waddled out of the trailer, sweat pouring down the back of my neck within seconds.

There were a surprising number of people gathered for our little soiree. Katy Nunez, the doughnut store gal, was there with what appeared to be a tribe of grandchildren. I recognized a few more Seepwillow natives who sipped bottled water and ate toast and jam. Of course the Escobar children were sprinkled around, their mother perched on a chair in the shade. What I didn't see, was many potential clients. Of course, the left eye hole on my chicken head was significantly smaller than the right which prevented me from seeing much of anything.

I took a tentative waddle into the courtyard. A dull thud caused me to do a one eighty. A young toddler was on the ground, having been plowed under by my tail. "Oh sorry about that." I scrambled to give him a wing up. The boy's eyes rounded in terror and he shrieked. Off he ran in a frenzy of fear.

Hmmm. Not the reaction Aunt Stella was hoping for. I did a few practice flip flop steps. It was so hot I was pretty sure any eggs I might lay would come out hard boiled. Nonetheless I attempted a cheerful wing flutter.

"Aren't you supposed to quack?"

I turned again to find Chaz standing next to me. His jeans were torn at one knee. A Cardinal baseball cap shaded his tanned face. He held an icy soda in each hand.

I was in no mood to be trifled with. "I draw the line at quacking. Aren't you supposed to be fixing something?"

He leaned closer to make out my words. "No, I'm helping with the ring toss game."

"Well why aren't you helping then?" The words were muffled by my orange felt mouth.

"What?"

"WHY AREN'T YOU HELPING WITH THE RING TOSS THEN?"

He smiled. "Because the kids are more interested in you."

I suddenly noticed out of my good eye that there was a row of pensive children, some sucking thumbs, some whispering, clustered just beyond the span of my left wing. They were apparently waiting to see if their young colleague survived his sanity threatening encounter with the giant poultry.

Chaz raised a thick black eyebrow. "I brought you a soda."

A sweet gesture, but I was far too crabby to be gracious. "How exactly am I supposed to drink that in this thing?"

He leaned forward again, his face within beak range. "What?"

"HOW AM I SUPPOSED TO DRINK IN THIS COSTUME?"

"Do you want me to pour it through the big eye hole?"

I peered intently through said hole. He didn't seem to be laughing at me, though there was a suspicious gleam in his dark eyes. "No thank you," I said in a slightly more civil tone. "I'll have one later, after I've fulfilled my duties."

"Suit yourself. Maybe you'd better try a quack or two so you don't scare the rest of them."

I glared at his wide back as he left, trying not to notice the wide expanse of muscled shoulders. I turned again to the children. "Er, quack?"

There was no response.

"Cluck," I tried.

Still no response.

"Cock-a-doodle-doo?"

Nada.

I opened the bag that hung around my neck courtesy of Aunt Stella. "Candy?"

Ah, candy. The universal word for happy.

The miniature people jumped up and down, transformed into a happy mob.

I clucked and passed out candy and posed for photos and waddled around. Then I joined in a rousing game of Pin the Beak on the duck. My role in this activity was supposed to be standing by the duck poster handing out pre pinned construction paper beaks. One of the Escobar boys would then blindfold the child and do a brisk turning around before the little tyke had a chance to try his luck. Things were going smoothly until I felt a prick on the back of my leg. I peered down to find an angelic child with a devilish grin doing his best to pin a paper beak on the back of my leg. I tried to shake him off.

"Shoo, shoo. Mrs. Ducky doesn't like that." I shook my leg but the juvenile barnacle remained stuck fast.

"Go play ring toss with Mr. Chaz," I quacked.

No luck. The boy continued to find a pliable spot in my leg for his pin.

"Ouch. Stop pinning me kid. Go find your mother."

I hopped on one yellow leg and shook the other one. "Help," I called. "Somebody get this kid off of me."

Katy looked up from her spot at the jam table. "Hey," she called in a thunderous voice. "Skip, you let go of that duck right now or I'll tell Mama and you'll lose your bike for a month."

Skip's eyes widened. He released my drumstick and trotted away.

I limped along for another round of clucking, candy distribution and posing. After an hour of this, I was about to be a rotisserie chicken.

Sweat poured into my eyes. My lungs behaved like they were filled with wet felt. The horizon swam in front of my eyeholes. I felt myself being taken by the wing and led into Aunt Stella's trailer. She was on the phone, listening intently. Who then, was attempting to loosen the death grip of the horrible chicken head? With a rip of Velcro, the thing gave way and Chaz stood before me with a bottle of chilled water.

"Here. You need fluids." He thrust the cold bottle into my hands.

I didn't require a second invitation. As I chugged, he undid the zipper on the back of the costume. The semi-cool air of the trailer felt like bliss against my sweat soaked tee shirt. Chaz helped me step out of the mess and tugged off the flipper feet.

He stood there, contemplating my sodden remains.

I watched him watch me. Even in my poached state, I noted the injustice in a person of the male persuasion having such a lush fringe of eyelashes.

Aunt Stella finally hung up the phone. "Simone, are you all right, honey?"

"She looked a little wobbly so I brought her inside," Chaz said.

He must have been keeping tabs on my condition. That gave me a tingle which I chalked up to dehydration.

Stella wet a cloth and pressed it to my forehead. "I meant to come and get you but I was distracted by the phone." She leaned toward me until her frizzy hair brushed my cheek. "Are you going to be okay?"

"Yes," I croaked, "but this chicken has clucked her last."

"Absolutely." She peered out the dusty blinds. "It looks like the crowd is petering out anyway." She continued to stare outside. There were worry crinkles next to her mouth.

"Is something wrong?" I asked.

"Wrong? No. No there's nothing wrong. Why don't you change out of that costume and have a snack? There's watermelon in the fridge and some more bottles of water. I'll catch up with you in a minute."

I knew something was wrong but I didn't want to press her on her big day. "Okay. We can talk later." I finished the last gulp of water. I turned to find Chaz. "Thanks for bringing me here."

But he was already gone.

A good half hour later I ventured outside again. The crowd had dispersed, leaving only a few stragglers behind. In a shady corner, Katy Nunez folded up the paper tablecloth. She packed the unsold jars of jam into boxes. "Sorry about Skip. He's a stinker when he thinks no one is watching. He takes after his father."

"Did the jam sale go well?"

"Not bad, if I do say so. We sold twenty-three jars. Some people bought six packs."

"What is the profit margin like?"

Her brown eyes rolled in her wide forehead. "Let's see, minus the jars and labeling, that makes...well about sixty dollars." The smile never left her face.

Sixty dollars. Only 52,940 dollars left to earn. I kept my gloomy thoughts to myself. "That's great, Mrs. Nunez."

"The really great thing is we rented out three of the trailers for next week."

I was stunned. "We did? That's amazing."

"The minister thought it would be a great place for the summer kid's camp."

"A kid's camp? Here?"

"Each trailer will sleep five. That will be just right for the twelve kids in the junior high class plus an extra bunk or two for the pastor and anybody else he brings."

Summer camps. I never would have thought of that. "What will teenagers do hanging around the Ruddy Duck all day?"

Katy smashed paper into a trash bag and rested plump fists on her hips. "There's plenty to see in the desert. You just gotta know where to look. You used to love it here. Don'tcha remember that race? What was it called? The Dirt Squirt. The whole town turned out to see you. We all hollered until we were hoarse."

I did remember. That was my first real race and I was killing them until the last whoop. Then over I went. Somehow it didn't matter a bit. The pride on my father's face wowed me more than any trophy could. I had a sudden glimpse of his wondrous smile, his eyes crinkled up in pleasure. "That was a long time ago. Do you need any help with the jelly?"

The smile drained from Katy's face. It was replaced by an openly hostile glint. "What do you want?" she hissed over my shoulder.

"Stella had to go on an errand," Chaz said. "She asked me to unplug the coffee pot."

"Well do it then." Katy folded her arms across her massive chest.

He disconnected the extension cord and heaved the ancient percolator into his arms. An uncertain look crossed his face as he looked from me to her. A dribble of coffee snaked down his tee shirt as he left.

Katy watched him go, eyes narrowed. "Stay away from him, Simone. He's no good."

"What do you mean?"

"It ain't my place to say. For your own good, you just stay away." She picked up a cardboard box and headed to her pickup.

What on earth was that all about? I knew Chaz was a moocher but he didn't inspire that much hostility in my gut. What did Katy know that I didn't?

The courtyard was empty. In the summertime, all the productive outdoor work has to conclude before twelve o'clock to prevent any melting of people. It was just before one so even the die hards had hit the road or holed up in their trailers.

Jojo trotted up, her cheeks flushed from the heat. "Quack."

"Uh, quack," I replied.

"Quack, quack."

I could see where this was going. "Did you have a good time today? I saw you playing ring toss."

She nodded. "I got three lollipops. Mr. Chaz let me pick my favorite colors. Two red and a green." She screwed up her face as she attempted to recollect the object of her mission. "Auntie Stella borrowed it."

"Borrowed what?"

"The case."

"What case?"

Jojo considered as she licked a green lollipop. "I dunno. Bye."

It was time to get out of the heat.

***

Katy Nunez had only known part of the great news. Apparently a cactus club from Des Moine had stumbled across my ad on the internet and booked four trailers for the fall. "Awesome! We are on a roll," I shrilled to my computer screen. While I celebrated with a happy dance, an instant message popped up.

Simone, please forgive me. I never meant to hurt you, really. Where are you? We need to talk.

My heart leapt when I read the words until I noticed the sender's address. The message was from Donna.

Not Doug.

My brain knew that Doug was gone. He had moved on with a charming young lady who liked his cologne. He wouldn't be contacting me with apologies or any other such sentiments. But my heart had not yet gotten the message. My heart, the fickle thing, dredged up a memory of the time Doug and I got stuck in the rain when I accidentally locked us out of the car after a Black and White ball. His tuxedo was ruined and my Anne Klein gown practically dissolved by the time I found a spare key.

Doug had laughed and thrown his arms around me. "Honey, I'd rather be in this mess with you than anywhere else in the world."

When had that changed? At what moment did I stop being The One and started being The Mistake?

Maybe it hurt more because I didn't feel like I'd been "the one" in the eyes of the man that should have mattered most. My father was just as much a stranger in life as he was in death. Except for one small thread that bound us together and that was broken now too.

Tears filled my eyes. Why was I never enough?

It was time to take action against the shroud of self pity that threatened to smother me. I shoveled these thoughts out of my head and reached for strong medicine. Whipped cream. Lots of whipped cream, the kind with a nozzle, baby. Nothing can make you feel quite as loved as spoon feeding yourself a nice plate full of whipped cream. Not squirting it directly into your mouth, mind you, that would be indelicate. I was desperate, lonely, confused, abandoned and generally emotionally volatile, but not indelicate.

Fortunately, I had been able to sneak into town before the duck fiasco, so I had plenty of whipped cream. Donna's message danced on my computer screen. It would be easy to scratch her off of my list of friends, to despise her for getting what should have been mine. Why *her*? Uh oh. This envy thing was becoming a trend. Come on, Simone. Get it together. I applied more whipped cream. When half the can was gone, I typed an answer to Donna's message.

I am okay. I know you did not mean to hurt me. I am visiting with my aunt in Arizona, blogging from there too. Things are okay, really. Talk to you soon. Simone p.s. I miss you.

I threw myself on the bed. I really did miss her. No one would appreciate the indignity I had suffered in the clutches of a chicken suit like my friend Donna. Donna was a gal who could collect all kinds of embarrassing personal info and keep it stored away safely never to be used against you. She'd never breathed a word to anyone about the time I walked through a restaurant with a six foot trail of toilet paper stuck to the bottom of my shoe. A true friend, that Donna.

If she were here right now I could ask her what she thought of Katy Nunez' strange remark about Chaz. What did she know about him that made her so angry? For the life of me I couldn't see the man as anyone sneaky or underhanded. He was just too...gorgeous and sincere for that. Or was it sincerely gorgeous? On the heels of that prickly thought, I fell asleep.

Chapter Six

"Aunt Stella?" I got no response to my knock on the trailer door. This wasn't much of a surprise as she could sleep through the crash of the Hindenburg. Yesterday had been a full day and we all pretty much went our separate ways after the big event. She was probably still sleeping it off, dreams of ducks dancing in her head.

I glanced at my watch. No, that theory was out the window. It was ten fifteen. I had slept right through the Sunday morning church service which Aunt Stella always attended at 8:00 sharp. She was like the postal service about church stuff. Maybe she had to stop in town after the service. My mind began to wander off to more depressing scenarios. Perhaps she had fallen and conked her head. Got stuck in the shower. Tripped over LeRoy on her way to visit me.

After one more round of vigorous knocking, I let myself in. "Hello?" There was no welcoming smell of instant coffee or Twirly Roni. No off key singing coming from the shower. The only sound was the ticking of her battered kitchen clock.

A pink paper napkin sat on the table, anchored by a box of instant mashed potatoes. It was covered with familiar blue scribbles.

Simone, I thought you needed to sleep so I didn't wake you for church. You did a fabulous job as the duck yesterday. All the kids were impressed. Mr. Barnett at the hardware store asked if you would appear at his Lucky Duck Sale. I said I didn't think so but I'd ask. He said he'd give you a free case of molly bolts if you'd agree to do it. I have to run an errand. Be back soon. Take care of any details that pop up today, will you? Tons of love, S.

There would be snow in a very warm place before I did any more appearances in a duck suit, molly bolts or no molly bolts. I reread the note. Funny she didn't mention any errand to me. A peek out the window revealed that her ancient Gremlin was missing from its parking place in the tangle of weeds.

She inherited that car after one of her tenants left it lifeless next to the trailer. Perhaps it was compensation for the fact that he skipped out without paying the bill. As it turned out, it was more than a fair trade because my aunt could rebuild any engine from the ground up while blindfolded, standing on one leg. Four new spark plugs and a repaired alternator and that Gremlin was raring to go. She taught me engine basics too. My girlfriends would never believe I could change a set of spark plugs faster than a pair of pants. And I would never tell them either. It wouldn't enhance my cosmo girl image at all.

Maybe my aunt had gone into town to replenish the Twirly Roni supply. I helped myself to a bowl of curly goodness and some instant coffee. The canned delight was beginning to grow on me. It was slightly sweet, slightly salty and you didn't really even need to put much effort into chewing it. The ring of the phone sounded loud in the small space.

"Hello?" The voice on the other end was high and soft. I ratcheted up my volume a couple of notches. "What? I can't hear you. If you're looking for Stella she's out for a bit. Call back later." I was about to hang up when I caught the next phrase.

"They'll be there around twelve o'clock," the voice said.

"Who will?"

"The Loving Doves."

"What's a Loving Dove?"

The lady on the phone introduced herself as the church secretary. She patiently explained that the doves in question referred to the Junior High school students that were scheduled to descend on our trailer park.

"Oh wait a second, there's been a mistake. I know my aunt is expecting them but they aren't supposed to come for another two days."

"I'm sorry, honey, but Pastor has to have a root canal so we moved up the camp dates. Stella said it would be no problem."

"When did you talk to her? I haven't seen her all morning."

The chipper gal was unphased. "No problem. She told us on her way out of town, to go ahead and send them."

The words thumped on my ear drums. A funny feeling crept into the pit of my stomach. "Out of town? Where did she go exactly?"

"She didn't say, hon. By the way you looked darling in that duck costume. Stella showed us a Polaroid before she headed out. Uh oh, I've got another call coming in. Anyway, the kids will be there at noon. Talk to you later."

That's when I noticed the message scrawled on the other side of the napkin.

p.s. Kids will be here at 12. Desert Life class at 8:00 p.m. Chaz will help with this. Have fun.

Desert Life class? Chaz will help? Loving Doves? What in the blue blazes was going on here?

I suddenly remembered Jojo's cryptic message. With my stomach floating just below my Adam's apple, I ran to the Escobars' trailer.

Mrs. Escobar answered my frantic knock. Her skin was pale. A sheen of sweat coated her forehead. "Hello, Simone. Can I help you with something?"

"I just wanted to talk to Jojo for a second. She said my aunt borrowed something and I wanted to double check with her." I hesitated. "Are you okay, Mrs. Escobar?"

She nodded, a string of damp hair falling onto her face. "I'm not feeling well today. Just a flu, probably."

I eyed her greenish pallor doubtfully. "Okay. Is Mr. Escobar helping out with the kids?"

"No, no. He's driving a load of tomatoes to Phoenix. He'll be back in the morning. Most of the boys left for summer camp today, too."

Jojo appeared around her mother's hip. "Hi, Simone."

"You will call her Miss Greevey, young lady," her mother said. "Would you like to come in and talk, Miss Greevey?"

"No thank you. If I could just ask Jojo a question that would be great. Then I've got to find Chaz. Have you seen him?"

"He was working on the electric box on Mr. Singh's trailer earlier."

She pressed a hand to her back. "I've got to sit down for a minute. Jojo, mind your manners."

The little girl nodded and bounded out the door. "Hi, Miss Peevey."

"It's Greevey. Hello, Jojo. Remember when you came to tell me that Aunt Stella borrowed something?"

The girl wrinkled her nose and stuck a finger in her mouth.

"Remember? You were quacking and telling me about your lollipops?"

"Oh, uh huh."

"What did Aunt Stella borrow, Jojo?"

"A case."

"What case?"

"The kind for clothes."

My peripheral vision began to blur. "A suitcase?"

"Uh huh. She's gonna bring it back soon. I think she needed it for her underwear and mittens."

"Did she say where she was going?"

"To Mars." She skipped away towards the spitting sprinklers.

I closed my gaping mouth. My aunt had gone to Mars. A gaggle of junior high schoolers was about to descend upon us, expecting something called a Desert Life Class. Worst of all, I was apparently in desperate need of a man whom I felt it best to stay far away from.

And I thought the chicken costume was rock bottom.

I hightailed it to Mr. Singh's trailer. Chaz lay on his back underneath a grey metal box. His jean clad legs were long and lean. The sun beat down on the both of us with no mercy.

"Chaz?"

He didn't answer.

"Chaz?" I resisted the urge to plant a foot on his solar plexus.

He continued his oblivious tinkering, whistling the tune from Oklahoma all the while. When he got to the O-K-L-A-H-O-M-A part I had had enough.

"Hey." I poked a toe into his shin.

He sat up abruptly, smashing his forehead on the metal box. "Owww." He clapped a hand over his thick brow. With the good eye, he squinted up at me.

"Hi, Simone. What can I do for you?"

"You can tell me what a desert class is."

Beads of sweat glistened in his dark hair as he rolled out from under the metallic box. "I'm guessing a class about the desert. Or maybe a class in the desert. Was it desert or dessert? Two s's puts a whole new spin on things."

"Whatever it is, you and I are supposed to teach it tonight to the Lovey Doveys or whatever they're called."

Now he squinted with both eyes. "Have you been out in the sun a lot today?"

Deep breaths. Do not mash your co-teacher. In with the good air, out with the bad. "Mr. Tagliola, perhaps we should adjourn to my trailer so we can discuss the catastrophe that is gathering around us?"

"Catastrophe? Uh, sure." He climbed to his feet, gathered up his tools and followed me to my trailer.

I plopped a cold soda in front of him after he squeezed his giant frame onto the narrow seat. I caught the tantalizing scent of warm male and spaghetti sauce. "Where is my aunt?"

The soda fizzed as he drank it. "I give. Where is your aunt?"

"If I knew that, would I be asking you?"

"I don't know. You ask a lot of strange questions."

I ignored this. Too bad I didn't have a lightbulb to beam down at him for this interrogation. "Did you know we're teaching classes to a church camp?"

"No."

"Did you know the Lovely Dovey Junior High class will be here in..." I consulted my watch, "approximately thirty minutes?"

"Is that what we're talking about? I thought they were coming next week."

"So did I, but apparently they've been rescheduled to accommodate a root canal."

"Oh. Pastor's finally going to have that tooth fixed. Good for him. He doesn't like medical procedures so he's been putting it off." He drank more soda.

His calm countenance annoyed the bejeebers out of me. "According to a napkin note we are responsible for teaching some sort of desert class to these people at 8:00 tonight."

"We?"

"Yes we." My voice was shrill. I wondered if that was a smile lurking behind his dimples.

"Okay."

"Okay? Well how do we do that exactly? What is there to see here in the middle of the desert that junior high kids would find remotely interesting?" I felt like my head was about to pop like a bottle rocket.

Chaz took a long drink and drained the can. Then he crumpled it and slam dunked it in the trashcan. "Come with me."

***

"Look at that." Chaz's voice was almost a whisper.

We were standing in the meager shade of a scruffy tree at the point where a gently sloping plane began. In the far distance was a whole lot more gentle sloping plane and in the way farther distance, the mountains. A barbed wire fence separated our side of the nothingness from the nothingness owned by someone else. I followed his pointed finger to the ground.

"What am I looking at?"

"That." He pointed again.

All I could see was a collection of ratty shrubs and a taller thing which I took to be a tree or a really ambitious bush. The ground underneath was strewn with rocks and what appeared to be the remains of a mouse. I took another step forward.

"Stop!" He stopped me with a stiff arm to the clavicles.

"Owww." I slugged him as high as I could reach, far below the clavicle zone. "Are you crazy?"

"You almost stepped on it."

"Stepped on what?"

He wasn't listening. The man looked like I had just thrown his new puppy out of a moving car. He peered closely at the ground.

Normal color returned to his face. "That was close. You know, if we're coming out here at night, I'd better tape this area off. You almost stepped on it in broad daylight. They are definitely going to want to see this."

"See what?"

"I think I've got some tape in my toolbox." He trotted off.

"WHAT? What am I looking at?" I screamed.

"The saguaro," he called over his shoulder. "Don't touch it or anything."

I peered at the ground and finally spotted it. A tiny hairy fingerling poked up through the detritus. It was no bigger than a stick of gum. "That's supposed to impress a bunch of teenagers?"

He was a good five yards away when he shouted again. "You'd better get back, Simone. Looks like the kids are here."

A caravan of packed cars was indeed pulling up at the Ruddy Duck.

My heart stopped.

As the dust settled under the tires of the battered van, large gangly youths with big shoes and backpacks began to pour from the vehicle.

The junior terrorists had arrived.

Chapter Seven

I was raised by a woman who does not believe in the word meltdown. Mother sails along, ramming her ship through crisis by sheer force of will. My father used to say her spine was made of steel. I recall a look of admiration on his face as he said it. It made me want to be strong like her.

At the moment, I didn't feel the slightest bit strong but I summoned up these ghosts of the past to firm up my own set of vertebrae, which were quivering like banana slices in Jell-0. I didn't know where Aunt Stella went, but I knew I couldn't let her down. Two calming breaths and I plastered a serene smile over my face. With calm, measured steps I walked back across the field and joined the gang that spilled out onto the sizzling ground.

"Hello," I said to the tallest person. "I'm Simone Greevey, Stella's niece."

He seized my hand and pumped it vigorously. "Hello. It's great to meet you. How very kind of you to have us. I am Stan Stanley, the pastor of Crosstides Church."

I thought at first he was a stutterer, until I saw his name printed on the leather strap that held the keys around his neck. Stan Stanley was a round man. His head was covered by a scant layer of fuzz. All his other parts seemed to broaden and meet somewhere around his belt before tapering off at his hiking boots. The smile he gave me was wide and sincere.

"Pleased to meet you." I eyed the dozen teenagers who seemed to be expanding to fill the available space. "Let's go in the office and I'll get you the keys. I'm not sure the trailers have all been cleaned yet, though. We weren't expecting you for another few days."

"No problem. No problem at all. We appreciate your flexibility."

We found the keys and returned to the parking area. I counted twelve teens, clothed in different variations of jean shorts. They all wore the same neon green tee shirts sporting a dove logo. Even in this detail they broke the role of uniformity. Some rolled up the sleeves, some tucked the shirts in and others left them out. A tall red haired boy seemed to have cut the sleeves off completely.

Pastor Stan called to the troops. "Everybody, this is Miss Greevey. She's Mrs. Bernard's niece."

"Hi." A young blonde girl waved. "Weren't you the duck at the party? My brother said you knocked him over."

"Oh gee. I did? Was that your brother?"

She nodded. "Don't worry about it. I feel like knocking him down all the time."

The red head bobbed a chin at me. "Nice to meet you, Miss Greevey. I'm Jack. Are we going to have lunch soon?"

The black girl next to him laughed, setting her beaded braids clacking. "He's always hungry."

"Lunch?" It hadn't occurred to me that the teeny boppers would need food. Of course, I'd only recently learned about the whole Lovey Dove adventure in the first place. "Oh, I thought you were bringing your own supplies."

"No problem, no problem," Stan said. "Stella said she would let us use an empty trailer as a lunch room slash meeting place. She said she left some groceries around here somewhere for us."

My mind ran like a hamster on Kool Aid. "Okey dokey. I'll just find the groceries and rustle up some lunch."

"Great, great. I'll send a few Doves over after we've unloaded to help you. Listen up, listen up!" he boomed to the kids.

I was beginning to wonder if Pastor Stan Stanley had a skip in his record.

"I'll just be going then." As I headed toward the trailer he continued to direct the troops.

"Everybody up and at' em! Gather up your gear and follow me. Let's go, let's go!"

***

In the last trailer I was confronted with a sight that would put any Seepwillow Food Mart to shame. Crowded against the wall were cartons of food, piled to the ceiling. Stacks of peanut butter jars, loaves of bread, vats of strawberry jelly, sacks of plates and towers of boxes that no doubt held other culinary treats. The couches and beds had all been folded up, leaving a good sized empty space. I climbed the mountain o' food and spread out on the counter to begin slapping sandwiches together.

I was ready to go find the chips when the girl with the braids showed up.

"Hi, Ms Greevey. I'm here to help."

"Hi, er... what did you say your name was?"

"Tanya." She inspected my handy work, her beaded braids clacking softly together. "You're going to need more sandwiches."

"Really? For twelve kids?" I counted sixteen sandwiches. "That's a big pile already."

"Yeah but Jack can eat seven all by himself."

"Really?" I said again. "How is that physiologically possible?"

"You should see what he can do at the all-you-can-eat place. It's not pretty. He's been banned from the Bountiful Buffet in town." She began to pull out more slices of bread and coat them with peanut butter. "So where are you from?"

I was taken aback by her easy conversation. "San Francisco."

"Oh wow. That's a cool city, even though I've only seen pictures. I'd like to go to college there. UCSF is looking real good."

"How old are you?" I hauled bags of chips out onto the counter.

"Fourteen. I start high school next year."

"And you're already picking out colleges?"

"Sure. You need to know what they are looking for ahead of time if you want to be competitive."

Zowie. I was mostly concerned with the label on the back of my jeans when I was fourteen.

"Do you like being in the, er, Lovely Ducks?"

She laughed, teeth white against her dark skin. "That's the Loving Doves. Yeah, I like it. It gives me a chance to hang out with other Christian kids and Pastor Stan is really awesome. He's helped me through some bad stuff. My mom says he's the nicest white guy she's ever met."

"Do you get any teasing from your non-Christian friends?"

"Oh yeah. They call us the God Geeks. We don't get invited to the cool kid stuff but there's always some youth group event going on to keep us busy. Last month we had a bowling night. That was really fun."

Just then the trailer door was flung open and a pack of voracious teens piled in.

Though the air conditioner struggled to keep pace, the dozen or so sweaty teens warmed the trailer to a balmy temperature. They sat in a cluster on the floor, paper plates balanced on their laps, chatting with gusto about Green Day and the price of Ipods.

Pastor Stan called for attention and prayer. He bowed his fuzzy head. "Father God, thank you for bringing us together for this fine meal. Thank you for providing for us always. In Jesus' sweet name. Amen."

Fine meal? I looked around, expecting to see the faces of disgruntled teenagers on the verge of rebellion, but they seemed quite content with their food. Most of them, anyway.

Jack set a glass container on the floor and added a heaping portion of marshmallow fluff to his sandwich, a curtain of red hair hiding his face.

Tanya noticed my amusement. "He never goes anywhere without marshmallow fluff."

He lifted his sandwich to me in salute. "Food of champions."

I laughed. Maybe the teenage species wasn't as terrible as I thought. I felt very proud of myself as I watched them gobble the sandwiches. They were delighted with my culinary skills. Me, Simone Greevey, Peanut Butter Queen.

Then round two began.

A boy with a shaven head stood up. "Hey, Miss Greevey, ma'am. Could I have another sandwich please?"

The short girl behind him stood up also. "Me too? Please?"

The chorus echoed through the room. More, more, more. I shot Tanya a "you were so right" look. "Uh sure. I'll just whip up another stack of sandwiches." I scurried to the counter with Tanya at my heels and began slopping out peanut butter until my arms ached. Tanya added a glop of jelly to each one.

A couple feet away Pastor Stan was deep in conversation with the shaven head boy whose name I discovered was Raul.

"It's the method, son," the pastor said. "We don't disagree on the concept, but Jesus would not condone the violence."

"I don't either, Pastor," Raul said around a mouthful of bread. "I'm just saying the whole thing hasn't been addressed in the political arena, no matter which administration is in office. Until the animal kingdom manages to secure the right to vote, their needs will never be considered. They take a back seat even to the other disenfranchised groups only they're even more helpless. I can see why radicals take the cause into their own hands."

My peanut butter spreader hand stopped for a moment. Political arenas? Sheesh. And to think most of my bloggers wanted to chat about the merits of whitestrips vs. bleaching gel for that dazzling smile.

I looked at Tanya. "Okay, spill it. What global cause are you passionate about?"

She drew thick eyebrows together. "Let's see. I'm really not happy about the coral bleaching thing. And the greenhouse effect is bad too. But I think the thing that bugs me the most is the way we handle disagreement."

"How so?"

"The fact that one person can't disagree with another anymore without slamming that other person."

"I don't understand."

"Let's say you and I differ on some issue. Prayer in schools for example."

"Am I for or against?"

"What do you prefer?"

"Well I prayed regularly and often in school. I'm quite sure that's how I passed algebra."

She laughed. "It doesn't really matter but okay. You're for and I'm against. We disagree. The trend I see these days is disagreement means that I decide you are evil and reject you as a person along with your ideas."

"I never thought about that."

"It goes on everyday from the school level all the way up to Congress and the world. We disagree and along with that we dismiss and disrespect. I don't think that's what Jesus was all about. He said love your neighbor, not just the ones you agree with or those of the same political persuasion. He even loved the person who hammered nails into his hands and spit on him as he died. If he could do that, surely we could try to at least tolerate people we disagree with."

Yet again, my peanut butter hand was stopped mid-spread. "Are you going to run for office when you grow up?"

"Nah." She returned to her jam dispersal. "I'm going to be a marine biologist."

Pastor Stan blew his whistle. The shrill noise made us all clap our hands over our ears.

The pastor blushed. "Oh, sorry. I got carried away. My wife just got me this new whistle."

The teens grabbed half empty bags of chips and the remaining sandwiches and filed out the door.

"See you later," Tanya called from the doorway.

I waved a sticky knife.

"I'll help with the hot dog roast before the bug lighting," she said before the door closed.

Hot dog roast? I sighed, looking at the stale crusts and smears of peanut butter everywhere. I wondered approximately how many hot dogs Jack and his cohorts could put away. Then the other half of her sentence sunk in.

Did she say bug lighting?

***

The little hand was five minutes past two when I finished cleaning up the cafeteria/trailer. I remembered that my paying job was awaiting me, namely my blogger duties. My internet career might not be much but I was determined to do it well. I was going to lift people up, ding dang it, if it killed me.

My laptop sat right where I left it. I plopped down in the lovely lukewarm air of my trailer and booted up.

Brandi, I need some advice. A friend of mine is getting married to a guy I can't stand. He makes racist jokes and demeans her all the time.

Everyone thinks he's a class A jerk except her. In her eyes, he's wonder guy. Should I warn her? Should I keep my mouth shut? Help. -- Cherry B.

Oh boy. That was a tough one. Of course my mean green gut would advise Cherry to go to her friend and tell her what a complete louse her boyfriend was. Then again, the less green parts of me thought about that whole mote in the friend's eye when you've got a beam in your own thingy. Obviously Cherry's friend saw her man in a different light, rightly or wrongly. Hmmmm. This Brandi thing was more difficult than mere fashion advice and restaurant recommendations. I spent a bit of time perusing my Bible before I answered.

Cherry, that's a tough spot to be in, friend. It seems to me your job is not to tell your girlfriend what she should think, but to listen to what she already does. You don't have to like the guy; you just have to love your friend. Brandi

Galatians 5:14

For the whole Law is fulfilled in one word, in the statement you shall love your neighbor as yourself. But if you bite and devour one another, take care lest you be consumed by one another.

Excellent advice. Tanya would approve. So why did I have an uncomfortable twist in my tummy? Oh yeah. The hypocrisy clause. Here I was dispensing righteous pearls to my followers but I wasn't loving my neighbor. Not my neighbor named Doug, anyway. Anger for him still burned hot and heavy. I wondered how I would have reacted if someone told me Doug was a louse before I figured it out on my own. I had a sneaking suspicion that I would have turned my back on them. Maybe my sage guidance was good then. If I could just learn to take my own advice.

No, not my advice.

His.

The knock at the door startled me.

I opened it to find a sweaty Katy Nunez clutching a giant cardboard box and a pair of oven mitts festooned with frogs.

She eased the carton onto one hip. "Where do you want this stuff?"

I peered into the box filled with jars, sugar and barbecue tongs. The proper question was *why* did I want this stuff? "What is it for?"

"The jam lesson."

"What's a jam lesson?" Sounded like a jam session, only more ominous.

She shoved the box into my arms. "We're doing a jam lesson tomorrow morning."

I stood aside to let her in. "Why would we do that?"

Katy heaved her considerable bulk down on my bed. The mattress sank almost to the floor. She took the glass of ice water I offered. "Stella thought it would be good to do a demonstration on how to make prickly pear jam for the kids. Using desert resources, I think she called it. She said she was going to tell you all about it. I bought all the supplies this morning."

So my aunt had given the matter significant attention before she disappeared. When she returned, she was going to get quite an earful from me. "She didn't get around to filling me in. By the way, where is my aunt, Mrs. Nunez?"

She drained the water. "She said she had to go pick up Bud."

Pick up Uncle Bud? At the airport maybe? How long could that possibly take? I heaved a sigh of relief. "Well she'll probably be back tonight then. She can do this jam thingy with you."

Katy raised a thick eyebrow. "Don't you know how to cook?"

"Me? Of course. I cook. Sometimes. But we don't have prickly pear cactus in San Francisco. It's not my specialty. We're known for sourdough and scallops and the like. We've got some killer sushi too."

"Uh huh. I'm sure you'll be able to handle a little desert cooking. You won't get hurt, if you follow directions."

Hurt? I pushed the bangs out of my face. "When is this class supposed to take place?"

"Tomorrow morning, six a.m."

I goggled. "Six? As in 6 a.m.? Why so early?"

"You really don't want to be boiling cactus in the middle of the afternoon, do you?"

I didn't want to be boiling cactus anytime, anywhere, with anyone. I was sure the only reason cactus was classified as a food was because some desperate desert native ran out of anything else remotely edible. If there were spare tires lying around those would have become a delicacy too. "Okay, well I'm sure Stella will be back tonight so I'll remind her about the class."

"Okay. I'll just keep the stuff here in the lunch trailer and I'll be back tomorrow. See you at six." She lurched down the front steps.

My watch read three o'clock. The Loving Doves were all engaged in some sort of quiet time in their trailers. Though I despised the thought of subjecting my skin to the broiling sun, I thought I'd better prepare for the weenie roast and bug lighting so things would be ready when Aunt Stella returned.

But what in tarnation was a bug lighting? I pondered this as I took stock of the coolers filled with hot dogs. I pictured dozens of black beetles with tiny Bic lighters in their hands. No, that wasn't it. Bugs didn't have hands. At least, I didn't think so.

I resolved to research the matter on the internet. There was no way I was going to ask Chaz for any explanations if I could help it. I still hadn't figured out what the great saguaro treasure at the edge of our property was that he was so hot about. Surely that scrawny bit of plant life wasn't much of a marvel. I was beginning to think the man was looney as well as cheap.

The squishy packages filled the cooler to the brim. Six dozen hot dogs. That ought to do it, even with Jack's appetite. Mustard, ketchup, pickles. Hmmmm. Something was missing. Hot dogs were not a regular part of my diet. I'm more the veggie wrap, sushi kind of gal but even I knew that hot dogs are better served on buns. There was not one single bun to be found.

I considered my options.

Option number one: go get buns.

Option number two: ask Chaz to do it.

Number three: Let them eat hot dogs sans buns. Option number three worked best for me. They were teens. They could eat the paint off a house and be content. They would be fine without buns. This was not my responsibility. I was in no way involved in the planning of this. This whole Loving Doves fiasco was dropped on me without my input or consent. Not my problem. No buns, no big deal.

I felt good about that decision for approximately five seconds until I pictured Jack without anything to hold up his marshmallow fluff. Then I fetched my purse and drove into town, on a mission for buns.

Along the way I scanned the reverse traffic for Stella's Gremlin. No luck. The only thing on the other side of that road was a speeding jackrabbit and piles of dirt that swirled in odd little cyclones. I thought I spotted a polar bear hiding in the blinding glare of sand but that could have been my imagination.

The Pick N Pack parking lot was nearly empty. I unstuck myself from the front seat of the rental car and walked as quickly as my half melted legs would go into the store. The blanket of cool air was delectable.

The oddly stocked shelves brought me back to my childhood. I remembered asking my aunt why the dry goods were grouped in such an unorthodox manner. Never in San Francisco had I seen coffee beans plopped next to the creamed corn.

"Mr. Bunko shelves all the dry goods alphabetically by their common names." Stella said it as if that was the most practical thing in the world. "He thinks outside the box, honey."

Way, way outside the box. I was just as fascinated in my adult years to see how the zany tradition had been carried on by Fred Bunko, Jr. I walked past the collection of artichoke hearts and anchovy paste and on past packages of barley and black beans. The buns were right where I expected to find them, sandwiched between barbecue sauce and chopped clams.

"Help you find something?" A black haired store clerk poked her head around the croutons. She was waif-like, the green store smock baggy on her slender shoulders. A smattering of freckles spangled her cheeks and nose.

I noticed the nametag pinned to her top. "Are you Katy Nunez's daughter?"

"Yes, I'm Gigi. You must be Simone. My mother said you were in town." She took a tentative step closer. "How are you getting along with the Loving Doves?"

"Fine so far, but they can put away more food than an NFL team. I'm here to stock up on buns."

She smiled. Two tiny dimples hugged the creases around her mouth. "They're buy one get one free. We've got a special on Twirly Roni too."

Even though the stuff was growing on me, my stomach churned at the thought. "I'll pass on that."

I wished I could ask her what her mother had against Chaz but I couldn't figure out how to get to that topic gracefully.

Gigi stood for a moment, arms wrapped around her chest. Her lips opened and she started to say something, and then reconsidered. "Okay, well let me know if you need help finding anything."

"Thanks," I called to her back.

I gathered up as many buns as I could carry. On my way to the checkout I stopped for a bag of apples, a Diet Coke and a side of yogurt. I would not be able to snag any sushi or Chai tea at this place, but at least I could supplement the canned food regimen with some pseudo health food. I staggered to the register and a teen boy rang up my purchases.

"You want any stamps?" he said around a wad of gum.

"No thank you."

"Lottery ticket?"

"No."

"Chewing tobacco?"

"Uh, no thanks. I'll just take these things."

He dutifully scanned the items. "Paper or plastic?"

"Plastic please."

"We're out of plastic."

"All righty. Paper will be fine then."

I scurried out of the store before he could inquire about any other subjects. I loaded the groceries into the trunk and cracked the cap on my diet soda, which was rapidly warming in the ferocious heat. Someone familiar caught my eye as I slithered into the front seat and set the air conditioning to mega blast.

Gigi stood under the overhang of the Pack N Pick. She was deep in conversation with a dark hunk of a man. I couldn't hear what they were saying but the look on Gigi's face wasn't a happy one. I watched in the rear view mirror as Chaz handed her a rectangle of paper. She took it, but when he reached a hand out to touch her shoulder, she jerked away and slammed back into the store.

Chaz looked down for a moment. Then he shoved his hands in his pockets and looked up. Just in time to see me drive out of the parking lot.

Chapter Eight

The ride home was like a trip through some fantastic painting. Though it was still hot enough to pop corn on the ground, the sun was lower, coloring the flatlands with a patina of gold. Distant cliffs rose in vibrant ochre waves against the blue sky. I drove past an enormous saguaro, lifting its prickly arms to the sky as if in supplication. Was this why people made their home in the desert? To be a part of some incredible natural work of art? The idea bounced around in my head and didn't last long as I coasted toward the molten asphalt of the Ruddy Duck parking lot. The heat poached those romantic notions right out of my cabeza.

Katy was right. Through my childhood eyes, Seepwillow was a fantastic place. My visits to this odd spot were never too hot, too quiet or too boring. I knew it was not the place that had changed. I saw it through the same eyes, and the view was unchanged, but I no longer felt it with the same heart.

Dad was dead and with him went some of the magic. Doug was gone. He took my trust and made me flee to this forsaken spot. Now Stella had disappeared too. I didn't see her car anywhere. Where in the world had she gone to pick up my uncle? It was as if she'd evaporated into the thin air. I gave myself a stern mental slap. "She's not gone, she's just...temporarily not here. She'll be back with Uncle Bud in tow in no time."

I noticed Chaz hadn't returned as I parked and off loaded bushels of buns. What was his mysterious business with Gigi Nunez? I remembered her mother's advice to stay away from him. No problem there. He may be my co teacher in this desert class debacle but after the final bell rang our connection would be severed. I intended to stay far away from Chaz Tagliola and his problems, whatever they were. Even if the guy was a smidge hunky and drove a sweet bike. I determined to be darn sure that he started to pay rent before I left.

The lunch trailer door opened. I found Tanya, fanning herself with a memo pad.

"Hi, Ms. Greevey. I thought you might need help getting the weenie roast underway."

"God bless you, Tanya. Do you help out this much at home?"

"Pretty much. Mom works full time and I have three younger sisters who can eat as much as Jack. I'm famous for my spaghetti and meatballs. Sometimes the Doves come over and I make fajitas for everyone."

I handed her two bags of buns. "You're hired. Did my aunt return, by any chance, while I was gone?"

"Haven't seen her around but we've been in Bible study most of the day."

We hauled the buns and condiments out to the picnic table that perched in the feeble shade of a tree. Pastor Stan and three teen boys started the campfire while the rest of the kids scoured the ground for roasting sticks. It was a tricky job with the lack of trees and the billows of acrid smoke wafting around. Several of the kids settled on wire coat hangers for cooking purposes.

A sharp hissing noise snatched my attention away from the fire. Two painfully skinny boys were hunkered down having a conversation with LeRoy the tortoise. I gathered from the loud turtle grunting that LeRoy did not appreciate their tone. Nor did he seem pleased when the shorter of the two stuck his hand under the steps where the animal was cornered.

"Ouch!" The kid stuck his finger into his mouth. "He bit me."

I wondered if I should do anything about this. Did Stella's liability insurance cover tortoise attacks? The finger was still attached and there was no river of blood, so I decided to leave things alone. LeRoy could hold his own against these young people better than I could. He had generations of survival under his armor plated belt. As long as they didn't turn him over, he'd be peachy.

As hot dog monitor, I made sure everyone had a few affixed to their skewers. When the wieners were sizzling, Tanya and I hauled out a zillion cans of soda along with bags of chips and cans of pork and beans. She went off to roast her own dinner, and I sank down on an old lawn chair to catch the eensy breeze that cut through the heat now and then.

Chaz materialized at my side. He carried a backpack in one hand and a fluorescent light in the other.

"Hi, Simone. I thought we'd take off about eight. That should give us an hour to get set up before sundown."

"Set up for what?"

"The bug lighting." He flipped his thick braid over his shoulder and knelt to put supplies in the backpack.

Ah yes. The bug lighting. What exactly was a bug lighting? I hadn't had time to check it out online. It didn't matter. If it had the word bug in the title, it was not for me. "Er, I don't suppose you need my help with this? I'm sure you can escort the Doves by yourself."

His eyes glinted coal black. "I need you to help with the photography. You can handle that, can't you?"

I pressed down the panic I felt at the thought of being in the same acreage as members of the insect family. A ripple of stubborn pride cut through the panic. Stella left me in charge, not this dimpled giant. "Of course I can handle that."

Photography. How hard could that be? If I had to go out into the desert at night, at least I would have a relatively benign task. Thanks to the beauty of the zoom function, I could stay far away from anything with an exoskeleton and six legs. "Fine. Eight o'clock then. I'm game."

There was a hint of a smile on his face. He nodded. "I'm glad you're coming along."

My cheeks warmed at the expression in his eyes. "I saw you talking to Gigi at the Pack N Go."

The humor vanished. He busied himself adjusting the straps on the pack. "Yeah. I've known Gigi for a long time. She's a real great gal."

Judging from her reaction to his touch, the feeling was not mutual.

"Did you go to school together?"

"Uh huh." He pulled on the pack. "I'm going to get some more gear. Don't forget to change your shoes."

I looked down at my Taryn Rose sandals. "And what exactly is wrong with my shoes this time?"

He heaved the pack onto his wide shoulder. "Nothing. I think your sandals look great. I just figured you wouldn't want to share any shoe space with scorpions."

When the blood returned to my aortas, I went to change my shoes. A ridiculous thought tickled my brain as I trotted along. Chaz thought my shoes were great. Clearly I'd been hanging around the junior high schoolers too much. "Get a hold of yourself girl. Who cares what he thinks?"

On the way back I ran into Jojo and her older brother, Ricky. She was hopping up and down with excitement.

"I'm going to the bug smiting."

The boy squeezed her hand. "Lighting, not smiting. Mom said she could go if I watched her."

"Good for you, Jojo." I took her picture. "I'm surprised to see you, Ricky. I thought all the Escobar men were at summer camp."

"I'm leaving after the bug lighting tonight. I'm at a different camp than the others."

"Do you think we'll see any real big spiders?" Jojo's enormous eyes were fringed with heavy lashes.

I held my shoulders steady against the ripple of horror. "No spiders. I'm sure there are no spiders in the desert. Spiders like tropical places with monkeys and coconuts. There's lots of spiders in Tahiti, I think. That's where Miss Muffet lives, I heard." Tahiti was the farthest place I could think of.

Ricky gave me an odd look and hauled his sister away.

We convened at the appointed hour. The kids swarmed around the picnic table, zipping their packs and testing flashlight batteries. The sky was a dusky orange. I was sweating in my jeans and long sleeved denim jacket. These garments would protect against insects and even though I wasn't going to get within spitting distance of one, it couldn't hurt to take extra precautions. I would have packed a flyswatter and a can of Raid if my pockets had been big enough. Come to think of it, I should have borrowed one of those bee keeper getups.

"Here." Chaz handed everyone a small notebook. "We're going to keep a record of all the living things we see tonight. Buddy up with someone. Everyone got a flashlight?" The man seemed to be almost as excited about this adventure as Jojo.

His excitement was contagious and the Doves all waved their lights in the air. Two guys in the back began to use them as Samurai swords until Pastor Stanley stepped in. He must have shared my sentiments about bugs because he wore long pants and sleeves and a camouflage safari hat.

Like a procession of cheerful ants, we walked. The ground was still hot underfoot but there was a blessed hint of coolness in the air. We paralleled the road for about two miles and then veered off on a sad excuse for a trail. It was almost dark so we used flashlights to pick our way along the sandy trail as it climbed upward. I could just make out the outline of a rocky cliff that rose several miles in the distance.

I whispered to the girl next to me. "Hey Tanya?"

"Yeah?"

"Did Chaz say anything about rock climbing?"

She pulled down her sleeves against the cooler air. "I don't think so. We're just here for the bugs."

I would rather climb rocks than face bugs anyway. I could just see the silhouette of our fearless leader several yards ahead. "If we're just here for the bugs, why is he carrying a baseball bat?"

Tanya shrugged. "I asked him the same thing. He said some night creatures are not as friendly as others."

I gulped and wondered for the hundredth time about the location of my aunt. No phone call, no e-mail, not even a napkin note regarding her whereabouts. How long could it take to retrieve Uncle Bud? The man weighed three hundred pounds. How far away could he have gotten? I would have worried more if I didn't know Stella's unusual sensibilities. The woman was going to get a piece of my mind for putting me in this close proximity to the insect world. And with a guy who couldn't even fix a plastic duck. Was he qualified to lead us into no man's land?

Jojo's brother hoisted her onto his shoulders and she laughed. Her giggles carried in the night.

After another mile of uphill hiking, we came to a broad stretch of flat nothing. There were a few scrubby trees, lots of spiky shrub balls and a whole lot of dry ground. The night painted everything in odd shades of black and gray. Chaz dropped his pack and unloaded a clothesline and two sheets. Jack and Raul helped him string the line between two trees and draped the sheet over the rope. He clipped a battery powered blacklight to the top of the fabric. The other sheet went down on the ground under the hanging one. Chaz turned on the light. The glow made his eyes glimmer in an eerie fashion.

"All right, troops. Now we need to move away and give them time to show up. Let's move back there." He pointed to a spot behind us.

Our tired platoon trudged several yards away and sat. I checked the terrain before lowering my behind. No bugs, snakes, or irate ants. Nothing but flat. Just to be extra sure, I took a plastic bag out of my pocket and set it on the ground before sitting down.

Once I settled in, I relaxed enough to breathe in the clean air. There was nothing but endless skies. A spangle of stars began to gleam overhead. I flashed back on a few nighttime rides with my dad. This spot would be a great place to open up the throttle. I wondered if Chaz had taken his Elsinore out here for a spin. The oddball desire to get on a motorcycle again momentarily overwhelmed me.

"Mr. Tagliola?" The pastor waved his flashlight. "I'd like to start our adventure with a word of prayer. Prayer, everyone."

We bowed our heads and Pastor Stan led us. "Father, open our eyes. Let us see and marvel at your awesome creations. And help us to never ever take your precious gift of life for granted."

One of the kids began to sing *Revive Me*. They joined in one at a time until the sound swelled and rose, splendid, into the night air. The desert was a strange and hostile place, but I knew no cathedral ever held such sweet music. I watched Chaz as he turned his eyes to the crescent moon and sang along. His face, awash in emotion, was a patch of light in the darkness.

The last note faded away. Pastor Stan finished with another prayer and a hearty Amen.

"Now open your notebooks and listen," Chaz said, in a confident teacher voice.

His demeanor surprised me. As far as I knew the guy was some type of handyman. I was not expecting any sort of structured presentation.

Maybe Stella left him some napkin lesson plans before she disappeared. I thought he was going to launch into a lecture but he didn't say a word. Instead he stabbed a thick finger toward the rocky precipice. Tanya started to say something but he silenced her.

"Listen."

Then we all heard it. Two high pitched shrills followed by a long wavering yodel. It sounded like wet fingers squeaking across glass. The cries echoed hauntingly in the desert air.

"What do you think?" Chaz asked, his voice low. "Guesses?"

"Coyote," Raul answered.

"You got it. Ever see one up close?"

"I have," Jack said. "A couple of them came sniffing around my Grandpa's hen house."

"How did you know they were coyotes and not wolves?" Chaz asked.

"Carried their tails low. Wolves carry 'em high."

I could barely make out Chaz's nod of approval. Okay, so the guy was a coyote expert. Maybe he did know a thing or two about this crazy desert.

The kids scrawled notes in their books.

I readied the camera for night framing, hoping all the while that the coyotes were content with their location at the far end of the rock promontory.

Chaz waited until most of the pencils were still again. "So what are deserts exactly?"

Tanya spoke up. "Places where it's really hot?"

"Sometimes, but the common denominator is precipitation, not heat. Deserts have very little rain, but they're not necessarily hot. That means there are frozen deserts too."

Deserts could be cold? This handyman was certainly well versed in all things environmental. Something brushed against my leg and I squealed like the proverbial pig. The noise carried beautifully. All the Doves stared at me.

"Sorry," Tanya said. "I was just passing you the cheese puffs."

My face burned hot in the darkness. "Oh, thanks. I, er, thought you were a bug."

Everyone laughed. In order to occupy my shaking hands, I took an enormous handful of cheese puffs. I stuffed them one after the other, hamsterlike, into my cheeks. Mr. Brain said, "*Are you kidding? Cheese puffs? Have you sunk from salmon on rice wafers to cheese puffs?*" I ignored this and listened instead to the voice of Mr. Mouth. He said, "*Hooray! Cheesy, salty goodness. Puffs. Give me more puffs, I say!*" Seepwillow was diluting my sense of class, all right. I passed the bag to Jojo.

We crunched and slurped from our water bottles until the darkness was profound.

"Okay." Chaz dusted off his hands and got up. "Let's go see who has come to visit."

We trailed him back to the lighted sheet. The Doves crowded together in an effort to get a good look. Their teeth and shoelaces glowed in the blacklight. There was a collective gasp of appreciation. I stayed several yards back, in the safe zone.

"Cool," one of the kids said. "Look at that beetle." He reached out a toe to poke it but Chaz stopped him. "Just look and sketch. That one is a darkling beetle. They don't fly because their wings are fused together to keep them from drying out. If you pester them they give out a pretty nasty odor."

"Awww man," Jack said, craning his neck to peruse the sheet. "No scorpions."

I couldn't suppress a shudder.

"Yeah, but look at those ants. And that spider. They're like, fluorescent."

The kids sketched and commented. Pastor Stanley was every bit as eager as his charges. "Look, look." He pointed excitedly to a moth that fluttered on the upright sheet. "Absolutely beautiful. And look there. Another type of beetle, crawling right up the sheet."

I zoomed my lens to take pictures of the acrobatic insects. True, I could only focus on the critters attached to the hanging sheet but that was more than enough, in my book. While the kids chattered on, I took a moment to examine the sky. It was inky black, flecked with brilliant specks of light. The sliver of moon added soft light to the tableau. The coyotes were silent now, probably waiting for the intruders to leave. Or busy eating some innocent night hiker they had brought down.

Chaz left the circle and walked over to me. "I'm impressed. These kids know a lot about insects already."

"So do you."

"You sound surprised."

"I thought you were a handyman."

His tone was curious. "I am a handyman. Does that exclude me from being other things?"

"No." I snapped off two more pictures. His shoulder felt rock hard next to mine. "I didn't say that."

"Are you sure?"

Raul jogged up to us. "Hey, Ms. Greevey. Can you get a shot of this? There's a fantastic scorpion that just showed up. She's got babies on her back and everything."

"Fine. No problem. I'll get a shot." I hurried away from Chaz.

The fact of the matter was I had assumed that he was a loser, a man with a menial job and no prospects. Guilt poked me in the gut. I deserved to feel bad. I was busy looking down my upper class nose at him. I should be punished.

Two seconds later, I was.

As I readied my camera to take the scorpion's picture, a tiny rat, about the size of a baby bootie hopped like a possessed thing across the sheet. Tanya, who was kneeling in front of the fabric, shot backwards into my oncoming legs. I toppled over her.

Though it only took a nanosecond, it felt like an eternity.

Down I went.

Down, down, down.

Onto the sheet.

Facedown.

Into a writhing pile of bugs.

Chapter Nine

I don't remember how I got back to my trailer. I think Chaz may have carried me over his shoulder but I preferred not to summon up this mental picture. I did remember much screaming, frenzied leaping around, and falling into contortions on the ground.

When I came to a proximity of my senses, I was on the bed with a cold cloth on my head and grit in my mouth. As soon as my eyes opened, the panic returned. I jumped out of bed and tore at my clothes screaming at an inhuman volume. "Get them off me! Get them off!"

Chaz, who was sitting at the kitchen table watching me, shot to his feet and came over to grab my wrists. "You're okay," he bellowed. "The bugs are gone. Stop, Simone. You're okay. All the bugs are gone."

He gave me a shake that rattled my teeth.

I stopped. For the first time I was able to focus on his face. His mouth was open slightly in shock, but other than that he seemed calm, controlled. Perhaps the bugs really had gone? My voice came out in a whisper. "Are you sure the bugs are gone? How do you know?"

His eyes were wide black pools, reflecting my panic in their darkness. He held my wrists up to his chest. "I got them all off. I promise. I checked very carefully."

"How carefully?"

"Er, extremely carefully."

I could feel the strong steady beat of his heart. My own heart was jackhammering its way into defibrillation. Beads of sweat popped out all over my forehead. I tried to do more therapeutic breathing but it came out in pants and gasps.

After a final squeeze Chaz gently let my hands go.

"I didn't know you had an insect phobia. I'm so sorry. I shouldn't have pushed you to go along."

The floodgates opened. I began to cry. I sank to the floor with a terrible wail. Words blabbered out without regard for grammar or syntax. "It's not a phobia. I just don't like bugs. Bugs are bad. Three part bodies, wiggly legs, stingers. Awful, simply awful."

He half nodded. "I can see they upset you."

My voice filled up all the empty corners of the old trailer. "Bugs should be upsetting to everybody. They sneak up on you in the dark and bite. Why do they say that anyway, bite? Bug bites. Don't let the bed bugs bite. I thought they stung."

"Uh, well I don't actually know."

A horrifying thought occurred to me. "Do bugs have TEETH?"

He eased down next to me and put an arm around my shoulders. Oddly, he smelled like marinara sauce. "I don't think so. I've never seen a bug with teeth. I promise there are no bugs here. If you happen to find one lurking outside, I'll come get it. All you have to do is call me."

More tears rained down my face accompanied by heaving, shuddery noises.

"It's okay." His breath was warm against my cheek. "It's okay. You're safe now."

Everything gushed out in the wake of the tears. "My Dad. It was a bug. Little hairy killers. I hate them."

His eyebrows crinkled in confusion and he handed me a big wad of Kleenex.

"Well, er, don't feel bad about that. Lots of people hate bugs. My mother is afraid of them. She makes my dad scoop them into paper cups and take them outside. Samoan bugs are big, too."

I did not want to be compared to this man's mother. I slapped his arm off of my shoulder. "It's not the same," I hissed. "Were any of your relatives sent to that great island in the sky because of an insect?"

Chaz opened his mouth and then closed it again.

"I didn't think so."

"I'm sorry. I was trying to think of something to say that would help you feel better." He passed me a trashcan for the soggy tissues.

"You could never understand. My dad was a great man, a handsome man. He was a Navy officer." I swiped at my runny nose. "I look exactly like him, just ask Aunt Stella."

Chaz did not appear to comprehend my wild conversation.

I hurled a ball of tissue against the wall. My shrill voice echoed in the small room. "He was killed by a bug. A BUG! A big strong man, the commander of a nuclear submarine, killed by a bug. How is that possible? Can you answer that question for me, Mr. Nature Lover? Hmmm? What universal laws can possibly govern such things? How can a grown man die from a bug?"

He hesitated only for a second. "What kind of bug was it?"

"A bee!" I shouted. "A puny bumblebee. My father was stung in the locker room and he died before anybody even found him. How is that possible?" The tears continued to course down my face.

Chaz cocked his head. "Anaphylactic shock?"

"Yes, it was." I focused all my anger into that calm, wide face. "What do you know about anaphylactic shock? Did you ever have anyone you know die like that?"

He shook his head.

"Well it's completely RIDICULOUS. My mother grieved as much about the WAY he died as the fact that he was GONE. She was mortified that her husband could die in such a ludicrous manner, brought down by a bumblebee. A great big man, gone in minutes." My whole body suddenly felt rubbery and I could hardly lift my chin off my chest. "I don't like bugs. That's why I live in San Francisco. Hardly any bugs. An occasional ant or butterfly, but that's it."

He started to put a hand on my knee and then reconsidered. "I'm sorry, I didn't know. How old were you when he died?"

"Twelve."

He continued to stare at me. I could not read anything in his face, nor did I want to. I felt limp and used like the soggy mass of paper in my trashcan. I was overwhelmed by a desperate need to be by myself. "Will you please leave me alone now?"

"Of course." His eyes were troubled as he pushed himself to his feet. "I just want to say again that I'm sorry for taking you out there. I knew you were reluctant and I shouldn't have pushed." Just before he got to the door, he closed his eyes and leaned his dark head against the door frame.

"What are you doing?" I asked with all the energy I could muster.

"I'm praying for you. Good night, Simone."

Great. I was being prayed for by a bug lover wearing eau de spaghetti. The door shut behind him and I sank into the quiet. There was no buzzing or humming of any insect intruders. I was safe.

I shoved away thoughts of Chaz and the bugs until only my father's face filled my brain. The tears started again, hot and fast and my body curled itself into a tight ball on the floor. When there were no more tears left, I stripped off my clothes and boiled myself in the shower, checking every square inch for hitchhiking bugs. Then I checked under the sheets, pulled the covers over my head, and slept.

***

Bang, bang, bang.

I was dreaming about a giant mosquito with a hammer.

Bang, bang, bang.

Could be a sledgehammer.

Bang, bang.

I sat up in bed. There was no mosquito, but the banging was real. I quickly scanned my bed for insects. Whew. No legs under the covers but mine.

The sunlight poking through the shades said it was Monday morning, but the clock did not agree. Five-thirty. No sane person would classify five-thirty a.m. as morning. Civilized folks knew morning did not arrive until nine-ish. Ten on weekends.

Bang, bang, bang.

This time a female voice followed the noise.

"Simone? Are you in there? Come on. We've gotta get set up for the jam class."

Uggh. My close encounter with prickly pears. Did that mean my aunt had still not returned from her mystery mission? I lumbered to the door and yanked it open. "Isn't Aunt Stella back?"

"Haven't seen her. Car's still gone. It's just you and me, honey."

"Mrs. Nunez, I really appreciate all that you're doing for the doves and all. I just don't think any kind of cooking project will work out this early in the morning. It's unnatural to make edibles at this hour."

She laughed until her chins wobbled. "That's a good one. I'll meet you outside in five minutes."

I pried open my eyes and slogged to the bathroom. The reflection in the mirror could not possibly be mine. Puffy eyes, blotchy skin, dark hair styled courtesy of static electricity. Visions of the previous night came back. I groaned at the memory of baring my soul to Chaz Tagliola on my trailer floor. The humiliation was too much. I would have rather been seen naked than offering up those personal neuroses to him. Not to mention the Loving Doves were no doubt convinced I was one pancake short of a stack.

What exactly had I said in my hysterical rant? I couldn't recall everything on account of being drunk with fear the previous night. Chaz's face swam before my eyes. I hadn't seen judgment there, or ridicule. There had been no disapproval, only compassion. Then again, maybe I imagined that and he'd run right to the nearest newspaper office to blab the juicy details. *Woman Lands in Pile of Bugs, Leaves her Sanity with the Scorpions.*

I winced at a loud clatter from outside. There was no possibility that the plus sized woman on my doorstep was going to let me shirk the jam session, so I wrapped my hair in a bandana and slapped on some moisturizer. A touch of gloss, a swab of mascara and swirl of powder and I approached human. Mentally unstable mind you, but passably attractive. The heat struck me with an angry fist when I made my way outside.

The long folding table was piled with bristly, rose colored fruits. Katy looked up from her precarious perch on the lawn chair. "I sent the Doves out to get these, since you looked kinda indisposed. I told 'em to come back with more in about fifteen minutes."

I eyed the pile of fruits in their prickled armor. "How in the world did they collect those things without bloodshed?"

She picked up a pair of barbecue tongs and clacked them together. "No problem there. Let's get a few of these prepped while the water is boiling."

A camp stove nearby heated the water in an enormous kettle.

"Here." She handed me what looked to be welding gloves. "You don't want to get any of them barbs in your skin. They're the devil to get out."

"Swell." I donned the stiff gloves without any further prodding. We began the tricky skinning process. Holding the things was like trying to do needlepoint with boxing gloves on. One prickly cone shot out of my hand and plunked off the side of the trailer. I struggled to get one peeled in the time it took Katy to knock out half a dozen of them. She whistled as she skinned, her chins covered by a sheen of sweat.

I was so focused on not impaling myself with the lethal lobes, I didn't notice Jojo until she popped up at my elbow.

"Hi," she said. Someone had taken the time to put her hair in a single ponytail that sprouted out the top of her head. She looked like a hispanic Pebbles Flintstone. "You freaked out at the bug smiting."

I took a cleansing breath. "Yes, I freaked out. But I'm okay now."

She nodded. "It was funny. Like you were doing a dance. You made some really funny noises."

Oh brother.

"Do you have some candy?"

That's the great thing about kids, I thought. They just take things at face value. No searching for deeper meaning. If the strange lady said she was okay, then she was okay. I would have patted the girl on the head if I wasn't wearing the gloves of doom. "I don't have any candy right now."

"I wanna go see it again."

"Go see what?"

"Where the bugs are."

The kid actually wanted to go trekking through the insect infested desert again? And I thought I was crazy.

Katy plopped a huge pile of cactus shrapnel into the boiling water with nary a splash. Red juice stained her fingers and wrists. "Go on and play, Jojo. I don't want you to get burned."

Off she went. This Mrs. Nunez was all right. She just issued a proclamation and kids obeyed without questions. When I gave direction to small children they menaced me with pirate swords or thumb tacks. I wondered if Katy heard about my major desert meltdown before Jojo's helpful report. She didn't say anything as she continued to peel.

I decided to indulge my nagging curiosity. "I saw your daughter at the Pick N Pack. She seems nice."

"Gigi is a good girl." The woman's face glowed with perspiration and pride. "She's finishing up her classes at the junior college. Then she'll go to a university to get her teaching credential. She'll be the first in our family to get a degree. Ain't that something?"

"That's fantastic. Did she go to high school with Chaz?"

Katy's head snapped around so quickly her chins took a second to catch up with her neck. "No. He moved here after high school. They met in junior college, unfortunately. Because of that louse, Gigi didn't start at the university right away. He stole her money so she had to stay at the j.c. for two more years."

Zowie. I never saw that one coming. Chaz, a thief? "He stole her money?"

"Not my place to spill garbage. Ask him if you want to know any more." She pressed her fleshy lips together.

Chaz stole Gigi's money? I had a hard time believing the guy would do something that callous. Then again, he was mooching free rent off my cash strapped aunt. But he seemed so earnest about everything. I finished peeling prickly pear number two. Somehow I was going to find out the truth about this odd little mystery.

And then the Doves flew in.

It was quite the assembly line. The teens were an interesting sight in their massive gloves, peeling and slicing another batch of fruit. They certainly had better dexterity with the knives and prickles than I did. After the cactus boiled for twenty minutes, they extracted the red blobs with slotted spoons and began to mash them with great enthusiasm.

"Come on, Jack." Raul poked his friend. "Put some back into it man, you mash like a girl."

"Yeah?" A blond girl with the name Alison written in puffy paint on her bandana looked up. She raised her sticky implement from the bowl. "Why don't you come over here and I'll show you what a mashing is?"

The boys exchanged some whispered comments and more laughter.

Katy supervised the removal of the small seeds and fibers that did not succumb to the masher. Then the whole mess went back into the drained pot along with an enormous amount of sugar and powdered pectin. In between tasks, Katy interspersed facts about the prickly pear which the Doves dutifully recorded in their notebooks. "The fruits are an important food for many animals and peoples. The O'Odham tribe for example."

The information impressed me. I couldn't imagine people performing this cactus mangling on a regular basis. How did they accomplish this in the olden days without the benefit of barbecue tongs, gloves or band aids? Must've had skin like iron.

"Now it's got to be fast boiled and poured into jars," Katy said, wiping her fingers on the apron that spanned her stomach. "Who's up for that job?"

Tanya stepped forward and began to stir the concoction with a wooden spoon. "It's the color of a red crayon. I bet this stuff will be great on our pancakes tomorrow."

"Pancakes?" The word caught my attention. "Where are we going for pancakes?"

Tanya raised an eyebrow. "Didn't you see all the griddles in the chapel?"

"Oh man." I sighed. I could only imagine how many pancakes Jack and his cohorts could put away. "I have terrible luck with vacations."

"Don't worry, Miss Greevey. We're only here for three more days and then you're home free. Besides," she gave the spoon a smack on the metal pot, "Mr. Tagliola was able to pick the scorpion out of your hair before he carried you back home after the bug hunt. That's pretty good luck, isn't it?"

***

Brandi, I decided to take the plunge. I'm going to grad school and leaving Bryan behind. It seems surreal. Will I regret it forever? I cry every day about it but, I think that's what is best for me now. I need some hand holding here. Did I do the right thing? Am I making the worst mistake of my life? -- Sister Sue

I don't know if it was my close encounter with insects or the fact that my day started at an inhumane hour, but I just couldn't seem to come up with anything helpful for Sue. I hoped someone else would put in their two pennies worth. The next post was from Glenda. I suppressed a lip curl. The last time I heard from her she was munching on truffled eggs with Mr. Perfect Ryan.

Hi guys. You'll never believe it. Ryan is a complete jerk. He said he wants more space, that he needs room to be himself. Can you believe it? He can't be himself when he's with me? And I thought he was an angel.

Jerk, jerk, jerk! -- Galpal

I tried to stifle the unholy satisfaction that welled up inside me. So Scrambled Egg man wasn't Glenda's love match? Welcome to the club. Been there, still wiping the yolk off my face. I readied my typing fingers but Cherry had already beaten me to the punch.

Don't let it get you down, honey. You're a great gal and if he doesn't realize that just cut the line. You're better off without him. -- Cherry B.

Well said, Cherry B. I cursored down to the next comment. It was a new post from a name I didn't recognize. Yay me, increasing the hits per week stats, even from my station in a desert wasteland.

Maybe Glenda was looking for something that only exists in the Savior. There's just one perfect, and it's not here on earth. -- D.F.

The message took me by surprise. I had to admit the words were true, but not the sort of thing a jilted lover wants to hear. Visions of my ex floated in front of my eyes. Was I looking for perfect in Doug? For a while I thought he was perfect for me. A perfect fit, a perfect complement.

A perfect disaster, my inner voice hissed, like the eruption of Vesuvius. It was partially my fault, as much as I loathed to admit it. There had been signs; broken dates, a lack of enthusiasm for wedding plans, a subtle distance between us. I'd been so thoroughly wrapped in my happy pre-marital vision that I hadn't noticed him falling out of love with me. Maybe if I'd paid more attention to the man that was supposedly my soul mate.

I sat back in the hard chair to cogitate. More of that uneasy self reflection stuff was zinging around my mind. Doug may have been a fickle faced frog, but he wasn't a liar. He hadn't hidden any character flaws from me. Doug never claimed to be perfect. Oh gee, I hated those moments of flaw recognition. My fingers snapped off a quick reply.

Sounds like you speak from experience. Do you have any other suggestions for Galpal? -- Brandi

I hit the send button with only a second of regret for my sarcastic tone. Hopefully my mood would not come clearly through the computer screen. The little spot behind my temple began to throb in the stuffy heat of the trailer. This was day eight without Starbucks or a manicure and my DNA was beginning to break down. Before I signed off, I checked my personal e-mail, hoping against all logic that there would be a message from Stella along the lines of "just pulling in to Seepwillow now, see you in five minutes."

There wasn't. Only another message from my freckled friend in San Francisco.

We need to talk, Simone. I'm taking vacation. Where exactly are you? Donna

My heart skipped over a large chunk of beating. There was no way I wanted Donna to come here, to see me in these conditions struggling to keep up with a bunch of prepubescents. It was just too humiliating.

Don't come. I'm really busy. I'll look you up when I get back. Simone

Thank goodness I didn't have a live video laptop. She'd never believe Simone Greevey, queen of the midweek apricot facial, was sitting in a sorely unexfoliated state in a broken down trailer without even an imported mineral water to ease her sorrow.

I signed off.

The view out my trailer window depressed me. The setting sun beat unmercifully on the flat ground. Heat shivered up from the scruffy grass like snakes ready to strike. No wonder the insects here were awful. How could such an inhospitable locale produce anything but horrifying creatures? The thought of a scorpion on my body made me quiver until I forced myself to take five deep cleansing breaths. It wasn't just my irrational fear of bugs. Any sane person would be in a hurry to leave Seepwillow.

The desert was not the place for me.

Not anymore.

"San Francisco, when will I see you again?" I wailed.

As if on cue, the phone rang.

Chapter Ten

It could have been my imagination, but even the ring of the phone had an ominous undertone. I picked up the ancient, shoe sized receiver. "Hello?"

The voice on the other end was barely audible over the static. "Hi honey."

"Aunt Stella!" I shouted. "Is that you? What happened? Where are you? Are you all right? Why haven't you called? I've been worried sick."

"Yes, I'm...."

It sounded like she said something about pork rinds. "What?" I shouted louder.

"I said I'm fine and so is Uncle Bud. I'm sorry I didn't call sooner. It took me a while to find a phone. We had a little trouble, but it's all worked out."

"Trouble?" My heart began to pitter patter. "What kind? Was there an accident?"

She used a word I took to be detested. There was more snapping and crackling on the line. "He detested what? I don't understand. This connection is terrible."

"Arrested," she yelled into the phone. "Your Uncle Bud was arrested. He was passing out Bibles and he wound up in jail. Law enforcement is crabby around here. He's all right though, they let him out this morning."

The vision of my rotund uncle shackled in some rat infested prison was too much to contemplate. This was the new millennium. I couldn't fathom a man being slapped in irons for distributing Bibles. Before my lungs filled up again, she picked up the conversational football.

"How are things going with the Doves?"

"Swell." I didn't even try to contain the sarcasm. "You didn't tell me I would be running a day camp for teens. I've spent the past few days making more food than the U.S. Army turns out in a week. And there are way too many bugs in this place. Where are you anyway? And when are you coming home?"

"What did you say, sweetie?"

"WHEN ARE YOU COMING HOME?"

"As soon as we can catch a flight. It's not easy to get one here. I'm sure you'll do just fine with the Doves until I get back. Chaz will help you with anything. Thanks so much, honey. It's such a relief to know the Ruddy Duck is in good hands. Could you be a doll and check my p.o. box in town? I don't think there will be anything too important but go ahead and open anything that you think needs a peek."

The woman was asking me to look after her mail. People who are planning to be home in a matter of hours do not ask others to do postal duty. I put that together with the phone scarcity and the fact that my uncle was in jail for evangelizing. "Wait one minute. Hold on. Exactly where are you calling from, Aunt Stella?"

There was a loud crackle and one word got through before the line went dead.

"Bulgaria," my aunt said cheerfully.

***

I finished up my temper tantrum just as the sun began to set. The word Bulgaria caused all my self-control caulking to bust loose. I was marooned in the desert with twelve teenagers, a handyman and sixteen cans of Twirly Roni. Who knew how long it would take my aunt to get a flight out of Bulgaria? They were hanging out at an airport at the other end of the universe. I could be here for months. It was too much.

To my credit, I only broke one dish in my emotional rampage. And because the whipped cream was all gone, I drowned my sorrows in a jar of dill pickles. Not nearly as satisfying as whipped cream, but the fat content was vastly better. The sour snacks matched my mood anyway.

Since the Loving Doves were headed back to church for a potluck, my cooking services were not required. I flicked on the TV and stared at it. The old thing only got a few channels and I wasn't in the right frame of mind to watch a bass fishing tournament. Then I stared at the walls. After an hour more of this ocular torture, I could stand it no more. The trailer door clanged shut behind me as I walked into the molten dusk, pulling on a jacket and hat to shield me from insect life.

My feet looked very nice in their Teva X-1s. You couldn't see the remaining delicate peach tint of my toenail polish, but the feet were stylish. They looked like feet that could run a marathon or do some athletic mall walking. Too bad they took me to the place I did not want to go, a place that haunted me.

The shed was even hotter than the night outside. A blast of air smelling of fertilizer and dry grass hit me. Piles of tools were scattered around. I stepped over a bucket of golf balls on my way to the shrouded bundle. My brain had not yet caught up with my feet: it was wrapped around an ancient memory.

My father rose in my thoughts just as surely as if he were standing with me in the shed. I pictured the hesitation that was forever painted on his face when he looked in my direction. He was always frightened of me. An odd word for a man who commanded a vessel ready to deploy a nuclear bomb at any moment. Maybe it was the extended tours at sea that prevented him from getting used to having a child. Sometimes I would see him out of the corner of my eye, watching me as if observing some rare natural phenomenon. When he saw me looking, he would turn away without a word.

As I grew older we found a few safe subjects: how was school? Did I brush my teeth? What did I want for my birthday?

"Will you take me to the park?" I would say.

"Uh, well, I think your mother is better for that, Simone."

Never honey, pussycat, sweetheart. Always Simone.

Until that one day.

The day I snuck into the garage.

I heard him in there, his tools banging and clattering as he worked. Head low, feet silent, I crept in. He finally saw me. I didn't say anything when our eyes met. His eyes locked on mine and for the first time, the only time, understanding passed between us. "Do you...want to help hon?"

I nodded. And that was the beginning of our secret. I sat, and watched his gentle hands coaxing that motorcycle to life. I listened to the throaty rumble of the engine that vibrated my sternum. We both lit up like search beacons when he got that bike roaring to life.

In the superheated shed, sweat trickled down my back as I reached for the fabric. I pulled it away and then I forgot to breathe. It was exactly like I remembered. All smooth curves and hot metal.

"I wondered who belonged to that bike."

I whirled toward the voice. "What are you doing here?"

Chaz peered over my shoulder. "I saw the door open. I thought I should check it out. That's a sweet bike."

I eyed the shiny black frame. "It's better than sweet; it's a XR75 mini."

His eyebrow shot up. "I know. I'm surprised that you do. You told me you didn't know anything about bikes."

My cheeks warmed even more. "I don't know a whole lot. Just the basics. My father was the bike guru. And Aunt Stella is a whiz with engines, of course. She taught me a few things."

Chaz sat on a wooden crate. His hair was loose, a mass of swirling black around his tanned face. He bobbed a chin at the motorcycle. "Did your dad give it to you?"

I nodded, because my throat clogged. The long ago moment was forever burned into my brain. I coughed and the words came out. "We didn't tell my mother. She didn't approve of his hobby in the first place. Dad used to drive me to Seepwillow to visit Aunt Stella. He had his motorcycle in the back of the truck. On the way he would stop and let me ride. On one trip he gave me my own bike."

"Excellent." Chaz wiped a trickle of sweat from his face. The open vee of his shirt showed a muscled chest, gleaming with moisture. "Is that why this bike is here? You didn't want your mom to know?"

"Yes." On that brilliant, scalding day as we drove to Seepwillow, my dad had pulled off the road.

"I've got something for you." He made me close my eyes and when I opened them, there it was, complete with sleek black helmet. The shiny body gleamed like a brilliant sun. I laughed so hard I cried. I thought I saw a bit of moisture in his eyes too.

Then we rode.

And rode.

And raced, zooming over bumps as fast as we could go, tasting the sweat and the sand in our mouths. It was pure exhilaration, pure joy.

Hours later when we piled back into the truck, I grabbed him around the neck. "I love you, Daddy."

He didn't say a word, but after I buckled up he squeezed my hand with fingers full of love. After so many years, I could still feel his warm hand on mine.

"Did you ever race?" Chaz's soft voice cut through my memories.

"Only once. They had an informal dirt bike race here once. The Dirt Squirt. I entered and crashed right before the finish line. But I got back on and finished second."

He looked at me without blinking. "And it was the best feeling you ever had."

"Crashing?"

"No, riding."

I tried to go for nonchalant, crossing my arms in front of my body. "Oh, I don't know. It was okay, a great childhood memory."

"It was more than that. I can hear it in your voice. You love bikes. They're in your blood. Why don't you ride anymore?"

Why didn't I ride?

Because I was an educated, accomplished woman. Because I was well groomed and classy, not some hardcore biker chick. Because it was not a part of my world anymore. I had reinvented myself without it. And without my father.

"I outgrew it," I said, finally.

"Too bad. I didn't think it was possible to outgrow bikes. My bike is about the only thing I own in the world." He cocked his head. "I was thinking we could go for a ride sometime."

For a second I pictured racing across the desert, sharing laughter and building memories with a special man. A man with M&M skin and a dimpled smile. I buried that weird thought in a hurry. Go for a spin with Chaz? The thought was laughable. "Thanks, but I'm just not into it anymore."

He looked down at his worn boots for a moment before he got up. "I see. No problem. Will Stella be back tomorrow?"

"No. She's in Bulgaria. They're trying to get a flight home."

He laughed. "Bulgaria? That figures. You can never really predict what she's going to do next. I found a napkin stuck in my toolbox with a note on it a little bit ago. I guess she arranged for a take-your-Loving-Dove-to-work-day so I'm giving them a tour of my office tomorrow."

"Your office?"

"You bet. Pastor Stan is driving the kids in the van but they're pretty full up. I was going to give Stella a ride on the back of my bike, but I guess that's out." He sighed. "I really could use another adult there to help out. You sure you don't want to ride shotgun?"

"I'm sure."

His eyes filled with disappointment. "I guess after our last field trip you're not too keen on going with me anywhere."

I felt a little smidgy less mad. "It wasn't your fault about the..." I swallowed "...bugs."

"Yeah, well, I still feel bad that you had to go through that. Sometimes I make some really dumb decisions. Anyway, I'll see you for pancakes in the morning." He ducked through the doorway into the night.

I pulled the tarp back into place. As I did so, my fingers skimmed the warm metal. I remembered the speed.

I remembered my father.

***

There was only one blog entry waiting for me.

Brandi-

Is it harder to forgive someone else or yourself? D.F.

I ate microwaved popcorn while I considered this. I had quite a list of people on my "to forgive" list at the moment. There was Audrey who sandbagged my career. Donna for taking my job without a moment's hesitation. And, of course, Doug, the man who popped my self esteem balloon with his Rachel pin. I knew Audrey and Donna had not harmed me intentionally. Come right down to it, neither had Doug, but I was having real trouble erasing him from my list. He was wrong to fall out of love with me, wasn't he?

As far as forgiving myself, I was pretty clear on that count. There wasn't much there to forgive. Oh sure, maybe a fixation on wedding details that prevented me from noticing my fiancé fall for another woman. And then there was the fact that I really hadn't embraced this whole Loving Dove experience. But that really wasn't too bad. Not like breaking any commandments or anything. Moses wouldn't hold it against me. I mean, he killed a guy and he still wound up being a moral compass and all that.

I shoveled in some more popcorn as a word surfaced in my mind.
Chaz.

Hmmm. I had painted a picture of him the moment Jojo knocked over his ladder. He was rough, unkempt and, the nasty phrase crept into my mind before I could squash it; blue collar.

The realization made me choke on a popcorn kernel. Was that why I didn't like him? The man was not on my socioeconomic or educational par? Ooooh. That sounded downright snobby. Did I need forgiveness for that too? I shook it off.

"There are plenty of reasons to dislike Chaz besides that," I said firmly. "I fell into a pile of bugs because of him. And he doesn't pay my aunt any rent. And Katy says he robbed Gigi. And every time I'm with him I say something dumb."

I looked at the screen again. Something about this D.F. was odd. This wasn't your typical blogger chick. The messages weren't following in the same vein as the rest of Brandi's flock. I couldn't put my finger on it but the hair on the back of my neck did a prickle dance.

I tapped out a return message.

Pretty deep thoughts, D.F. I think forgiveness is a good thing, regardless. Did you need some personal advice on the subject? -- Brandi

That ought to do it. Ball's back in your court, honeybunch. I'm supposed to be directing the questions here, not fielding someone else's volley. It's called Bloggin' With Brandi, girlfriend.

An odd flicker in the window caught my attention. A beam of light danced across the darkness for just a moment and then disappeared. I hoisted the crooked shade and peered out. Nothing but blackness. As I was about to turn away, the light swooped by again in a luminous zig zag.

I grabbed a flashlight and poked my head out the door. Having seen the nocturnal creatures in action, I resolved to go no further than the porch step. I waited, listening. There was a quiet buzz of crickets and the faraway moan of a coyote. I thought I heard a snatch of laughter but it was gone before I could pinpoint the sound.

There it was again. Near Aunt Stella's trailer. A flash of light that made a glowing arc for the briefest of seconds. Oh sheesh. As much as the thought terrified me, it was my duty to look after this little spot of nowhere. What if it was a robber breaking into the office trailer? Or aliens landing? If it was aliens, they should have used Mapquest. They'd missed anywhere significant by a hundred miles.

I procrastinated for a while longer. Somebody had to go check things out and I was the only somebody present and accounted for. Another good reason why I should never have come to the desert in the first place.

It would be okay, I told myself. As an extra precaution I put on long pants and tucked the legs into some sweat socks. Then I wrapped a kitchen towel around my neck and put on my shower cap. Too bad I didn't have a ski mask handy. No bug was going to have access to any square inch of Simone Greevey, ever again. I would rather face an armed thief than a naked beetle.

I took a fortifying breath and stepped out of the trailer. My shoes made soft crunching noises as I crept along. The odd flash of light danced ahead, around the next trailer. I sidled up to the wall of Mr. Singh's trailer and inched along, step by step until I was even with the edge. The light continued to flicker just ahead of me.

Feeling like a character in a bad police movie, I leaped around the corner, brandishing my flashlight.

"Hold it right there," I hollered.

The beam of my flashlight blinded the poor victim. He stood frozen in the glare. Then he started to hiss and snap his beaky mouth. Poor LeRoy. The Loving Doves paid him back for that bite all right. They fastened a flashlight to his back with wide bands of electrical tape. LeRoy was his own fantastic light parade as he wove his way around the trailer park. That explained the laughter I'd heard earlier.

"That'll teach you to bite teenagers. You are now officially the laughing stock of the entire tortoise brigade. Come here and I'll help you, naughty boy." I grabbed the not hissing regions of the angry tortoise. With a bit of elbow grease I was able to untape the flashlight and carry him over to the porch step. His spindly legs swam helplessly through the air. When I put him down next to the porch he gave me a hostile glance and burrowed under the step, wiggling madly to get his rear end down the narrow hole.

With LeRoy safely ensconced in his sandy burrow, I breathed a sigh of relief.

Then it hit me.

Watching that turtle jam himself into the hole jarred loose a memory. The realization swept through me faster than a run in pantyhose.

I was correct when I guessed that my new cyber pal was no ordinary blogger.

I knew who D.F. really was.

Chapter Eleven

The smoke from the burning pancakes did not rouse me from my daze. It wasn't until Tanya grabbed the spatula and flipped the crispy thing that I noticed the charred smell. The Doves were busy wolfing down pancakes smeared with scarlet prickly pear jam. Jack added a layer of marshmallow fluff in between his towering mountain o' breakfast. They all had giant backpacks on the floor, ready for the Tuesday adventure, a visit to Chaz's office.

"Are you okay, Miss Greevey?" Tanya asked, as she expertly flopped three pancakes from the electric griddle onto Raul's waiting plate.

"Me? Oh sure, sure. I was just thinking about something else." That was an understatement. My realization on the previous night sat in my head like a live grenade. I knew that D.F. was not your typical blogger. As a matter of fact, D.F. wasn't even a woman. The mysterious blogger was none other than my ex fiancé, Doug.

The matter became crystal clear when I watched LeRoy wiggle his way down into the hole. It brought me back to Doug's annoying hobby. His mother got him a metal detector for his birthday and he took it everywhere. For months it was a permanent fixture in the trunk of his car. I gradually grew to loath the ugly contraption. The final straw was a day at the beach when he proceeded to dig a hole so deep that I could only see his legs sticking out.

I was mortified that someone would debase themselves in search of a quarter or an old watch. It just looked so... desperate. When I could take no more, I transformed momentarily into his mother and shouted, "Douglas Franklin Mitchell. If you do not climb out of that hole right this second, I will snap your metal detector like a pretzel."

Douglas Franklin Mitchell emerged, grinning.

"No one calls me that, not even my mother. I hate my middle name so Mom just calls me D.F. when she's ticked. I can't stand that either."

Good old Douglas Franklin.

So D.F. wanted to discuss the search for perfection. And forgiveness. On my blog. With me. After he dumped me for the multi-talented Rachel. Why would he do such a thing?

"Here." Tanya thrust a plate of pancakes and jelly into my hand. "Maybe you should have something to eat."

The jam was lovely, I had to admit. Sweet, but not cloying with a tiny smidge of tang. And there weren't even any kitchen utensils or bits of finger floating around in it. Katy Nunez would be proud. I made it through half a pancake by the time the kids were packed up and ready to go. They tossed their sticky paper plates and headed out to the waiting van in a loud swarm. Through the open door I could see Chaz outside, next to his red Elsinore.

"Are you coming with us?" Tanya finished washing her hands.

"Uh, no. You can tell me all about it when you get back."

She nodded and followed them out.

I was alone with my rampant thoughts.

Doug.

How dare he come and pancake flip my life. Again.

First he loved me. Until he loved Rachel. Then he was out of my life. Now he was...what? Looking for reconciliation? Forgiveness? Fashion tips?

A nugget deep down inside of me warmed up. "Just desserts," I sniped. He had realized his mistake. Rachel wasn't the love of his life. She wasn't Miss Perky Perfect. How supremely satisfying.

I watched the kids cram into the van. Pastor Stan fired her up and a big belch of smoke spat out the back.

Chaz straddled his bike and strapped on the helmet. He was dressed in tight jeans and a green tee shirt. I wondered again what sort of office he belonged in. The extra helmet was secured on the back. I could picture Gigi sitting behind him, her long hair trailing in the desert wind.

"What is happening to me?" The words bounced against the walls of the empty trailer. One week ago I was in San Francisco with a comfortable life and cemented plans. In the space of a few days the scenery changed from bayside to barren wasteland and I had gone from someone's better half to knee deep in sand all by myself. And now...what?

Forgiveness? The word danced around my head. How dare he change my whole life and then drop in on my blog, hiding behind another name. The blood pounded behind my eyes. He betrayed me and now he wanted to slink back into my world. He had no right to control me. If I wasn't good enough before, that was his loss. I used to be a strong person long before I mutated into Doug's fiancée. I used to know who I was and what I wanted out of life.

An odd feeling flared inside of me, a stubborn fire that burned its way up to my brain. I was going to be that person again.

I shot out the door and grabbed the helmet off the back of the bike.

Chaz whipped around. His eyes were wide. "Hi, Simone. Did you change your mind about the field trip?"

"Yes," I called above the engine. "But I'm driving."

***

It wasn't exactly like my childhood rides. I looked much more stylish now in my Roxy jeans and Tommy Bahama tee. The helmet was emblazoned with a picture of a desert fox on the back which wasn't my style, but anything looks good on top of a cherry red Elsinore. But the feeling was the same, an amazing rush that vibrated every nerve with a glorious energy. It was as if I'd never stopped riding as we flowed over every curve and turn.

As we headed down the highway, Chaz tightened his arms around my waist. He didn't say anything, but I could feel the hammer of his heart against my back. After a while, all of those details melted away. Even Doug lost his place in my head as the engine roared under me. There was open road, the hot wind on my face and speed.

I didn't break any laws, but I pushed the bike as fast as legally possible.

"Where are we headed?" I finally shouted to Chaz.

"Just follow the van," he hollered back.

The bike handled like a dream. The two stroke engine had plenty of punch and all my early riding technique came as naturally as putting on lipstick. I could hear my father's voice echo in my ears.

"Stay centered over the bike, Simone. Ride on the balls of your feet and weight to the outside on the turns."

I must have been a bit too enthusiastic on some of those turns as I felt Chaz mold his body tighter against mine. The temperature suddenly jumped a few degrees. I caught the ever present aroma of marinara sauce. After a few miles we had left the van far behind.

"Slow it down a little, Simone. Speed limit's sixty here."

Though it pained me to do so, I slowed. We were in the middle of nowhere as far as I could tell. No buildings, only a few cars, not even a gas station for miles. Unless this office building was buried under three tons of sand, I could not figure out where Chaz was taking us. Finally he squeezed my arm and pointed left. We turned in next to a sign that read *Saguaro National Park.*

I pulled over and slid the bike into a narrow parking lot. We hopped off.

Chaz pulled off his helmet which sported the same tacky fox on the back. His hair was held back into a ponytail but damp strands stuck to his face where the helmet rested. His face creased into a grin.

"That was some ride."

"I will take that as a compliment."

"That's how it was meant. What made you change your mind about coming along?"

I smoothed my hair. "Woman's prerogative. So where's your office?"

He swept a hand to the acres of parched land that spread out on either side of the road. "Here it is. The Saguaro National Park."

"This is your office?"

"Yup. Ninety one thousand acres and a doozy of a view. Not bad for a handyman, eh?"

I blushed. "What exactly do you do here?"

"Nothing today, it's my day off. The rest of the time I'm a Naturalist.

I teach classes at the visitor center and give guided hikes and campfire programs. Sometimes I collect fees or do trail maintenance."

The words fell out of my head before I could filter out the snob factor. "I thought you had to have a four year degree to do that."

He cocked his head. "If I wasn't such an easygoing guy, I might feel offended by that remark."

My face grew even hotter than it already was. I searched for something to repair the damage and found nothing. "Oh boy. Did I really say that?"

"I believe you did. You know, somebody who saw you tearing through the desert on a dirt bike might make some snap judgments about you too, in spite of your trendy clothes."

"I apologize."

"Okay. I take it the perfect man in the Simone guidebook has a college degree and an indoor office?"

"Not necessarily." I picked a piece of imaginary lint off my jeans.

He smiled. "Good. I'd hate to think you had such a narrow view of what is acceptable. I mean, if every man followed those guidelines, who would be left to work on the bikes?"

I flashed him a hostile glare. "I get the point."

He pulled a bottle of water out of his bag and handed one to me. "You're right, by the way. You do need a college degree. Mine's in herpetology."

"I thought you went to community college with Gigi."

"I got my B.A. before that. When I moved here I decided to add on a business degree. Gigi was getting her general ed stuff done before she transferred to a state college." His gaze traveled over the ground.

"Did you finish the degree?"

"Nah. I had a loan I needed to pay back so I dropped out." He drained the water. "Here come the Doves."

The teens piled out and collected in clusters in the shade of the van.

"Oh man," Jack said. "That was some sweet riding, Ms. Greevey. I didn't know you could handle a bike."

"Why do you sound surprised?" Tanya said.

He tossed a mop of hair out of his face. "Oh, you know, she just seems kinda...girly and prissy. In a real nice way, of course."

Allyson smacked him in the shoulder. "Oink, oink."

"What?" Jack said. "What did I say?"

"Something stupid," she said.

Raul shouldered his pack. "Come on, Allyson. You have to admit, women tend to focus on the material."

"And men don't? What about your tools and computer toys?"

"Tools are not toys."

Allyson fisted her hands on her hips. "An iPod is not a tool, Raul."

Pastor Stan came to the rescue. "All right, all right. Let's get ourselves ready for the tour. Everyone has water, hats, sunscreen and umbrellas?"

They all nodded.

I leaned over to Tanya. "Why do we need umbrellas? Is it going to rain again?"

"Chaz said it's important for desert survival."

I looked over at the big man who was efficiently organizing the troop, suddenly wishing I had packed my umbrella too.

Chaz rallied the kids together. "Here's the deal. I'm going to take you on a hike. Not a stroll or a meander. A hike. The desert houses the most complex, intricate ecosystem on the planet. It's extremely fragile and deadly at the same time. So make sure you have water and don't wander off. In the desert it's real simple; you follow the rules or you die. Is that clear?"

Everyone nodded.

Visions of insects suddenly swam in front of my eyes. My fierce determination waned a bit. I hoped they didn't hear my gulp of suppressed panic.

"All right. You're responsible for yourself and your partner. We're headed for an amazing spot that will rock your world. It will be a long hike but we'll stop frequently. Is everybody ready?"

I was too embarrassed to say what was on my mind.

The Doves gave a cheerful shout and shouldered their packs.

Chaz gave us all a thumbs up. "Let's go."

***

I realized about one mile into the trek that I was totally unprepared. No backpack, no hat, not even an umbrella. I had raced out to the bike in a fit of Doug induced hysteria. Now, as I hiked along behind Jack and Tanya, I began to feel another stab of concern.

It was still early morning but the sun blazed like a mega watt laser beam. The jacket I'd grabbed as I flew out of the trailer was tied around my waist and sweat poured down my back and soaked my tee shirt. At least I'd remembered my sunglasses.

Distracted as I was by my slow roasting, I was impressed by the wide open space around me. We were following a narrow, flat trail that wound along past a mesquite lined wash on either side. I expected only browns, beiges and sizzling whites, but the color palette was peppered with the vivid green of shrubby trees that Chaz identified as Palo Verde. After an hour of hiking, we stopped under the shade of a few of these specimens for a break.

I carefully lowered my posterior onto a flat rock. The kids were taking long pulls on their bottles of water which they had frozen the night before. The cool beads that dropped onto the ground as they drank reminded me that I had no liquid substances, save the lip gloss in my jacket pocket. I tried to think of other things, like the angular hawk that drifted in lazy circles in the brilliant sky. No dice. My mouth was dry as the sand.

A lovely cool drop landed on my arm. Chaz stood over me with a chilled bottle of water. "Here. I brought extra."

"Thank you." I drank the water greedily and watched him. He stood there, brown face turned up to meet the sun. He looked at home, as though he was a part of this strange rugged space. "How long have you lived in the desert?"

He seemed surprised by the question. "Me? It seems like forever. We moved to Phoenix from Samoa when I was a baby. Dad worked in my uncle's shoe factory until he couldn't stand it anymore. Then he and Mom went back to the island and my brother and I stayed with my uncle to finish school."

"Is your brother still here?"

"No. He's got a medical practice in San Diego. It's been really successful for him. He sends money home to my folks every month. Last summer he bought them tickets to come and visit the states."

There was an odd expression in his eyes. Was it a touch of regret? Shame? "But you stayed here instead of moving back to Samoa?" I prodded.

"Yeah." He drained his water bottle and put it back in his pack. "I belong in the desert."

"Is that why you have a desert fox on your bike helmet?"

He brushed away a fly. "That's a leftover from another time, the name of a business I was into for a while."

"What business?"

At that moment a bird with long tail feathers and speckled wings barreled along the trail and disappeared into the bushes. Chaz snapped into teacher mode. "Okay, who had their eyes peeled? What type of bird was that?"

Allyson spoke up. "A roadrunner?"

"Right. They eat a lot of moist food, insects, scorpions, lizards, rodents, so they don't require much water. They can run up to fifteen miles an hour which is about the top speed of that old van you guys drove here."

"Yeah, well we didn't have Speed Racer driving like you did," Jack said. "Pastor Stan gets the brake and the gas pedal mixed up."

"What's that?" The pastor looked up from his notebook. "There's a gas pedal?"

The laughter sounded small in the wide open space.

"Come on then, you landlubbers." Chaz grabbed his pack. "Let's move."

***

We spent another few hours recording all the wildlife that we stumbled upon. I regarded the wonders of the Patchnose snake from a distance, preferring to note instead the bits of mica that shone like glass along the pathway. I tried to hide my alarm when we came upon the warning sign for Africanized bees. There was a picture of a hideous looking winged creature with a stinger. Chaz must have heard my heart, which beat hard enough to hammer its way out of my chest.

"Africanized bees are dangerous, but if we stay on the path we'll be fine," he said. "They aren't a problem unless you disturb them. I've worked here for years and never had any trouble."

Raul looked excited. "Killer bees? Aren't they the kind that swarm and sting until you die?"

I squeezed my eyes shut. Hard. I was hoping for an I Dream of Jeanie moment. She could always blink her way out of trouble. It didn't work. When I opened them I was still in the desert discussing murderous insects. That swarmed. And stung things. Repeatedly.

"They're like every other animal," he said, eyeing me. "They don't attack unless you provoke them. It's not in their interest to have a close encounter with people."

That satisfied Raul and the group moved along. Chaz hung back and fell in step next to me.

"Are you okay?"

I nodded. "Sure."

He put a hand very gently on my arm.

"If you want to go back, we'll turn around. I can bring the Doves here another day. No problem at all. I'd be happy to do it."

For some reason I felt comforted by the pressure of his massive hand on my wrist. The old Simone was fearless. I was going to find her if it was the last thing I did. "I'm okay. As long as you promise there are no killer bees in my future."

He smiled. "I wouldn't take you anywhere that I thought you could get hurt."

"You wouldn't? Why not?"

"Because...because Aunt Stella would never forgive me."

"Are you afraid of my little aunt?"

"No, but I wouldn't ever want to hurt or disappoint you."

Awww. Warm fuzzy feelings.

I looked into his dark eyes and he returned my gaze for a moment before he dropped his hand. Then his expression changed. "Uh, Simone? You did put sunscreen on today didn't you?"

"Sunscreen? Of course. I wear sunscreen everyday," I said somewhat haughtily to erase the weird fluttery sensations. Back on solid ground. I didn't know a roadrunner from a rhododendron but I knew all about skin care.

"Oh. You just look kind of pink. That was SPF 50 at least, that you put on, wasn't it?"

"Of course it was."

He nodded and returned to the front of our merry band.

That left me to wonder. That moisturizer, the one with the aloe and orange extract. The one that I put on my face every day to prevent the damaging UV rays of the mild San Francisco climate. Wasn't that the moisturizer with a whopping sun protection factor of fifteen?

I wondered if killer bees liked their victims well done.

Chapter Twelve

We arrived at our breathtaking destination just after two o'clock. On the way we stopped for lunch which was another item I had neglected to bring. Tanya shared her peanut butter sandwich and trail mix and Chaz supplied me yet another bottle of water. The contents of that magic backpack would make Mary Poppins positively green. Jack even offered to share some of his marshmallow fluff. Helpful, these Doves.

"Here it is," Chaz said, sweeping a hand toward the prickly plateau. "The cactus forest."

I squinted, trying to ignore the stinging on my nose now shaded by Tanya's Cardinal baseball hat. Try as I might to embrace the drama of the moment, I was not moved a bit by the sprawling scenery. It was, well, a bunch of cacti, sprinkled in between creosote shrubs, clinging here and there in clumps to the rocky ground. It wasn't my idea of what a forest should look like, not a single leaf anywhere.

"Come on," he said. "Everyone find a partner and go look at a cactus up close. I want a good sketch and notes about your observations. Look in the guidebook to identify the species. Stay where you can see me and we'll meet back here in thirty minutes. If you need help, holler."

The kids scurried off, leaving me alone with Chaz. I followed him up a gentle slope to the shade of another Palo Verde tree. He seemed impervious to the heat, only having eyes for the green monster that stood next to the scant shadow of the tree.

It was at least fifteen feet tall. The saguaro was as big around as a motorcycle tire with a dozen or so spiked arms. The skin was marked and pitted with what looked like scabs. I tried to summon up the proper tone of awe before I broke the silence.

"It's a saguaro, right?"

He didn't take his gaze off the massive plant. "Yes. Over two hundred years old." He shook his head. "Can you believe it started out as a seed the size of a pinhead?"

"Er, no. It's a wonder it survived."

"Exactly." He turned to look at me. "Exactly. They usually only survive if they grow under a nurse tree, like this one that shelters them from the elements. They only grow a quarter inch a year. It takes seventy five years before they sprout their first arms."

Man. Talk about your delayed gratification. Imagine if it worked that way in the human world. It could have some advantages. The murder rate would drop significantly if people had to wait until age seventy five for their arms to sprout. I wiped my sweating forehead. "It's not easy being a cactus."

"Right. They get eaten, trampled, struck by lightning, or frozen. At every stage of life they're vulnerable. But they are absolutely crucial to the desert ecosystem." He touched a finger gently between the jagged spikes.

I was curious about this alternately charming and exasperating man. "Why do you love the desert so much, Chaz?"

He sighed and wiped his forehead. "I've thought a lot about that Simone. I think it's because the desert has all the answers. It's written down here, in this place. All the important truths, together in one spot."

"What do you mean?"

He pointed to a flat section in the distance. "If you came here in the spring after the rains, you'd see blankets of wildflowers over there, colors exploding all over the place. People come to photograph them because it's such an unbelievable sudden beauty. But if you come back two weeks later, they're gone, every one. They're annuals. They exist only when the environment is favorable, when life is good to them." He waved a hand at the acres of cactus that surrounded us. "Then there are these guys, the patient perennials that cling to life in good times and bad. They grow and flourish in the wet season, and conserve their resources through the months of long drought. They survive through the bad and thrive in the good with an incredible tenacity."

He looked at me. "Is there a clearer message from God than that?"

I looked from Chaz to the prickly mountain of green next to us. I don't know if I was more amazed by the intricate survival techniques of the giant plant, or the perception of the man that recognized it. I pegged him for a handyman, a guy who fixed plastic ducks and mooched a free place to stay from my aunt. He was much more than that. Much more. "But they're plants. Plants don't love God, do they?"

"Maybe not but they sure hold onto what He gave them. That's why I like it here. There's just life and God and nothing in between. No careers, social status issues, money or college degrees, it's all pared down to the important stuff."

I peered closer at the nearest spiky individual. The cactus looked like a grizzled old man, covered with silver prickles. For a second, it seemed to stand up a little straighter. Thrive in the good and survive through the bad. "That really is something."

He nodded his head and very gently brushed a strand of hair out of my face. "I was hoping you would think so."

His touch left a trace of tingles on my cheek. I moved closer to his lips which were moving towards mine.

Tanya and Allyson trotted up. "Come on. Wait until you see what we found."

Chaz heaved a sigh as we followed them past the toppled body of another immense cactus. It was dry and stripped of green. In places the long internal ribs showed through the withered skin. The desiccated capsule looked like the ruins of an ancient Egyptian mummy.

The girls stopped in front of an upright saguaro with six inch spines. About halfway up the waxy trunk was a small hole.

"Look inside," Allyson whispered.

Tanya must have caught the expression on my face.

"It's not a bug or anything. Just look."

Chaz and I stood on tiptoe, heads together, and peeked in. The air near the hole was cool on my face. Three tiny faces peered back, blinking and silent.

"A nest of Whitewinged doves," Chaz whispered. "They've found a spot to beat the heat."

"It feels like they've got air conditioning," I whispered back.

"It can be almost twenty degrees cooler inside a cactus than out. Thick walls make good insulation."

We stepped away. From a distance you would never know that a teeny bird family made their home inside the massive cactus. Soft down hidden by ferocious spikes. What a place of contrasts.

The green cactus arms splayed wide against the sharp blue sky made me blink. The cactus seemed so exposed, vulnerable, like Jesus when he journeyed to the wilderness to be closer to his Father. Chaz was right, there was no buffer here. This strange place butted right up against God, with no place to hide. In spite of the heat I shivered.

Tanya hunkered down in the shade of the cactus to write in her notebook. "Mr. Tagliola? I came after the rains last year with my uncle. The cactus were all swelled up like sponges. Now they look skinny."

Chaz nodded. "They have pleats so they can fill up with water when they get the opportunity. Cool, huh? Talk about taking advantage of God's blessings while you have them."

The girls and I agreed. "Cool," we said in unison. I was amazed to find that I really meant it. As frightening as I found this place, it was definitely awe inspiring.

By that time the rest of the gang collected back at our meeting place. The kids buzzed with excitement, eager to share their findings with the group. We spent a little over an hour sipping water, nibbling our remaining snacks and talking. Everyone was surprised when Pastor Stan looked at his watch and sucked in a breath.

"Oh boy," he said. "It's almost four o'clock. Imagine that, four o'clock. I'd better be getting you kids turned around. There's a good two hour hike back to the van." He secured the top on his water bottle. "I promised everyone a stop at Burger Barn on the way home. Burgers anyone? Who's still up for burgers tonight?"

Jack whooped with joy and he and Raul each grabbed one of Pastor's arms and hauled the portly man to his feet. We fell into a messy line and began the long hike back to the entrance.

It was still more than hot as we edged our way along, but the brutal sun was lower on the horizon and a small breeze teased us as we walked. My skin was still tingly. Tanya had mercifully slathered sunscreen on my nose and the back of my neck during our lunch stop, so I was hopeful the damage wouldn't be too bad. One of the kids began to sing and soon the whole gang was engaged in an upbeat version of *Blessed Be Thy Name*. The tune vibrated in the thin air.

Blessed be Thy name.

It was a thought that I hadn't entertained in a while. I had been too steeped in Doug depression and desert mayhem. Thoughts of my fiancé evaporated out of my head in the intense heat of this wild place. Maybe that was the real beauty of the desert: it stripped away the extraneous. But how many layers did I want to slough off? Deep down that was the crux of my dilemma. I loved God without a doubt, but did I really trust Him? Did I really want to be freed of all my lovely superficial layers and plans?

I thought about the wildflowers. Had I been guilty of contingent gratefulness? A thankful heart only when my life was the way I wanted it? The way I'd planned it? I felt an uncomfortable flutter as I recalled the words of my fickle man, D.F.

Glenda was looking for something that only exists in the savior. There's only one perfect and it isn't here on earth.

The soft voices bounced along the flat ground, echoing off the distant canyon walls. Had I only flourished because I had pieced together my own perfect little world? Perfection was a hefty burden for a regular guy to shoulder. Doug couldn't hold up against that kind of pressure. I didn't know any man or woman who could, come to think of it. I envisioned him to be the perfect guy because I hadn't taken the time to see all of him. And sadly, I hadn't let him see all of me either.

The realization poked me in the gut. Why did I have to come to the middle of a fiery furnace to identify this character flaw?

The blog entry came back again.

There's only one perfect.

Another mistaken judgment. I hadn't realized Doug was that perceptive. I always figured his faith was more intermittent than instructive. Maybe that was a product of my flawed vision too. Would he look different to me if I saw him again? I wasn't so sure about anything.

We stumbled into the parking area and visited the little campers' room. My reflection in the warped bathroom mirror scared me enough that I actually cried out.

"I look like poached salmon," I shrieked, tearing off the baseball hat. The ointment that Tanya had slathered on after the poaching was well underway served to accentuate the swollen, medium rare look.

Allyson and Tanya peered into the mirror over my shoulder. "Oh wow," Allyson said. "That's not going to be pretty in the morning."

Tanya put a gentle fingertip to my neck. "And it's going to hurt like crazy."

I blinked back an onslaught of tears. A few salty drops escaped and burned a trail down my ruined face.

Allyson wet a paper towel and patted my neck while Tanya rubbed comforting circles onto my back like a mother does for an upset toddler. I looked from my horrible skin to the sympathetic girls behind me. "Thank you," I mumbled.

They handed me Kleenex and led me back to the parking lot, where the group was waiting, bags already loaded.

"Do you want to meet us at the Burger Barn?" Pastor Stan asked, swiveling his eyes quickly away from my tear sodden face.

Chaz looked at me.

I opened my mouth, then closed it again as I felt the tears return.

"Uh, no thanks, you go ahead. I have a..uh...thing that I need to do. We'll head home," Chaz said. "See you tomorrow morning for a debriefing over French toast."

The kids loaded up the van and drove away in a shower of dust and gravel.

I couldn't hold it in anymore. My emotional dam broke and a swell of tears gushed out past my swollen eyelids.

Chaz looked at me open mouthed. He raised an arm and then dropped it. He started to speak and then stopped. Finally he shoved his hands into his pockets and cleared his throat. "What's wrong?"

The tears stung my burned cheeks. My nose began to run. "I don't...know how..."

"How to what?" He bent over to look into my eyes.

"I can't..."

He tried to read my lips.

"I don't know how to make French toast!" I wailed.

He put his arm around me very gently and smiled.

***

It took about a half hour to reassemble the remaining fragments of my mind. Chaz parked me on a bench in the rosy glow of a setting sun and disappeared, returning shortly with two cold sodas. I couldn't imagine where he'd found them and I didn't ask. I pressed it to my heated cheek. We sipped in silence. He cleared his throat a few times and took a breath to speak, but apparently decided against it.

We settled on silent sipping.

I could not think of anything to salvage my dignity short of waking up and finding out the whole Seepwillow saga was a disturbing dream. This did not seem likely. The sky was almost completely dark and the temperature dropped with every passing minute. I drained the soda, handed him the empty can and unknotted the crumpled jacket from my waist. "We'd better get moving, don't you think?"

The poor man looked supremely relieved. "Oh right. Yeah, it's about two hours to the trailer park. Do you er, want me to drive?"

I had lost the rash confidence that landed me on the bike earlier. The desert had ironed that out of me too. "Yes, please."

I gingerly eased the helmet over my broiled flesh. I climbed onto the bike behind him and held onto his waist. He revved the engine. We took off.

I didn't think about much as we sailed along under a brilliant half moon. The air was cool against my exposed cheek. The other cheek rested against Chaz's tee shirt. His hard back felt safe, a wall to keep out my uncertainties. I wished I could hide my face against his muscled shoulders and stay there. The rumble of the engine was like a lullaby as the miles went by. I saw a set of yellow eyes peer back at me from the darkness on the side of the road. Other than that that it was a flat road and fast bike.

After about an hour of driving, Chaz sucked in a quick breath and without warning, accelerated. "Hold on," he yelled as we zoomed off the road onto sandy ground.

"What are you doing?" I clung to his back like a frightened limpet. It was all I could do to hold on with all the bumps and jerks.

He didn't answer. We barreled toward a set of dim headlights several yards ahead. Then he slammed on the brakes and jumped off in a hail of gravel. With an exclamation which I didn't catch, he threw the helmet onto the ground and ran.

Whatever could make a giant man move that fast must be something to see. I took off my own helmet and hurried after him, keeping one eye out for snakes and other icky insect nightlife. Ahead I could see the headlights of a battered pickup truck. Three men with shovels were hard at work digging at the base of a human sized saguaro. When they saw Chaz careening toward them, one guy jumped in the pickup and turned the key.

Another man, a skinny white guy, held up his shovel to stop the Chaz train from splatting him. "Whaddya want?"

Chaz grabbed the shovel and tossed it several yards away. "You can't take that cactus. They're a protected species."

"What are ya? Some kind of a do gooder? They're cactus. There's million of them around here."

"You are an ignorant fool but I'm not going to debate with you. I'm a Park Ranger and you're not going to take any. You got me pal?" His voice vibrated with rage. He was so angry he lost track of one important detail: the third guy.

"Lookout!" I yelled with all the volume I could muster. "Chaz, behind you!"

Too late. Guy number three circled around and brought his shovel down on top of Chaz's skull with a dull thwack. Chaz toppled forward onto the ground.

The two upright men joined their buddy in the pickup and sped away into the night.

"Oh no," I panted. "Oh no, oh no, oh no!" I sank down next to him, my heart lodged in the back of my throat. A black trail of blood snaked down his neck, under the braid. "Chaz, are you alive? Please don't be dead. I'm no good with dead people."

My fingers were clammy as I felt around in the sticky blood for a pulse under his chin. I couldn't find it. The chin, not the pulse. His shoulders were hunched up and I couldn't find the spot where the happy jugular beat was supposed to be located. The night heat seemed to squeeze the air out of my lungs.

I leaned down close. "Oh Chaz. You've just got to be alive. Wake up right now, you crazy park ranger. This is darn inconsiderate of you to do to a girl."

No answer.

"If you're dead I'm going to steal your Elsinore. Do you hear me? I'll drive it from here to San Francisco. Then I'll chop it up and sell all the parts for scrap. You'll never see that bike again, especially if you really are dead."

His pitiful groan filled me with joy. I almost wet my pants, I was so relieved. "Thank you, God," I breathed.

He tried to get his arms under him but they didn't want to cooperate. Instead he rested his weight on his forehead, bunched up his knees and rolled over. I helped him to sit up.

The front of him didn't look any better than the back. His face was covered with dirt and there was a scrape across his chin and forehead. A stream of blood leaked out of his nose. He had sort of a glazed expression. It finally occurred to me to whip out my cell phone to call the people trained to handle such problems.

"Oh great. No service. You'd think they could hook up an antenna to one of these cactus thingys, wouldn't you?"

Since there was no way to summon help, I did the next best thing. I fished a Kleenex out of my jacket pocket and tried to wipe away the grit. Not very high tech, but the best I could offer. As I dabbed, I gave him another kind of strong medicine. "I don't know what came over you, but that was the stupidest thing I've ever seen a grown man do. You must have left your brain in your other pants."

He blinked. "Is that supposed to make me feel better?"

"No." I crawled around behind him. "I'm sure you don't need anyone to help you feel better. I'm sure you're feeling just peachy, after getting jumped by thugs and smashed in the head with a shovel."

I left him there and returned to the bike where I grabbed the first aid kit from his backpack. The six by six gauze pads would have to suffice. I pushed his hair aside and pressed the bandages on his scalp as gently as I could, ignoring his gasp of pain. Then I wrapped a strip of gauze around his head and under his chin, I kept wrapping until the gauze ran out. "There. That will have to do until we get back."

He looked like he had just had a facelift. And the parts that did show in between the bandages weren't looking too good. He tried to stand up, but his eyes squinched shut and he sank back down.

"Take is easy, Paul Bunyan. Just sit for a few minutes. It won't do you any good to collapse."

He opened his eyes and tried some deep breathing. I breathed along with him for moral support.

"Do you want to tell me why you decided to take on three guys in the middle of nowhere? Why exactly was this necessary?"

Chaz cleared his throat. His voice was rusty. "No choice. They were rustlers."

"Rustlers?"

"Cactus rustlers. They dig up specimens and sell them to landscapers and collectors."

I would have laughed out loud if he hadn't looked so forlorn. "I've never heard of cactus rustlers. I didn't even know that crime existed. It sounds like something from a Looney Tunes cartoon."

"It's more than a crime, Simone. They get top dollar for these things on the black market." He pointed to the cactus. "One hundred years. One hundred years to grow and thirty minutes to dig up. A couple of crooks can do irreparable damage to the ecosystem."

"Okay. Cactus rustling is a big problem, I get it. But did you have to take them on all by yourself? You couldn't call the police or something?"

He shook his head slowly. "They'd be gone before anyone showed up. I guess I sort of bungled the rescue."

Bungled? How about behaved like a complete idiot in the face of certain danger? How about let your testosterone get the better of your brain? We were far beyond bungled. I opened my mouth to let him have it until I noticed how the moonlight shone on his bruised face. He looked so tired, so defeated. I took another deep breath. "Oh, I wouldn't exactly say bungled. I guess you did pretty well. You saved that one, right?"

We both took a moment to admire the cactus, framed in intricate spiny shadows. An owl swooped low in the night sky. Far away came the chitter of a lonely beetle.

Chaz heaved himself onto all fours and began to crawl toward the cactus.

I was too surprised to speak for a moment. "What are you doing?"

He reached the base of the cactus and began to push the dirt back into the hole the rustlers had made.

I couldn't believe it. The man had nearly been killed and here he was on his knees trying to protect a pile of prickles. I folded my arms and watched him. His hands were clumsy and he had to stop and catch his breath. Then he began to feebly pat the earth back into place. He stopped for a second time, to rest his forehead on the ground.

I put down my load of judgment. God gave these giants what they needed to survive. And He gave man power to go and screw it all up. I was familiar with that whole business. When Chaz finally lifted his head again and continued his task, I crawled over next to him and helped tamp the earth back against the precious roots. Our hands touched.

His smile shone for a moment in the blackness. He leaned over and kissed me. His lips were soft and gentle, just like his heart. My pulse quickened until he made a little pained noise. I pulled away and he held a hand to his head for a second.

We finished our task and moved well away from the reach of the spines. I tried to help him to his feet. This was along the lines of trying to straighten the Leaning Tower of Pisa. He swayed and sent us both crashing to the ground.

"I'm sorry, Simone. Did I hurt you?" he said when he made it to his knees.

I picked myself up and pulled a stick out of my hair. "Fortunately I'm tougher than I look."

He managed a half grin. "I'll say."

I hooked a shoulder under his arm and we tried again. This time we made it over to the bike, with only one stop for more breathing therapy. I eased the helmet on his head. He grunted but did not cry out.

"You realize this means I am going to have to drive again."

"Yes, ma'am," he said. "Just try to keep it under a hundred."

"You got it," I said, over the roar of the engine.

Chapter Thirteen

I drove slower than my natural tendency because I was afraid he would slip off the back of the bike and I'd leave him on the highway somewhere. It was nearly midnight by the time I dragged the battered cactus lover back to the Ruddy Duck. He refused to go to the hospital with the sane injured people in spite of my badgering and threats.

We discussed it as we stumbled up the path to my trailer.

"I don't need a hospital. I'm okay."

"Not to be rude Chaz, but you must have hit the ground pretty hard when you fell. You look like someone ran over your face with a tractor."

"Thanks. That gives me a nice visual."

"Hospitals have everything people need in these sorts of cases: bandages, nightshirts with little ties in the back, lovely pain reducing medicines, cable TV. And oh yes, there are the x-ray machines for detecting skull fractures and such."

"I don't have a skull fracture. I don't need a hospital." There was a stubborn set to his scraped chin.

"Men," I grumbled. "Fine, you can stay with me then." I shoved him through the door, banging his head in the process.

He clapped a hand to his cranium. "I'll be fine in my own unit."

"I'm not going to go to your trailer tomorrow and find you dead of an untreated head injury. If you're going to die tonight, I want to know about it right away so I can dispose of you. I'll have to roll you up and put you in the freezer until Aunt Stella gets back. She wouldn't want your cadaver hanging around, taking up floor space."

I steered him toward the bed and helped him lie down.

"If I die, I'll be sure to let you know first."

"Thank you. It's the least you can do." I retrieved a plastic container and towels. I filled the bowl with warm water and eased a towel under his head. "Roll onto your side. No, the other side."

I peeled off the bandages and rinsed the wound. His long black hair clung in sticky clots to the cut. With no Florence Nightingale tendencies to speak of, I managed to ascertain that the wound wasn't all that deep, and only about the length of my pinky. It must have hurt to have it reopened, but he didn't make any noise. I didn't either though my nose wrinkled at the sight of the blood.

"You do realize you could have a serious concussion."

"Unlikely," he said. "I have a head of granite."

The water in the bowl was murky with blood as I continued to sponge. "I have no trouble believing that."

"That's what most people would say."

"I'm going to have to wake you up every couple hours to check for signs of life. I read that somewhere. Or maybe I saw it on a TV show. Anyway, it's the only thing I can recall about head injuries so we're going to go with the waking up plan."

"Uh huh," he mumbled against the pillows. His eyes began to close.

I looked at him and wondered at this strange creature who loved cactus and motorbikes. Who was he? It occurred to me that there was so much about him I didn't know. I decided to take advantage of the gap in his defenses. "Chaz, what was the business you wanted to start? The one that didn't work out?" For a moment I thought he had fallen asleep.

"I wanted to buy a motorcycle outfit, start a tour company."

I thought about the helmet logo. "You were going to call it the Desert Fox?"

He didn't answer. Then he sort of sighed, a long, sad sound.

"What went wrong?"

"I got taken. Paid for the shop and four bikes and the guy skipped town with everything. Lost it all and it wasn't even mine. All I got left is the helmets."

I squeezed out the cloth. "What wasn't yours?"

His voice was soft. "The money. Borrowed it from Gigi. She trusted me, and I lost it all. I thought I would be able to return the money with interest in a few months. What a dope. I'm still trying to pay her back."

"You've been paying her back?" That explained the check he gave her at the Pack N Pick. I had to lean down to catch the last phrase.

"Slowly. Working here and the park. Some nights at an Italian restaurant."

"Ah ha. That's why you always smell like marinara."

He sighed. "Yeah. I should have it paid off next month. Then I can start giving Stella some rent money."

He was planning to start paying rent? I might have to change his title from Chaz the Moocher.

I considered the plight of Gigi. As much as I hated to admit it, I could understand why someone would feel kindly enough toward Chaz to loan him money. He did have sort of an odd kind of charm. Still, Gigi must have been devastated when her college plans were derailed. There wasn't that much opportunity for a girl to make a career for herself in this tiny town. Without college, she was going nowhere fast. "So that's why Katy hates you, because you lost her daughter's money."

"I don't blame her. I'd hate me too, I think. I've grown up since then, changed a lot, but I still feel terrible about Gigi."

"I guess Gigi, isn't, um, interested in you anymore?"

He began to snore softly.

I inched the towel from under his head and covered him with a light blanket. I closed the door to the bedroom but did not pull it tight so I could hear him if he called.

How had Chaz changed? Maybe the same way I had. Being humbled in front of everyone can certainly alter your outlook. After Doug dumped me, I obsessed about what everyone would say. *He met another girl. How humiliating for her. What's the other woman like? Two years of dating wasted. How will she show her face in public?*

Turns out they didn't say anything, to my face anyway. Too polite I guess. Their comments would have been nothing compared to my self chatter anyway. For some reason I didn't care so much about the opinions of San Francisco society at the moment.

The sensation of my burned skin brought me back to the present. It itched just under the hairline. But the feeling that overrode the discomfort and the worry about Chaz was the thrill of being back on a bike. Twice in one day. Me, Simone Greevey, back on a motorcycle. My grin was wide in the darkness.

I eased my body down on the tiny couch and composed a letter in my head.

Dear Simone,

Remember our time in the desert? You looked so free riding that bike, as if there was nothing in the world but speed. I hope you always have unfettered joy. That is my greatest wish for you. I love you.

Love,

Daddy

I was not sure my father would have used the word unfettered. Frankly, I wasn't sure he would have even said he loved me in writing. But he did. I knew that. He loved me the only way he could. Riding the bike today brought back that feeling.

I hoped I would remember it when I woke up the next morning and surveyed my flambéed face. The time was just after one. Chaz breathed deeply and sighed. I would give him two hours before I checked for signs of life. When the little alarm on my watch was set, I drifted off to sleep on the couch.

***

"Chaz? Can you hear me?" It was dark but I could just make out the outline of his wide shoulders under the blanket. I tiptoed into the bedroom and poked him in the nearest scapula.

"Uhhhh," he grunted.

"Who are you? What's your name?"

"Whaaaaa?"

"What's your name?"

"Chaz."

"Chaz what?"

"Chaz Timothy."

Timothy? Not what I expected for a giant's middle name. I figured on a Cliff or Rocky or something rugged. "Chaz Timothy what?"

Snoring sounds.

I poked him again. "Chaz Timothy what?"

"Tagliola."

"Okay." I settled the blankets up over his shoulders and went back to the couch.

***

"Chaz? Can you hear me?" I asked two hours later.

"Hear? Huh?"

"What's your name?"

"Chaz Timothy," he muttered.

"Chaz Timothy what?"

"Tagliola."

"Okay. Go back to sleep."

***

"Chaz? Can you...?"

"My name is Chaz Timothy Tagliola and I will name all my future children after you if you will please stop waking me up."

It didn't sound like he was suffering from any brain malfunctions. "All right then. Good night, Chaz Timothy Tagliola."

He was already snoring.

***

The smell of French toast greeted me when I tumbled off of the sofa two hours later. Those Doves must have gotten tired of waiting for the chef to arrive. It took me a second to remember why there was a man lying on my bed. It all came back to me. What if Chaz was dead? What if his brain swelled up and popped like a balloon in the night? I could not make out any encouraging breathing movements. Uh oh. This could turn out to be a really bad day.

I tiptoed over to check for signs of biological function. As I leaned in close, my hair tickled his face.

"Chaz Timothy Tagliola," he mumbled before he went back to sleep.

He might be the victim of a concussion, but at least the guy didn't pass away on my watch. With his black hair curled around his face, he looked all of ten years old. Yielding to crazy impulse, I kissed him softly on a spot of unscraped cheek before I headed towards the shower.

He must have been a heavy sleeper because my scream didn't wake him up.

The cascade of hot water on my shoulders reminded me of a painful truth. I had been cooked the day before. Not poached, but flat out deep fried like those poor helpless egg rolls that never did anything to anyone. I turned the water down to tepid and washed as best I could without dislodging any body parts. Pleased that my nose hadn't fallen off and swirled down the drain, I searched through my cosmetic bag for something, anything that would help stop the sizzle.

Moisturizing lotion with aloe. Soothing. Gentle. Cooling. Perfect.

I slathered my face and any other exposed parts before I ventured to the mirror.

The sight that greeted me was not quite along the lines of a horror flick but close. Very close. My face looked like a side of bacon. I had never considered myself excessively vain, but the sight propelled my heart right down to my feet.

The jumble of beauty products seemed to jeer at me. *Ha ha*, they said. *If beauty's only skin deep, you're out of luck, baby.*

Don't worry, Simone. Be brave. There's some sort of facial spackle here that will work. I pulled my hair up into a bun and contemplated my cosmetic choices. The aloe was kind of sticky so foundation was not a good option. It might turn into a cement mask. Go au natural? Not even a remote possibility. I settled for mascara and lip gloss. Still scary, but I didn't feel quite so naked.

I perked coffee in the tiny pot and drank a cup. Through the blinds the day looked to be progressing from hot to hotter. The skin on my arms and face felt like it had been put through a cheese shredder, raw and angry. Though I knew it was ridiculous to hope, I searched for my aunt's car. No luck. She was still in faraway Bulgaria. Rats.

That left me with a bruised cactus fanatic on my bed and an energetic horde of teenagers. Which was a better choice on this sizzling morning? Frankly, I could do without either one. I was beginning to have a few odd feelings about Chaz that I didn't want to deal with. He was nice, sure, but he lived in a place I couldn't wait to get away from. Seepwillow wasn't the town for a twenty something with big plans. Or anybody with big plans.

I wanted to go back to San Francisco where the air was cool and the clothes were tailored. Of course, that would mean facing Doug again. In the face of his extended cyber hand I wasn't sure what to do. Admit my mistakes and move forward? What about his really big mistake? The one that involved dumping me. Things must have gone bust with Rachel the cologne connoisseur if he was sending out blog feelers.

When had things gotten so all fired complicated?

Chaz rolled over and groaned but did not show further signs of consciousness.

My laptop beckoned me. Would there be another message from D.F.? An admission of guilt? A plea for forgiveness? The fire in my skin and the lack of sleep drained all my courage away. I grabbed my purse and headed to town.

***

The coolish air of the Pack N Go was luscious. Gigi wasn't there. I selected some apples for my basket. I wondered how she would feel when Chaz paid back the money he borrowed from her. Would there be forgiveness then? A reconciliation? Maybe they would become a couple.

Whipped cream materialized in my stash, along with some yogurt. Fruit and yogurt for health and whipped cream for insurance in case of further disasters. With all bases covered, I headed off to collect Aunt Stella's mail.

On my way to the post office I saw a familiar figure.

Mr. Singh shuffled along, head down, brown arms clutched around a paper bag. His white hair shone brilliant in the sunlight. He mumbled something to himself as he stepped off the curb.

"Hello, Mr. Singh."

He jumped with such violence that the bag toppled out of his hands. His 'hello' sounded rusty as if he hadn't tried to speak in a millennium or two. The items from the bag rolled in all directions.

I retrieved a roll of duct tape that fell near my feet. "I'm sorry I startled you. Here you go."

He stuffed a reel of wire back into the bag and avoided my eyes as he took the tape from my hands. After a mumbled thank you he turned to go.

"Is everything okay?" I said. "With your trailer and all? Stella asked me to take care of things until she gets back."

He crinkled shaggy brows the exact same shade as his hair. "Everything's okay." He walked away.

I wondered what it would be like to lose your family all in one moment. Did he worry that they felt pain at the impact? Did he regret the last words that passed his lips before they died? I was sure he wondered why he lived when they had not. I watched him shuffle away before I noticed an item that had fallen out of his bag and lay unnoticed in the gutter.

It was a knife. A very sharp hunting knife.

He puts bodies in the trash bags, Jojo said.

A ripple of fear raced up my back. Grief could change people. It could twist good hearts and morph them into something sick and evil. My lungs burned from holding my breath.

I wrapped the knife in a wad of Kleenex and shoved it under the container of yogurt.

A few minutes later I was rolling back home, air conditioner on super blast and a pile of mail next to me. I tried to focus on that instead of my Mr. Singh terrors. There was plenty to focus on. My aunt, it seemed, was a member in good standing of every catalog retailer in the contiguous United States. There were catalogues for chocolates, gardening supplies, book clubs, and motocross. Aunt Stella was even a valued customer of the Snow Shop where you could buy everything from skiis to snowmobiles. A handy resource for someone who lived in Seepwillow.

Underneath all this colorful advertising was one small brown envelope from the Phoenix Valley Bank. It was very official looking, addressed to Mr. and Mrs. Bud Bernard. I wasn't sure if I should worry more about Mr. Singh or the letter. Both were disturbing in their own way.

There was no sign of the old man when I let myself into the trailer. Chaz was gone too. That was a good sign. We had enough togetherness recently. I sat down at the table and fired up the lap top. The bank letter sat there, leaking bad vibes which I decided to ignore for the present. I opened up the blog.

Brandi, what's up with this toenail fungus thing in nail salons? Is it safe to get my pedicure? I desperately need some pampering. -- Jilly J.

I peeked at my own sadly neglected toes. They were about the only part of my body that wasn't burned. Fortunately, Cherry B. took on the toenail question for me.

Jilly J., Just make sure you watch them take the tools out of the sterilizer and go to a good place. You'll be fine. You can even bring your own tools if you want. I had little daisies put on my big toes to show off my new Steve Madden sandals. Sooooo cute! -- Cherry B.

Steve Madden sandals? The thought made the envy Slinky unwind in my gut. I wanted Steve Madden sandals and floral toenails. If I spent any more time in the desert I might forget about the joy of pedicures altogether. Courage, Simone, courage. Stella would be back any minute. She had to catch a flight sooner or later.

I decided to earn my paycheck for the week and add a summery, cheerful note to the blog. Besides, now that I knew Doug was on board, I had to sound perky. No one need know that I was now in a position to lose a beauty contest to the Bride of Frankenstein.

Blessings all! I am vacationing in Arizona, learning about the wonderful world of cacti. God's at work here, all right. I know because I am still alive and the temp is approaching one hundred two. When I get back I'm heading straight for the salon! Daisy toes, here I come! -- Brandi

The perfect ratio of perky to practical. I hit send and retrieved a semi cool soda from the fridge. There was a message waiting when I returned. My heart beat faster when I saw the name of the sender.

What do you see there, Brandi? -- D.F.

What did I see? What kind of a question was that? I looked around. I saw a dingy trailer with a banged up refrigerator. In the mirror, my reflection screamed of raw hamburger. On the table was an ominous letter from the bank which did not bode well for my aunt. Perched on the counter was a wrapped knife, sharp enough to split an atom. I didn't think these details were exactly what Doug was after. What did I see in this desert? In the hideous place of inhuman extremes?

I thought about the lone saguaro standing sentinel on a moonlit night. In my mind, I saw a giant of a man put his safety on the line for this one silent being that seemed to be much more than just a plant. My fingers danced along the keyboard.

I see things struggling to live the life that God gave them. -- Brandi

His message materialized a few minutes later.

Lucky. -- D.F.

Lucky?

How was it lucky to be dumped by one's fiancé in Sunday school and booted out of a job by your best friend? Not to mention landing in Seepwillow for sympathy and instead inheriting a decrepit trailer park and a bunch of teenagers. He had some gall telling me I was lucky.

A motor gunned outside. I looked up to see Chaz roaring away on his bike, the bike I got to fly on the day before.

There were no further messages so I signed off.

The letter could be avoided no longer. I read it with teeth clenched. Aunt Stella was right. She did have a balloon payment due at the end of the year in the amount of fifty three thousand dollars and ninety eight cents. There was a place to apply for a six month extension but that was about it in the way of wiggle room. There was no way we were going to come up with that kind of money by selling prickly pear jam or attracting the odd cactus club.

I paced back and forth. What could we do to draw people here? What did this dilapidated trailer park have to offer the world of sane people? I couldn't think of a thing. It was possible that there might be an undetected oil well or emerald mine on the property but that was on par with winning the lottery. I paced another couple of laps until I couldn't stand it any more.

The outside air hit me like a sledgehammer as I made my way to the office.

The Loving Doves had afternoon bible study so I spent the day taking messages from the answering machine and looking out the window for Stella. Of course, there was no sign of her.

I attempted a nap. My burned spots proved a challenge. By late afternoon I gave up and joined the Doves for another weenie roast. There was still no sign of Chaz. Maybe it was his Italian restaurant night.

He had made an idiot of himself by losing Gigi's money on a scam, but I had to give the guy credit. He was sure working hard to make it right. And I knew he really was sincere about coughing up some rent money after his debt was paid off. As the kids settled in around the campfire to sing and harass each other, I saw movement in Mr. Singh's trailer.

In spite of my pounding heart, I retrieved the knife from my place and walked to his door. He couldn't murder me right there in the open, so I figured it was safe to risk it. Besides, I had to know if the guy was a killer. Aunt Stella would never suspect anyone of wrongdoing, even if they carried around a pocket full of fingers. He might murder them all after I returned home. I could hear the headline. Stella Slain by Singh in Seepwillow. I felt the mantle of responsibility on my crispy shoulders.

I wiped my clammy palm on my shorts and knocked. "Mr. Singh? It's Simone. I have something of yours."

It was quiet for a long minute.

I knocked again.

The door opened a crack.

"Yes? What is it?"

"You dropped this outside the Pack N Go." I handed it over handle first. I tried to peer around him into the dimly lit trailer, but his body blocked the way.

His eyes widened and he took the knife. "Thank you."

We stood like that for a moment, each one of us trying to think of something else to say.

"It was...kind...of you to return it," he said finally.

"No problem. Would you like to join us for hot dogs?" Best to keep an eye on him, but I'd have to be sure he got a dull tipped roasting stick.

"No, thank you. Goodnight."

I tried to peer between his legs. "Goodnight."

The draft of the door ruffled my hair as it swung closed.

Later that night one tiny detail about our encounter gnawed at me. The image would not go away.

Behind Mr. Singh, on the floor of his trailer, was a young child's shoe.

Chapter Fourteen

I spent the rest of the day and night doing nothing productive. By Wednesday evening, this bout of unproductivity had sapped my vital juices. Even though my mind was chewing on the scary Mr. Singh problem and my aunt's looming fiscal catastrophe my body was done for the day. It said, "I am going to cease all bodily functions if you do not put me to bed, post haste."

I followed directions, after showering as best I could. The bed was lumpy and the mattress thin, but it felt like a cloud to my weary limbs. So what if it was only eight-thirty? That meant it was a respectable midnight somewhere in the world. Though I was exhausted, fifty three thousand things kept me awake for a while until my body took over.

Sleep. Blissful sleep.

A pounding on my door startled me awake. I uncemented an eye and checked the clock. Just shy of midnight. The pounding continued. Maybe Chaz had died and someone was coming to tell me they found his body. Not likely. Oh no. Could it be that Mr. Singh decided to come for me with his knife? My heart began to hammer.

Wait a minute. Why would Mr. Singh knock if he was coming to kill me? And why were there sounds of adolescent angst on the other side of my door?

I heaved myself upward and out of bed. Tanya stood outside my door with Allyson who was red faced and teary. "Wha...?" I said.

"He like, totally dissed me," Allyson wailed. "I'm like, so humiliated. It's just unreal."

I looked at Tanya who mouthed something at me which I didn't catch.

"I'm so done." Allyson sobbed and sniffed. "He dumped me because I so wasn't fun and he wanted to go with someone who could totally let loose and Diane will totally go to clubs with him and I won't because of my parents and he thinks I'm all nice and all that but he doesn't want to go with me and he dumped me." She began to wail again.

Tanya patted her on the back and I went for tissues. While Allyson blotted and blew, Tanya translated for me. "Her boyfriend Jake broke up with her. He texted her cell phone and said he isn't into her anymore."

"Oh, that's nothing." I gave her a squeeze around the shoulders. "My boyfriend dumped me while I was teaching Sunday school."

Both girls stared at me.

Then Allyson resumed crying.

She must have been well hydrated because at one o'clock she was still going strong. I struggled to keep my eyes open and offer consolation at the same time.

"I can't face the others," Allyson wailed. "Everyone will totally know. I am so humiliated. I can never show my face again."

I should have told her all those mature bits of advice. You'll find another boyfriend. You're better off without him. Men are pigs. Instead I settled on the comfort my aunt had given me. "He'll always regret giving you up."

She shot me a watery smile.

Tanya nodded, impressed.

"It's because I'm not like the other girls," Allyson continued in a shaky voice. "My mom doesn't let me stay out late or wear lots of makeup." Her look turned from sad to horrified. "What if he calls me a God Geek now too? How will I face him in school? Oh man. I'm going to see him with HER everyday when school starts. And I'll be....ALONE." Her face crumpled and she began to wail anew.

I applied more Kleenex and stifled a yawn. "That's not for another few weeks. Let's just take one thing at a time. Why don't you sleep here on my couch tonight and we'll sort this out in the morning?"

Allyson nodded and blew her nose. Tanya said good night and promised to return first thing in the morning.

I found it hard to sleep with the sustained snuffling coming from the couch. Poor girl. The teen years were nothing but a foggy memory to me, but I could relate to her grief. I guess heartbreak doesn't hurt less just because you're young. We both drifted into an exhausted sleep.

The next knock was quieter, and lower down. I ignored it at first. If it was a fire or nuclear bomb, it could wait until I got at least four hours of shut eye. The knock was persistent but irregular. Knock. Knockity knock. Knockity knock knockity. Worse than Chinese water torture.

I sprang out of bed, lurched past a sleeping Allyson and threw open the door. There was no one there, at least not in my line of sight.

"Hi, Miss Peevey." Jojo fingered the edge of her Big Bird pajamas. "Your face is squishy."

I looked down. "Hi, Jojo. My face isn't awake yet. Do you know what time it is?" Actually, I didn't know myself other than it was still dark so it had to be way early.

"No."

"It's not daytime." I pointed at the sky. "See? No sun yet."

"Uh huh." She stuck her finger in her mouth.

"Well aren't you supposed to be sleeping?"

"Uh huh."

We stared at each other for a while. "So, what did you want, Jojo?"

"Do you have any lollipops?"

"No. Go back to bed."

"Okay. Mommy said to tell you she's in favor."

"In favor of what?"

"Dunno. Bye."

Off she skipped.

I flopped back down on the bed just in time to hear a knock. Knockity knock. "Ahhhh," I moaned as I yanked the door open again.

Jojo was in tears this time. Snot ran down her upper lip and into her mouth.

"What's the matter?" I asked.

"LeRoy. A fox is gonna eat him."

"LeRoy?" I had to think a minute. One of the teens was being devoured by a fox? No, that wasn't right. Try again, brain. LeRoy, LeRoy. Aha! "The tortoise? Nothing is going to eat him, honey. He's like a knight. He has his own suit of armor."

"But he's turned over and all his legs are up in the air. The fox is gonna eat him. You gotta save him."

I took a calming breath. "Why don't you get one of your brothers or sisters to save him?"

"J.R. is on a trip with Daddy. The rest went to summer camp. Pleeeease." Jojo let loose another gusher. "I don't want LeRoy to get ate up."

It was clear that there would be no diverting this preschool drama. I was just going to have to wade through the emotional river to get to the mattress on the other side. "Okay. Okay. Stay right there." I pulled on a pair of shorts and a tee shirt and grabbed a flashlight. Allyson slumbered on.

Jojo insinuated her sticky fingers in mine. I tried not to contemplate where those digits had been. We rounded the corner of trailers and found LeRoy. He was indeed on his back, hissing like an overturned tea kettle. A gray fox stood a few feet away, dancing towards the prone turtle and then away to avoid the snapping mouth.

When he saw us, the fox cut his yellow eyes in our direction. We locked peepers for a moment. His ears pricked and then he turned tail and streaked away. This was a good thing as I had no idea how to scare a fox, unless he was alarmed by my roasted face.

When we were sure the fox had gone, Jojo and I approached the crabby LeRoy.

"You have got to be the weakest link in your evolutionary chain." I grunted as we flipped him back onto his feet. "First you let kids make you into a searchlight, and then you're bested by a fox. I know mammals are higher on the food chain than you are but really. Have you no self respect?"

He shot us a malevolent look and trundled off. No such thing as reptilian gratitude.

"Easy peesy," Jojo sang.

Chaz emerged from his trailer wearing only a pair of blue sweat pants. The faint light gleamed against his bare chest.

My eyeballs ogled his gorgeous pectorals before I pulled them up to his face.

He looked like he was in one piece, though the emerging dawn caught the dark smudges under his eyes. The scrapes and cuts were vivid against his skin. He held a hand to his head as though to prevent it from flying up into the atmosphere. "Was that LeRoy?"

"Yes." I turned away from Chest, I mean Chaz and directed my attention to the child. "Jojo, if you have any other problems in the next six hours, knock on Mr. Tagliola's door, okay? He knows all about nature things. He'll be happy to help you. I'll bet he has candy too."

"Okay." She walked over to Chaz and hugged him around the knees. "We saw a fox. He was going to eat LeRoy. Me and Miss Peevey scared him away."

Chaz twirled her pony tail. "It's a good thing you saved him, Jo. LeRoy needs a little help sometimes."

"Uh huh. Mr. Chaz, my mommy is in favor."

"In favor of what?" he asked.

"In favor of the baby."

He looked at me for clarification. I shrugged. "I don't speak toddler."

He dropped to one knee and looked her in the eye. "Tell me again, what your mommy said."

Jojo wrinkled up her nose. "Mommy is sick because she's in favor. She's making sad sounds. She told me to go and get Miss Peevey."

Chaz shot to his feet, his eyes locked on me.

"You don't suppose she means..." I started.

"I think we better call an ambulance," Chaz said as he ran inside for a shirt.

***

It was way too late for an ambulance.

When we got to Anna Escobar's trailer, things were happening that were not fit for the faint of spirit. She lay on the floor panting, her face flushed and sweaty. There were bodily fluids on the linoleum that definitely didn't belong there.

The fabric of her nightgown actually undulated with the contortions of whatever was under it. I was reminded of some awful alien movie. The thing inside Anna wanted out. Now.

Jojo's eyes widened. "See? I told you she was sad."

"Uh, not to worry honey. This is all..." I tried to remove the disgusted wrinkle from my nose, "...perfectly natural stuff. Uh, you just wait right here on the porch for a minute."

I turned and yelled loudly enough for Tanya to hear me and come running. I guided Jojo down the porch steps. "Take care of her and call an ambulance. Mrs. Escobar is in labor and we need to get her to the hospital."

Tanya scooped up the girl and ran.

Chaz put a pillow under Anna's head to create a cushion between her cranium and the floor. "Are you okay Mrs. Escobar?"

"Noooooooooooo," Anna wailed. She took in a deep breath and wailed some more. "No, no, noooooooooo."

He looked at me. "I don't think she's okay."

"Thanks for the insight. Should we put her on the bed?"

"I...can't...move," Anna gasped.

"Okay then. No need to move anywhere. We'll just, er, make you comfortable right here." I got some towels from the bathroom and sort of wedged them underneath her hips to keep her from rolling around.

"I'll go get a wet cloth for her head," Chaz said.

"Don't worry, Mrs. Escobar." I looked into her panicked eyes. "Uh, it's going to be okay. They've called for an ambulance. It will be here any minute."

"The baby is coming now!" Her face was a mask of pain.

"Now? Oh boy. Are you sure? I don't suppose you could, er, kinda hold it in until the parmedics get here?"

She screamed.

I screamed.

Chaz jumped and ran over to us.

"What? What is it?"

Anna screamed again. The noise seemed to come up from her ankles and work its way along until it exploded out of her mouth. "Help me, please."

I tugged on his pant leg. "I don't think she's in favor of babies anymore. Sit down here and hold her hand."

He knelt by her shoulder and wrapped his huge fingers around her slender ones. "It's going to be all right, Mrs. Escobar. We'll take care of you."

I shot him a "what do I do" look.

He shot me back a "I haven't the foggiest notion" glance.

I beamed a "I'm going to pretend like I know what I'm doing so she doesn't freak out" expression.

Chaz gave me a doughnut look, eyes round and glazed.

"Mrs. Escobar," I said, "I'm just going to, er, take a peek, you know, to see what's up. With the, er, baby and all."

She bit her lip and nodded.

After a deep breath, I peeked under her nightgown. "Chaz," I hissed, "I think she's having the baby."

"Right now?" His eyes were nearly as wild as Anna's. "Are you sure?"

"Well I'm not positive but that's what it looks like to me. If you want sure, you don't pick a blogger to do the work of an obstetrician," I snapped.

He let that sink in before he whispered, "Well what should we do?"

"How should I know?" I hissed back. "Just because I have a uterus doesn't mean I know anything about having a baby." I scanned the room. "Maybe we should boil some water."

"Why?"

"I haven't the slightest idea. To make tea or something? It's in every old movie where people are having babies in weird places. Just go do it."

He grimaced. "I can't."

"Why not?"

"Because she has my hand in a death grip. She's breaking my thumb."

If the situation wasn't so serious, I might have laughed to watch delicate Anna Escobar pin Chaz to the floor by twisting his thumb. It could have been a great spot on one of those wrestling events.

The door opened a crack and Pastor Stan stuck his head in. "The ambulance will be here in five minutes. Do you...?"

That was as far as he got before he took in the view. His eyes rounded and all the color drained from his face. He went over backward like a felled pine.

"Oh, for the love of cheese." I pushed the door open to find Pastor Stan on the ground and six Doves dashing to his aid. Jack and Raul were in the front of the pack. "Guys, we're kinda, er, doing a thing in here. Do any of you know anything about delivering babies?"

Raul blanched. "Human babies?"

"No, Raul. Gorilla babies. OF COURSE HUMAN BABIES," I screeched. The stress was getting to me.

"Uh, no," Raul said. "I can't help you there."

I turned to Jack. "What about you?"

Jack couldn't get a response past his lips.

"Don't they teach you people anything in Boy Scouts anymore?"

All I got in response to my comments was a look of sheer terror from the two teens. "Okay. I was just asking. Can you take care of him?" I pointed to the unconscious pastor.

Jack's eyes darted around for a second. "Yeah. Raul, you and Peter get his head. Allyson, help me with the feet. Let's get him to his trailer. Don't twist his neck."

"That's one problem taken care of," I muttered as I turned back inside.

Anna was still groaning. "I've...I've...got to ...push," she grunted.

"Oh, uh, are you sure?" I wiped my forehead. "Maybe we could hold off on the pushing. Pushing sounds less than optimal. I'm really not comfortable with the pushing plan." As a matter of fact, I was struggling to keep my stomach where it belonged.

Chaz grimaced as she bent his finger even farther.

"Instead of pushing, how about we go for some sustained clenching?" I suggested.

She grabbed the towel with one hand and squeezed Chaz's hand with the other. His face twisted in pain. Then she pushed.

We all screamed together.

The sound reverberated in the tiny space. There was a moment of synchronized panting while we collected our wits. I peeked at the business end of things again. Man oh man. There was a reason this stuff was done in the privacy of hospital rooms. "Anna, I can see a head. I think that's a head. It's kind of sticking out. I guess that means we're committed at this point. Maybe you should push some more."

She sucked in a huge breath and pushed again. The head popped out up to the neck. The little eyes were closed and so was the mouth. It looked like a doll, a very still lifeless doll. My stomach clenched into a knot.

Oh God in Heaven. Please help me. I don't want this baby to die because of me. He deserves better than that. Help me help this baby, sweet Jesus.

I pressed down the fear. "Okay Anna. Let's get this done. You push again and I'm going to pull him out. On the count of three we do it. Ready?"

She nodded faintly. Her eyes were glassy and bloodshot.

I put my hands on either side of the sticky face.

"One..."

She leaned slightly forward.

"Two..."

Chaz tucked his knees under her back to give her more leverage.

"Three!" I shrieked.

She pushed.

I grabbed hold of the tiny cheeks as gently as I could and pulled. He didn't move a millimeter. How could he be wedged in there so tightly?

Still no breathing or crying, except from the grownups.

The panic began to push upward from my gut into my heart. "You have to push one more time. Harder, Anna."

I counted fast this time but Anna didn't move. She lay panting, her face pale and drawn.

Chaz caught my terrified look and snapped into action. He lifted her shoulders higher onto his lap and grabbed both of her hands. "Come on Anna. We're just about there. One more good push and the baby will be out. We'll do it together. One, two, three..." They both tensed as she bore down one last time.

The baby slithered out in a pile of goo.

I didn't have time to be properly disgusted because he was very still and bluish.

I turned him face down on my leg and whacked him between the shoulder blades. I had only seen this done in movies but it was the best I could come up with. Two whacks and a bunch of stuff dribbled out of his mouth onto my shorts.

He started to cry.

I was never so glad to hear someone cry in all my life, even if I did have to burn my Nike shorts. Baby began to cry in earnest, a thin wail that filled up the corners of the trailer.

Cry, little baby. Let all the world hear that you are alive.

I looked at Chaz. He looked at me. Anna looked at us both and the three of us locked eyes on the shrieking infant.

Then we all joined in the crying so he wouldn't feel self conscious.

Chaz extricated his fingers from Anna's clutch. He laid her gently down on the pillow and crawled over to me. "Here's my shoelace," he said as he wiped his eyes.

"I deliver a baby and you give me a shoelace? I'm insulted. Shouldn't you at least take me to dinner or something?"

He laughed. "I think you're supposed to tie it around the umbilical cord."

"You are? Why?"

"So the blood doesn't go back from the baby into mom."

"How do you know that?"

"I just remembered it from a first aid video I saw a couple years back."

"You might have trotted out some of that helpful medical information a half hour ago." I handed him the baby. My hands still trembled from the whole ordeal. Chaz held Escobar, Jr. as if he was a hand grenade, his face a mingling of fear and awe.

I tied the shoelace in a lovely bow and double knotted it for good measure. Then I retrieved the angry wrinkled bambino, wiped his face with a towel and handed him to Anna. Chaz was going to have to find some scissors and finish the job. There was no way on this spinning planet that I would be doing any snipping of cords. Just the thought made my guts do the rumba.

We both watched the little tyke for a moment. His balled fists flew back and forth in front of his face as if they had a mind of their own. He opened his mouth so wide we could see clear down his angry red windpipe.

Chaz handed the snuffling baby to Anna and covered them with a blanket. She smiled, through her tears. "Thank you," she whispered.

"Easy peesey," I said, over the sound of an approaching siren.

***

The paramedics loaded up Anna and baby and took them to the hospital. I promised to bring Jojo along as soon as I decontaminated and called Mr. Escobar to relay the news.

Pastor Stan refused professional medical treatment. He settled in under the care of the Doves who plied him with cold compresses and sodas. When I stopped to check on him he blushed, two pink blotches in his still pallid face. "Sorry about that, Miss Greevey. I've never been able to handle the sight of, er, fluids. Even nose bleeds send me straight to the floor."

"Don't worry about it. The Doves handled everything like professionals."

Even Allyson rallied to help Tanya prepare a pancake breakfast for the troopers since our bizarre night had now morphed into Thursday morning. She waved a pancake flipper at me as I walked by the chapel trailer.

I left Jojo with Chaz and headed to the shower.

Standing under the warm water I began to shake and tingle all over. The steam swirled around my head. I had delivered a baby. I had been a part of the miracle of life, a child's first earthly moment. I saw with my own eyes and felt with my own hands the birthing of an actual infant.

Ewwwwwwwwww!

I scrubbed as much as I dared until the water ran cold. When I was pink and shriveled, dressed in a clean denim skort and polo shirt I felt my life juices return. I stood in the middle of the kitchen, unable to figure out what to do next. After that kind of a morning, my synapses were fried.

I contemplated eating a can of whipped cream, but my stomach was still a bit squiffy.

Should I go help Chaz with Jojo? Probably, but I felt a strong urge to be alone for a moment. My computer friend beckoned me from the kitchen table. I grabbed hold of the comfortable familiar and logged on.

No new blog entries so I reread the last few messages.

What do you see there?

What a question. Since the wee hours I had seen a desert fox duke it out with a tortoise, a group of teens rally to help their stricken pastor, and a woman give birth on my lap. In one morning I'd witnessed enough to fill up a whole lot of blog entries. But what could I put down in words?

I could still hear the sucking sound of the baby's first gasping breath.

I see things struggling to live the life that God gave them.

I could feel again the tiny lungs fill under my trembling hands.

Lucky.

I smiled and closed the screen without typing a word. Then I went to find pancakes.

Chapter Fifteen

The first three phone calls to Jaime Escobar went unanswered. The party I was trying to reach was not in service at that time. Sheesh. So much for global communications. The guy might as well have been on the moon. The next two calls connected me with Jaime's trucking company and a gum chewing woman named Roz.

"I am looking for Jaime Escobar. I need to talk to him about his wife."

"Hang on one sec, hon." There was a click and then a dial tone.

I redialed and repeated my request.

"Escobar? Hang on." Click. Dialtone. Blood pounded in my ears as I redialed.

This time the lady smacked a few times. "Does he work for us?"

"Yes." I heard some clicking fingernails.

"Are you sure?"

"Pretty sure, yes." The day's events caught up with me. "Shouldn't you know who works for you?"

She snapped her gum. "Don't get testy with me. We've got plenty of people to keep track of around here. I'm doing the best I can."

That was scary.

"Oh yeah," she said. "Here he is. He's on a trip to Southfork,

Wyoming. The truck broke down so he's waiting for a part."

I groaned inwardly. "Can you please give me a number where I can reach him? I can't get through on his cell phone."

"Are you sure you're not some stalker person?"

"I'm sure. I'm trying to give him a message about his wife."

"You are, huh? Well how do I know you aren't some jealous girlfriend or something? You wouldn't believe the wackos we get calling in here. If you're some sort of home wrecker, I won't lift a finger to help you, do you hear me? Jaime is a good guy and he's got a passel of kids to feed so don't go thinking you're going to throw a monkey wrench in the works, honey."

I took a steadying breath. "Ma'am, my name is Simone Greevey. I'm a friend of his wife's. She's in the hospital and I need to talk to him."

"Oh yeah? Well anyone could call and say that. How do I know...?" she began.

My self control busted with an audible snap. "HIS WIFE DELIVERED A BABY ON MY SHORTS AND I NEED TO TALK TO HIM NOW, NOW NOW!"

The gum smacking stopped for a moment. "That's gross. Okay then. Here's the number of the hotel where he's staying."

"Thank you." I hung up, exhausted.

The next phone call went much better, at least from my perspective. I got Jaime on the first ring. "Hello, Mr. Escobar. It's Simone Greevey, Stella's niece. I wanted to tell you that Anna had the baby, a boy. She's in the hospital. She asked me to call you."

The poor man was speechless. I could only hear gasps and puffs for a minute. Then he began to lament in Spanish. At least, I think it was lamenting. I didn't exactly rip through my high school foreign language requirement. There was just enough English mixed in to keep me in the loop. Something about a cheap transmission line causing him to miss the birth. He inquired anxiously about Anna's health, in both languages. I reassured him the best I could. "They're both fine. Just come home as soon as you can. We'll take care of Jojo and Anna until you get back." I gave him the hospital phone number and hung up.

Chaz poked his head into my trailer. "Hey, Simone. I called the hospital to check in. Anna has an infection. They asked us not to take Jojo there right now."

I wasn't surprised about the infection. Just thinking about the place we birthed that kid gave me the willies. And not a rubber glove in sight. "Oh boy. I hope it's not something too bad. I'll go and check on her. I've got to tell her I reached Jaime. Can you keep Jojo for a while?"

He nodded. "You bet. She wants to go hunt for LeRoy anyway."

"Look for a pathetic critter on his back with all four legs wiggling."

"You've got Leroy pegged."

I grabbed my handbag. Chaz still lingered in the doorway.

"Simone," he said, then stopped.

"What?"

"I just wanted to tell you something." His cheeks darkened. "You did a great job in there, with the baby. I was really impressed. I know you were just as scared as I was, but you really came through."

I felt my cheeks heat up a degree or so. "Thanks. You turned out to be pretty helpful yourself. Never would have guessed about the shoelace trick."

He flashed a shy grin. "I really would like to take you to dinner to celebrate."

I stared at his tired face, still decorated with scratches from the cactus incident. The man was half crazy. But the other half was sweet. "Okay. You may take me to dinner. Be forewarned that I do not eat any place where the meal comes with a plastic toy."

He laughed, teeth white against his dusky skin. "I was thinking about a picnic."

"Hmmmm. Sounds sort of rustic. Can you promise no bugs?"

"I think I know a place with no bugs."

"Okay. Maybe tomorrow. Between Allyson, Jojo and Baby Escobar, I hardly slept last night. I'm running on fumes."

His smile was huge. "You're on."

I headed off to the hospital thinking about picnicking. Picnics were fun, right? Fresh air, lovely scenery, thermoses and portable food. What could be bad about that? Then I had another thought. Chaz and I snuggled up together on a picnic blanket. A shiver tickled my backbone as I drove down the sizzling highway.

***

Anna appeared loads better than she had on the floor of the trailer, but she was still not back to her cheerful self. Her eyes were puckered and she looked more tired than I was. Various tubes connected her to an i.v. bag. Baby Escobar slept in a plastic bassinet thingy next to her. At least, I assumed it was him. All I could see was a critter wrapped up like a burrito.

I mouthed a hello to Anna who gestured me in. I tiptoed over to the baby and peeked under the layers. His face was as round as a melon, a shock of black hair stood straight up on the top of his head. For a moment I watched the gentle rise and fall of his chest, just to be sure. Yep, he was alive and well. I hadn't dreamed the whole thing. We really had produced an actual living person. Imagine the Lord equipping a couple of bumblers like Chaz and me to do that. Mind boggling.

"He's beautiful, Anna." This wasn't a total lie. I did think he looked kind of like a potato, but there was definitely an angelic quality about him.

She managed a smile. "Thank you. He's a little over seven pounds. That's smaller than the other five were but the doctor said he's in perfect health."

"And what about you? How are you feeling?"

"I have some kind of infection. I will have to stay until the medicine starts to work." Her hand fell limp on the blanket, as if the effort of speaking left her drained.

I nodded. Hospitalization was probably a good thing as she didn't appear to have enough energy to lift her head, let alone manage a baby and Jojo. I relayed the message from Jaime. "He wanted to know what you named the baby."

Her smile was shy. "Mateo." She hesitated. "Mateo Simon. The Simon is after you."

"Me?" Oh gee. I alternated between warm tingles and worry. A baby named after me? I sure hoped he didn't get beat up when the other kids found out his middle name.

"I wanted to thank you, for everything."

"No problem. It was definitely a moment I'll never forget. Chaz too. He's got to buy a new set of shoelaces."

Her fingers pulled at the still covers. "You were both guardian angels to us. I am afraid...there is another thing I must ask of you."

It couldn't be bigger than what we'd already been through. "Shoot."

The worry crease in her forehead deepened. "Since Jaime cannot come home, I need someone to watch Jojo, until I am let go from here. Her brothers are away at camp and my sisters will take a few days to get here from Texas. I would ask Stella, if she has returned?"

I shook my head in a negatory fashion. Aunt Stella might have set up residence in some nice Bulgarian bungalow for the amount of time it was taking her to return. I thought about all the helpful teens swarming around the Ruddy Duck who would be delighted to take on the precocious Jojo. Tanya could handle the kid with her eyes closed.

"Don't give it another thought. We'll take good care of her, Anna."

She passed a hand over her face. A sheen of moisture collected in the corner of her eyes. "And Saturday is Jojo's birthday. I am so sorry to ask it, but could you maybe, buy a little cake for her? There is money behind the sugar canister on the kitchen counter. Six dollars. That would be enough for a small cake from the market." Her words came out in a rush. "It is not right to have you do it, but it has been hard for Jojo through this whole pregnancy, with her Papa being gone so much and no friends to play with. Please forgive me for asking so much of you. I have no one else."

A birthday party for a five year old. And I thought delivering a baby was tricky. "Well sure," my mouth said. "No problem. We'll have a cake, and er, sing the birthday song and maybe have a game or two. What do kids like to play? Gin Rummy? Backgammon?"

A tide of relief swept through her body and she sank down into the mattress. "Thank you again, my friend. How can I ever repay you?" She coughed into a Kleenex and then her eyes lit up. "Wait. I have an idea. Do you like Mexican food?"

"I love it." True enough. Donna and I spent many lunch hours scouring San Francisco for the best place to find a chimichanga. And those pockets of dough with sweet stuff in the middle. And the amazing shredded beef. And...

Anna pulled me back from my culinary fugue.

"Yes? Then I will cook for you. We will have a big feast in your honor. I'll prepare my best dishes." A smile lifted her face.

"Do you make those little corn husky bundles?"

Her brows knitted for a moment. "Oh tamales? You like tamales?"

"I love tamales, with the pocket of meat stuff inside." My stomach did a happy jig just thinking about it.

"Then that is what we will do." She clasped her hands joyfully. "They tell me my tamales are very good. They're Jaime's favorite too. I will make them for you and Chaz. We will invite everyone. The kids too, the doves."

I smiled at the happiness that infused her face. "That sounds great, Anna, but let's get you well first. I'll call and check on you tonight. Maybe if you're better tomorrow we can bring Jojo to see her new little brother." I wrote down the number of Jaime's hotel.

"Thank you, Simone."

I touched a finger to Mateo's satiny cheek. "Goodbye, baby. Let Mommy get some sleep."

His lips curled into an almost smile. I wondered if he liked tamales too.

***

Back at the ranch I propped myself against the trailer wall and pondered what to do with Jojo. For the moment, she was digging a hole in the late afternoon sun. Chaz sat on the porch step and watched her. Obviously she couldn't sleep in his trailer, as the guy was hardly ever there. Mr. Singh was out on account of his knife and children's shoe fetish. The Loving Doves were busy with the last three days of activities. That left, I suppressed a shudder, my trailer.

Presumably Allyson had recovered enough from her jilting to return to her own sleeping place so the couch was available for Jojo. But sharing a trailer with a kid? I liked Jojo well enough but children were just so...childish. And they were prone to having tantrums and spewing contagion everywhere. The last time I hung out with kids my fiancé dumped me. Kids and I just weren't simpatico.

I was too tired to give the matter much thought. I gave it up to God. *Lord, help me with this Jojo thing. She's a wily one and I'm pooped.*

It was barely dinner time and I had all the energy of an overcooked noodle. My senses registered that someone was grilling something. The unmistakable perfume of roasting meat. In the distance I saw Pastor Stan rolling hot dogs around the barbecue. Boy, these Seepwillow residents really enjoyed their frankfurters.

I meandered toward the cooking fumes and sat down next to Chaz. Tanya came out to put paper plates on the picnic tables. Allyson chatted away behind her, seemingly recovered from her trauma.

"How did it go at the hospital?" Chaz asked.

Jojo trotted over. "Where's Mommy?"

"Mommy is fine, honey," I said. "She's at the hospital with your baby brother. His name is Mateo. That makes you a big sister now."

Jojo was unimpressed. "I wanted to name him Peaches."

And I thought Simon would be a difficult name for a boy. "Mommy has to stay there for a few days so Mr. Chaz and I will take care of you."

"Where's Daddy?"

"Daddy is with his truck but it's broken so he can't come home right now."

She looked at me for a minute. "Can I have a lollipop?"

Chaz ruffled her hair. "Maybe after dinner. I see hot dogs and chips. Let's go get some." He picked her up and put her on his shoulders. She squealed with delight. "Do you want to come along, Simone?"

"In a while. I'm just going to hang out here for a minute."

A minute turned into a half hour. When I woke up, I was still in the same spot, leaning against a big, oregano scented shoulder. I sat up with a jerk.

"Uh oh. Did I fall asleep?"

He nodded and handed me a napkin wrapped object. "Yup, but I saved you a hot dog."

"Thanks," I said, wondering if I had drooled on the man or talked in my sleep. "You didn't have to be my pillow. You should have woken me up."

"That's okay. It was kind of nice."

I ducked my head to hide the flush that crept across my cheeks. The funny thing was I thought it was kind of nice too. That was weird. I nibbled on my hot dog. How did he know I liked mustard only?

The sky was an incredible swirl of melting sherbet colors. For a brief moment, everyone stopped eating, talking and laughing to look. I knew why people came to the desert to paint. There was an intensity here, a sense that things were stripped down to their barest elements. For a second, we were a part of a fantastical vibrant landscape.

Then again, I might have been suffering from fatigue induced sentimentality. I finished my hot dog and retrieved Jojo from the pile of rocks she had collected.

"Okay, honey. Let's get you settled in for the night in my trailer."

"I get to sleep with you?" she squealed.

"You get to sleep on the couch. Won't that be fun?"

"Will you sing to me?"

"Uh, well, we'll see."

Chaz looked amused. "Come knock on my door if you need anything. I'll see you in the morning."

"Right. But not too early."

Jojo led the way to her place where we retrieved toothbrush, jammies and a story book. Someone, I suspected Chaz, had cleaned up any signs of Mateo's unceremonious entrance into the world.

By the time we got back to my bunk my legs felt like lead. We brushed, we read, we sang Old McDonald four times.

"Do you know any more songs?" Jojo said.

"Not unless you can sing the Gilligan's Island theme."

"What's a Gilligan?"

I kissed the top of her head. "We'll sing more tomorrow. Good night, Jojo. If you wake up real early in the morning, just look at your story book. Okay?"

She nodded. We said a short prayer before I tucked her in.

Her little fingers searched for something under the sheets.

"I want Mr. Soupy."

I yawned. "Beg pardon?"

"Mr. Soupy."

"Who's that?"

"My octopus. Mr. Soupy sleeps with me. He's in the trailer."

My eyes were beginning to sag closed. I scanned the room in desperation. I handed her the first helpful item I saw. "Here you go. This is Mr. Oven Mitt. He's really nice and cushy, see?" I stroked my cheek with the fabric. "Mr. Oven Mitt will stay with you tonight. Nighty night, Jojo." I heaved myself into a nightshirt and collapsed on the bed.

"Thanks, God. For letting Mateo live and for everything else about today that I'm too tired to remember. Amen."

There was no knocking. No adolescent wailing outside my door. No turtles that needed rescuing. Only blissful sleep.

Until three o'clock in the morning.

When my bedroom light was snapped on.

And a child materialized in my bed.

A child with tears running down her face.

"Mrs. Peevey." Jojo snuffled as she poked me in the ribs. "Are you dead?"

"Yes."

She processed this for a minute. "How do you talk if you're dead?"

"I don't know. Mrs. Peevey is very tired. Please go back to sleep and leave her alone."

An unearthly wail came out of the child's mouth. "I want Mr. Soupy."

A spattering of hot tears splashed my cheeks. I rolled over. "Mr. Oven Mitt is keeping you company. He's a gem, a fine figure of an oven mitt."

"I don't want Mr. Oven Mitt. He smells funny."

"That's his Twirly Roni perfume."

More tears dropped onto my face. "I want Mommy. I want Mr. Soupy."

I suppressed a series of unfriendly comments. "Please, just stop crying. Mommy wouldn't want you to cry all over Mrs. Peevey."

Jojo looked at me with brimming eyes and stuck her three middle fingers into her mouth. "I want Mommy," she said in a very small voice.

Oh gee. Even in the wan light of the trailer the child looked completely pitiful, like a puppy in the pound. "If I go get Mr. Soupy for you, will you sleep on the couch the rest of the night?"

She nodded.

"All right." I didn't bother to put on a robe before I grabbed a flashlight. I was too tired even to worry about the nocturnal insect population. "Where is Mr. Soupy?"

"He's in my bed. Under the pillow."

"Fine. You stay right here. I'll be back in a minute. Don't go anywhere. Do you understand?"

She nodded again.

I stomped down the trailer steps. This was ridiculous. How could a person survive on no sleep? My head was spinning as I slammed into Jojo's trailer. Mr. Oven Mitt didn't smell right. How good could a stuffed octopus smell anyway?

I found Jojo's bed and sure enough, there was Mr. Soupy, stashed under the pillow. I held him by one pink tentacle. He looked like a relic from World War I. How many generations of bacteria thrived amid his tangled arms? As far as aroma went, I was too disgusted to take a whiff. On my way out the trailer, I slammed my foot into the door jamb and dropped the flashlight. It rolled under the front step. "Owwwww," I hissed to myself.

I hopped up and down, nursing my bruised foot. The darkness closed in around me. I peered under the porch step, thinking about the millions of insectoid creatures that probably inhabited the same space as my flashlight. Forget it. Mr. Soupy and I would navigate by starlight. I limped towards my trailer.

Something black and heavy flew over my head. I dove face first on the ground. The sound of my terrified breathing filled my ears. I waited for the next bombardment, but nothing else came. No more night bombers. Probably a bat, another one of nature's marvelous desert creatures. The gravel was now imbedded in my knees and forehead. Mr. Soupy lay nearby, laughing at me no doubt. I heaved myself up, brushed off the mess and grabbed one of his ugly legs.

That's when I noticed the light in the office trailer.

No sign of Stella's car.

No Loving Doves lurking about with flashlights and duct tape.

None of the tenants had reason to be in the office.

I remembered the small box of cash we kept on hand.

The last straw broke.

I was dirty.

I was tired.

I was stubbed and burned.

And now, the office was being robbed. On my watch.

Fury rose from my bruised toe and grew as it winged its way up my scraped knees to my head. The injustice was too much. I wanted to be in San Francisco, the land of pedicures and designer handbags. Instead, I was stuck in Seepwillow; stuck for all eternity in this bubble of weirdness. Common sense and rational thought escaped out my ears with a hiss of angry steam. I actually heard my mind snap like a dry cactus rib.

Swinging Mr. Soupy in circles around my head, I raced to the office door, screaming as I went. My voice echoed throughout the miserable trailer park.

"That is it!" I hollered as I charged. "I have had it. I don't know who you think you are, you pitiful excuse for a felon, but I have had enough drama to last me a lifetime. I am done, do you hear me? D-O-N-E."

I pounded up the steps.

"I have fallen on bugs. I have been kept awake by crying teens. I've been left to run this dump by my aunt who has skipped off to Bulgaria. My skin is unraveling even as we speak. And I haven't had a pedicure in ages. So whoever you are," I shrieked as I flung open the door, "be prepared to meet the business end of Mr. Soupy!"

Chapter Sixteen

That could have gone better.

The criminal in the office trailer screamed and then began to laugh. Not a sinister, up-to-no-good laugh, but a hysterical, amused chortle. She laughed. And laughed until tears ran down her freckled face. As she stood there, convulsed with amusement, Pastor Stan arrived wielding a baseball bat followed by Chaz armed with a rolled up motocross magazine. A few Doves piled in too until the trailer was jammed tighter than a Macy's on the day after Thanksgiving.

"What's going on here?" Pastor Stan huffed. "I heard shouting. Who is this? Are you okay?" His eyes darted back and forth like a rabbit's before they settled on me and Mr. Soupy. "Simone, are you okay?"

Chaz ran over and grabbed my forearm. His expression was stuck somewhere between confused and amused. Then he looked at the criminal. "Who are you?"

Donna attempted to catch her breath and introduce herself. "I work with Simone. I flew in from San Francisco this afternoon. She told me her aunt ran this trailer park so I came looking for her and I figured I would start hunting in the office. Simone, what's happened to you?" She looked me over from my stubbed toe to my burned face, to the bedraggled octopus in my hand as she wiped the stream of tears from her face. "Is that an octopus?"

"His name is Mr. Soupy," I said with dignity, tucking the unfortunate sea critter under my arm. "What are you doing here, Donna? I thought you were a burglar." We hugged each other.

She tried to swallow her laughter but more giggles came out anyway. "I had to come and talk to you. I took a few days vacation. Your website for this place had a great map. I didn't get lost even once."

Miraculous, for a person who needed a global positioning system to work her way through the mall. We hugged again. I couldn't help but notice how chic she looked. Green belted capris. A soft clingy tank. Metallic sandals. Tiny hearts on her big toes. "I think you're nuts to come here, but I am so glad to see you."

I tried surreptiously to straighten my wild mop of hair.

By this time, Pastor Stan had lowered the bat and Chaz unfurled his magazine. I introduced them and the assorted doves to Donna. She flashed a dazzling, lip glossed smile and shook hands all around. "Pleased to meet you," she said to Chaz.

"Good to meet you too. We seem to attract all kinds of San Franciscans these days."

Donna looked at the magazine in his hand and then at Chaz again. "Are you into motocross? I've always been curious about it."

I stepped between them and grabbed Donna's elbow. "Never mind that now, I said. "Let's go to my trailer and we can talk after I hand over Mr. Soupy. Jojo is waiting for him." I apologized to the men folk for the disturbance as we left making sure not to turn around to witness the hilarity that was no doubt accumulating in our wake. I pulled her toward my trailer.

Donna tripped over a rock. "Your life has changed since you left California."

"You don't know the half of it."

It was no small irony that Jojo was sound asleep, sans Mr. Soupy. I deposited him next to her anyway and Donna and I sat at the kitchen table with a candle burning between us. I plopped a cool bottle of water in front of each of us.

"So you're in charge of the little girl?"

"Yes, and so far it's been like herding cats."

Her eyes wandered over my face. "Last time I saw you, you were a together, well manicured type. Now you're, well..." she stumbled to a halt.

"A total wreck?"

"I wasn't going to say that. Not a wreck, exactly. You just look more relaxed, now that you've put down the octopus, I mean."

"I've had a bit of trouble here in good old Seepwillow. My aunt had to go to Bulgaria and she left me to run the place. There are teenagers everywhere and you wouldn't believe what kind of weird things live in the desert."

"Why is she in Bulgaria?"

"My uncle was busted for Bibles."

"That sounds like some bad, low budget movie." She pointed at Jojo. "How did you manage to become the child's caretaker?"

"Caretaker? That's nothing. I delivered her baby brother on the floor of a trailer."

Her eyes widened. "You are not serious."

"I could show you my shorts to prove it but I had to incinerate them."

She sipped her water. "Unbelievable. You actually delivered a baby? What was it like? Magical? Miraculous?"

"Messy. There were some really cool moments mixed in with a lot of gross parts. All in all, I'm not keen to do it again."

Her eyes sparkled in the candlelight as she shook her head. "Why don't you put that stuff on your blog? It's a hoot."

"Somehow I don't think that's what the twentysomethings want to hear"

She laughed. "You underestimate them. But what happened to your skin? You look like you've been in a toaster oven."

"I got burned on the way to the Cactus Forest."

"Uh huh. Is that anywhere near the Emerald City?"

In spite of myself, I chuckled along with her. "Probably. So you really drove all the way to Seepwillow to see me?"

She suppressed a yawn. "Believe it or not. I felt really bad about the way we left things. I hurt you. I never intended to, but I did."

I shrugged, pleased to find that my anger about the subject had waned. "I understand. It wasn't your fault they didn't give me the job."

"I know. But I still felt bad. You're my friend, and it didn't seem right. Anyway, things have changed at Rock Your World."

"What things?"

She yawned again. "Maybe we could talk about it in the morning. I'm really bushed. I can stay until Sunday so we can catch up on all the important stuff, if that's okay."

"If you think you can handle three days in the desert, I'd love for you to stay. I'm afraid Jojo has the couch so you'll have to bunk with me."

"As long as you keep those sandpaper feet on your side of the bed."

I pulled a lock of her red hair. "I missed you, Donna."

She removed a stick from my frizzy follicles. "I missed you too, Simone."

***

Jojo was the first one out of bed. The resourceful child fixed herself a bowl of whipped cream and olives. Breakfast of champions. When I finally emerged from the shower, Donna was seated across from her at the table, her chin propped on her hand.

"Hi, Mrs. Peevey." Jojo sucked cream off her finger.

"Hello, Jojo. I see you've met Miss Foster."

"Yes. She has red hair," the child said, solemnly.

"I know."

"Mr. Soupy and Mr. Oven Mitt had a sleepover party."

"That's nice." I turned on the coffee pot and slid in next to her at the table.

Donna shot me a look. "I offered to fix her toast but she said no. She's been telling me there's a man here who carries baby legs in trash bags."

A quiver shook my vital organs. "Uh, yeah. Jojo could tell you a lot of things. We'll talk about that later."

Through the tiny window, I saw Tanya setting up for breakfast. I opened the door and asked her to watch Jojo for a while. The child trotted off after I made her deposit Mssrs. Mitt and Soupy on the couch. There was no way I was going on another nocturnal reconnaissance mission. Those critters were under house arrest.

"Okay, spill it Donna. What's changed at the magazine?"

"For one thing, everyone misses you."

"I miss them too. Cyber commuting is just not the same as going to the office. You miss out on all the water cooler chit chat." I poured us both a cup of coffee with milk. "But that's not why you came down here. What else?"

"Audrey is leaving."

I almost dumped the java on the table. "What? Where is she going?"

"Nepal."

"Audrey is going to Nepal? Why?"

"To climb Mt. Everest with her sister."

I sipped and swallowed. Somehow that seemed to fit right in with my mental picture of Audrey. The Sherpas had no idea what they were in for. "Wow. That's certainly a lofty goal, no pun intended. Who is going to run Rock Your World?"

Donna raised coppery eyebrows. "Me."

"You?" I squealed and abandoned my coffee to give her a hug. "Congratulations. What an opportunity. You'll be a smashing success."

"Yes, but I'm going to need a good special features editor. Are you up for the job?"

My stomach did a yee haw somersault. "Really? Me? You mean it? Me?"

"Why else would I come all the way to Seepwillow to ask you?"

Waves of excitement prickled my skin. "I can't believe it. When would I start?"

"Next month. Audrey will be off to Nepal then and I'll be at the helm. I've got a whole folder full of really intriguing new ideas. We're going to take this e-zine right to the top. What do you say?"

What did I say? There was only one thing to say. "I'll think about it," I said. What? Did that really come out of my mouth? I meant to say "Of course, you bet, yes sirree bob, no problem, I'm your gal." It wasn't like I had better offers on the table. The Ruddy Duck would be back in Stella's hands by then. A picture of Chaz swam into my muddled head. Chaz was a friend, a weird desert friend that was all. He belonged here with the cactus and I didn't.

Donna was not put off by my answer. "Okay," she said with a laugh. "You can let me know in the next few days. Your blog is going well. I really liked that last entry about the cactus."

"Well there's plenty of material around here to write about. The place is insane." I topped off our coffees. "Have you followed the messages from D.F.?"

She frowned. "D.F.? Oh the real short ones. I didn't take much notice. Why?"

I put down my coffee. "Brace yourself Donna. You won't believe this but D.F. is my ex fiancé, Doug."

Her mouth fell open. "Doug? Are you sure?"

I nodded. "It's crazy, but I think he realizes he made a mistake when he dumped me. Why else would he be blogging on my site? I think he wants to reconcile."

Her face was a mask of confusion. "Reconcile? Oh I don't know about that. I think you may have misread those comments, Simone."

My words flowed out in a rush. "The thing is, I don't know if I even want to speak to him again, let alone reconcile. It just feels too strange to think about getting back together when I'm really not sure I ever saw him clearly in the first place. Plus there's the anger about being dumped at Sunday school of course. It would be hard to get over that bit of humiliation."

Donna's eyebrows drew together. "I don't think Doug is interested in reconciliation."

"What makes you say that?"

She stood up and fished around in her tote bag. "Because he asked me to give you this."

The paper swam in front of my eyes, heavy weight ivory with a shiny vellum overlay, a beautiful embossed cake on the front.

Douglas Franklin Hobart

Rachel Anne Perkins.

Honor of my presence.

Holy matrimony.

Candlelight reception to follow.

R.S.V.P.

I looked at Donna.

She looked at me.

"He invited me to his wedding?"

She nodded gently. "I'm sorry, honey."

"He doesn't want to get back together with me."

"It doesn't appear that way."

I fought a wave of nausea. "I am an idiot."

"That's kind of a strong word, Simone. I can see how you might have jumped to the wrong conclusion."

"Those blogs, they weren't even from Doug, were they?"

"Well, I guess they could have been. Maybe you just misunderstood the message behind them."

"I knew he wasn't that deep. So Doug and Rachel are getting married." I looked again at the invitation in my hand. "They're registered at Crate and Barrel."

She twiddled with her pony tail. "Nice store."

"That leaves me with just one question."

"What's that?"

I swallowed hard. "Should I get them a crate or a barrel for a wedding present?"

We both began to laugh.

Chapter Seventeen

So Doug wanted me to come to his wedding. The thought burbled through my head throughout the day as I hunkered down in the chapel trailer, preparing stacks of peanut butter and jelly sandwiches for the afternoon activities. I wondered how to tactfully say I-would-rather-be-rolled-in-honey-and-coconut-and-presented-on-a-platter-to-cannibals than attend your wedding. Perhaps a simple 'cannot attend' on the response card would be enough.

I thought about the beautiful dress that hung in my closet in San Francisco. It had little pearls dotted all over the bodice. Rachel would no doubt look stunning in her bridal gown. Oddly, the thought did not stir up my angry, jealous demons. Instead I felt flat, disappointed in myself for even entertaining the thought of reconciling with Doug. I didn't want Doug back, I just wanted him to want me back. No matter what Donna said, I was an idiot. An idiot with a wedding dress hanging in her closet. There was nothing more pitiful than an unworn wedding gown.

The kids piled in and got a load of my towering stack of sandwiches.

"Wow, Miss Greevey." Raul nodded in approval. "You've got this lunch thing down. Too bad we're leaving on Sunday morning."

The words startled me. I had begun to think of the teens as a permanent noisy fixture. In two days the Doves would fly the coop. Then what? I looked down the line of scruffy kids. Jack was busy trying to hang a fork in Allyson's hair while she wasn't looking. The turtle boys shared the earpieces on an Ipod. And Tanya, wonderful Tanya, held Jojo who twirled the older girls braids in her fingers.

A detail poked at my brain as I took in the scenery. Something that I was supposed to do, besides make sandwiches. Something that involved preparations. Hmmmm. It was gone before my little gray cells could catch hold of it.

Chaz barreled through the door. The white tee shirt he wore accentuated his muscular arms. "Good morning everybody. Grab your lunch and your backpacks. Time to take a hike."

The kids groaned, but not too loudly.

"Come on, you couch potatoes. It's a short hike, just to the end of the property. And don't forget your umbrellas."

They loaded the sodas and food into their packs.

Donna looked at me. "Why do we need umbrellas? Is it going to rain?"

I shrugged.

Chaz came up to the sandwich table and gave her a dimpled smile. "It could rain later, but the umbrellas are for emergency shade. Would you like to go with us?"

Donna's face lit up. "Oh sure. Thanks for the invite. I haven't been to the desert before. I'll go get my hat."

Chaz turned to me. "Well, Ms. Greevey? Are you up for a short hike?"

Hike? My skin hadn't recovered from the last solar flaying. Donna would be happy to keep Chaz company on the long walk. "Why not?" I said recklessly. "Do you think Jojo can make the trip with us?"

He grinned. "You bet. I'll carry her if she gets tired. You can share an umbrella with your friend. You are still friends aren't you? Even after you tried to clobber her with Mr. Soupy?"

"Funny." I capped the peanut butter.

His breath tingled my skin as he whispered into my ear. "Are you sure you two will be able to keep up?"

"We'll try our best but Donna's not much of a hiker."

He laughed. "Well, neither are you."

I threw the towel at his retreating back.

Donna's decision to come along surprised me. I explained about the bug factor, the need for SPF 3,000 and all that, yet she still chose to accompany us. She even rustled up some stylish hiking boots and a pair of banana yellow shorts. With her red hair twisted up on top of her head, she looked only slightly older than Jojo. It annoyed me.

This time I was careful to slather myself with mega sunscreen and smash a floppy brimmed hat on my head. Sturdy walking shoes, gallons of insect repellant and a backpack with other vital necessities. This time, I would be ready for anything.

Donna eyed my preparations. "I have to go home soon so I might as well see the wonders of the desert and all that. Chaz seems like a capable guide. You two have a good rapport."

"He's very knowledgeable. I didn't know you were into the great outdoors."

"Chris has taken me hiking in the Marin Headlands."

"How are things going with Chris anyway?"

"Pretty good. He's really busy but we make time for each other. He's in New York right now but we're going to visit his parents when he gets back." She patted her hair.

"His parents? That sounds serious."

She smiled, a rose sheen infusing her cheeks. "I think it might be." Then she shot me a look. "Does that make you feel bad? I'm sorry. I shouldn't have said anything."

I had to admit a wistful twinge there for a second. "You know, I am just happy that you're happy." I was amazed to find that I really meant it.

She clasped me around the neck for a quick hug. "All right then. Let's go see this desert of yours."

We hit the sandy trail.

***

Something odd hovered in the sky over our heads. It took me several yards of hiking to decide it was a cloud. The puffy gray sprawling thing looked out of place in the brilliant blue. And kind of ominous, like an envelope from the I.R.S. or something. Cloud not withstanding, it was still plenty hot as we shuffled along.

Donna was probably warmer than I as she received extra solar energy from the sun reflecting off my wall of sunscreen. Her skin was shiny and her cheeks flushed but her cheerful smile didn't waver.

We meandered upward over a rocky plateau. The ground was sprinkled with scrubby mesquite and lizards sucking in the sunlight. Their leathery sides were the only body parts that moved as they watched us tramp past. Gravel crunched underneath our sneakered caravan.

Donna hiked along, the sweat glistening on her face. "It will be great when you're back at the magazine. We'll have a staff meeting as soon as I hire a new person to cover the blogging thing."

I felt a momentary twinge. Who knew I would begin to feel maternal about the Blogging With Brandi gig? "Oh, I'm sure I could still do the blogging."

"I didn't think you'd want to."

"It's kinda grown on me."

She fished a rock out of her boot. "I've got some amazing new ideas."

"Tell me about them."

"What about vodcasting?" Her eyes sparkled as she eyed me over the top of her sunglasses.

"Sounds like a Transylvanian thing to me. Does it involve aliens or vampires?"

She poked me with her elbow. "It's an automatic video sent to subscribers via the internet. We could change the topic each month. Maybe round up some guest stars and all that."

I could feel her excitement. "I've heard about vlogging. That might be something to try too. It would be awesome to convert the blog into a video web log, except that I wouldn't be able to work in my pajamas anymore."

"Yeah, that's a great idea. You see? It's synergy. We make an awesome team. How long are you committed here?"

If the Ruddy Duck stint went on much longer, I would be committed here permanently, to a rubber room with clothes that tied in the back. "I know my aunt will be back soon. She was trying to get a flight from Bulgaria last I heard."

"I still can't believe there are places where people can get thrown in the clink for giving away Bibles. Your relatives live amazing lives."

"Stranger than fiction, I'd venture to guess."

The collection of sweating people came to a stop in front of a bizarre cactus. It had the requisite spines and green barrel trunk, but its arms were splayed into scallops and strange loopy tendrils.

Jack shoved a half pound of trail mix into his mouth. "What happened to it? Or is that the way it's supposed to grow?"

Jojo prodded at the plant's crazy shadow with her ducky umbrella.

Chaz gazed up at the odd cactus. "Two schools of thought on that. One says it might have been struck by lightning in its formative years. The other is that it's some sort of genetic mutation. It's called a crested cactus."

Donna took a picture of the giant thing while the Doves sketched in their notebooks. "Simone, stand next to Chaz and let me take your picture in front of the cactus."

"I don't..." I managed.

Chaz dutifully stood next to me.

"Closer," Donna said.

I edged a bit nearer.

"Closer," she said again. "I can't fit you both in."

She ignored my poisonous look. Chaz snuggled up and put his arm around my shoulders. His muscular side was hard against my warm skin. He smelled like a very nice calzone, the kind that's all filled with melty cheesy goo.

"Your friend is funny," he breathed into my ear, sending tingles down my ribs. "Are all of you Californians so different?"

"We're not different. You desert dwellers are the odd ones." I held my breath, waiting for Donna to focus.

"I wouldn't bet the farm on that." He planted a tiny kiss behind my ear before he returned his grin to meet Donna's camera.

"There," she said finally. "That is one good picture. Do you want to see?"

"No," I said, trying to stabilize my shaky kneecaps. Chaz headed off to round up the group. "What are you trying to do?" I whispered to her.

"Me?" Her eyes were round. "What do you mean?"

"You know what I mean."

"I was just taking a picture. I've decided to start scrap booking for my new hobby." She put her camera into her fanny pack. "Come on. Let's catch up."

We came to the edge of a rocky cliff. It was a mountain of giant boulders and soft patches of silvered grass that plummeted into a rocky gorge below. The smell of long baked earth hovered in the air.

Chaz materialized at my elbow. "Your aunt tells me her property ends over there, just beyond that cottonwood tree."

I followed his pointed finger, down the ravine and up the other side. An unenthusiastic tree squatted on the far side, wishing it was a cactus.

"So Aunt Stella is the proud owner of this patch of desolation too?"

Chaz's dark eyes registered surprise. "Desolation? Are you kidding? This place is a treasure trove. I've been wanting to explore all the nooks and crannies for a long time but I just haven't done it. You know what kind of wildlife lives in a place like this?"

"No, and that's the way I'd like to keep it."

He sighed. "You are still resisting the desert charm, aren't you?"

Jojo saved me from answering. She craned her neck to look down into the gorge. "Where's the treasure?"

We looked down at her curly pigtails. "What treasure?" Chaz asked.

"You said it was a treasure trove," I reminded him.

"Oh." He went down on one knee next to her. "I meant there are all kinds of creatures living there. Those are God's treasures. They're way more important than money and jewels."

She nodded. "Can I go down there and dig? I want to give Mommy some treasure gold."

"No, Jojo," he said. "There isn't treasure like that." He shot me a desperate look.

I shrugged with no help to offer on the subject of adult/tiny tot communication.

He patted her head. "Maybe when you're older we can go down there together and I'll show you what I'm talking about."

"Okay." She trotted off and asked Jack if he had any candy.

Chaz marshaled the troops toward a semi shady spot a few yards away.

Donna sidled up to me. "You've got some explaining to do, Simone Greevey. Tanya said you drove Chaz's bike the other day. I didn't know you could ride a motorcycle."

"I am a woman of mystery." I took a swig out of my water bottle and fell into line behind Jack and Jojo.

She followed. "I'll say. I knew you were good with makeup and fashion, but motocross?"

I drank busily.

"Well what else haven't you told me? Do you ride bucking broncos or disable land mines?"

More drinking.

"And what about Chaz? He's adorable. Muscles and those sultry black eyes. Whew. Even if we weren't in the desert, he'd be hot."

I drained the bottle and quickened my pace.

Donna trotted to keep up. "Well? Spill it. Are you interested in him?"

"Of course I'm not interested in him. He's a ...desert person."

"What's wrong with a desert person? He's got a passion. He's good with kids. He's Christian. What more do you want?"

I turned to face her. "I don't want to have this conversation."

"Why not? What are you afraid of?" She cocked her chin and waited for the answer.

I looked her square in the eye. "I don't know."

The kids stopped again to do a sketch of the resurrection moss that clung to the hot gray rocks. More clouds moved in to accompany the first one. They rose in puffy splendor like an enormous tiered cake.

Cake!

The forgotten bit snapped back into my mind. I stopped dead and clapped a hand over my mouth. "Oh no. Oh no, oh no!"

Donna hopped up and down in front of me. "What? What is it? Are you getting heat stroke? What should I do? Should I apply pressure somewhere or take your pulse?"

"Tomorrow is Jojo's birthday. I promised her mother I would have a party for her." My watch read three thirty. "How am I going to put a party together this late in the day?"

Donna sighed with relief. "Oh, is that all? I thought you were dying or something. No problem. It'll be an afternoon party. Let's see. You can pick up the cake tomorrow morning. I'll drive into Yuma and buy her a present. No offense but the selection in Seepwillow isn't the greatest. The girls can decorate the chapel trailer and find some music while someone keeps her occupied elsewhere. Then, voila! A party."

I looked at her in amazement. "You are a force to be reckoned with."

"Nothing to it. Parties are a snap. I threw together a surprise party with two dozen guests in an hour once. This will be no sweat. Besides, I love party planning."

We hustled over to fill Tanya and Allyson in on our plans.

"Oh that will be fun," Tanya said. "We can play musical chairs. My sister always loved that one at her parties."

"Yeah." Allyson chewed on her fingernail. "We have to get party hats and those little blower thingies. You can't have a kid's party without those."

I volunteered to pick up hats and thingys when I got the cake. In a matter of minutes the details were all firmed up. What a relief to be surrounded by a bunch of women. Men are great for plenty of things, but for party planning, a gaggle of cheerful chicks was unbeatable.

The sun was full in the sky and the troopers settled down in the shade of a huge creosote bush to have a snack. Jack and Jojo stood at the top of the ridge several yards away.

Chaz hollered to them to join the group. When he looked back they were still standing there.

I saw Donna trying hard to leave a spot next to Chaz for a Simone sized bottom. "I'll go get them," I volunteered, much to her dismay.

I jogged up the super heated incline and walked over to Jack. "It's lunch time guys. Let's go eat."

"Okay." Jojo jogged past me on her way back to the group, clutching her ducky umbrella. "But Jack can't come now."

"Why not?" I didn't hear her answer.

I took another two steps until I was even with his shoulder. "Jack, why aren't you coming?"

My next glance filled me in completely.

Chapter Eighteen

The *Croatalus atrox* comes from the Greek word *Crotalon*, meaning a rattle or little bell. This was a charming fact I learned the week before from Aunt Stella's nature books when I was too bored to sleep. Less charming was the Latin word *atrox* meaning hideous or savage. Little bell. Hideous savage.

Those Latins had it right on the money because the thing that lay in front of Jack's feet was hideous and savage. In addition, it appeared to be highly disgruntled. The snake was at least six feet long with a triangular head and black diamond blotches sprinkled over his taut length. The rattles in the rear end worked overtime, vibrating into a frantic blur while the front of his body was elevated off the ground in an angry 's' shape.

Another helpful fact from Stella's book snapped into my head. I recalled at that moment that the bite of the Western Diamond Back Rattlesnake is generally fatal in a matter of minutes.

Swell.

This never happened in San Francisco.

I tried to keep myself together with limited success. All of my important body juices froze up. Terror balled itself up in my stomach. I couldn't see the front of Jack's face, only his profile, but my bet was his stomach was in the same fix. "Jack," I whispered. "Maybe we should take a tiny step backwards, real slow."

The boy did not answer. He didn't even blink.

"Jack," I murmured again. "We've got to move back."

Still no answer.

In an agonizing slow motion I put out my hand on his back and grabbed hold of his belt. "Jack," I whisper pleaded, "please. We have to get out of here."

Donna trotted up. "Come on you guys. I think your trail mix is melting. Let's..." She got a good look at the snake.

"Don't move, Donna," I hissed. "Stay absolutely still."

"Aiiiiiieeeeeeeeeee!!!" she screamed as she turned and ran, her high pitched hollers echoing down the canyon.

Uh oh.

Now the snake's head was quivering and its mouth was beginning to open. Two needle sharp fangs emerged from the folds of pink flesh. For a second I felt hypnotized by the gleam of ivory against the rosy flesh. My fingers tensed around Jack's belt. "Jack, on the count of three we run."

He didn't answer.

Praying he heard me, I tightened my grip. "One."

The snake mouth opened wide.

"Two."

I could see the viper head pull back slightly, a band of coiled strength.

"Three!" I yelled.

Everything happened at once. Jack and I leaped backward. Our legs tangled and we crashed to the ground.

The snake moved in for the kill.

Simultaneously, Chaz darted in front of the snake, unfurling Jojo's ducky umbrella as he moved. The snake struck out. His fangs sank deep into the nylon fabric and remained there, dripping. The rest of the snake was not satisfied with the situation and thrashed wildly, trying to free its evil choppers from the umbrella.

Jack and I lay on our backs. We panted in unison as we watched the snake dangle from the umbrella. The only sound was a small whimper that emerged from my mouth. Or was it from Jack's? I couldn't tell.

Chaz's face was wild as his eyes shifted from the snake to us. "Did anyone get bitten?"

It seemed like a long time before my mouth started to work again. "Nn, no," I managed. "I don't think so. Jack, you ...you aren't bitten are you?"

Jack managed a jerky head shake.

Chaz breathed heavily for a moment. "Good. That was way too close."

We watched the snake swing like a pendulum.

A slow smile spread across Chaz's face. "You see? I told you never to leave home without an umbrella." He hauled the snake umbrella over to the edge of the crevice and used another umbrella to gently disengage the critter from the nylon. When he was finally free, the creature darted away about as fast as we did, for fear it might somehow hop up that incline and finish us off.

"Are you two sure you're all right?" He bent to check out our limbs for puncture holes.

Jack nodded, his face pale. "Awesome. I never saw a rattler up so close. Cool."

"They don't seek out confrontation but they're extremely defensive. It was probably napping and we scared it somehow." Chaz stood there for a moment, hands on hips. His breath came in pants and sweat rolled down his face.

Most of the kids still peered down the slope to watch the snake make his getaway so they didn't notice Jack dart away a few steps and throw up on an unfortunate prickly pear before they turned back to him.

Raul thumped him on the back. "Man, that snake was huge."

Jack wiped his mouth. "Yeah, it was pretty big, I guess. Cool to see one so close. Is there any snack left?" He was escorted off to the dining area by a cluster of Doves.

Suddenly, I wasn't feeling well either. My knees began to shake. I had goose bumps in spite of the triple digit temperature. My head spun. Visions of that gaping pink mouth and the curved fangs swam before my eyes.

Chaz took me by the hand and sat me on a rock in the shade of a Palo Verde tree. He left for a minute and returned with a bottle of water and a clean sock. He soaked the sock and handed me the remainder of the bottle. "Drink this."

While I drank he applied the cool fabric to the back of my neck.

I took a few gulps and my nerves steadied a bit. His fingers were gentle on my neck.

"Are you feeling better?" His eyes were anxious.

"Yes, I think so. I may have to add snakes to my list of phobias. They're just as bad as insects."

He smiled. "It's my fault. I shouldn't have let the group separate. I should have been first on the trail. The snake was probably sunning itself and Jack didn't notice." He shook his head. Dark hair fell across his cheek.

He looked a bit on the peaked side as well. I reached out and took his hand. "No harm done. You did tell us to stay together and we didn't exactly follow directions."

His black eyes met mine and he covered my hand with his. "I wouldn't want you to get hurt. Ever."

I met his glance until the swirly stomach feeling intervened. "But you know," I struggled to my feet, "we really should go back."

He helped me to my feet. "You're not up for any more adventure today, huh?"

"That, and the fact that we've got to find Donna. She may be halfway back to San Francisco by now."

"I was wondering why she bolted. I figured I'd better check on you two before we took off after her. She missed her calling. She could have been a track star. She was halfway back to the trailers before I made it to my feet."

"It's a useful skill back home. Especially at those department store sales." My knees held and I stood long enough to receive a gentle squeeze from Chaz. I clung to him for a moment longer than was strictly necessary, enjoying the way his torso filled up all my hugging space.

We rejoined the others. Pastor Stan asked for a moment of prayer. We bowed our heads and thanked the good Lord for delivering us from the rattlesnake.

Now that the snake was safely back in slithering territory, I could appreciate the humor of the situation. Leave it to God to provide a ducky umbrella for snake rescue service. I snuck a look at Chaz as he shouldered his pack. And a man who wasn't afraid to use it.

***

Donna moved pretty quick for a girl who is more at home in pumps than hiking boots. We found her a mile down the path, walking towards us.

She threw her arms around my neck. "I'm so sorry. I panicked. I can't believe I left you there to be devoured by a rattlesnake. Did anyone get bitten? Was Jack hurt? Will you ever forgive me?"

"Everyone is fine and there's nothing to forgive. I would have run if my feet were cooperating." I squeezed her back and told her all about the umbrella rescue. She looked from me to Chaz and back to me again.

"This is the weirdest trip I've ever taken in my entire twenty seven years of living."

"And this is only day two of your visit," I said.

"You should put this on your blog."

"Do you think anyone would believe it?"

Donna considered. "Probably not."

Out of the corner of my eye, I saw Tanya scurry after Jojo who was headed back towards snake country. She hoisted the girl on her shoulders and returned to the group.

"Where were you going, Jojo?" I asked.

"I gotta go get some treasure. That snake messed up my umbrella and I need a new one."

Chaz laughed and twirled her pony tail. "I'm sorry about that Jo. I'll make sure you get another one before the rainy season."

"Okay. Do you have any lollipops?" He gave her some carrot sticks instead.

It was almost five o'clock before we staggered back to the Ruddy Duck. Chaz carried a sleeping Jojo to my couch and put Mr. Soupy within arm's reach.

"Okay," he whispered, "how about six?"

"Six what?"

"Six o'clock, for our picnic."

"Oh right. I forgot about it with all the snake trauma. Okay. I'll be ready at six. Um, I know you promised no bugs, but can you guarantee no snakes too?"

He laughed. "Yes, ma'am. No bugs or snakes."

Donna entered as Chaz left. "Six for what?"

"I'm having a picnic with Chaz."

Her eyes lit up. "Really? Oh that's so romantic. Just you and the stars."

"And the bugs and snakes."

She shivered. "Ick. Well I'm sure he won't take you anywhere with snakes. So are you two an item or what?"

I plopped onto the kitchen chair. "No, Donna, for the last time, we are not an item."

"Why on earth not?"

"We run on different wavelengths. He's Mr. Nature and outdoors. He wants to open a desert touring company."

"Sounds cool. Why is that a problem?" She raised a coppery eyebrow.

"I am a city girl, shallow to the core. I like pedicures and sushi and expensive clothing. He likes...lizards."

"Uh huh. So?"

"It just wouldn't work."

"Because he's not a white collar professional?"

"Of course not. That has nothing to do with it."

"Good. Because I would hate to think snobbery would come between you and a great guy."

I stalked to the refrigerator. "You're one to talk, Donna. Your boyfriend is a structural engineer. Not exactly dating a construction worker are you?"

She sighed. When she started talking again, her tone was soft, tender. "You're right. But you know what? I almost married a mechanic. He was one of the greatest men I've ever known, next to my Dad."

That surprised me. "But you broke up, didn't you?"

She rubbed her freckled nose. "Denny died of leukemia six years ago. That pretty much ended our engagement."

My mouth opened but no words came out. I thought I knew Donna inside and out. "I'm sorry. I'm really sorry."

"Me too, but I don't regret one moment I spent with him. I could have been very happy being a mechanic's wife."

"Oh Donna. I didn't know." I clasped her in a tight squeeze around the shoulders.

"That's okay. I don't bring it up generally because it still hurts a little." She got up from the table. "I'm going to go take a shower while you're still here in case Jojo wakes up." The waning sun lighted her freckles like bits of bronze. "Just think about all the reasons you're saying no. Make sure they're reasons God would agree with."

I sank down in the chair again. Chaz was wrong for me. God would agree. We were like the city mouse and the country mouse. Oil and water. Sweat socks and strappy sandals. There wasn't enough in common between us to go beyond a tenuous friendship. And some sort of physical attraction. Besides, I'd recently been planning to wed another man. It was not the time to go forward on some sort of crazy romantic adventure. I put that mental folder back in my cranial file cabinet and opened my computer.

Brandi girl, you're in the desert? Oh wow, which one? The closest I want to be to the desert is Las Vegas and that's inside an air conditioned hotel. I might consider Palm Springs too. Are you anxious to get home? -- Jilly J.

Cool, Brandi. I've never been to the desert but I want to go to Egypt someday. I just picture this broad expanse of nothingness with camels and dunes. How does it compare to San Francisco? -- Cherry B.

How did Seepwillow compare to San Francisco? What a question. I typed in my response.

How does it compare? Like horseshoes and hand grenades. About the only similarity is the people. The Christian community is alive and well here too! Desert dwellers seem to have the same struggles that city folks do. And yes, I am very anxious to get home. Do you know how long it's been since I had a facial? -- Brandi

p.s. No camels in this desert but some of the bugs are close to camel sized!

I looked at the last blog with my heart in my throat. It was another one from D.F. Now that I knew I had totally misinterpreted all of Doug's previous e-mails, I wasn't sure if I wanted to read it or not. After a tortured moment of indecision, I took the cyber plunge.

Brandi,
Blessed is the man who trusts in the Lord
And whose trust is the Lord
For he will be like a tree planted by the water,
That extends its roots by a stream
And will not fear when the heat comes;

But its leaves will be green,
And it will not be anxious in a year of drought
Nor cease to yield fruit.
Jeremiah 17:7,8

Jeremiah? That didn't sound like Doug at all. And besides, he was getting married. So what was all this blog fellowship stuff? Guilty conscience? My head spun.

I read the passage again. The heat had come for me all right. Drought too, and the odd killer snake. But here I was, still standing. I always thought I trusted in the Lord but maybe I was only playing at it. Like the wildflowers that spring up when there was water.

This was the time of drought all right. What should I do? Whom should I trust? This man had let me down in a big way, but I wasn't ready to offer forgiveness. I chewed my lip. I wondered how many times I had let God down. How many times had He been disappointed with Simone Greevey?

What was Doug trying to tell me? How come I hadn't seen these parts of him before? Perhaps it was all just a cruel way of taunting me now that I had been dumped. Tears sprang into my eyes. I blinked hard and went for the whipped cream.

A little voice piped up from the couch. "Why are you eating that, Miss Peevey?"

I swallowed quickly and hid the plate behind my back. "Eating what?"

She rubbed her eyes. "The whipped cream."

I put the can down and walked over to the couch. Caught with my hand on the nozzle. "Mrs Peevy is having a bad day, honey."

"Cuz of the snake?"

"That and some other things."

"Oh." She grabbed her octopus by one battered arm. "Do you want to hold Mr. Soupy? You could sleep with him tonight if you want."

My heart filled up at the sight of that disgusting stuffed Petri dish. I sat next to her with Mr. Soupy in my lap until she fell asleep again.

When she was safely unconscious, I returned Mr. Soupy to her embrace, shut my troublesome laptop and grabbed the cell phone to check on Anna. I got through to her room after a few minutes.

"Hello, Anna. It's Simone. How are you feeling?"

"Better. The doctor said I can come home on Sunday. How is Jojo behaving?"

"She's doing just fine. We went on a hike today." I decided to leave out the snake part. "My friend from San Francisco is visiting and they're getting along famously. She's going to help me with the birthday party tomorrow."

Anna sighed into the phone. "You have been so good to me and my children."

"How is Mateo?"

"He's fine." She chuckled softly. "He eats all the time, just like his father."

"Will Mr. Escobar come back soon?"

"He should be here late Saturday night, God willing."

I heard the gusty wail of a baby near the phone. "Sounds like Mateo is hungry again."

"I guess so. He will grow like a weed if he keeps it up at this rate." There was a sound of phone juggling. "I've already planned out your dinner in my mind. We'll have tamales and arroz con pollo. My sisters will come and help. We'll invite the whole trailer park and Jojo can have a second birthday party. I thought maybe Wednesday. Will you tell everyone?"

"Well sure Anna, but don't you think you ought to take some time to rest and recuperate?"

"With six children? This is as much rest as I'm going to get. Besides, I need something to lift my spirits. We could all use that, I think."

"I couldn't agree more. I've got to sign off now. Do you have my cell phone number handy in case you need anything?"

"Yes, I do. Gracias, mi amiga."

"You're welcome, Anna. Kiss Mateo for me."

***

Donna dressed me. I was going for jeans and a matching top but she put the kibosh on that.

"You can't wear that on a date," she said over my shoulder. "How about a skirt? Where is your suitcase?"

"In Bulgaria, and it's not a date. My clothes are in the closet."

"This skirt is great. He'll love it." She held up a white Eileen Fisher.

"We're going on a picnic."

"So?"

"There are bugs in the desert and I'm not giving them easy access to any body parts."

She walked by me and peered into the closet. "I see your point. Okay, these then." She picked out a pair of Jones New York stretch jeans in a fetching shade of green with a coordinating striped halter top.

"Cute, but the bugs might still get my arms."

"So you'll wear bug repellent and a sweater." She shoved me into the bedroom. "This shows off your beautiful shoulders and that olive complexion. Change."

"I don't want to show off anything, Donna. It's just a celebration for bringing a baby into the world intact. Chaz is just a friend."

"Well then treat your friend to a nice view. Now change."

I grumbled as I donned the outfit. Who knew Donna could be such a fashion fascist? "Well I'm not wearing sandals," I called. My sneakers certainly did not send a "come hither" message, even if they were sporty Cole Haans.

"Fine by me," Donna said. "He won't be looking at your feet anyway."

The mirror reflected a face that was more human looking than it had been the day before. I applied lip gloss, powder and eye enhancement before I emerged for the fashion critique. Jojo was awake, playing with blocks on the table. I twirled so she could get the full effect. "What do you think, Jojo?"

"You need an umbrella," she said.

What a revelation. I spent all that money on fashion and all I really needed was an umbrella.

Donna laughed. "You look great. He'll love it."

I shot her a dark look. "Are you two going to be okay here?"

"Of course. I've got a Barney movie and some Jiffy Pop. We'll be fine."

"Where is Mr. Soupy?"

"Safely tucked under the pillow with Mr. Oven Mitt. Now go along, young lady. And be home before midnight."

***

I blinked against the sinking sunlight. Then my jaw hit my clavicles.

Too many days in the desert had finally caught up with me. I was experiencing a mirage. It was a pretty impressive mirage, though. Standing in the golden light was a motorcycle. The light glinted off the aluminum tank and fenders. My mouth watered as I stumbled out the door of my trailer.

Chaz pulled up on his bike right next to my mirage. "Do you like it?"

"Is it real? I thought I was seeing things."

He laughed. "Sure it's real. I borrowed it from a guy I work with. It's a..."

"A twenty-eight horsepower 250 Elsinore," I finished.

"Yeah." His laugh was deep and musical. "Do you want to ride it?"

Oh boy. Moral dilemma. Ride that bike? I wanted it more than my next breath. But I didn't ride anymore unless it was an emergency or something. That was my other life. And even if I did, I wouldn't ride with Chaz. That would be like both of us drinking from the same cup. My stomach knotted.

I could feel two sets of eyes watching me from the trailer. "Uh, well, no. No thank you. I would not like to ride. No."

"Okay. Then you'll have to hop on the back of mine."

I thought about putting my arms around his taut waist. I'd done it before, but that was earlier, when I thought of him as a harmless lunatic. And then again when I thought he might drop dead of a head injury. Things were different now. I stood there in tortured silence.

He continued to gaze at me. "Sorry, but I don't have a car. The picnic spot is about three miles from here and that's a long walk."

Oh man. What to do, what to do. Ride with Chaz?

Ride the 250?

Back out of the whole deal and look like a moron?

A lightbulb went on. "I don't have a helmet."

Problem solved.

He extracted a blue one from the other side of his bike and held it out to me. "I've got a spare. Here."

Those eyes peeping through the trailer window bored into the back of my head. "Get going, you ninny," I could hear Donna thinking. "Are you waiting for an engraved invitation?"

"Oh, well, I uh, think maybe it wouldn't be a good...okay." I grabbed the helmet and straddled the bike. Donna was no doubt picking her mandible up off the floor. I kick started the engine and yelled over the roar. "Let's go."

Chapter Nineteen

We flew.

All right, we didn't exactly break any land speed records but that's what it felt like. I trailed him for a while, relishing the push of the wind against my body. Then that inside part of me, that odd shaped piece that didn't fit in my puzzle, broke loose. I cut around Chaz's bike. His surprised grin followed me as I took the lead.

The low sun hovered close to the horizon in a smear of orange and red. For a while, I felt like part of the canvas, superimposed on the giant panorama that unrolled under my wheels. I vibrated with life and laughter. The yellow lines on the road blended into one luminous finger pointing the way to who knew where.

Then the practical side kicked in. Being in front would make it kinda hard to follow Chaz to the picnic site. I reined in my wild horses and dropped back behind him. Though it was still hot, a cool rush of air bathed my face as we swept by miles of flat, decorated with pockets of dwellings and the occasional cottonwood tree.

Chaz slowed as we approached a weathered road sign. He pointed and we pulled off in the town of Snap. I looked for nearby villages called Crackle and Pop but no dice. Snap was a little bit of civilization amidst a whole lotta nothing. As far as I could see they didn't even rate their own

Starbucks.

"Why do they call it Snap?"

"After Maynard Snap, a miner who founded the town," he called over the idling engine. "He used to hike all over these parts, looking for gold deposits. Told some wild stories about a bunch of giants who lived in the canyon."

"The man saw giants?" I shook my head. A lunatic around these parts. What a shock.

Chaz pulled back on the uneven road. "It's just a little farther."

I surveyed the area as we rolled onward. It was a lot like Seepwillow. One gas station, one post office, a grocery store and a tiny doctor's office. Small houses slouched in clusters leading from the main drag. We continued on away from the optimistically named Main Street until we came upon a feed store and a three- story warehouse-like building fronted in brick. The windows were boarded over and a scalp of dried grass in front of the place spoke of better times. Chaz rode his bike around the side of the brick building and parked.

I followed, looking around for anything resembling a picnic site. I pulled in next to him and we removed our helmets.

"Uh, Chaz? What are we doing here?"

His eyes crinkled as he looked over the two-story structure. He grabbed his backpack. "This is my building, such as it is. The beginning and the end of my fancy business plans. Come on. I'll show you."

I followed him into the dark space.

It took a moment for my vision to adjust to the gloom. The carpet was conveniently mold colored, well suited to the place. The walls were covered in peeling paint. Speckles of dust danced in the beams of sunlight that poked through the shuttered windows. There was no furniture except for a metal folding chair. The only decoration was a poster of a stylized fox on top of a green motorcycle. *Desert Fox Tours*, the sign read. *Come see the wonders of the desert from the comfort of a bike.*

Chaz turned in a slow circle. "This is it. The building I bankrupted myself and Gigi for. Of course, the place I thought I was buying was the business office down the street. That was nice. Plush carpets, wired for computers, air conditioned. The whole nine yards."

"Must have stung when you figured out what happened."

"More like humiliated than stung. I showed up with my keys in hand only to find they didn't work on the office down the street. They fit the lock for this dump. And the six bikes I bought vanished along with the guy who set up the deal." He shook his head. "I still can't believe I was such an idiot. I'll bet he's still laughing."

The defeated look on his face tugged at my heart. "He probably swindled lots of other people too."

"I'm sure you're right, but that doesn't make me feel any better."

I looked around for some sort of silver lining. Even silver plated would do. "This place is yours, right? Why can't you build a business here? Fix it up and buy the bikes gradually?"

He smiled. "Because I'll never have that much money in my entire life. But thanks for saying that anyway."

I looked away. "There is always the possibility of a business loan. The place has potential."

"The potential to be a fire trap maybe, but it does have one nice feature. Follow me." He shouldered his pack again and led the way to a door which opened onto rickety metal steps. In a moment, he vanished up the staircase leaving me to follow.

There were no bugs at large in the dusty space so I climbed up after him. I emerged onto the flat roof, bordered by a three-foot cement wall. From that vantage point, I could see for miles. Far off mountains lay in deep brown folds as if they were made of vintage cloth. The sky was ruffled with clouds and in the distance a golden eagle soared on enormous tapered wings.

I turned to Chaz. "I was right. The place does have potential."

He laughed as he spread out a checked blanket from his pack. "Well, I figured you wouldn't get ambushed by a rattlesnake up here." He pulled out plastic plates, cups and a Thermos. "Do you want to sit down?"

I eased myself onto the blanket thinking it was a good thing I'd left the skirt at home. He handed me a cup of lemonade. "How is Anna feeling?"

"Better. She is going to have some sort of giant fiesta on Wednesday. The whole trailer park is invited. She asked me to tell the Loving Doves to come back too, for the occasion."

"I admire her fortitude. Just being there for the birth was enough to make me want to lock myself away in a bunker somewhere."

"That makes two of us. At least you didn't lose a nice pair of cargo shorts."

We both laughed. Then the conversation skidded to a halt.

He looked at me over the top of his cup until my cheeks warmed. "What? Why are you staring at me like that?"

"I was just thinking that you are an interesting person."

"Hmmm, interesting. Is that like saying a girl has a nice personality with the face of a St. Bernard?"

"You don't have the face of a St. Bernard."

We sipped until the silence threatened to smother us.

"So do you take lots of girls up here on the roof?"

"No. You're the first."

"Should I feel lucky or nervous?"

He laughed. "I'm not sure. I meet lots of girls, but nobody like you. I've got to admit I don't really understand what makes you tick."

I fiddled with my cup. "What's not to understand? I'm a city girl trapped in the desert. I like pricey clothes, gourmet food and all the shallow pleasures of life."

"And you like bikes. Don't forget that one."

"I used to have a thing for bikes. Not now."

"Why not?"

"I don't know. It was, a phase. My father gave me a bike so we'd have something to talk about. After he died, there wasn't anyone around who spoke that language." I sipped my drink. "It just doesn't have a place in my life anymore."

He didn't answer. His eyes followed the lazy progress of the eagle overhead.

"Go ahead and say it," I said.

"What?"

"What you're dying to say but don't want to offend me. Come on. I can see those wheels turning. Let me have it."

He took another sip before answering. "I wondered if you gave up biking because you were mad."

"Mad? At whom?"

"Your father, for dying."

I blinked. "That's ridiculous. I didn't really even know my father."

"Precisely."

My mouth filled with a snappy retort but nothing came out. Mad at my father? A man who tried to love me? A man who died before he really got the chance? I thought about the pile of letters I wrote to myself in my father's name. Feelings of anger and embarrassment floated around my gut. "You should stick to cactus."

"Probably."

Anger won out over embarrassment. "So all this time you've been trying to psychoanalyze me? Maybe you should spend some time on yourself. Why do you graffiti your Bible anyway?" I snapped.

"What?"

"The day I met you you were trying to fix the duck. You dropped your Bible on my head, remember? It had ink and chicken scratch all over it. What kind of a person writes in a Bible?"

"The kind who reads it."

Hmmm. I'd never written in a Bible before. Then again, I hadn't exactly been reading mine a whole lot lately either. I couldn't figure out whether to be furious or curious. I settled on the latter.

The breeze ruffled my hair. I pushed it out of my face. "Chaz, I know you feel close to God here and all..."

"Yes?"

"What did you think when He made your dream go up in smoke? The bike touring thing?"

"I thought it was lousy, unfair and pretty all around devastating. Then after I got over that, I realized His job is to give me what I need, not necessarily what I want."

"That's hard to accept when your dream goes down the tubes. You didn't think He was trying to tell you to go to Phoenix and be an engineer or something?"

"No. He would have made me better at math if that was His yen."

All my inner confusion resolved itself into one crystal clear question. "Don't you find it hard to give it up to Him? To give Him control of your life?"

He smiled. "In view of the fact that He may not have the same plan for me that I do?"

"Exactly."

"Sure. It's difficult, but there's also a freedom in it. I can't even fix a plastic duck, so I know I don't have the skills to be responsible for my own destiny. God is God and I'm not. Simple as that."

The wind picked up, muffling our laughter. Clouds began to mass along the horizon.

"I'm not mad at my father."

"Okay."

"It's not his fault he was allergic to bee stings."

"True."

I batted at an airborne leaf that danced in my face. "I don't want to ride motorcycles. It just doesn't fit my image."

"Too low brow or it reminds you of what you've lost?"

I didn't answer.

"Look, I'm sorry if I sound judgmental. It's just that you've got an amazing joy that surrounds you when you ride." His voice dropped. "And I've never seen anything as beautiful as you on a bike."

I was dumbstruck. Thrilled. Scared. Embarassed. Overwhelmed. Did I mention thrilled?

He let the silence linger for another few minutes. "It looks like a storm is on the way. Maybe we'd better eat."

He reached for my hand and we bowed our heads to give thanks. I hoped he didn't notice my fingers trembling. Why was it being close to Chaz reduced me to a frazzled idiot?

He handed me a salami and cheese sandwich. "Sorry it isn't fancier, but that was the best I could fit in my backpack."

"It's good." I had to admit the guy had a way with condiments and cold cuts. The ordinary activity of chewing seemed to whet my curiosity again. "Chaz," I said after a swallow of sandwich, "why do you stay here? In the desert? You could move other places, with more opportunity and such."

He raised an eyebrow. "I thought we discussed that."

"I was just thinking that God gave you free will and all. Maybe he didn't mean for you to stay here. I mean, this place is kind of...inhospitable."

"Not to me." He chewed thoughtfully. "It seems harsh on the surface, but there's everything I need here. You just have to put down roots far enough to reach the good stuff."

"Why don't you like the rest of the world where the good stuff is on the surface? Say, Las Vegas for instance? It's in the desert but they have all kinds of lovely things. Movie theaters, malls, Starbucks."

"I guess that's the reason, it's all on the surface. In the desert you get what you see."

I got up and walked over to the edge to look at the sweeping panorama. Far below there were acres of land and life, but very little noise and business.

He followed me. "Don't you have roots in San Francisco? A place where you feel connected?"

"Yes," I said. My lips tripped over the word. "No. I don't know. I thought I had a niche carved out."

His shoulder touched mine and he sighed. "I know that feeling. I thought I had my Desert Fox plan all figured out too. I was going to combine my love of bikes and the desert and make money at it. What could be better than that?" The wind played with his thick braid. "Things changed for you too?"

I nodded, my throat thick. "The man I thought I was supposed to marry dumped me. The job I knew was mine went to my best friend so I ran away to find my aunt but she ran away to Bulgaria. So here I am in the desert, feeling sorry for myself, wondering why me, God?"

"That's a lot to deal with all at once. Are you...do you have any chance of reconciling with your fiancé?"

"I would tend to doubt it, as he's getting married. He even invited me to the wedding. They're registered at Crate and Barrel."

"Ouch."

"Yeah, ouch. I thought I had it all together until the bottom fell out of my life." I looked down at our bikes, standing together like an old married couple. For some unaccountable reason, my eyes filled with tears. "I guess that makes me a wildflower, right? I bloom with the rain and then shrivel up in the dry season."

"No it doesn't Simone." He turned me gently and wrapped me in his arms. "That just makes you human."

I cried. Then I cried some more. After that there was more crying with a sobbing chaser. After a while I couldn't really tell what I was crying about. Doug? The job? My Dad? My ruined pedicure? It all melded into one salty, soggy grief. Through a haze of tears, I felt Chaz take my hand and lead me to the blanket. Then he gave me some paper napkins to blow my nose. He didn't say much as he fished around in his backpack. Out came the best medicine money could buy wrapped in a yellow paper napkin.

"Here's a double chocolate chunk brownie, no nuts."

I inhaled the healing scent of chocolatey carbohydrates. Could have been my fragile mental state, but the brownie was the exact color of his eyes. "Thank you, Chaz. You are a very sweet man."

He gently wiped a tear from my cheek. "Don't let it get around."

I wanted to talk, to tell him all the things that swirled around inside. He would understand, I imagined. Those gentle eyes would take it all in and not lavish judgment. I opened my mouth, and then I chickened out. I finished the luscious hunk of therapy instead. Drained by my torrent of tears, I lay down and let the setting sun ease my grief away.

***

A drop landed on my cheek. I ignored it and snuggled further into slumber land. Three more drops of liquid cold convinced me I was not dreaming. My eyes popped open. A brilliant pocket of stars greeted me, sandwiched between two ominous cloud banks. Stars. And rain. Using my deductive skills I figured out I was lying on my back on a blanket. Next to me, snoring softly, was Chaz, hands folded behind his head.

The raindrops began to fall in earnest. I checked my watch. "Two thirty!" I shrieked.

Chaz bolted to a sitting position. "What? What is it?" he blabbered.

"We fell asleep!" I shrieked again. "It's two-thirty Saturday morning!"

"Oh man." His eyes rounded to Oreo size as rain splattered onto his forehead. He leaped into action, shoveling the picnic remnants and blanket back into his pack.

I helped cram in the soggy mess.

We ran to the roof door.

It was locked. Or jammed. Or just ornery. Whatever the reason, even Chaz's considerable bulk could not make it budge.

Cold water snaked down the back of my shirt along with a trail of fear. "Please do not tell me we are stuck up here in a rainstorm for the rest of the evening."

"Nah. We can get down."

"Whew. You had me worried there for a minute."

"We just can't do it the same way we got up here."

My soggy eyebrows drew together. "What are we going to do?"

"How do you feel about fire escape ladders?"

I gave him a "you are completely nuts" look.

His shoulders slumped. "Not good? I'm sorry, Simone. Trust me, this isn't how I expected the evening to turn out. The only way down is the ladder. I can go first and catch you if you fall."

The poor man was serious. I should have been furious with him but I couldn't ignore the lines of regret that etched his face. I wondered at precisely what moment I had gone from disliking Chaz to caring about his feelings. The rain began to come down in sheets, plastering our hair against our faces. A howling wind rose over the sound of the deluge.

There didn't seem to be a plan B. "Okay. You go first," I shouted.

He did a "thumbs up" and stepped over the edge of the rooftop onto the ladder. I could hardly make out his dark head through the pounding rain. I waited for a few minutes before I clutched the wet metal and headed down after him.

"Yet another good reason I didn't wear that skirt," I muttered. The bars were slippery. I held on like a monkey with the last banana. Remembering the don't-look-down rule I kept my face pointed towards the sky. That left me in an excellent position to take in the blinding display of lightning. I froze. "Chaz," I shouted. "That was lightning. Does that mean there's thunder next?"

No answer.

"Swell. I'm clinging to a nice wet piece of metal in the middle of a lightning storm." I could only hear the howl of the wind. My question was answered a moment later when an enormous rumble of thunder shook the ladder. Another stab of lightning illuminated my soaked body. Water poured down the back of my neck. I braced for the thunder, continuing my downward progress at the same time.

Chaz's voice finally rose above the storm. "You're doing great, Simone. Only eight more rungs to go."

Two more cycles of thunder and lightning had me trembling from head to miserable toe. The next time Chaz suggested a picnic I was going to have to give the matter some serious thought.

I stepped down one more rung. The lightning came again, only this time it was much closer to home.

It struck the rod on the roof with a horrendous crackle. The noise scared me so badly I lost my death grip on the ladder.

I watched in horror as my hands detached from the ladder.

I fell.

Chapter Twenty

Chaz did not catch me.

He did, however, provide a moderately comfortable landing spot. I fell backward off the ladder and crashed on top of him, knocking us both to the muddy ground. I heard a soft grunt from my human cushion as I flattened him.

I rolled off and peered into his face. "Did I kill you?"

When he regained the breath I'd stomped out of him, he opened his eyes and started to laugh. "No, but I think you smashed the rest of the brownies."

Then we were both laughing, victims of weather induced hilarity.

Chaz pulled my face to his and kissed me.

I should have been surprised but for some reason it all seemed quite natural.

His face was cold but his kiss warmed me all up inside. A funny flutter welled up in my heart reminded me of a long ago feeling. I kissed him back and my lips felt as if they'd always known his. After a moment, I pulled away. "You certainly do plan some interesting field trips, I'll give you that."

The moonlight caught a sparkle in his eyes. He grinned. "At least there weren't any bugs. Or snakes."

"The evening isn't over yet."

Chaz led the way back into the decrepit building where we stayed until the worst of the storm passed. We talked and laughed and listened. It was a whopper of a tempest, raging against the walls like an angry monster, but it only lasted a scant half hour. When the downpour faded to a pitter patter, we emerged from our hidey hole and headed out to the bikes. Fortunately, they started up without a problem.

For the briefest second before we took off, I looked up at the roof and thought about what Chaz said. Had I put away part of my life because I was angry at my father for leaving me?

"Come on, Simone," I chided myself, "now is not the time for self analysis. Now is the time for a hot bath and fuzzy slippers." I eased my formerly cute jeans over the clammy seat and revved the engine. Chaz waited until I pulled out onto the slick road before he fell in behind me.

The ride home gave me time to collect my soggy thoughts. A simple picnic had turned into a night of drama. Aside from the embarrassing aspect, I felt a strong connection to this strange but sincere man. As for the kiss, it stirred up feelings I was not supposed to have. A woman recently scorned should not be smooching a man, especially a man that was so different than her almost husband. Nonetheless, I couldn't forget that kiss. I didn't want to.

The rain pattered gently on my helmet. What had happened to my life in the past week? Things were easier to understand in San Francisco. They ran nicely along the superficial universe. No introspection or self analysis. Suddenly I had a terrible craving for a latte.

We pulled into the trailer park at precisely three-thirty in the morning.

"Thank you for the picnic, Mr. Tagliola."

"You're welcome. Sorry about the rain and all. And the fire escape thing. " He looked me up and down. "I have to say, though, those jeans look just as good wet as they did dry."

I blushed, only slightly pleased. I jumped off the bike and scurried up the steps.

"No problem. I'm sure my outfit will recover."

He watched me with one eyebrow raised in amusement. "Sleep well, Simone."

"You too, Chaz."

I tiptoed my way into the trailer. Jojo slept with Mr. Soupy. She had him in a chokehold. My clothes had dried to the point that they weren't oozing all over the floor, but my shoes made squelching noises with each step. I took them off and continued in stealth mode to the bathroom.

As silently as possible, I stripped off the damp articles and wrapped my frozen limbs in a sweat suit. I gently lowered myself onto the bed. Nothing. I hadn't woken Donna. Thumbs up for super sneaky Simone.

"Do you know what time it is young lady?" a voice whispered in the darkness.

I groaned. "I know, I know. We were on a rooftop and we fell asleep. It started to rain. Go back to sleep."

She thought for a moment. "Well that must be true because it's just too lame a story to be fiction. Your feet are freezing. What did you do? What did he say? Did you have a good time?"

I shivered and pulled the covers up. My ribs ached from the fall off the ladder. I was pretty sure my shoes were ruined. But another detail was foremost in my mind, an imprint of that kiss. "Yes, I did," I said, and I meant it.

***

The morning came mighty early even though I didn't slide out of bed until nine thirty.

I peeked through the blinds to find Chaz gone and the extra bike too. Donna was already eating pancakes with Jojo and the Doves when I arrived. She sidled over to me. "So, you had a good time, eh?"

"Yup. Are there any pancakes left? I'm starving." Tanya piled some onto a paper plate for me.

"Your voice sounded funny last night." Donna drizzled more syrup on her breakfast. "Like a girl who has been on a great date."

"We got poured on and I fell down the fire escape."

"Sounds memorable to me. By the way," she whispered in my ear, "Katy Nunez is going to take Jojo in a few minutes so I can go pick up her present. We're going to meet here at 12:00 for the party. Tanya and Allyson are going to decorate and make sandwiches."

I choked on my pancake. "Oh gosh. I forgot. I've got to go get the cake. Meet you back here later." I slam dunked the plate and ran to get my keys.

I drove as fast as I legally could. The sun was already ferocious by the time I got to the Pick N Pack at ten thirty. I waited anxiously for Gigi to unlock the front doors.

"Hi, Gigi."

"Hello. Come on in." She began to set up a giant tower of canned peas.

I headed to the bakery portion of the store. The glass cases were stocked with dozens of ...doilies. I waved at the woman in the baker's hat. "Excuse me. Where are all the cakes?"

"There aren't any."

"What do you mean there aren't any? How can you have a bakery without cakes?"

She gestured with a spatula. "The oven is broken. It should be fixed later today. Check back after 4:00."

My stomach dropped to my shoes. Four o'clock? All I had to do was pick up a measly cake and now that plan was Plutoed. Put on your thinking cap, Simone. You've got to make this work for Jojo.

I checked my watch again. If I bought a mix and some frosting, I could take it home and whip up a cake. The old brain did some quick math. Half an hour back home. An hour to mix and bake. Another hour to cool and frost. I would never make it.

I scanned the counters in all directions. Not a single cake anywhere except for some ice cream cakes in the freezer. That wouldn't work. They would be reduced to mush by the time I got them to the car. We'd have to hand out straws.

Then I saw my salvation. Twinkies. What kid doesn't like Twinkies? A diabolical plan formed in my brain. I grabbed three boxes of the spongy delights and a couple of tubs of vanilla frosting. I raced to the checkout counter, peeling money from my wallet as I went. Bag in hand, I ran to the car.

Wait a minute. No candles or blowy thingys.

Back in I went. They only had two varieties of birthday paraphernalia. One was a collection of black stuff with "Over the Hill" emblazoned on them. The other sported a dinosaur motif. No plain, pink, flowered or polka-dotted stuff anywhere. "Dinosaurs it is."

I headed to the checkout again.

Gigi smothered a smile. "What about balloons?"

I blinked, money suspended in my hand. "Balloons?"

"They're kind of important at a kid birthday party. My little brother didn't even want to open his presents. He just wanted to play with the balloons."

"Balloons," I repeated. "Do you have any?"

"Sure. We don't have too many choices but I can inflate them for you. Girl or boy?"

"Girl. It's for Jojo Escobar."

"Okay. Be right back." She disappeared into the back.

I checked my watch. Almost eleven. This was more stressful than a root canal. When Gigi returned with one pink and eleven green balloons, I snatched them from her hand.

"Sorry, we only had one pink one left. The green will match your dinosaur candles though."

"Thanks so much for the help, Gigi." I paid and left.

Somewhere around mile five of my frantic drive, the balloons cut loose from their moorings and bobbed all over the car. I elbowed them back but they persisted. One hovered in front of my face until I was forced to pop it with a pen I had under the sun visor.

Three balloons met an untimely end before I pulled up at my trailer again. Tanya stuck her head out of the chapel as I drove up.

"We thought you weren't going to make it."

"Come get these balloons while I stick the cake together."

She shot me a look as she came to fish the balloons out of my car.

I hauled my junk food into the kitchen. 11:25. Oh boy.

I grabbed a plate from the cupboard before I unwrapped a bunch of Twinkies. The tub of frosting was slightly melted. I forged ahead, slathering each one with goo and sticking them into a sort of Twinkie bee hive. Then I spackled that layer with frosting and stacked more Twinkies on top. Three layers later and the thing was beginning to teeter.

I ripped open the tiny freezer door and threw out a box of popsicles and a bag of frozen peas. In went the quivering birthday cake. That should do it. I sighed with relief and washed my hands. The cake crisis was resolved.

Way to go Mrs. Peevey.

I ate two of the leftover Twinkies and glanced at my computer. Would there be another cryptic message from Doug? No time to worry about that. I fished my creation out of the deep freeze.

The clock read two minutes to twelve as I jammed the dinosaur candles into the giant blob and headed out. When I opened the door of the chapel trailer, a crowd of people jumped up and shouted "surprise!"

I narrowly avoided launching the cake into the air.

"Oh, it's you." Donna lowered her party blower. "We thought it was Jojo."

"You don't say." I deposited the cake on the table.

Her eyebrow crinkled. "What kind of cake is that?"

The kids crowded around to witness the work of culinary wonder.

"It's a Simone original."

"Very original," Chaz said with a smile.

"It looks like Mt. Vesuvius," Jack said.

"I'll take that as a compliment."

"Is that marshmallow fluff?" he asked, poking a finger at the white mass.

A car crunched to a halt in the gravel. Everyone scurried back into their hiding places. I leaped behind the nearest file cabinet. This time the "surprise" had the desired effect. Jojo squealed, jumping up and down. "For me! For me! A birthday for me!" she chortled as Mrs. Nunez pushed her through the door.

I blinked back a tear at her emotional reaction. Or maybe it was a response to the fact that the top layer of cake was sliding off onto the plate. She giggled and squealed as they all honked their party blowers in her direction. Even Mrs. Nunez embraced the moment and donned a dinosaur party hat.

The Doves presented her with a group gift: a new ladybug umbrella and a matching hat with little antennas sticking out of the top.

"They didn't have any duckies," Allyson explained.

Donna's gift was wrapped in shiny paper with an enormous purple bow. The child made short work of the trimmings as she unveiled a large green stuffed sea turtle. Donna beamed. "He can play with Mr. Soupy. It's from Miss Greevey too."

Jojo cradled the turtle. "She's so nice. I'll name her Mrs. Soupy."

There was another present from Chaz: a plastic piggy bank in the shape of a bear. She shook it and coins rattled in the bottom. "Thank you Mr. Chaz."

"You're welcome."

She opened a few more presents from the Pastor and Mrs. Nunez.

Donna eyed the disbanding Twinkies. "Let's cut the cake."

We gathered around and sang to the birthday girl. Donna circled the cake, knife in hand, like an explorer looking for a passage to the new world.

"Oh let me do it." I grabbed a spoon from the kitchen, scooping, rather than slicing. Plates were passed and the group began to devour my creation.

"I've never had anything like it." Pastor Stan wiped a sticky white trail off his chin. "Delicious. It definitely satisfies the sweet tooth. Definitely."

Jack nodded in agreement. "I want one for my birthday."

A knock at the door made the room go quiet.

"Come in," I called.

Mr. Singh stuck his solemn face into the room. "Oh, I er, I will come back later."

I gulped. There didn't seem to be any weapons in his hands. No duct tape either. "We were just having some birthday cake for Jojo. Would you like some, Mr. Singh?"

His eyes darted around the room. "No, no. I was just going to check the calendar, to see what day was her birthday."

Aunt Stella's kitty calendar hung over the bookshelf. It listed all the tenants' special days from anniversaries to baptisms. I didn't believe the man. His face was dotted with sweat and he looked like his heart was going to leap out his mouth any minute.

"Come in," I repeated, figuring he couldn't do anything too nefarious with that many eyes on him. "Anna is going to have a big coming home birthday party on Wednesday. She told me to invite you. This is just a little celebration to tide Jojo over." "No. Thank you, no." He jerked his head out of the room. The door closed with a thump. Gradually the conversation resumed. I went to the window and watched Mr. Singh scurry back to his trailer. Checking the calendar, huh?

The cake was eaten until only the gooey bottom layer remained. Some of the Doves sat on the floor, playing cards in one corner and others piled building blocks in the other with Jojo. I sat next to Chaz on a worn sofa.

"That was some party," he said. "I think it meant a lot to her."

I nodded.

"Looks like you dried out from our excursion last night."

"Yes." I did not move away from his shoulder as it brushed against mine. "Did you suffer any ill effect from my landing?"

"No. The Tagliolas are sturdy folk."

"Oh that's right. Heads of granite."

We watched the festivities for a while. I replayed our rooftop conversation in my mind. Looking around at the people clustered in the trailer, I began to wonder if he was right. Maybe the desert did have some good stuff, deep down, if you could put roots down far enough to reach it.

Suddenly my spine stiffened. I had heard that particular phrase before.

Wait a cotton pickin' minute.

I got up from the sofa, my legs matching the contortions of my brain.

Blessed is the man who trusts in the Lord.
And whose trust is the Lord
For he will be like a tree planted by the water
That extends its roots by a stream.

Chaz appeared at my elbow. The faded fox on his tee shirt seemed to sneer at me. "Hey, Simone. Is something wrong?"

I picked up the cake. "You'd better believe it buster," I shouted as I smooshed the cake into his face.

Chapter Twenty-One

I didn't stick around to watch the cake shrapnel slide down his cheeks. One minute longer and I would have grabbed other things to throw. I sailed past the open mouthed teens, stomped over to my trailer and wrenched open the door. Inside, I tried to comfort my lungs which were busy gasping for air. The blood boiling in my veins drowned out the sound of knocking a few minutes later.

The nasty toad.

Chaz was the mystery blogger.

The D.F. was for Desert Fox, not Douglas Franklin. I didn't realize it until I recalled his phrase about sending out roots and all that. How could he? What would possess him to break into my blog with all that psycho babble and make me think he was my fiancé? My ex fiancé. And I had actually kissed the man...and liked it!

The hand on my shoulder made me jump. I screamed.

Donna screamed. When she stopped screaming she interrogated.

"What in the world did you do that for?"

No words came.

"Simone, are you having a mental breakdown? Why would you smash the cake into Chaz's face? Was it some kind of psychotic collapse?"

"I did it," I said finally, "because he's D.F."

She frowned. "You are having a breakdown. Sit down and put your head between your knees. In with the good air, out with the bad."

"Donna, Chaz is the one who has been blogging me, the person that I thought was Doug."

Her eyes darted around in her freckled face. "Oh. Really? How did you figure that out? Did he tell you?"

"No. Some things he said sounded familiar. Desert Fox is the company he tried to start. That's what D.F. stands for, not Doug Franklin."

"Oh," she repeated. "Okay. So he's been posting to your blog. Is that any reason to ruin Jojo's cake?"

A wave of guilt washed over me. "Oh no. I lost it for a minute. Was she upset?"

"Actually no. She thought it was the funniest thing she'd ever witnessed but that's not the point."

I sighed with relief. Then the anger flared again. "He tricked me. Sneaking into my personal blog. Using a false name. Asking questions about what I thought when he could have asked me himself."

She folded her arms across her chest. "Would you have answered him?"

"I don't know. That's not the point. He tricked me."

There was a knock at the door. It was Chaz. "Simone? I'm getting the sense that you're upset with me. I don't know what I did but whatever it is, I'm sorry."

I didn't answer.

He waited a few moments. "Simone? I need some help. Talk to me. I don't understand why I've been caked."

"Oh you don't, don't you?" I shouted through the door. "Well you can just wear those Twinkies all over your face until you figure it out."

His voice rose a notch. "Please open the door. I've got to go to work in a minute. I don't want to leave things like this."

"It doesn't matter what you want," I bellowed.

Donna whispered to me. "I don't think you're being fair."

"Of course I'm not being fair. Was he fair when he snuck into my life and TRICKED ME?" The words bounced around the small space. "You tell him to go away and stay away."

She exhaled noisily. "This is very junior high school. I'll go out and tell him. You stay in here and take some cleansing breaths until your sanity returns. Don't touch any more edibles for a while."

I was left with a head full of steam and a quiet trailer.

***

Donna must have gone to help clean up after the birthday party because it was dinner time when she came back. She pattered around to the side of the bed where I lay sprawled and waved a foil wrapped parcel over my head. "Are you hungry?"

"No." My stomach growled, branding me a liar.

She unwrapped the plate. The food aroma made my mouth water.

"Hot off the grill. Hamburgers. Baked beans and potato chips." She waved the plate over my head. "No Twinkies."

"All right." I snatched the plate and headed to the kitchen table. "Where's Jojo?"

"Allyson is reading her a bedtime story. She's completely tuckered out. They'll be along in a minute."

"Is the louse gone?"

"Chaz?"

"He is the louse I am referring to, yes."

"He's got to lead a group on an overnighter at the park. He won't be back until tomorrow."

"That will be too soon for my taste."

"He also said he'll call you tonight and for whatever he did he is sincerely sorry. He asked me what he'd done but I thought it best to stay out of it."

"How can he be sorry for a sin he doesn't even remember committing?"

She slid into the seat next to me and took my hand. "Lord, thank you for this food to strengthen and nourish Simone. Please help ease her heart, and give her peace. Remind her that forgiveness is blessed by you. Amen."

"Dirty trick, throwing that in with the grace," I said around a mouthful of hamburger. "God would agree with me that Chaz is a louse."

"Are you sure about that Simone? Really sure?"

I crammed in a mouthful of baked beans. "He has no business chatting on my blog."

"Why not?"

"What do you mean why not?"

"Why doesn't he have the right to blog with Brandi?"

I chewed some more. "Because he's not in the group. We talk about teeth whitening and control top pantyhose."

"The mission statement of Rock Your World says we're there to reach out to Christians, not just girl Christians. Besides, maybe he did you a service, setting the bar a little higher than pantyhose."

My mouth dropped open and a bean fell out. "Don't tell me you think he should blog with us? He didn't even have the good grace to use his own name."

"Neither do you, Brandi."

The bean went down the wrong way and I coughed. "That's different."

She snitched a chip off my plate and chewed. "Think about it. Cherry B., Galpal, Sister Sue. Are those their real names? How many women do you know named Galpal?"

I waved a crust of bun at her. "That's immaterial. The fact is he deceived me. I've been with the guy every day. He should have told me he was blogging."

"All right, all right. He didn't disclose his blogger i.d., but he didn't say anything on the blog to embarrass you or put you on the spot. He never mentioned your escapade with Mr. Soupy the night I arrived. He could have garnered some very amusing comments about that one."

"Why bother posting to the blog anyway?"

"My guess is he just wanted to get to know you."

"Why?"

"Because he's interested, Simone, and you are harder to read than the fine print on a medicine bottle."

"I don't want to talk about this any more."

She opened her mouth for another volley when Allyson came in with Jojo. "Hi. We finished reading. I think Jojo is tired." She shot me a puzzled look. "Are you...okay?"

"Fine. Just fine. Thanks for the story time. I'll tuck her in."

"Okay." Allyson gave me another look like I was a three headed dragon or something. Then she left.

I helped Jojo into her pajamas and brushed her teeth. When she was safely tucked in with Mr. Soupy on one side and her new stuffed turtle on the other, she yawned so wide I could see her tonsils.

"That was funny what you did at the party." She giggled. "Mr. Chaz had cake up his nose!"

"Never mind about that part. I'm glad you had fun. Good night, Jo."

"Why did you splat him?"

I sighed. I guess it was too much to hope that she would forget about the nasty cake smashing incident. "I was angry."

"Oh. That's bad. Mommy says you should never hit anyone, even if you're mad. You were naughty."

"Your Mommy is right. I was naughty. I shouldn't have done that."

She giggled again. "That's okay. It was real funny. Could you do it again so Mommy can see?"

"I don't think so." I kissed her on the forehead and turned off the kitchen light.

Donna was nowhere to be found. I heard strains of campfire songs. She had probably gone to join the Doves for their final night in camp. I should have done the same. Aunt Stella would be out there right now singing with callous disregard for pitch or tone. I didn't have it in me to join them. My heart felt like it was made of plaster.

Instead I booted up my computer and read the D.F. blogs again, now that I knew who they were really from.

There's only one perfect and it isn't here on Earth.
What do you see?
Is it harder to forgive someone else or yourself?

What an idiot I'd been. It was completely obvious the messages were not from Doug. Of course they were from Chaz. The phrases positively reeked with his deep philosophy. Patient perennials. Roots down to the water. Mad at my father. What gave him the right to barge into my blog? My life?

The whole thing made me want to consume copious amounts of carbohydrates.

Chaz didn't need to talk to me like I was a child. I knew I wouldn't find perfect here or anywhere. Something niggled at my gut. Expecting perfect wasn't right, I knew that, but refusing to see imperfections wasn't either. I'd made that mistake with Doug. In my mind he was who I wanted him to be, rather than who he really was. Man. I went to splash water on my face

A disgruntled woman scowled at me in the mirror. I wasn't going to repeat that error. There were *plenty* of imperfections in Chaz. He smelled like spaghetti sauce, for one. He wouldn't know the first thing about how to fit in the real world. His disastrous plans for a touring company proved he had no business acumen. He was unsuccessful in all the ways that I'd ever used to measure achievement.

The phone rang ten times before the caller gave up. Good thing I hadn't given him my cell phone number. The room settled into silence except for Jojo's regular breathing.

Forgiveness, he said. Forgiveness for what? For trusting someone who didn't deserve it? I had done that twice with both D.F's, fool that I was. I flopped down on the bed and grabbed a notepad and pen.

Dear Simone,

Daddy loves you. Daddy loves you. Daddy loves you.

I wrote until the tears blurred the words on the page into a sad, dark stain.

***

Sunday morning I awoke to the sound of slamming car doors. It was the Doves preparing for their final flight. I emerged with Jojo to find them loading bags and backpacks into the dusty van.

Pastor Stan came over to see me. "Well, Miss Greevey, we sure had a great time this past week, a real great time. Thank you for your gracious hospitality."

He no doubt considered it wise not to bring up the cake smashing incident. "You're welcome. I'm sorry to see you all go."

I was too. Weird. Sure the teens taped flashlights to LeRoy and ate more than any Roman legion, but they kind of grew on me. "Are you all coming back Wednesday for Anna's feast?"

Stan nodded and Jack added his own enthusiastic approval of the idea.

Tanya and Allyson distributed hugs to Jojo and me. Allyson whispered in my ear, "Maybe I'll try that cake smashing thing on my jerky ex boyfriend."

I gave her a squeeze. "I wouldn't recommend it. You only feel better for a minute."

"Yeah," she said with a grin, "but it sure got his attention."

Donna joined us. I hoisted Jojo on my shoulders and we waved until the van was out of sight.

The Ruddy Duck trailer park fell into a deep quiet. I looked around. The Doves were gone. Chaz was on a trek, no doubt still picking frosting out of his eyebrows. Aunt Stella was A.W.O.L. and Mr. Singh was holed up in his trailer of doom.

Donna helped me lower Jojo to the ground. "Hey guys. I've got to get my stuff together. I'm due at the airport at noon."

Off she went.

My best friend was leaving me too. Depression settled around my ears as I contemplated my lonely destiny.

The phone rang in the trailer. Donna poked her head out. "Simone, it's for you."

"Is it the louse?"

She sighed. "It's Chaz. He wants to talk to you."

"Tell him I am not granting an audience to people of the louse persuasion at this time."

"Simone. Is that really the way you want to behave?"

I stuck my chin in the air and refused to answer.

She shook her head and disappeared.

"What's a louse?" Jojo said.

"Trust me honey, you don't want to know."

Chapter Twenty-Two

"Are you sure you can't stay longer?"

Donna zipped her suitcase. "I really can't. I've got to start getting things organized at work. Speaking of which, you never gave me a straight up answer. Can I expect you to start next week?"

I took a minute to ponder. What was left to do here? Aunt Stella needed some sort of divine financial intervention, but there was very little I could do to make that happen. Jojo's mom would return soon and the doves were safely back in the arms of their parent birds. There was nothing left with Chaz that I needed to bother about. It was time to head back to San Fran. "Sure. I'll start on Monday unless Aunt Stella isn't back by then. She's got to come home sometime."

"Great." She gave me a squeeze. We helped her haul the luggage out to the rental car. "Are you sure you'll be all right here by yourself? I keep picturing that awful rattlesnake."

"No sweat." I nodded with a confident nod. "Jojo will keep me company. She's got a new umbrella we can use if the situation presents itself."

Donna's voice dropped an octave. "That's kind of what I meant. Do you know how to take care of a child all by yourself?"

"Of course I do. We've been getting along fine so far."

She raised an eyebrow. "Yes, but you had Chaz and a park full of teens to help you."

"I am offended. It's babysitting, not rocket science. I handled Sunday school didn't I?"

"Mmmm. I seem to recall something about inappropriate playdough usage." She hugged us both one last time. "I'm sure you'll be fine. See you soon, Simone. Bye, Jojo. I'll send you a card in the mail."

"Can you send candy too?"

Donna laughed as she settled into the seat. The car rattled over the gravel and out to the main road. One more wave and she was gone.

The silence settled upon us.

"When are my brothers coming back?" Jojo asked.

"Your Mom said they'd be back on Tuesday."

"When is Mommy coming home?"

"Real soon." I had an inspiration. "Do you want to go visit her and see your new baby brother?"

"Just Mommy, not the baby."

"Fair enough. Let's go."

***

Anna looked much improved. She wrapped Jojo in an enormous hug. "Hello, niña. I've missed you." She pointed to the bassinet next to the bed. "Did you say hi to your new brother Mateo?"

She peered inside. "He looks like a frog."

I smothered a chuckle. "Something tells me you're in for some sibling rivalry."

Anna laughed. "I think you are right." She played with Jojo's ponytails. "Have you been a very good girl for Miss Greevey?"

"Oh yes. We had a birthday party. I got lots of presents and Mrs. Peevey made me a cake and then do you know what she did?"

I stepped forward hastily. "I'm sure Mommy doesn't want to hear about that. Why don't you tell her about the gifts?"

The child recited a list of her birthday booty. When she came to the end she jumped off the bed to play with a stack of Dixie cups.

"Have you heard from Jaime?" I asked.

Her face cracked into a smile. "Oh yes. He was so sorry to have missed the birth. He'll be here tomorrow and I'm to be discharged in the afternoon. We will all go home together."

"That's great." I felt a swell of relief at the thought of handing Jojo back over into her parents' care. "I've been meaning to ask you something. Have you ever noticed anything odd about Mr. Singh?"

"He keeps to himself. I don't think I've ever talked to him more than a few words. Why?"

"Nothing in particular. He just seems...mysterious." I thought about the knife and the tiny shoe I'd seen in his trailer. A shiver wiggled my shoulders but Anna did not seem to notice.

"One of these days your aunt is going to get him to come to a bible study. Then she'll have all his secrets out."

We both laughed. "That I can believe."

"Is Stella home from her trip?"

"Not yet. I keep expecting to see her arrive at any moment."

A nurse popped in to announce the end of visitors' hours so we said good-bye and left.

I checked my watch. Four thirty. "Do you want to drive into town and have dinner?"

"Can we have ice cream for supper?"

"Why not?" I promised to keep her safe, not nutritionally balanced.

The Nicely Icely Ice Cream Parlor provided us with a couple of giant hot fudge banana split sundaes complete with sprinkles and whipped cream. I hoped the proprietor didn't rat me out to the kid's mom later. We stopped in the Pick N Pak afterward. My plan was to stock Anna's kitchen with some of the things she might need to plan her feast. If she was going to feed that many people on Jaime's salary, anything would help.

We perused the expanse of choices. "What does your Mommy use for cooking?"

"Pans."

"I mean what does she put in the food? What ingredients does she use in the kitchen?"

"Are you going to buy stuff for Mommy?"

"Yes."

She screwed up her face. "Mommy uses jellybeans and chocolate."

"Your mother cooks with jellybeans and chocolate?"

Her ponytails flapped as she nodded. "And popsicles."

And she had such an innocent little face. "Hmmm. Well let's look around and see what we can find."

We tootled up and down the aisles. In the spirit of the alphabetical organization system we started at the 'A' section and worked our way toward 'Z.' I grabbed boxes of cereal for the rest of the Escobar horde, packages of corn husks, eggs, flour and a bag of jelly beans for good measure plus the biggest containers we could find of jam and peanut butter. Two gallons of regular milk plus one of the chocolate persuasion. We added bottles of soda. In went tomatoes, tortilla chips and tamarinds. I had no idea what tamarinds were, but Jojo got all excited when we spotted them.

I paid for the stuff and we hauled it to the car. When Jojo was strapped safely into her car seat, we headed for home. It was almost six o'clock. I had successfully frittered away an entire afternoon. Yea me. This kid care stuff wasn't so bad. I gave myself a mental slap on the back.

"Mrs. Peevey?" Jojo said from the backseat.

"Yes?"

"I don't feel so good."

"You don't?" Alarm bells began to chime in my head. I immediately slowed and pulled over, scrabbling in my purse for a plastic bag, wishing Tanya was along to help. "Just breathe deeply, honey. In with the good air out with the bad."

Victory!

I dumped my tube of moisturizer out of the Ziplock and turned around, just in time to watch Jojo vomit her hot fudge sundae all over the seat. I sat there, frozen in horror, the bag suspended in my hands.

"Jojo. You just threw up all over the car."

She nodded. "Uh huh. I feel better now."

I exited the vehicle in a calm, sedate manner. Inside, I was having a meltdown of epic proportions. Ewwww, ewwwie, ewww, ewwww! It was way beyond gross. Thoughts raced around in my head like a greyhound after a rabbit. Maybe someone would drive by, someone with an industrial suck and dry vac. Or perhaps, a sympathetic mommy with decontamination kit in her vehicle.

There wasn't a car anywhere in sight.

If I called 911 would they send a fire engine and personnel? They had those rubberized suits for the really icky jobs, didn't they? Though in my mind it was definitely an emergency, I wasn't sure the fire department would see it that way.

Perhaps I had dreamed the whole nasty episode.

A peek through the open car window disproved that fanciful notion. The child sat there covered from head to foot with yuck.

I could call Chaz and ask him what to do.

No way. I would not give him the satisfaction of knowing I was desperate. Besides, I didn't have his cell number.

There was no help for it. I approached the vehicle warily, holding my breath. "Unbuckle yourself, Jojo," I said before I went back to holding my breath.

She fumbled with the straps. "I don't know how."

With a whimper I shoved my hand in the plastic bag and used it like a glove to free Jojo from her gunky straps. She got out of the car and we retreated behind a cluster of mesquite by the roadside.

I offered encouragement while she stripped off her shirt and pants until she was down to her bunny undies. Then I used six dozen handy wipes to clean the car seat before I almost passed out from lack of oxygen. "Just put your dirty things in a pile by that rock and let's get you back in the car."

"What about my clothes?"

I nudged them with a toe into a neat pile. "We're going to leave them here."

"We are? Will the police get mad?"

I looked at the horrible pile. "I think they'll understand."

"Will Mommy get mad?"

"I'll buy you a new outfit, Jojo. I promise." I used my fingertips to strap her into the car. I doused myself once more in hand sanitizer before sliding behind the wheel.

Even when all the windows were rolled down, I tried to drive with my head sticking out as far as possible. What was I thinking letting Donna leave me with a child? I forgot about the juvenile tendency to leak bodily fluids at any given moment. I needed Tanya. Aunt Stella. Chaz. Anybody.

Jojo hummed the only two lines she knew to B-I-N-G-O.

"B-I-N-G-O and Ringo was his name-o," she chortled.

"That's Bingo."

"What?"

"Bingo, not Ringo. Ringo was a drummer."

"I thought he was a farmer."

"No, the farmer's name is, er, Farmer and his dog is named Bingo."

"Okay." She continued to sing about Ringo and his name-o all the way back.

The bunny underwear went into the trash and Jojo went into the shower. I squirted her all over with body wash and commanded her to lather up with the cloth I provided. I went into the kitchen to wash my hands yet again.

"I'm done," she called.

I brought a towel to the bathroom. She stood there completely covered in mounds of white suds. "Well wash off the soap now."

"Okay." She commenced the rinse cycle.

When she was dressed in pajamas, I sat her on the couch with a coloring book. "I need to go clean the car. You stay here until I come back."

I donned a pair of yellow rubber gloves and filled a bucket with soapy water. For good measure I tied a bandana around my face before I grabbed the scrub brush.

Jojo laughed. "You look funny, Miss Peevey."

I waved my rubberized hand and went out to the car. Now I understood how those Hazmat guys felt when they had to go clean up toxic waste or plutonium or whatever. I removed the car seat and plopped it on the porch step. Then I scrubbed and rinsed and blotted until both the car and the seat were passably clean. I filled the bucket with fresh water and rinsed the seat. There was a loud hiss from beneath the porch step. I poked my head under.

"Sorry about that LeRoy."

The tortoise glared at me and hissed again.

"Trust me, if I didn't wash this stuff, by tomorrow we'd have to quarantine the whole trailer park."

He turned his back and flipped me off with his spindly tail. Naughty tortoise.

As I shook off the scrub brush, the sun slipped below the horizon. Once again the sky was filled with the lush iridescent colors I'd noticed on the inside of seashells.

What do you see? The words circled in my mind.

I exhaled and the tension melted off of my shoulders. "Thank you, Lord, for this breathtaking sunset. Thanks for putting me here to see it, even if I did have to scrub vomit. I love you, God."

The sun lost itself in a swirl of lovely.

I wondered if Chaz was looking at it too.

***

The whole ice cream sundae throw up thing was instructive. When Jojo asked for cookies for dinner, I wisely said "no way, kid." We ate buttered toast and scrambled eggs. I figured if they made a return appearance, at least there would be no fluorescent sprinkles languishing about in the mess.

After a rigorous game of Candy Land and several stories, I tucked her in. She folded her hands under her chin. "God please turn Baby Peaches into a dog. I've already got some brothers. Amen."

The darkness hid my smile.

"Miss Peevey? Are you still mad at Mr. Chaz?"

"Who me?" I faltered around looking for an answer. Bad enough she had heard me call the man a louse. That probably broke several cardinal rules of child rearing. And the whole cake episode wasn't a great modeling behavior either. "Uh, well yes I'm a little bit mad at him but only a little."

"Why?"

"It's a grown up reason."

"Okay."

I slipped Mr. Soupy under her arm and headed for my own bed. A tiny red light on the answering machine blinked.

Message number one was from Anna. "Hello, Simone. The doctor said he will discharge me at 2:00 tomorrow. We should get back home around 3:00. Will you be okay with Jojo until then? If this is no good, call me and I will try to find someone to watch her. Thank you so much."

Three o'clock tomorrow? What was I going to do with her until then? That was practically a whole other day. I decided to delay that panicky thought until the morning.

The next two were from Chaz.

"Hey, Simone. I think I figured out what I did. Was it the things I said about your father? It was presumptuous of me to talk about that. I apologize." There was a pause. "Was that it? Or was it because you had to climb down the fire escape in the rain? Are you there?" A heavy sigh. "Okay. I'll keep thinking on it. Bye."

He sounded tired in his second message. "Is it the blog thing? I called Donna in San Francisco and she said something about cyber stalking. Is that it? I didn't mean to stalk you or anything. Are you there?" Static silence. "Man, this is really tough over the phone. I'll talk to you tomorrow. Goodnight, Simone." Click.

A high voice from the sofa piped up. "Why is Mr. Chaz a celery stalker?"

"Never mind, Jojo. Go to sleep."

I tried to do the same.

Chapter Twenty-Three

We faced off at the kitchen table after Monday morning eggs and toast. The monotonous tick of the clock proclaimed it a few minutes after nine.

"So what do you want to do until Mommy comes home?"

"Go find the treasure."

"Treasure?"

"The treasure where the snake was."

I recalled the lovely cliff where we found a rattlesnake and lost Donna. "There is no treasure honey. Mr. Chaz just meant it's sort of a natural treasure, like a real nice cactus or pile of rocks."

"Let's go dig it up. I know where there's a shovel."

This logic business wasn't getting me anywhere. "We can't, Jo."

"Why?"

"Ummm, the snake is probably still mad about the umbrella thing. He probably got laughed at by all his snake friends."

"Oh." Her eyes squinched up in thought. "Do you think he would bite me?"

"Yes."

"I could bring my umbrella. I could use it like Mr. Chaz did."

"Not today, Jojo."

We lapsed into silence again. "How about some t.v.? What do you like to watch?"

"Mommy doesn't let me watch t.v. She says it makes people dumb."

Another Mommy rule. Like not eating hot fudge sundaes for dinner. Well she'd been right on with that one so I grudgingly decided Anna might have a point about the t.v. too. A light bulb went off. "How about I paint your nails? I have three different colors in my bag. Girls like to have their nails done."

"No. I like mine plain."

"Hmmm." I was hit by another stroke of genius, or was it desperation? "Do you want to help me clean out my purse?"

She shook her head.

We sank back into deep quiet. I could not figure out a single thing to talk to the child about. It was like trying to communicate with a space alien. I just did not speak preschool.

"I want Mommy." There was a dangerous catch in her voice. She sighed and put her head down on the table.

Panic descended on me. It was hard enough having a preschooler around, let alone a crying preschooler. I walked to the window and scanned the grounds. My eyes came to rest on the shed. I thought about another grown up, from a long time ago, who found a way to connect with his little girl.

"Jojo," I said over my shoulder, "did your Mommy ever make a rule about motorcycles?"

"I don't think so."

I turned around to face her. "Have I got an idea for you."

***

Once I moved the lawnmower, the rusted rake and elbowed aside a plastic Santa Claus, the bike rolled right out of the shed. I filled the tank with gas from a container I found with the lawnmower. We got a bucket and sponges and washed it until it shone.

We stood back to admire the black and silver surfaces of the XR75 mini. The sun dazzled metal made us both squint.

"What do you think?" I asked.

"It's really shiny. What are we gonna to do with it?"

I thought about my father. In my memory, he stood there on the shoulder of the road, watching me ride, his face a mixture of uncertainty and pride. "Jojo, we're going to ride it."

"We are?"

I nodded.

Her eyes were round as ping pong balls as I strapped on her helmet. Then I climbed onto the small seat and scootched forward so she could squeeze in behind.

"You need to hold on tight around my waist." I kick started the engine. As the motor throbbed to life, Jojo's arms cinched around my ribs in a tight hug.

"Are you scared Jojo?"

"Yes, Mrs. Peevey."

"Do you want to get off?"

"No, ma'am."

We did a few slow circles around the shed. Then I guided the bike around the entire perimeter of the park. Under the shade of a cottonwood I craned my neck around. "How are you doing back there? Having fun?"

She nodded, her face tiny in the sturdy helmet. "Can we go faster?"

"You bet. Just hold on tight."

I did a couple of faster loops until I heard her laughter over the engine noise.

"Are you ready to go for a real drive now?"

"Yes, Mrs. Peevey," she yelled.

It was a five-mile drive to the nearest rest stop. Jojo squealed on and off the entire trip. Though the sound was shrill in my ear, I didn't mind. She laughed and gasped and hollered, just like I did my first time on a bike. After fifteen minutes or so I eased off the road and cut the motor. She hopped down and we unstrapped her helmet. Her brown eyes sparkled. "My brothers never rode a motorcycle. You won't take them for a ride, will you?"

"No way. This is just for you and me, girlfriend."

She wiggled around in a happy dance. "I rode a motorcycle. I rode a motorcycle."

We stopped at the potty and then drank cool sodas from the vending machine. The day was approaching scorching. "Do you want to go back now?"

She emitted a giant belch. "No. Can we go to find the treasure?"

"No treasure, Jo. But we can ride for a few more miles before it's time to go home."

"Can I drive the bike?"

"Do you have a license?"

She frowned. "I don't think so."

"Then you'd better leave the driving to me."

I kept off the main highway, choosing instead the small back roads that wandered by ramshackle houses and the occasional gas station. We stopped at a store called Top Togs. Jojo picked out a pants and a shirt in a fetching shade of green to replace the clothes we'd left on the side of the road. I threw in a cool pair of bumblebee sunglasses just for fun. After our fashion adventure we continued on a few more miles.

When we got to Snap, we turned around. I flashed on the guy Chaz told me about who said there were giants in the area. I made a mental note to tell Jojo the crazy story when we got back. On second thought, she might demand that I take her to see the imaginary giants. It was hard enough diverting her from her treasure hunt fever.

Though the air was habanero hot, we drove as fast as I dared, letting the wind whip against our flushed cheeks. At times, we both squealed from the pure joy of it. When we slowed for the last turn before the Ruddy Duck, Jojo launched into a rousing chorus of Ringo was his name-o. I joined in at the top of my lungs.

We crunched up the driveway to find a crowd of people staring at us with open mouths. First was Anna, cradling baby Mateo. Jaime stood next to her with a suitcase in his hand. Then there was big brother Enrique whose eyes threatened to jump out of his sockets.

"Miss Greevey?" Anna called out. "Is that you? Jojo! Have you been riding with Miss Greevey?" She patted the baby on the back.

Busted. I'd meant to have the kid safely home by the time her parents arrived. "We only went on the back roads, and very slowly. I pulled over anytime there were other cars. It was very safe."

Anna stared at me for a moment. Jojo ran up to her and enveloped her in a giant hug. "I rode with Miss Peevey. We got sodas and new sunglasses." She cast a look at her brother. "I rode a motorcycle," she said with a sly grin.

Anna and Jaime took another moment to reconnoiter before they both laughed.

I sagged in relief.

"Say thank you to Miss Greevey, Jo," said her father.

She ran over and laid a hug on me too. "Thank you. Maybe we can ride to get some treasure later."

We chatted for a moment. Anna looked happy but her face was lined with fatigue. Mateo began to wail. The sound was surprisingly loud for a pair of lungs that had only recently been activated.

Anna put the noisy load to her shoulder. "I'd better get him inside. Thank you again, Simone. I'll talk to you soon."

Jaime added his thanks and they left.

That's when I noticed the other person standing against the shaded wall of the office trailer, a person dressed in the khaki drab of a park ranger.

Chaz shoved his hands into his pockets and walked over to me.

"Wow," he said.

"Is that all you've got to say for yourself?"

"No, that's all I've got to say for you. Jojo looks like she just won the lottery."

"She had a good time, I think."

"I'll bet."

The silence stretched out. Chaz started to say something and then stopped. The turmoil on his face was clear. He wiped the sweat off his forehead.

My head began to pound under the weight of all that solar energy. "I'm too hot to stay out here. My synapses are liquefying."

He nodded. "Mine too."

"So let's go inside and I will expound on all the ways you are a louse."

"Can I have a soda while you expound?"

"No, but maybe I'll get you some water. No ice, you understand, room temperature only."

"Yes, ma'am."

We settled into chairs at the kitchen table. I supplied Chaz with a glass of tepid water, no ice. I opened a diet root beer for myself.

"How was the hike?" I asked. "Did you lose anyone to snakes or scorpions?"

"No. One guy had an allergic reaction to nuts in his granola bar. Broke out in hives all over. Fortunately it was a mild allergy. That was about the worst of the damage."

"Good. Wouldn't want anyone to have an up close and personal with a rattlesnake. The one I met was a smidge antisocial."

"Yeah." He raked a finger through the hair which hung loose around his face. The park ranger uniform he wore was remarkably clean for a guy who had spent the night in the desert. Judging from the dark smudges under his eyes, he hadn't gotten much sleep.

The silence stretched into the awkward zone.

"Do you have to do another shift at the park?"

"In a couple of hours. I signed up for overtime this month. I'm on a lunch break right now."

"And you drove all the way back here? Why?"

His eyes rounded in exasperation. "Because of you. I did something to hurt you and I'm trying to fix it."

I busied myself with my soda, to cover any nervous twiddling.

"Well? You can't keep quiet forever. It was the blog thing wasn't it?"

The words exploded like popcorn from a popper. "You snuck onto my blog and tricked me into thinking you were my fiancé."

His jaw dropped. "You thought I was your fiancé? How did I do that?"

"Because, Mr. Park Ranger, his initials are D.F."

Chaz slumped in his chair. "Oh man. I just used D.F. because that's my nickname."

"Desert Fox. I know that now." I refrained from adding "you big toad."

"Unbelievable." He shook his head. "Who would have guessed D.F. was the initials of your ex? And you thought my blogs were from him? The guy who dumped, er, broke up with you?"

"Yes." There was ice in my tone. Then it melted. "Well sort of. Doug doesn't have the same level of cognitive function that you do."

He half smiled. "Cognitive function? Does that mean I'm an intellectual?"

"No. It's just that you think of different things than he does."

"I'm sure he's a swell guy." He drained his glass of water. "Simone, I didn't think joining in the blog was a bad thing, honestly. I remembered you saying you worked for Rock Your World and I looked it up on the web. Stella told me about the Brandi blog so I started reading it."

"And?"

"And, I didn't understand any of that stuff about exfoliating and mascara wands. I certainly don't want to know what a Brazilian wax is. I just wanted to know what you thought about things."

"Why?"

"Because." He lowered his gaze to the table and dropped his volume. "You fascinate me."

I sucked the soda down the wrong pipe. I gasped in between coughs. "I do?"

"Yes, you do. You are courageous, temperamental, witty and totally in denial about yourself."

"I am not in denial about myself. Oh wait, that sounded like a denial. Scratch that."

He laughed. "You see? You imagine yourself to be this fashion plate city girl, with a perfect grasp of what's important. But inside you're a ferociously loyal woman who stepped in to run a dumpy trailer park for her aunt and wore a duck costume in August."

"It was a chicken costume and I'll thank you not to mention it again."

"And you love bikes. It doesn't fit in with your mental picture of yourself, does it? Biker chick doesn't work for you."

"Let's not get off track here, buster. You should have asked me about myself, not snuck onto my blog and tried to ferret out information." I whacked my soda can on the table for emphasis. A stream of liquid spewed out the top and splashed Chaz in the face.

He wiped the root beer out of his eye. "Do I look like a ferret to you?"

He didn't. There was nothing ferret-like about Chaz Tagliola. Bullish maybe, but not ferret. "You were sneaky."

"You're right." He sighed. "But not because I wanted to trick you. Because I wanted to know you, and I didn't think you would let me."

I felt a pang deep inside. The last of the anger trailed away. "I probably wouldn't have."

Chaz reached for my hand across the table. "I'm sorry, Simone. I am a moron when it comes to women. It was stupid of me to join in the blog."

I sighed. "No it wasn't. As Donna reminds me, that's what the blog is for, to connect Christians, not just Christians with pedicure dilemmas."

He squeezed my fingers in his massive hand. A tiny beep from his watch made him pull away. "I've gotta get back to the park. I have a cactus club coming at 5:00. They can get prickly if you keep them waiting."

"I believe it." I walked him to the door.

He stopped and turned back to me. The heat from outside barreled in the open doorway, blasting us both. "So, am I still a louse?"

"Probably."

"Well would you consider an apology kiss from this louse?"

"Probably."

His lips met mine. After a few seconds, my insides were as melted as my outsides.

Chapter Twenty-Four

The giants were chasing me in my dream. They looked like enormous Twinkies with spongy pectoral muscles. The faster I ran, the closer they got. One more minute and my goose was cooked. When the hand touched my shoulder I screamed.

My aunt fell off the bed and onto the floor. "Ack. You scared me."

I sat up with a jerk. "Aunt Stella. Is that you?" I looked around for giants, figuring they might have the ability to mimic my aunt's voice.

It was really her. She sat on the bed again, thinner, and looking exhausted, but not a Fig Newton of my imagination. With a shriek I threw my arms around her shoulders and she returned the squeeze.

I wiped away my tears of joy. "I missed you so much. Why do you smell like garlic?"

"Bulgarians appreciate their garlic. I think it might still be leaking out of my pores." She held me at arm's length. "Simone, are you okay?"

"It's been quite eventful around here but I'm fine. Where's Uncle Bud?"

"Looking for food."

A peevish tone crept into my voice. "What happened? I thought you were going on an errand and you call me from Bulgaria."

"Oh honey, I'm so sorry. I never in a million years imagined it would take so long to fetch your uncle. Why don't you get dressed and join us for breakfast. I'll try to explain everything." She kissed me again. "I uh, noticed the note from the bank on the table. I took it, just so you know."

There was a glimmer of fear in her eyes that I hadn't seen before. I wanted more than anything to soothe that frightened look away. I squeezed her hand. "It'll be all right, Aunt Stella. We'll figure something out. I know it."

She nodded. "Come over for breakfast. Bud can't wait to lay eyes on you. See you in a few minutes." The door closed softly behind her.

***

Uncle Bud filled up the entire space in the tiny kitchen trailer. He hadn't lost any weight during his overseas adventure that I could tell. The Bulgarian prison system hadn't even made a dent. A "Cookin' With Gas" apron strained to make it all the way around his waist.

His voice boomed. "Simone! Come here, sweetie face." He wrapped me in a giant hug. "I haven't seen you in ages. How are you? Let me look at you. What a beauty. You were right, Stella. She turned into a real angel. Hard to believe you were a scrappy little kid the last time you were here."

"Hi, Uncle Bud. I'm so glad you're home." I removed a sliver of onion skin from his straggly hair.

"You and me both. What a time we've had of it trying to get back here." He took a moment to swirl a spatula around the eggs he was cooking. In another pan was a pile of white cubes, sizzling with garlic, parsley and peppers.

"What are you cooking?"

"Kyopulo. At least, I think that's what it is. Eggplant mostly. Those Bulgarians know how to eat. You've gotta try some bob chorba some time. Bean soup with vinegar and chili. Smells kinda suspect, but let me tell you..." he kissed his fingertips before working the spatula again. "You need to eat, my lass. Don't they have food in San Francisco? You're skinny as a pick."

I laughed and joined Aunt Stella who handed me coffee at the kitchen table.

She stirred her coffee with a fork. "How did things go with the Doves?"

"Pretty good. They're great kids. I think Le Roy was happy to see them go, but I sort of miss them. They'll be back for the big fiesta tomorrow though. Did Anna tell you about that?"

She nodded. "And she also told me you and Chaz delivered her baby."

I nodded and sipped. "Word travels fast in the desert."

"Amazing."

"You're telling me. That's not an experience I'll soon forget."

"Jojo said something about you smashing a cake on Chaz."

My cheeks warmed. "Oh, well, er, that was sort of a misunderstanding. We made up." I thought about the kiss the night before and my cheeks heated up even more.

"She also told me you drove her on the motorcycle."

I tried to read her face. "Only on the side roads. Very slow. Very safe."

"I'm just glad that you took out your bike again. I think your dad would be proud."

The coffee burned my throat as I gulped. "You do?"

"I do. He loved nothing better than being able to watch you ride." She covered my hand with hers.

Uncle Bud slid plates in front of us piled high with scrambled eggs and the vegetable concoction. We munched for a few minutes. Though I'm more of a yogurt for breakfast kind of person, the kyopulo wasn't half bad. It was definitely a nice change from Twirly Roni."Tell me about your trip."

Uncle Bud waved his knife in excitement. "It was amazing. The people there are so courageous. Imagine, risking imprisonment and worse to spread the Gospel."

"Hard to believe, compared to what we have here," Stella added. "Those poor folks have lived with communism for so long that their hearts are hardened. They desperately need some discipleship. There's a small group willing to put their freedom on the line to minister to the others."

"How did you get thrown in jail, Uncle Bud?"

"I was with a group of young ministers who were trying to plant a church. We were at a small coffee house, talking to a bunch of young folks. All of a sudden soldiers came barreling in and off we went to the big house." He shook his head. "The jailers were quite nice actually. I think they might have come around if I had more time."

"I'm sure they would have honey, but we were needed back here." She wiped her mouth on a paper napkin. "I went to the jail daily and spoke to just about everyone in the penal system. None of them was interested in letting him go. It seems they were going to make an example of him to discourage other missionaries. I even tried bribery."

"Did that work?"

"No. They took the money, thanked me very nicely and sent me away."

"So what made them let him go?"

Uncle Bud's eyebrows zinged up. "The Holy Spirit."

"That, and they couldn't stand one more day of *This Little Light of Mine*. Your uncle sang that song all day and most of the night until the guards couldn't take it anymore. They said it was worse than torture."

He laughed. "For some reason, that was the first song that popped into my head so I started in. Do you remember when I taught you that one, Simone?"

I held up my candle finger. "Don't let Satan blow it out, I'm gonna let it shine."

"That's my girl." His chins wobbled with laughter. "I guess those guys just don't appreciate good music. Let it shine, let it shine, let it shine."

"Good thing they didn't enjoy your singing or you might still be there. I'm sorry we were gone so long, honey. What did you do to entertain the Doves?"

"Chaz did most of it. Hikes and classes and such. The kids loved it. He's a really good teacher."

"Yes, he is. Did you get a chance to know him better? He's an awfully nice young man." Her eyebrows hovered upward, reminding me of Donna's.

"You're right. He really is a good guy." I continued in a rush. "My friend Donna came from San Francisco. She offered me an editor's position at Rock Your World. I'm going to start next week." The thought made the breath catch in my throat.

Aunt Stella smiled, but it did not reach her eyes. Her fingers drummed on the tabletop. "An editor's job? Oh that is wonderful. Of course, we'll miss you terribly, but I know it's what you want."

"Yes." I watched her nervous fingers.

"So, I don't suppose hordes of people booked trailers while we were gone?"

"No, I'm afraid not. The Doves paid their bill before they left." I wished I had better news, but for the life of me I couldn't think of any reason why people would come to Seepwillow to stay in World War II era trailers while keeping an eye out for scorpions.

"It doesn't really matter. Even if we rented out all the trailers this month we'd face the same problem the next." Her eyes misted over.

My heart squeezed itself into a blob of pity. With her head turned away, her face was transformed into a sad little girl's, much like my mother's childhood pictures. A thought struck me. I don't know why I didn't think of it before. "You know, I'll bet Mother would give you a loan to payoff the bank."

My aunt exchanged a look with her husband. "Your mother doesn't exactly approve of my business ventures," Stella said.

"Maybe not. But you're her sister, and I think she would help." At least, I hoped she would. Deep down I knew she loved her sister even though they were from different galaxies.

"You're probably right. But it would only delay the problem. The loan would have to be repaid to your mom and we just don't seem to be able to attract customers to the Ruddy Duck. I guess most people don't love the desert as much as we do."

"Oh, Aunt Stella. Just think about the loan thing. That will buy us more time to figure things out. There's got to be a way. We'll find it." I got up from the table and hugged her from behind.

Uncle Bud smiled. "That's what I've been saying. I'm going to lay off the mission trips until after we get this thing settled. We'll put our minds to it and sure as Bob's your uncle, we'll have a solution. You'll see."

She nodded and wiped her eyes with the napkin. "I guess I hoped some miracle would happen while we were gone. Silly, I know. I think I need to face the fact that we are going to lose this place."

I squeezed her again. "No, no. Don't lose heart."

"The worst part is we planned with our Bulgarian friends that they would come and stay next summer. We were going to have a Bible study camp for the ministers and teens and our Loving Doves. Wouldn't that have been great? I can see it in my mind's eye. Two groups from opposite ends of the world meeting here to experience God's word."

"It's a fantastic idea Stella." Uncle Bud thumped his glass on the table. "We'll come up with a way to make it work."

Stella carried the dishes to the sink. "You're right. I don't know why I'm such a gloomy Gus today. Must be jet lag. Or maybe it's the thought of you leaving, Sisi."

"I'll only be an e-mail away. Promise you'll let me teach you how to use the internet before I go."

She laughed. "I'm not sure this old dog can learn that new trick, but I'll try."

"Me too. Is it anything like the telegraph system? I used to know a thing or two about that." Uncle Bud set to work on the dishes.

This was going to be harder than I thought.

Stella joined Bud at the sink.

"Speaking of computers, I'll go check the website and see if there are any more bookings. Those ads have had more time to reach people by now." It was a futile gesture, but at least it made me feel like I was doing something.

"Okay, honey. I think we're going to take a little nap anyway."

The mid morning air hit me like a backhanded slap. Ridiculous. The extreme temperature still caught me by surprise. It was hard to break the habit of reaching for a sweater before I headed out the door. In San Francisco, every season was sweater season.

There was no sign of Chaz and his bike. He was probably at the park again. I wished I could talk to him about the whole bank problem. I sat on the porch step for a moment, letting the sun bore into me. Maybe it could blast away my current set of fifty-three thousand worries. I had never seen my aunt so down in the dumps, but the letter from the bank sucked the joy out of her, at least for the moment. Just thinking about the Ruddy Duck quacking its way into oblivion made a lancing pain my heart.

I knew my mother had the money and I was pretty sure she would loan it, in spite of her strained relationship with her sister. On the other hand, I could also understand Stella and Bud's unwillingness to replace one debt with another. They wanted to stand on their own two feet, or was it flippers?

A movement caught my eye. I watched a roadrunner pelt across the landscape. He stopped in the tangle of scrub near the tree before he streaked away. I wandered over to the clump of dry grass, carefully lifting the orange tape that Chaz posted to keep unwary feet from trampling his spiked baby.

After much hunting, I found it: the tiny finger sized saguaro, covered with a fuzz of miniature spines. I crouched down to look. The term patient perennial certainly described this guy. A whole year of growth and the thing was a whopping one quarter inch tall. After another fifteen years, it might hope to top a foot.

I put a finger very gently on its prickly top. "Hello, Mr. Cactus. I hope there's someone here to see you in fifteen years. If you can struggle through this crazy desert climate, you definitely deserve to live."

Sweat poured into my eyes, a good signal that it was time to head for air conditioning and cold water. The thought that followed me back to the trailer unsettled me as much as the looming debt. I was returning home in a few days. Not that I was going to miss the heat and the odd collection of deadly wildlife, mind you. I was giddy at the thought of cool foggy mornings and cups of steaming latte in my freshly manicured fingers. It was the people I would miss, one person in particular.

To distract myself from uncomfortable thoughts I revved up the old computer and cracked open a bottle of water. The last batch of blogs popped up.

Hey Brandi. My friend has come to her senses and called off the engagement to icky man. I didn't have to say a word, thank goodness. Now I just listen and pray with her. She doesn't see it yet, but God is definitely saving her from a big Humpty Dumpty fall. -- Cherry B.

That's great Cherry. Brace yourself for my big news! I'm back together with Ryan. He took me to the Japanese Tea Gardens. That's where we first met. He gave me a beautiful gold bracelet with a little teapot. He asked me to forgive him and said he can't live without me. Couldn't you just die? -- Galpal Glenda

This whole discussion depresses me. I wonder if grad school was the right choice. I'm going to miss Charlie so much. How do I know if I am following God's plan for me? Maybe I'm just following my plan for me. God's plan? My plan? How do you tell the difference? Brandi? Are you out there? Back from the desert yet? I need some advice. -- Sister Sue

I typed an entry.

Yes, I'm here. Still in the desert, though not for much longer. How do you know if you're following God's plan? Because if you aren't, he'll close the door and open a new one for you.

I thought with a jolt that God had certainly closed my marriage-with-Doug door. Slammed it, was a better term. For some reason that thought didn't summon tears anymore. I still had a weak urge to mash him, but it was more anger than hurt. Too bad that sometimes you get your fingers pinched when God closed the door. I resumed typing.

Go try out the grad school thing. Give it your best shot, Sister.

Whatever your hands find to do, do it with all your might. Ecclesiastes 9:1

-- Brandi

Restlessness drove me from the computer into the fridge. Not much there but yogurt and olives. I stuck a fork in the olive jar and slurped them down, one by one. What had my hands found to do in the desert? Lead a group of teens. Take care of a little girl and her mother. Meet a new man who challenged my beliefs about myself. But these things would be memory in another week. I was going home. Back to San Francisco, where I belonged.

Six olives later, I drove my mind back to the problem my hands had not been able to fix. Even with the new website, people were not interested in coming to the Ruddy Duck Trailer Park. The smoldering desert just didn't scream vacation destination. There was no grand canyon to see, no world class golf courses or spas. Not even a movie theater to escape the heat. Try as I might, I could not figure out a way to change that.

Maybe there wasn't a way. Maybe God was closing the door on the Ruddy Duck so Aunt Stella would move on to something new. It would hurt her, but she would survive, with God's help.

I sat back down at the computer.

The hard thing is accepting when God closes a door, that it's for our

own good. I met a cactus recently. A good sort of plant, but very small. He will stand there and hold on through ferocious winds and searing drought. Why? Because that is the life that God gave him. In the wake of summer rains, he will grow and flower. Why? Because that is the life that God gave him. If the lightning strikes and sears his branches, he will funnel his remaining spirit into the parts that are not blighted and he will survive. Why? Because life is good and precious and he will cling to the one that God gave him.

My father died when I was small. I wanted him to love me the way other fathers loved their kids. He didn't, but he did love me in his own way. I miss him, but I am not angry at him anymore. Why? Because that is the life that God gave him and I am thankful that I was part of it for a while. -- Brandi

I moved the mouse to the send arrow and hesitated. This was not the typical Brandi blog. Not sarcastic. Not witty. Not hip. It was something new.

I took a breath and clicked my message into cyberspace.

***

Later that afternoon I checked on my relatives. They were still napping. This sounded like a stroke of brilliance to me. I lay down on the bed when a familiar knockity knock sounded on my door.

I let Jojo in. "Hi, honey. How are you getting along with your new brother?"

"He's not a dog."

"Well that's true. He's better than a dog."

"He won't fetch."

"Hmmm. Maybe he will someday with the proper training."

She put her cheek on the table. "Dogs are better. My aunties and uncles are coming tomorrow. They're bringing a piñata for me and Peaches."

"That's great. A piñata will be fun, won't it?"

Her nose wrinkled. "There should be two pinatas. Peaches can have his own. It's my birthday. But Mama said it's too expensive and we have to share."

"Well Mateo is too little to eat the piñata candy anyway, isn't he?" She was unswayed by my logic.

"It's my piñata. I want it to be my birthday."

I patted her on the hand. "It's hard to share."

Big tears welled up and spilled on the table. "I don't want another brother."

I continued to pat.

She sat up suddenly. "Can I live with you?"

"Me? Oh I don't think so. Your Mommy would miss you, and Daddy would too."

"No they wouldn't. They've got Peaches now."

"But I'm leaving, Jo. I'm going back to San Francisco in a few days."

"Can I come?"

"I don't think so."

"Why not?"

I did some quick mental calisthenics. "Because I don't have a car seat."

"Oh. Okay."

The sound of stuttering water made us both look out the window.

"It's Mr. Chaz." She jumped up and down, shaking the whole trailer. "He made the sprinklers work. I'm going to get my bathing suit." The door slammed open as she catapulted out.

Chaz looked up from his fiddling. Water dripped from his hair and spattered his worn tee shirt. He waved a wrench and grinned.

I waved back. "God bless you, Mr. Chaz."

***

Jojo's mother slathered her with a liberal coat of sunscreen. She waved to me as the child streaked to the feeble sprinklers. It was late afternoon so the sun was scorching us from low in the sky.

Jojo jumped back and forth in front of the water streams until Chaz and I were wet too. We sat down in the shade to watch her.

"How's she doing with the new baby thing?"

"She wanted a dog."

"Uh huh. Mateo is falling short, I take it?"

"Yes. He's terrible at fetching and he's horning in on her piñata. All that and he can't even hold his head up yet. Wait until he can walk. She asked me to take her to San Francisco with me when I leave."

Chaz looked sideways at me. "When are you heading out?"

I swallowed. "In a few days."

He stayed silent. "I wish..."

He was interrupted by the sound of something being dragged across the ground. Mr. Singh staggered along, hauling a box up the path to his trailer.

Chaz sprang to his feet and ran to the man. He grabbed a cardboard flap. "Here, let me give you a hand with that, Mr. Singh."

"No." He held out a hand, pushing Chaz away. "I don't need help."

"Are you sure? That looks heavy."

"No. No help." He continued to lug the box up the steps. His door closed with a bang.

I suppressed a shudder. "Not a very friendly guy."

"Yeah." Chaz stared at the closed trailer. "Weird though."

"What's weird?"

He shook his head. "Oh never mind. That can't be right."

"Never mind what?"

"Nothing. I just thought I saw...I'm probably mistaken."

"What? What did you think you saw?"

His brows furrowed. "I'm sure I'm wrong, but I thought I saw a pencil sketch in the box. And it looked just like Jojo."

Chapter Twenty-Five

The aunties arrived on Wednesday, a good six of them in all. They were followed by a trail of uncles, a gaggle of cousins and a collection of family friends. Someone even schlepped along a fat dog, much to Jojo's delight. The Escobar summer camp siblings returned on fiesta day, too. I sipped my morning coffee and watched the procession from my trailer. Though I knew Anna was probably exhausted, her face was wreathed in smiles as she greeted each person with a shower of hugs and kisses.

Aunt Stella and Uncle Bud emerged from their trailers to mingle. It was nice, actually. The park had been so quiet since the doves left. Now that it was filled with noise and laughter, everything seemed all right. Maybe my aunt would be able to forget the debt that hung over her head and enjoy herself. I was eager to join in the stream of cheerful people.

After a quick shower, I hopped into a tank top and denim shorts and joined the melee. Anna hurried over to introduce me to the hordes. "Simone, I want you to meet my family. Everyone, this is the woman who delivered Mateo and took care of Jojo." She began the ponderous round of introductions.

I had no hope of remembering the string of names so I smiled and nodded. My hands were shaken and my cheeks kissed until I felt like a celebrity. A woman everyone called Auntie Shoo Shoo pressed a cold soda into my hand and offered me chips and salsa. I took one to be polite, scooping up some of the blood red tomato concoction. It was the best salsa ever to cross my tongue. It required serious restraint not to ask for a spoon.

She smiled. "Anna is a fine cook, no?"

"She sure is, but I feel bad that she's going to all this trouble right after having a baby. She should be resting."

Auntie Shoo Shoo laughed until all three chins wobbled. "Feeding people is not work for Anna. She gets her joy that way. She's like our Mama, God rest her soul."

I looked over to the awning which shaded a gaggle of women. Some of the gang drained the corn husks and filled them with tiny spoonfuls of meat. Anna was in the middle, mixing some sort of white glop. Her face was shining with sweat and happiness as the ladies joked and teased. Some of the younger teen girls were taking turns cradling Mateo and cooing to him.

For a moment, the scene filled me with sadness. I had never had any siblings to share my life, or a hands-on mother for that matter. But it was good to be welcomed into this warm rambunctious family. I felt blessed to be a part of their joy.

Jojo tugged at my arm. "Come here, Miss Peevey."

She dragged me over to the tree where a pink and blue piñata hung. "It's my birthday piñata." Her little eyes shone with excitement. A pile of presents sat nearby, many of them wrapped in baby paper. She picked up an enormous blue package. "Does it say my name, Miss Peevey? I bet it's a dog."

I consulted the shiny card. "I'm sorry, honey. It has Mateo's name on the tag."

Her face crumpled. "But it's the biggest one."

"There are lots of others with your name. Look." I picked up a frilly yellow gift bag and shook it. "This one is for you. What do you think it is?"

"I don't care. I hate Peaches." She burst into tears and ran off.

I wondered if dogs ever experienced sibling rivalry. Did they measure the size of the milk bones to see who was the favorite? Maybe once Jojo showed Mateo who was the alpha kid things would be better. I had just started after her when a van pulled up.

The Loving Doves piled out, followed by a sweaty Pastor Stan.

"Hello, hello. We're back everyone. Prepare for the invasion." In a moment he was swallowed up in a sea of aunties and uncles. They immediately took him to a shady chair and plied him with food and drink. Tanya and Allyson ran over and gave me a hug.

Tanya's face split into a wide grin. "Hi, Miss Greevey. Your sunburn looks much better. How did you survive the last few days without us?"

"I barely managed. I almost commandeered a vehicle to come pick you all up again. Allyson, how are things going?"

She pushed her hair into a pile and secured it with an elastic band. "Awesome, Miss Greevey. I've got a new boyfriend and he's way better than Jake. We're going bowling tonight."

I laughed. "Glad to hear it."

Tanya's eyes scanned the crowd. "Where's Jojo?"

"That's what I'd like to find out. She's not doing too well with this new baby brother thing. Do you think you could keep an eye out for her?"

"Sure. I'll tell the others too." The girls walked over to Jack who was retrieving a jar of marshmallow fluff from his backpack. I settled in the shade of the trailer next to Aunt Stella. We quietly sipped glasses of tea.

"Are you looking forward to going back to San Francisco, honey?"

Her question startled me. Was I looking forward to starting my new job? Certainly, but how about taking up my old life where I had left it? Not so sure about that one. The thought of explaining to everyone about the demise of the Doug-Simone union pained me, though his wedding to Rachel would probably be a big tip off that we weren't a couple anymore. Leaving behind the freedom and, dare I say it, joy I had found in Seepwillow would be painful. "I'll be glad to get out of the blazing heat but this place kind of grows on you."

She laughed. "Yes it does."

"You know, I've been thinking." I stopped to sip before I verbalized the nutty thought that had been poking at me. "I was sort of muddling through maybe getting myself a new bike and riding down here a couple times a month to see you and keep up with your computer issues and all that."

"Really?" She reached over and threw an arm around my shoulders. "I'm so glad. We would love to see you more often and there's nothing I like better than watching you ride. It's like all the world has been lifted off your shoulders and you've found your joy again."

"That's what it feels like to me, too." Why had it taken me so long to discover that?

Her face clouded over. "I just wonder if we'll still have a place here for you to visit."

It was my turn to put an arm around her. "Don't give up on the old duck. We'll find a way. God will help us, I know it."

Tanya trotted up with Raul who carried a mountainous plate of chips, salsa, and watermelon slices.

"I can't find Jojo, Miss Greevey." Tanya's brows pulled together. "But her brother says she hides all the time when she doesn't get her way."

"I'll have to try that next time things don't go the way I want them to."

Raul gave me a sly look. "Or you could just smash a cake in someone's face."

Tanya elbowed him.

The weather felt suddenly warmer. "I can't imagine what you're talking about, Raul."

Anna saved me any further embarrassment. She walked over to join us in the shade. "The tamales will be ready soon. I thought you would like to hold Mateo, maybe?"

"I'd love to." I took the baby in my arms. One of Anna's many sisters called to her. "I'll be right back." She hurried away.

Aunt Stella and I peered at the bundle of baby. Mateo Peaches Simon Escobar was asleep. His eyes were closed and his tiny hands clasped under his chin. He smelled of baby powder. My heart melted with an audible sloshing sound.

"He's so cute, just like a doll" Tanya touched his dimpled hand. "What's his name?"

"Mateo Simon. He's named after me." I could not keep the note of pride out of my voice.

Stella laughed. "Wait until he's old enough to ride on your bike. You'll be his favorite auntie for sure."

"I'll have some stiff competition." I gazed down at the perfect face. "You turned out pretty good for a guy who was born on a trailer floor." His pouty lips puckered and a frown arched his delicate brow. I could not tear my eyes from the baby. Then a strange rumbly noise began to emanate from the angel's nether regions.

Tanya and I looked at each other. The noises increased in volume.

"Uh, Anna?" I called.

She looked up from her place by the tortillas.

"Something is happening south of the equator."

She looked confused. I pointed at the diaper zone.

A series of indelicate explosions followed the rumbles. I was surprised the blanket didn't inflate with all the gaseous emissions. Mateo's eyes popped open and he began to cry. I held the precious bundle away from me. Too late, a wet spot darkened my lap. Man, these babies were rough on shorts.

By this point, Raul was collapsed to the ground in hysterics. Apparently bowel activities were amusing to the junior high school male population. I handed the baby to an apologetic Anna and went to change my clothes. Again.

On my way back to the party, my feet took me on a field trip. I meandered along trying to stick to the shelter of the sparse trees. In the distance the cliff dropped away into a pile of boulders and molten sand. A flicker of shadow danced into my peripheral vision and then disappeared. One of old man Snap's elusive giants, no doubt. A sudden whisper of wind cooled my cheeks. A wall of clouds gathered in the distance. I wished Chaz wasn't at the park until late.

A hand on my back made me jump. "Chaz. I thought you were working."

I hugged him.

He held onto me until I wriggled my way out of his embrace.

"I traded with a guy so I could come to the big bash. It's your last hurrah here in Seepwillow, isn't it?"

The glimmer of sadness in his eyes made me uncomfortable and pleased at the same time. "I guess so."

"Why aren't you back at the party?"

"I just have this uneasy feeling. Jojo kind of lost it and ran off. I'm worried about her." The wind picked up. "Do you think it's going to rain?"

He squinted up at the clouds. "I wouldn't be surprised. I'm sure Jojo is hiding in a trailer or something. She does that when she's mad."

"So I've been told." The panorama was beautiful as the clouds made the colors shift and blend. "Chaz, what's going to happen to the saguaro if my aunt loses the property?"

He bent and moved the grass aside. The tiny plant was still there, snuggled in its grassy bed. "I don't know. I would hope the new owners would protect it, but there is no guarantee." He straightened. "Do you really think Stella is going to lose the place?"

I told him about the fifty-three-thousand-dollar payment. "I don't see how the picture is going to change anytime soon."

He sighed. "Yet another reason I wish my bike company hadn't gone up in smoke. I could have helped out, maybe. I would have paid rent all this time, that's for sure."

A hawk circled the air far below the patchwork of clouds and then dove into the canyon. I reached down and took his calloused hand. "You've done all you can for this place. Too bad there isn't a real treasure down there."

"There is. You just can't put it in the bank."

"Tell that to Jojo."

We walked, hand in hand, back to the party.

***

The tamales brought tears to my eyes. Not because they were spicy, but because they were divine. The meat and masa filling was succulent and perfect. I felt like Jack as I piled my plate with as many as I could fit. Someone turned on the music and the crowd ate, sang and laughed. Mateo lay in his bassinet and slept through the whole thing. Fortunately one of the cousins snapped a boatload of pictures to capture the moment.

I found myself briefly next to Jaime. "Mr. Escobar, have you seen Jojo?"

He took a swig of soda. "Her mother told her to go lay down until she could be a nice girl. I think she fell asleep."

I breathed a sigh of relief. "Oh that's good. But she's missing out on a great meal."

He laughed. "Somehow I think there will be plenty of leftovers."

Judging from the piles of tamales, beans and rice and corn on the cob, he was probably right. He went to secure the awning which had come loose in the increasing wind.

Chaz sat next to me with his plate piled high. "This is the best meal I've eaten in a long time."

"What? You don't count our rooftop picnic as a culinary high?"

He grinned and kissed my forehead. "Well the food wasn't four-star but the company was priceless. I'll have to ask Anna to cook the food for our next picnic. Did you find Jojo?"

"Her dad said she's napping."

Raul, Jack and Tanya approached. They sat on the ground on a blanket. In between jokes and jibes, they inhaled bushels of Anna's excellent cooking.

Jack swallowed the wad in his mouth "So will you take us on a bug lighting tonight, Mr. Tagliola? We brought our notebooks and flashlights."

"Oh, I don't know." Chaz shot me a look. "I think it's going to rain and I'm enjoying hanging with Miss Peevey."

"Don't worry about me. Go ahead with your bug lighting. You can tell me all about it when you get back."

"You don't want to come?" There was no teasing in Tanya's question.

I suppressed a shudder. "I'm still recovering from the last one. You go on. Have fun, kids."

"All right then. We'd better get over there before the storm comes in. We've only got few more hours of calm, I'd guess." Chaz slam dunked his empty plate. "I'll go get my backpack. See you later, Simone."

I wiggled my fingers at him.

The kids hurriedly finished their food and headed after their fearless guide.

The group was still going strong, eating and chatting. Aunt Stella and Uncle Bud were taking turns rocking Mateo's bassinet. I felt the weight of the numerous tamales I had ingested. If I didn't move soon, I would become one with my lawn chair. Easing out of my seat I went for a stroll.

The clouds were thick now, the air oddly humid. I passed LeRoy busy shoveling sand out from under the porch step. Good thing the Loving Doves hadn't spotted him or he'd be sporting another flashlight on his back.

The sun was low and shadows crept along the ground. I rounded the corner to find Jojo sitting on Mr. Singh's front step.

I felt a surge of relief. "Well there you are. I've been looking for you."

Jojo didn't answer. She was still.

Very still.

In fact, she looked completely lifeless.

Chapter Twenty-Six

My stomach muscles clenched. Something about Jojo's posture as she knelt on Mr. Singh's porch seemed unnatural. I stepped closer a few paces. "Jojo?"

She didn't answer.

"Jojo? It's Miss Peevey."

I was two yards away. She should have responded. Though I had the desire to run, fear of knowing slowed my feet to a stagger. The air thickened around me in a humid blanket. "Answer me, Jojo."

Mr. Singh stepped out of his trailer. He blinked. "She cannot answer you."

My brain exploded with images: duct tape, knives, a child's shoe.

"Why not?" My voice was shrill with fear. "What did you do to her?"

He blinked again. His face was a roadmap of crisscrossing wrinkles. Then he took the girl by the shoulders and turned her around. "I did not do anything to her. She can't answer you, because she is a doll."

I found myself staring into the face of an exquisite porcelain doll. She was a replica of Jojo right down to the precocious pout. Even the leather sandals looked just like the pair Jojo often wore. "It's a doll? Did you make it?"

He nodded, taking her from my hands and gently straightening the pinafore dress. "I have been teaching myself. I gather up old dolls people throw away and I sculpt the molds. I study the way the eyes are painted until I figure out how to do it. I thought it would be a good present for Jojo's birthday."

My surprise was complete. The man I had pegged for some kind of maniac had been spending his time making Jojo a present. That's why he wanted to check her birthday on the calendar. And that's why I saw the tiny shoes in his trailer when I returned the knife. And no doubt why Chaz saw a sketch of Jojo in his box. "Mr. Singh, I'm so sorry. I never guessed you would do such a nice thing for Jojo. I misjudged you."

He looked down at the doll, eyes filled with an insurmountable grief. One wrinkled finger traced the delicate porcelain cheek. "She was five, my Rajitka, when she was killed. I wish..." A tear slid down the side of his face. "I wish I had made a doll for her." He cleared his throat and looked at me. "Is Jojo back yet? I would like to give it to her."

"Back? What do you mean?"

"She came by about an hour ago but the doll wasn't ready. I told her to return when she was done."

"Done doing what?"

"Finding the treasure. She said she had to dig it up and bring it back for her Mother."

My heart thudded to a complete stop. "Mr. Singh, was Jojo carrying an umbrella?"

He squeezed his eyes closed in thought. Then he opened them. "Yes, she was."

I thanked Mr. Singh and walked away. Goosebumps pricked my skin and there was a lead ball in the pit of my stomach. Jojo had gone off to the edge of the property to dig up treasure, to the place where a highly disgruntled rattlesnake lived. Who knew what other dangers lurked there.

Then again, maybe she'd changed her mind and gone to find a hidey hole. Thinking about the girl's determined personality it didn't seem likely. Her mental train was not easily derailed. Strains of happy music floated along the ground, punctuated by laughter. Should I go tell the family my suspicions? What if I was wrong? The whole gang would be thrown into a panic for nothing. The party would be ruined.

I looked up at the clouded sky. It would be dark in another hour.

The cliff was about thirty minutes away by foot. I stood there, paralyzed with indecision.

Ricky, one of Jojo's big brothers, walked by carrying a gallon jug of punch.

I ran over to him. "Has everybody left for the bug lighting yet?"

He nodded. "About fifteen minutes ago."

"I need you to do something for me, something very important."

"Sure. What is it?"

"Please go find Chaz and tell him Jojo went to find the treasure and I'm going after her. Did you get all that?"

"Jojo's gone to find treasure and you're going too." His black eyebrow arched. "What treasure?"

"Long story. Can you please find Chaz as quick as you can and give him that message? He'll know what it means."

"Okay." He put the jug down on a porch step and trotted away.

It would take him at least fifteen minutes to catch up to Chaz and the Doves and another half hour for them to make it back to the cliff. As for me, there was only one way I was going to make it to snake country in time to stop Jojo's wild adventure.

I wheeled the bike out of the shed and away from the festivities, after checking to make sure the extra helmet was strapped to the back. When I was far enough away that the sound wouldn't carry, I kick started the motor. If the party goers looked up I knew they would think it very ungracious for a guest of honor to flee the party on a motorbike. I prayed that I'd have a funny story to tell when I got back with Jojo safely in tow.

The air hung thick and heavy as I whipped along. In spite of the clouds, I was slicked with sweat after only a few yards. A bead of water splatted my face as I charged around a bend in the trail. Five minutes later it was raining hard. The drops were the size of cherries. I bore down on the gas as much as I dared on the slick road.

As I approached the spot where Donna freaked out I slowed, frantically searching for signs of Jojo. I pulled over and got off, scanning the ground for footprints. The idiocy of my actions stopped me. Who was I kidding? Even if the kid had stepped in fluorescent paint I wouldn't be able to find footprints in the mucky mess. Not to mention the fact that it was almost dark and I had no detective skills whatsoever.

A bolt of lightning sizzled overhead. I snatched the flashlight that

I'd had the foresight to grab before I began my crazy rescue mission and ducked under a cottonwood, trying to remember my storm safety tips. Were you supposed to shelter under a tree during a lightning strike or did the tree just direct the lightning to your measly hiding place? I had no scouting skills either.

I couldn't hear anything but the roar of the storm. Bits of airborne sand stung my eyes. A sodden branch, pushed by the wind, whacked me on the side of my face like a backhanded slap. That did it. My intellectual ship broke loose from its moorings and began to snap into small pieces. In the space of time it took to get slapped by a tree, I lost my mind.

"This is not..." I shouted as I hopped up and down, "what I am supposed to be doing!" The wind whipped my words around. "I am a CITY person. I do not go out in storms with bugs and cactus to rescue people. I am NOT THAT KIND OF PERSON. You've got it wrong, God. I can't be the person you want me to be."

I jumped and stomped and growled. I threw a vicious punch up at the sky. The momentum knocked me over into a rock strewn puddle. Icy water seeped into the seat of my pants.

Cold water.

On my wedding.

On my promotion.

On my life.

Tears streamed down my cheeks to mingle with the rain water. I felt too defeated even to rise from my puddle.

The moon came out briefly from behind its cloudy earmuffs and the rain slowed. Everything was painted in a silver sheen. From my soggy seat I could see a nearby saguaro silhouetted against the light. Each spine held a drop of water on its tip, glittering like a star. I fixated on the massive cactus.

That silly plant survived, flourished even, in this harsh place. I felt the sudden urge to kick the nasty green thing.

"Well you're just a cactus anyway," I snuffled. "What do you know about life?"

I stared some more at the giant, festooned with a shiny coat of silver. I got the strange sensation that if it had a mouth, the thing would have answered me. "What *do* you know about life?" I whispered.

Chaz's words echoed in my ears.

God doesn't always give you what you want. He gives you what you need.

What did I need?

I wasn't sure. I thought I needed Doug, a wedding, a job, regular visits to the spa and Starbucks, but all those things were all gone, like spring wildflowers and I was still here, surviving, like that mega cactus.

I wasn't at all sure what I needed, but I was beginning to get a clearer picture of what I didn't need.

All the extraneous stuff, the distractions as Chaz would say.

I'd lost a fiancé, and a job and I was still standing. Well, sitting, but alive, anyway. A warmth pressed through my chilled innards, a little spark of something I hadn't felt before. My life was not what I pictured, or even what I wanted, but maybe, just maybe, I'd been given what I needed. Me and the saguaro. We were built to live the life that He gave us.

A weight lifted off my shoulders and flew into the clouds. I turned my face to the rain. "I'm sorry, God. I've been afraid to give you control. I didn't think you'd really give me what I wanted. I forgot that isn't your job."

I felt a wee bit better.

Still scared, mind you. I was a smidge worried that He might have some more spiritual cleansing in mind and I wasn't sure how much more of that I could take. I still longed for those wonderful worldly things like pedicures and facials and lattes with plastic sippy lids. But wanting and needing were two different things.

I took another look at the massive cactus. A little blob of resolve began to form in my gut. I didn't know what I needed, but I knew what God needed from me at the moment. Jojo's life might just depend on it. It was time to get out of my puddle.

I wasn't sure Jojo was down in the gorge, but I knew I had to go find out and fast. I couldn't wait for Chaz to arrive. She could be lying in a pool of blood or being eaten by a rattlesnake with delusions of grandeur. The thought of those needle sharp fangs made me shudder. "Don't panic, Simone. One foot in front of the other, woman."

The rain started up again, splattering down in relentless sheets. I did a slow count to three and dashed from underneath the branches. The edge of the cliff swam in my vision. Plenty of sharp boulders, lots of thankful shrubs and pools of watery gravel but no little girl that I could see.

"Jojo?" My scream sounded very small amidst the howling storm. Though I strained an ear muscle listening, there was no answer. Maybe she wasn't down there. I felt a surge of uncertainty. My foot crunched down on something. It was a lollipop wrapper. Uh oh. That was definitely a Jojo sign.

I screamed her name again. The sound bounced back to me. I took a deep cleansing breath and stepped down over the edge of the cliff into the abyss.

Immediately, my shoes skidded against the gravel and down I went, bottom first into the grit. There went another pair of shorts. A rock poked me in the fanny.

I struggled to my feet and called again. "Jojo? It's Mrs. Peevey. Are you down here?"

Nothing.

I climbed over a boulder. The air smelled of wet soil. I called her name after every painful step. A sound made me freeze. Was that a rattle? I crouched in silence but the noise didn't repeat. I edged around another gargantuan rock and something shot by my leg.

I screamed.

No doubt the lizard would have screamed too if he wasn't so busy trying to get away from me. Then I heard another noise, the ominous sound of many determined rocks moving in unison. I ducked down as low as I could to avoid the shower of stones that came shooting down the path, probably dislodged by the rain. They clattered by, pinging over my head and shoulders. Nothing bigger than a marble came shooting down, fortunately.

Now I was wet, dirty and scratched and headed for a mental breakdown. Who knew how many years that lizard had taken off my life? Maybe the next shower of rocks would be skull crushing size. My only positive thought was that the insects were probably all hunkered down underground in their nice tidy bug bunkers. I eased out from behind the rock and shrieked.

Jojo sat under her umbrella in the shelter of a massive rock over cropping. "Hi, Miss Peevey. It's raining."

I gulped and gasped and swallowed before a word finally squirted out. "Jojo."

"Did you come to help me dig up the treasure?" She pointed to a small shallow that glimmered in the moonlight at her feet. "I started but then it rained. Now it's all filled up with water. Do you think the gold will float?"

I slithered over to her and slung my arm around her shoulders. The conversation in my mind ran along these lines: *You naughty girl. How could you possibly do something so dangerous and worry me half to death? Your mother will be frantic when she knows what you did and by the way how did you ever make it this far without help? And do you have any idea what this rain is doing to my hair?* Instead I squeezed her. "I'm so glad to see you. I was very worried, Jo."

She nestled into the crook of my arm. "Me too. The thunder was kinda scary. Do you have any candy?"

"Not on me, but let's go back now. I'll bet they're getting ready to cut the cake and sing to you. They probably have piles of candy out by now."

"Okay. I'm too cold to dig anymore." She folded her umbrella.

We made it to our feet just as the earth above us gave way. A giant river of rocks and gravel began to slide down the cliff face. I grabbed Jojo and pulled us both behind the boulder, covering her with my arms. There was a crash and rumble that shook the ground. The rock behind our backs vibrated as the debris rained down all around us.

Our screams were drowned out by the awful noise. We held tight in a shivering ball of arms and legs.

Then it was done, leaving behind only the sound of the rain and our gasps.

Jojo's heart hammered against mine. "That was really scary, Miss Peevey."

"Yes it was." I swallowed hard before I peeked out from around the rock. It wasn't good news. The pathway that brought us both down to this precarious place was gone, buried in piles of loose rock. A vein began to throb somewhere in my temple. My cactus courage began to fail me.

"I want to go home." Jojo began to sniffle. Her blotchy face was just visible in the veiled moonlight.

I put my hands on her cold cheeks and looked her square in the eyes. "We will go home Jo, but we're going to have to find another path. I'm going to climb up to the top of the ridge and see if I can find a new way out. You need to wait right here. Can you do that?"

She nodded. "Will you come back?"

I squeezed her cold hands and gave her the flashlight. "I'll come back." I sincerely hoped my body could live up to my bold words.

I steeled myself not to look back at those fear filled eyes as I crept away. Mercifully, the rain slowed again. The clouds broke apart leaving enough of a gap for the full moon to shine through. I picked my way along, headed upward to the outcropping that loomed fifty feet above my head.

"Mr. Rattlesnake," I whispered, "if you're around here somewhere I apologize sincerely for trespassing." Then I added a more important request. "Hey, God. Looks like I got myself into another mess here. Please keep Jojo safe. She's a pain, but I kind of love the little stinker. Help Chaz find her, find us both. You know I have no sense of direction and zero survival skills. I'm going to need some divine intervention here. I am officially putting my life in your hands. Sorry it took me so long. Amen."

The rocks tore at my hands as I climbed. A stumble left my knee scraped and bloody. Inch by laborious inch I made my way to a relatively flat projection of rock. It must have measured seventy feet across, dotted with shrubs and yucca. I figured if I could reach it, I would be able to see all the way across the canyon. Hopefully by that time Chaz would find us or at least I could see a way to climb out. Maybe I could light I a signal fire or something.

With that idiotic thought, I eased my body along until I reached the rock shelf. With a sigh of relief, I slid myself up and lay on my belly trying to catch my runaway breath. Then I walked to the edge of the outcropping and looked out. The view was quite lovely. Down below was a broad expanse of moonlit desert, washed clean and glittering with momentary moisture. For a second, I forgot my dire predicament. This was the desert at its most breathtaking and it felt like sneaking a peek at God's easel. His paint box must be unimaginable.

My awe was cut short when the rock under my feet gave way with a crash.

**

Chaz was calling my name.

I wondered how he got into my dream. I couldn't picture the guy having a mud bath, but somehow he was there calling to me over the earthy fumes in my dream spa.

His voice floated down from the outcropping above. "Simone, can you hear me?" Are you hurt?" There was an edge of fear in his words.

I sat up. The mud bath disappeared. The world whirled in a series of blurs and sparkles. I squeezed my eyes together until the psychedelic display was over. When my head stopped spinning, I tested my parts. My arm and legs were cramped and sore but most of them seemed to be cooperative. Where was I, anyway?

Chaz called again, louder. "Simone? Answer me, please." His request echoed oddly.

I eased to a sitting position. An enormous rock cavern swam into focus. Overhead I could see the hole that I had fallen through. Then I got a gander at the other occupants of the space. Nope, I wasn't all right after all. I must have sustained a terrible head injury. I clamped my eyelids together and then reopened them.

It was not a hallucination.

They were all still there.

Lovely as a sunrise, their arms outstretched to the heavens.

I wasn't sure whether to laugh or scream.

Mr. Snap wasn't crazy after all.

I had found his giants.

Chapter Twenty-Seven

It took Chaz a good half hour to figure out how to get down to me. He finally did, thanks to a very long rope tied to the back of a Pastor Stan's van. All of a sudden there was a scrabbling sound and he swung gently into the cavern and dropped to his feet on the sandy floor. His eyes fastened on me. Then they darted over to the giants and then back to my face.

He sort of shifted back and forth for a moment as if his feet were motivating him in one direction and his heart another. His heart won out and he knelt beside me. "Simone, are you okay? Are you hurt?"

I assured him I was relatively functional.

His eyes slid back to the wonder next to us. "What did you find here?"

We looked out across the wide space. It was a huge oval shaped cavern, concealed from above by the rock promontory. One side faced the canyon leaving it open to the elements. I had crashed through a hole in the roof of the place. In the middle of the space, standing in a silent cluster, were the Snap giants.

They were saguaros, bent and twisted into graceful human shapes by their efforts to reach the sun. Each was several heads taller than Chaz. Their slender arms were raised toward the sky as if in prayer. At one time the cactus must have encountered lightning or frost which sculpted the top of their heads into coiled knobs, like intricate sections of hair.

I tore my eyes away with difficulty. "Where's Jojo? Did you find her?"

"She's fine. Ricky got us and we high tailed it back here. We found her singing the alphabet song. Pastor Stan and the doves took her back up to her parents while I came to find you." His fingers moved gently over my head and shoulders and down my spine, dark eyes peering intently into mine. "Are you sure you're not hurt? Do you have pain anywhere? Tingling? Any numbness?"

"I'm fine, apart from some bruises and another ruined pair of pants."

Chaz nodded and stared up at the towering cactus.

It seemed at any moment they would lift their roots and begin to glide along the smooth ground. Even the air smelled of something important, something ancient and mysterious. Something that only God would understand. Chaz helped me up and we wandered among the giants, silent and awestruck.

After a while we stopped and did some more quiet wondering.

Finally Chaz found his voice and his eyes glittered with moisture. "To think...to imagine these saguaros, living here, hidden, all this time."

"A real miracle, right under our noses."

He cleared his throat. "I have never seen anything like this in my entire life."

"I haven't either but I think..." My throat clogged.

He looked into my eyes. "What is it Simone?"

"I think that God brought me here to see this, to remind me that He is a much bigger God than I believed."

Chaz smiled, a wide, peaceful smile. "Is that what you needed to see?"

I nodded.

Arm in arm we did another slow tour around the cactus clan.

Chaz looked them over from top to bottom. "Besides Maynard Snap, I bet we're the only people to see these guys."

"Yup, but I bet a lot of people would like to."

He swiveled around to look in my face. "What's going on in that lovely head of yours?"

"Do you suppose there would be a way to allow people to come here to see these giants? Without damaging them, I mean."

His teeth flashed white in the darkness. "We'd have to manage it carefully, but I know some people from the National Park Service who would help us. I'm pretty sure we could figure something out."

"This might be just the thing that would bring people to Seepwillow, don't you think?"

Chaz laughed. "I do indeed, Miss Peevey. I do indeed."

Silence filled the chamber again. We were both startled when a rope slithered down into our space with a blanket and a backpack tied to the end. Chaz shouted a thank you and untied the goods.

"What's all this?" I watched him unfurl a checkered blanket and wrap it around me.

"It's not safe to try to get you out in the dark while everything's wet. We'll wait until morning. It's only a few more hours until sunup."

"I have to spend the night here?" I looked at the graceful figures, their spikes glistening in the moonlight and at the tired man who settled down next to me. My heart filled with contentment. "Not a bad way to spend an evening."

He smiled and handed me a cup of cocoa from the Thermos.

"Here's to you and the giants."

***

Thursday morning the sun and I woke up at the same time. I hauled my bruised body from the shelter of Chaz' arms. He sat up and blinked. "What...was it real? It wasn't a dream?"

"Nope. We're still here, you, me and the big guys."

He rubbed his eyes. "Are you okay, Simone? Still not having any pain or anything?"

"Only the pain of facing the morning before a hot shower. Other than that, aside from the odd scrape and bruise, I am feeling fantastic."

The morning light bathed the giants in a golden hue. They seemed to expand, to open their arms a little wider to embrace the sun. I leaned against Chaz's warm shoulder. He pulled the blanket more securely around my shoulders and we spent a while longer ogling.

"Our rescue team will be here soon. I'm going to go scout a path," Chaz said with reluctance as he stood up. "I'll be back soon." He kissed me on the cheek and his glance lingered on our twelve silent companions before he left.

I snuggled deeper into the blanket. This would be an interesting addition to my blog. Really though, how would I coalesce all this craziness into words? Could I capture the majesty and wonder of this place? No. I knew that this moment was mine. It might be the vehicle that would save the Ruddy Duck, but there was something more here than that.

Chaz's words whispered in my ear.

"It's all written down here, in this place. All the important truths, together in one spot."

He was right. There was no clearer declaration of God's love than the survival of these ancient giants. They survived, because that is the life that He gave them.

It was time for me to start living the life He had made for me, instead of the one I'd fashioned for myself.

I folded my hands. "Thanks God, for being way bigger than I could ever imagine."

In my heart, the cactus giants added their amen.

***

We traveled up and out with relatively little trouble. My uncle and aunt, along with Pastor Stan and the doves were all waiting for us. Aunt Stella fluttered around, alternately squeezing me and looking me all over for contusions.

"Oh Simone. You could have been killed. Are you sure you didn't break anything? No sprains? No fractures? To think you were out here in the storm while we were all at a party. I nearly had heart failure when they told me."

"It's all right, Aunt Stella. I'm pretty sure everything is still in one piece. How is Jojo?"

"Just fine. Her mother gave her a scolding and then handed her over to the aunties for fussing. She was too tired to tell us much about her adventure. She didn't even ask about the piñata candy. I think she's still asleep."

Uncle Bud listened to Chaz relate the story with wide eyes. "Down there? On our property? Are you sure?"

"I'm sure."

"I've got to see it. Right now." Uncle Bud headed toward the cliff.

"Hold up there, Bud." Chaz scrambled to catch up with him. "Let's take care of a few things first. I think we'll be okay on the path, but let's take a few precautions just to be on the safe side." He handed a radio to one of the doves and clipped the other to his belt. Then he checked the rope where it was tied onto the truck before turning to the group. "Okay. Who else wants to see the giants?"

Everyone raised their hands, myself included.

He laughed. "Fair enough, but we'll have to do this in shifts." His voice changed to park ranger tones. "And it goes without saying that no one lays a finger on these cactus. No flash photography, no one gets close enough to breath on them. Understood?"

The crowd caught the dangerous gleam in his eye and nodded meekly.

I was in the first group to go down, in honor of my having found the things when I practically landed on them. The path was still damp and uneven in some places but not too treacherous in the watery sunlight. Even so, Uncle Bud was huffing like a steam engine when we collected at the mouth of the cavern.

The morning sun clothed the giants in luminous splendor.

Stella approached the nearest cactus with halting steps. She stood, with arms raised to the glittering figure. Tears streamed down her face. "I can't believe it. They look like angels. And they were right here, all the time. Right here and we didn't even know."

I placed a hand gently on her shoulder. "They'll save us, Aunt Stella. I know it. You'll still have to borrow the money from my mother to pay off the loan in the short term, but we'll take pictures and people will come to Seepwillow to see them. These cactus will inspire people from all over the country."

Her gaze was still fastened on the saguaros. "Could they really save us? Is this all real or am I dreaming?"

I laid a hand on her shoulder, looking at the silent colony in front of me. "It's real, all right. Wait until your friends from Bulgaria get a load of these guys."

Stella turned. Her face was a mixture of wonder and joy. She threw her arms around me and Bud added his meaty embrace to the mix. There was laughter and tears and prayers of thanksgiving.

Chaz gave us a minute before he cleared his throat. "Of course, you know the protection of this cactus will be paramount. We'll have to limit the number of visitors and keep them under constant supervision. Someone will have to make sure that these saguaro won't suffer from human contact."

Bud grinned. "Of course. And I just happen to know the perfect man for the job."

Our laughter echoed through the forest of spiky arms.

***

Friday I was packed. The car was ready to take me back to San Francisco. Except for an auntie or two, all of Jojo's relatives had gone, so the Ruddy Duck was quiet. Jojo sat in the shelter of a tree, talking to her porcelain friend.

"Hey Jo. How do you like the doll Mr. Singh made for you?"

"She's not my doll. She's my new sister. Her name is Pruney. She's five. Say hello to her."

"Hello, Pruney." I shook the doll's hand. "Nice to meet you. It looks like you and Jojo are going to get along famously."

She looked at my waiting suitcase. "Are you going?"

"Yes. I'm going back to San Francisco today."

"Why?"

There was a sudden catch in my throat. "I... belong there."

She cocked her head. "Why?"

"I have a job there, and a home."

She sat Pruney down and smoothed her hair. "Do they have lots of candy in San Cisco?"

I laughed. "Definitely."

"When will you come back?"

Chaz spoke from behind me. "I'd like to hear the answer to that."

We left Jojo with her silent sister and walked away a few paces.

"So when are you coming back, Miss Peevey?"

I cleared the clog from my windpipe. "I've been thinking about that actually. I thought I would come back a couple times a month to help Aunt Stella handle the whole giant business. She's going to need someone with computer saavy to update the website and handle advertising. I'm sure Donna would be okay with me working away from the office. I've managed to keep the blog afloat long distance."

A sparkle danced in Chaz's black eyes. "I thought you didn't like the desert."

I felt a warmth in my cheeks. "It has some hidden charms. Of course, it's really far away from the civilized world. Such a long distance to travel."

"You could drive your bike."

"I thought about that too."

"It would make for a short trip, that's for sure."

I laughed. We lapsed into silence for a minute.

Chaz scratched his chin. "You know, I've been doing some web searching myself. As it turns out, you have a pretty good desert there in California. I figured maybe if you weren't going to come here, I could move to a desert closer to San Francisco."

My heart thudded to a stop. "But Chaz, you belong here. It's who you are. Why would you think about leaving?"

He turned to face me. His adam's apple zinged up and down. "Because I love you. I know I should come up with some clever romantic banter right now, but I can't think of any. I love you. I love the way you look riding a fast bike. I love the way you rise to whatever challenge comes your way. I love the way you love the people around you and I love that nutty mix of humor and stubbornness."

My eyes filled to the lashes.

He fisted his hands on his hips. "Depending on how you feel about this love stuff, I am prepared to do whatever I need to so we can be together. If you want me to, I mean. That is, you know, if you feel sort of the same way and all."

I realized my eyes were the size of silver dollars. I forced myself to blink back the tears and take a deep breath. He was still staring at me, waiting.

A look of worry flittered across his face. "So? What do you think Simone?"

I swallowed. Hard. "I think that when I ride to Seepwillow, I'm going to need to slow down so you can meet me halfway."

His smile was huge as he kissed me under the hot desert sun.

* * * * *

Books by Dana Mentink

Trouble Up Finny's Nose (2008)
Fog Over Finny's Nose (2008)
Treasure Under Finny's Nose (2008)
California Capers (2008)
Killer Cargo (December 2008)
Flashover (January 2009)
Race to Rescue (September 2009)
Endless Night (January 2010)
Betrayal in the Badlands (October 2010)
Turbulence (February 2011)
Buried Truth (August 2011)
Escape the Badlands (upcoming)

* * * * *

About Dana Mentink

Dana Mentink lives in California where the weather is golden and the cheese is divine. She has published more than eight books with Harlequin's Steeple Hill imprint. Dana is an American Christian Fiction Writers Book of the Year finalist for romantic suspense and an award winner in the Pacific Northwest Writers Literary Contest. Her recent romantic suspense, *Betrayal in the Badlands*, is a Romantic Times Reviewer's Choice Nominee.

Dana loves to hear from her readers. Feel free to visit her website at www.danamentink.com or her Facebook Reader Page.

www.ingramcontent.com/pod-product-compliance
Lightning Source LLC
LaVergne TN
LVHW011948060526
838201LV00061B/4250